EARTH WITCH

BOOK TWO OF THE FRONTIER WITCHES SERIES

ANNETTE GRANTHAM

RAVENOUS SQUIRRELS PRESS

To Twilight, my energetic little black dog, who I will hold in my heart to the end of my days.

Prologue

Sunday, November 16, 1880 Tin Creek, Montana

The relentless Montana wind, harbinger of the looming winter, lashed through George Perkins's thinning hair, a chilling caress that belied the sweat dotting his brow. Laboring with his axe, George wrestled with stubborn logs, his efforts a race against the impending frost that threatened to clutch Tin Creek in its icy grasp. The owner of the town's solitary dry goods store, he found himself perennially caught unprepared for winter's onslaught, his resources stretched thin and insufficient.

"Damnation! No way can I gather enough firewood before the winter sets in. Gonna freeze to death," George grumbled, his voice a blend of defeat and exasperation. He dropped his axe, the tool landing with a thud that echoed his frustration. The mournful toll of the church bell punctuated the quiet Sunday morning, its somber chime a stark reminder of his predicament.

With a sigh of resignation, George hoisted the axe again, cleaving another log in his relentless battle against the cold. His movements were sluggish, weary from the effort. His eyes, wandering in distraction, landed upon the willow tree standing sentinel behind his store.

Its branches hung heavy, laden with blood-red leaves that shrouded the gnarled, blackened trunk.

"That blasted tree," he seethed, a bitter edge to his words. "A constant reminder of Mary, that accursed witch of a wife. Good riddance to her." His foot lashed out, striking the pile of firewood in anger. "Ever since her death, my life's been a living hell. Her curse, it haunts me."

Memories of Mary surfaced unbidden. She had nurtured the young willow, transplanting it from the Bitterroot River's edge. Under her care, it flourished, its canopy a haven for children's laughter and lovers' whispers. George had always scorned her rituals, her communion with the tree, her belief in its sacred nature.

But after Mary's demise, the willow transformed. Its leaves darkened to the color of dried blood; its bark contorted into sinister, blackened gnarls. The once gentle leaves became as sharp as blades, warding off any who dared approach. Mary's garden, too, succumbed to a dismal fate, its healing herbs and colorful flora replaced by hostile brambles and thorns, as if in sympathy with the willow's malevolence.

Rumors of Mary's mysterious death circulated among the townsfolk, some suspecting George's involvement, especially after he sent their daughter away to Chicago. But George remained indifferent to their suspicions; he was their sole lifeline for supplies in this isolated frontier settlement.

Consumed by resentment, George approached the willow, axe gripped tightly. Warily, he navigated the razor-like leaves, his movements cautious. He swung at the trunk, but the axe glanced off, sending him stumbling. Cursing, he tried again, only to be repelled. As he struggled to regain his footing, the tree seemed to awaken, its branches ensnaring him in a vengeful embrace. Lifted off the ground, George flailed helplessly as the branches whipped and lashed at him, his cries for help swallowed by the deserted morning.

The ordeal stretched for hours, the willow relentless in its torment until nightfall shrouded the sky. Finally, it released him, dropping him unceremoniously to the ground. Bruised and battered, George crawled back to his store, his defiance crumbling into a vow of silence. He raised a fist in an ultimate gesture of defiance but then halted, the realization dawning that he would never again provoke the wrath of the willow, nor the memory of Mary.

As he tended to his wounds, George's loathing for his cursed existence deepened—a life damned by the legacy of a witch and a vindictive tree.

Chapter One

Isobel Perkins navigated the cobblestone path with swift purpose. The imposing silhouette of her brownstone residence loomed large, standing as a monument to the city's burgeoning wealth and ambition. Drawing nearer, a wave of anticipation stirred within her, carried on the crisp evening air. She was awaiting a correspondence that held the key to her most fervent aspiration, one she harbored silently—a place at the nursing school.

Her fingers, clad in gloves, quivered as they clasped an envelope, its surface marked by the emblem of the institution she longed to join. The shadow of potential rejection darkened her thoughts for a moment, but with a practiced motion, she concealed the letter within a secret pocket of her bustle skirt, ensuring its invisibility.

Isobel earmarked the earnings from her position in the dress shop for this very dream. Her uncle Henry, a titan in the textile industry, had never once proposed funding for her academic pursuits. Instead, his inquiries veered towards the prospects of her social calendar, his outlook entrenched in the bygone era of Regency expectations. He feared for her marital prospects, even going so far as to suggest arranging a match that would secure her future. But Isobel's spirit was not so easily corralled; not a single suitor had captured her attention.

In defiance of her uncle's antiquated views and societal conventions, Isobel stood on the threshold of claiming her own path. Aunt Stella, ever the matriarch of their indomitable lineage, reinforced the belief that while marriage might be in their stars, submission was not. They were descendants of a robust lineage of women who, when united in matrimony, did so on their own terms, unshackled by the expectations that sought to confine them.

Upon entering the grandiose foyer of her relatives' domicile, Isobel was enveloped by the inviting glow of gaslight chandeliers. Their light danced across the lavish wood parquet flooring, crafting shadows that played on the walls like ethereal specters. Aunt Stella, her presence as commanding as ever, navigated the room with a grace that seemed to defy her years. Strands of gray ran through her chestnut brown hair, now styled in the contemporary Gibson Girl updo, a testament to her unyielding spirit and her subtle nod to the times.

"How did the day find you at the shop?" Stella inquired, her vibrant green eyes sparkling with an intensity that seemed to mock the passage of time. Despite the opulence that surrounded them, Stella chose a life less dependent on the labor of others, her preference for personal autonomy over a household staff clear.

"The shop kept me on my toes," Isobel confessed, as she adjusted her hat and smoothed down her red hair, flushed with the kiss of the cold, contrasting vividly against her delicate, Irish skin.

With a flick of her wrist, Stella drew back the heavy curtains, allowing the day's dying light to fill the room. "Your uncle will be joining us for the evening meal. He's buzzing with something he wishes to discuss, likely another prospective match he's conjured up.

The man does fancy himself quite the matchmaker," she said, a note of amusement in her voice.

Isobel's heart sank at the notion of suitors and matches. In their circles, the tradition of arranged unions lingered like a ghost from a bygone era. Isobel's spirit yearned for more than predetermined paths; she was driven by a legacy of strength and independence passed down from her mother, further nurtured by Stella's guidance in herbal lore and the wisdom of walking one's own path.

Stella poised herself to address the more mundane tasks awaiting her attention. "I must see to the candles on the dining table before your uncle makes his appearance," she remarked, her voice trailing off towards the task at hand.

"Will you be using your gifts?" Isobel inquired, a playful tone lacing her words.

"Naturally, my dear. How else should I light them?" Stella retorted, feigning the action of lighting a candle with a mere breath, her eyes twinkling with mischief as she offered Isobel a conspiratorial wink.

Isobel smirked in response. "But when he arrives, it's the flint that you'll turn to, concealing your magick as if it were a clandestine lover."

As Stella turned to depart, she executed a subtle gesture with her hands, seemingly inconsequential, yet it conjured a breeze within the confines of the foyer. This breeze quickly escalated into a gust strong enough to snatch Isobel's hat from her head, sending it sailing up the staircase in a defiant dance.

Isobel, now hatless and momentarily distracted from the conversation, gave chase to the rogue headwear. The impromptu chase served as a vivid reminder of Stella's power and her playful warning.

Yet, for Isobel, the immediate concern shifted towards the letter, burning a hole in her pocket. The need to discover her destiny, her fate as dictated by the nursing school's decision, outweighed even her uncle's intentions for her future. Resolved, she ascended the stairs, her thoughts already unraveling the possibilities that awaited in the written word, ready to face her fate on her own terms.

Before Isobel could reach her sanctuary upstairs, the resonant chime of the doorbell echoed through the grand hall. With Aunt Stella absent, likely attending to some final dinner preparations, it fell to Isobel. Peering through the door's beveled glass, she recognized her uncle's silhouette, bracing herself for the evening's inevitable discussions—those of unwelcome matrimonial prospects rather than the contents of the envelope burning a hole in her pocket.

Opening the door, she greeted him with warmth unmarred by her internal turmoil. "Uncle Henry!" Embracing him, she offered, "Let me take your hat. How are you?"

Henry surrendered his hat. "Thank you, my dear. I'm doing fine. And how is my favorite niece doing?" Isobel relieved him of his distinguished black top hat, placing it with care on the coat rack that stood sentinel in the foyer. He leaned his cane, an item more a statement of style than need, against the wall and shed his coat. Isobel glimpsed at the fabric's fine quality, a testament to his success in the textile industry, as she took his coat to hang.

Her laughter, light and genuine, filled the space between them at his endearment. She was, after all, his sole niece. "I'm doing very well. I hope you are hungry. Aunt Stella is out-doing herself today." The thought of her aunt's culinary prowess offered a brief respite from her apprehension about the discussion that would unfold over dinner.

Henry, embodying a blend of gravitas and weary experience, made his way into the parlor with measured steps. The richly adorned Persian rug underfoot, a kaleidoscope of intricate designs and bold colors, captured his attention, reflecting perhaps the complexity of his own thoughts. "I'll take a whiskey. Make it a double," he announced, his voice carrying the heft of a day burdened with unforeseen trials.

Isobel, taken aback by the depth of his request, quipped, "A double. That good of a day." She extended her senses, a subtle skill nurtured under Aunt Stella's tutelage, to perceive the emotional atmosphere surrounding him. Encircling Henry was a shroud of pale gray melancholy, punctuated by the erratic dance of orange orbs—each a spark of worry. This visual manifestation of his internal state evoked in Isobel a profound empathy.

Absorbed in contemplation, Henry's gaze wandered, eventually settling on the fireplace mantel, a masterpiece of craftsmanship. "Things rise and fall. Nothing ever stays the same," he reflected, a note of resigned wisdom in his words that resonated in the space between them as Isobel turned to fetch his drink.

In the dining room, she poured his whiskey, the liquid's rich hue catching the light, before heading to the kitchen. "Uncle Henry wants a double today," she relayed to Stella in a hushed tone, barely audible over the culinary sizzling of the roast in the oven.

Stella, her hands encased in oven mitts, tenderly retrieved the roast, infusing the kitchen with a delectable blend of rosemary, potatoes, onions, and carrots. "Oh, that's bad news," she responded, her voice rich with concern.

"It smells wonderful! I'll let him know we are eating soon," Isobel declared, a swell of familial pride lifting her spirits. She returned to the parlor with the whiskey.

Henry paused his contemplation of Aunt Stella's jade egg collection, each piece a testament to Alfred's business journeys. These artifacts, with their polished gleam and deep, verdant hues, seemed to anchor the room with a sense of history and exploration.

Isobel watched him, the subtle lift of her brows and a thoughtful tilt of her head betraying her concern. She sensed the weight of undisclosed troubles pressing on him, marking the gathering clouds in his usually serene disposition. It was as if the very air around them thickened with the unvoiced worries that shadowed his features.

Offering the whiskey, she glimpsed the usual tranquility in his eyes, now veiled by a tempest of thoughts. "Here you go, Uncle Henry. Aunt Stella pulled the roast out, so we'll be eating soon. Do you want to take a seat now?" Typically bathed in a light of unwavering calm, today, Henry seemed adrift in a sea of turmoil.

As he accepted the glass and moved toward the dining room, he scanned the table. "Doesn't this look fabulous? Should have known. You are always on top of things. You will make some young man a good wife," he said.

Isobel, tensing at the mention of marriage, managed a subtle eye roll. Her voice carried a hint of playful defiance, a soft rebuttal to the path he envisioned for her. "The Rockefellers keep their table set all the time. It's the latest trend. Why keep beautiful china locked up when you can look at it any time you want?" she said, skillfully navigating away from the sensitive subject of marriage.

"I did not know that. Maybe I should tell Eleanor. Can't be looking shabby now," Henry mused.

When Aunt Stella swept into the dining room, carrying a platter that hosted the evening's roast to perfection, Isobel's admiration for her aunt's abilities swelled within her. "I fixed some of that new Jell-O for dessert. Did you know you need an icebox for that?" Stella declared, setting down the meal with a flourish that seemed to light up the room.

Henry, having taken his seat, draped a linen napkin across his lap with a gesture of refinement. "I've heard about Jell-O. People molding it in different shapes. Almost like art," he said, then, almost as an afterthought, he produced a letter from the depths of his jacket, laying it down next to his plate with a nonchalance that belied its potential significance.

Isobel, eyeing the letter with a mixture of curiosity and dread, found herself momentarily lost in thought. The possibility that it heralded some unsolicited match made by her well-intentioned but misguided uncle sent a shiver down her spine. She took her place at the table, her mind awash with speculations, even as her fingers discreetly confirmed her own much-awaited correspondence.

Seizing a moment of distraction as Stella urged Henry to begin, Isobel excused herself under the guise of a forgotten necessity. "Oh, we forgot the bread!" she claimed, making a swift escape to the refuge of the kitchen. There, against the cold assurance of the icebox, she allowed herself a moment to collect her courage. Drawing the letter from its hiding, her whispered exclamations of joy were a private celebration of her admission into the nursing program, her spirit doing a dance of triumph.

With the letter safely stowed once more, Isobel returned, her arms cradling the warmth of freshly baked bread and the aromatic promise of herb butter. Setting them down with a precision that masked the storm of emotions inside her, she returned to her seat, her expression a carefully maintained mask of composure. Grateful for Aunt Stella's discreet respect for her privacy, despite the older woman's uncanny perceptiveness, Isobel navigated a sea of feelings—pride at her acceptance, excitement for the path ahead, and a niggling worry about what the future might demand of her.

As the meal progressed amidst the grandeur of the dining room, adorned with artifacts of wealth and taste, the discussion meandered through topics of immediate relevance and triviality. But Isobel's mind wandered far from the room, ensnared by visions of her future in nursing, a beacon of hope that now flickered ever more brightly within her.

The ambient sounds of dining—the gentle clinking of silverware against fine china, the murmur of conversation—were a familiar, comforting sound, yet Isobel found herself adrift in thought, only half-anchored to the present moment. The mention of a letter from George, her estranged father, snapped her back to the room, his name evoking a complex web of emotions, a mixture of distant pain and indifferent curiosity.

"George didn't write it, but it says he is sick and needs help," Uncle Henry revealed, a shade of genuine concern tinting his voice, breaking through the ordinary cadence of dinner chatter.

Aunt Stella voiced her worry with immediate warmth, "Oh, no! What could be wrong that he couldn't write himself? Do you think it's serious?"

The proposition that followed from Henry, however, landed with the weight of an unexpected storm. "Well, I think Isobel needs to travel there to help him. It would be a good time for her to spend time with her father." This suggestion, laid out with the simplicity of setting a chess piece on the board, seemed oblivious to the tidal wave of implications it bore for Isobel. His words, steeped in the societal norms of duty over personal desire, presented a crossroads that directly challenged the path Isobel dared to dream of.

As Uncle Henry unfolded the crudely written letter, the simplicity and urgency of its message cutting through the room's air, Isobel's world tilted. The abruptness of his proposal, casting a long shadow over her freshly illuminated path to nursing school, felt like a punch to her stomach. She brought a hand to her mouth, her breath catching in a tangle of shock and indignation.

"I got my acceptance letter for nursing school," she announced, her voice threading through the dense atmosphere with a blend of triumph and challenge. This dream, nurtured in secret and now blooming into reality, was hers alone to claim, not to be eclipsed by obligations to a father who was more myth than memory.

"You did?" Stella and Henry echoed, their reactions intermingling surprise and bewilderment.

With a renewed sense of resolve, Isobel squared her shoulders. "The letter came today. The first term starts in September." It was more than a statement; it was a declaration of her independence, her right to shape her own destiny.

Henry's rebuttal, though swift and steeped in the norms of their era, dismissed her ambitions summarily. "Why would you do that? You don't need to work. If you let me, I'd find you a fabulous husband, a great provider."

The patronizing tone ignited a fire within Isobel. A flush of defiance warmed her face as she pushed back the tears that threatened to spill. "I'll marry when I fall in love without help," she said, her voice trembling with emotion. The thought of forsaking her aspirations for a father who had remained a ghost in her life, in favor of conforming to societal expectations that didn't resonate with her, was intolerable.

"You want me to sacrifice an opportunity to take care of a complete stranger in Montana?" Isobel's voice, now laden with both plea and indignation, sought understanding, acknowledgment of her right to dream and to follow those dreams. She concluded her plea, lips pressed in a firm line, a silent declaration that this discussion was over.

The atmosphere thickened with the weight of Isobel's defiance, her stand not just a rejection of an outdated duty but an affirmation of her right to choose her destiny. She watched the silent exchange of looks between Stella and Henry, the tension manifesting in a dance of conflicting emotions and expectations.

As Henry met Isobel's steely gaze, his demeanor shifted, the usually unyielding edges of his authority softening. "I'm sorry. I don't know what has gotten into me," he conceded, vulnerability bleeding in his voice for the first time. His head bowed, eyes shadowed by a rare admission of fallibility. "I am proud of you. It's just I didn't realize you applied."

Isobel stood firm, her hands braced against the table's sheen, each word she spoke a cornerstone of her declaration for self-determination. "That's because you are too busy trying to marry me off instead of listening to me, listening to what I want in my life." The air vibrated with the strength of her conviction, reverberating against the walls of tradition.

Henry leaned back, his posture relaxing as he mulled over her words, the sharp angles of conflict in his expression giving way to contemplation. "Maybe your father only needs help for a short time," he proposed, attempting to find middle ground. "And you'll come back home to attend school."

Yet, Isobel sensed the inner discord within Henry, torn between his pride in her achievements and his adherence to societal conventions. She stood at a crossroads, acutely aware of the expectations that she should conform to the traditional role of a woman. However, forsaking her dreams for a life devoid of personal meaning and love was anathema to her.

In this moment of truth, Isobel grasped the essence of her struggle. She envisioned a world where women's ambitions and voices mattered, where the pursuit of professional and personal dreams wasn't stifled by outdated norms. She longed for Henry's understanding, for him to see the evolving landscape where women thrived not just in the home, but in the broader sphere of societal contribution.

Isobel took refuge in the ritual of cleaning up, her actions measured and thoughtful, creating a distance from the heavy atmosphere of the dining room. The simple act of washing dishes, the sound of water splashing against the porcelain, provided a comforting rhythm to her turmoil. As Stella's voice echoed from the next room, scolding Henry with a blend of disappointment and concern, Isobel took solace, knowing that her dreams were not entirely out of reach.

With each dish she dried and placed away, Isobel fortified her resolve to follow her path, to reach for the dream that shimmered on the horizon, despite the thorns that lay in her path.

Stella swept into the kitchen, her arms laden with linens, and with a casual flick, she sent the remaining dishes flying back to their places—a small showcase of magick that drew a fleeting smile from

Isobel. For Isobel, magick was a tool for more personal, introspective work, particularly in the quiet growth of her garden.

Leaning against the counter, Isobel's voice broke the silence, a soft admission of the conflict within her. "I'm sure my father has the same opinions about women as his brother," she pondered, the weight of her duty to a father who was more a concept than a presence heavy on her shoulders. "I should want to help my father, but he's a stranger." The cool indifference to the task set before her contrasted with the warmth she had felt upon learning of her acceptance into nursing school.

Stella's warm words of support cut through the fog of uncertainty, lighting the kitchen with a soft but unwavering belief in Isobel's choice. "I think it's wonderful you're going to nursing school. You always wanted to help people," Stella affirmed, her smile illuminated by the lamp above, her eyes shining with pride and conviction. "You'll come back in time to start school. I'll insist on it. Wow, a nurse. Your mother would be proud of you. Your uncle is in the past, and you are the future. It may take some time for him to see that."

In that moment, Isobel found a beacon of hope in Stella's words, a reminder that her journey was her own to forge, in defiance of the shadows cast by the past.

As Stella turned to leave the kitchen, she paused at the doorway, her silhouette framed against the dimming light of the hall. "We need to have a talk, dear. I have something to give you. I hadn't planned on you leaving this soon. But it can wait until tomorrow after dinner." Her voice trailed off, leaving a trail of intrigue and anticipation in the air.

Isobel, pondering what Stella might have for her, strolled through the dining room, her mind a whirlwind of thoughts. She noticed the absence of her uncle's heavy, conflicted emotions, which had hung in the air like a dense fog earlier, but now the remnants of his presence faded away like a distant foghorn. Isobel glanced at the seat where her uncle had sat, the cushion still bearing the imprint of his form, leaving behind a space that was both empty and filled with unspoken words and unresolved tensions.

Isobel's heart was heavy yet hopeful as she navigated through the familiar surroundings. The room, a witness to so many family discussions and decisions, now stood as a testament to her newfound resolve. She was stepping into a future that she chose, one where she could forge her own identity and make a difference in the world.

Isobel's steps were measured and thoughtful as she left the dining room, each footfall a step closer to her future. The uncertainty of the journey ahead was daunting, yet the support of her aunt and the strength of her own convictions bolstered her. Isobel admitted that the path she chose wasn't only about pursuing a career; it was about honoring her true self and the legacy of the strong women in her family.

Chapter Two

Isobel embraced the briskness of the early April morning, a chill lingering in the air as she ventured into the garden. Clad in her cherished blue woolen shawl, which gently compressed the puffed fabric of her leg-of-mutton sleeves, she cradled a steaming cup of herbal tea. The pebble path crunched under her feet, leading her away from the porch and onto the frost-kissed grass.

A vibrant assembly of early spring flowers - grape hyacinth, snowdrops, and Siberian squill - heralded the season's awakening. Isobel's daffodils, their buds swollen with potential, seemed to beckon for her attention. With a graceful sweep of her hand, she encouraged them, and they blossomed in a synchronized dance of yellow and white. Extending her influence beyond her own garden, she coaxed neighboring blooms to life, a discreet display of her earth witch abilities.

Despite the joy her garden brought, Isobel's thoughts were clouded with uncertainty. Even her loyal winter bloomers, the camelias of red and white, could not ease her troubles. The internal debate between fulfilling her uncle's wishes and pursuing her own desires weighed heavily on her.

Why am I so gutted by what my uncle wants?

The prospect of traveling to Montana to care for her estranged father was both daunting and intriguing. Is this journey an opportunity for growth and exploration? Perhaps she was too hasty last night.

Her contemplation led her to the potting shed nestled in the garden's far corner. After setting her tea aside, she scooped birdseed into a small tin can and scattered it along the grassy path. A chorus of birds - titmice, chickadees, and wrens - descended, chirping and hopping about in a lively feast. She watched until the birds left to flutter between the bird bath and lilac shrubs.

Isobel pondered the implications of leaving Chicago and the potential delay in her nursing studies. The thought of postponing her dreams for another year was unbearable. Isobel would miss Aunt Stella, Uncle Henry, and home. Then there was safety. Aunt Stella had expressed worry because they read stories of shootings in the newspaper. *Will I need a gun? I don't even know how to use one.*

Returning the can to the shed, Isobel resumed her garden stroll, her teacup warming her hands once more. She recognized the responsibility of doing the undesirable for the greater good sometimes.

Uncle Henry, who had been a father figure, often pushed her beyond her comfort zone, instilling a resilience she both resented and appreciated, like when he had put her on a pony, even though it terrified her. She ended up riding every summer since then.

She sought Uncle Henry's approval while also standing up to him, akin to a daughter with her father. The lack of parents was a void she felt deeply.

But she resolved to ensure her return to Chicago ahead of her first nursing school term. That was her non-negotiable condition.

Alone in the garden, with no prying eyes from neighboring houses, Isobel seized the moment to show her earth witch prowess. Isobel sat on the garden bench, sliding her hand along the side of each button-up black leather boot, savoring the sound as 16 buttons released magickally. The boots lined up under the bench with a flick of her hand. After her stockings slipped off, she placing them beside her. She removed her shawl, bracing herself for the cool touch of the grass under her bare feet.

As the energy of the earth surged through her, Isobel's shivers gave way to a warm, pulsating force within her. She moved her arms elegantly, orchestrating the growth of tulips. Stems emerged, buds formed, and blooms unfurled in a spectacular display of colors. The garden transformed into a vibrant tapestry, a testament to her connection with nature.

Exhausted yet content, Isobel redressed and returned to the porch. Wrapping herself in her shawl, she savored the remaining tea, her eyes drinking in the beauty of her handiwork. The myriad colors of the tulips resonated with her soul, creating a symphony of harmony and peace amidst her tumultuous thoughts.

When Isobel entered Stella's sitting room, a space reflecting the Victorian era's fascination with the exotic and the occult, adorned with ornate tapestries depicting geometric designs from far-off lands. The tapestries, likely bought during her Albert's travels, hung alongside elegant portraits framed in gilded wood, showcasing the affluent and eclectic tastes of the period. The room was lit by oil lamps that cast a warm and inviting glow over rich velvet upholstered furniture.

Stella, a figure of grace and wisdom, sat on an intricately carved settee, an exquisite example of the period's craftsmanship. Her familiar, a black cat with white paws named Boots, laid content in her lap, adding to the room's mystical ambiance.

The scent of sandalwood and myrrh incense burning in a brass burner, a common practice in homes to seek a connection with the spiritual world, struck Isobel. The scents, considered both exotic and therapeutic, relaxed her and center her thoughts.

Stella, who had been Isobel's guardian and mentor since she arrived at Uncle Henry's door, traumatized and mute, had always been her pillar of strength. Her wisdom and nurturing had coaxed Isobel back to life, helping her overcome the nightmares and silence that had gripped her after the traumatic events of her youth.

Stella gestured for Isobel to sit beside her on the settee. "I can't fathom why Henry thinks you should go to Montana. You barely know your father! And sending a young woman alone on such a journey..." Stella's concern was obvious, her protective nature always at the forefront.

Isobel, wrestling with her own mixed emotions, responded, "He may be a stranger, but he's still my father. And my goal has been to heal others. I can't ignore that, even if it means going to Montana."

"Your mother didn't belong there. It was too dangerous for her and for you, too. And you know why. I don't have to spell it out." Stella giggled. "Oh, look at me. I made a pun."

"Yes, you did." Isobel chuckled. "You've always told me to be cautious and I have and will be careful. I'll only use my gifts discretely to help others and not myself. Do you think someone discovered she was a witch?"

"No. Your mother was splendid at keeping them under wraps even when she misused them. But maybe..." Stella trailed off.

Isobel placed her hand on Stella's. "Aunt Stella? Are you okay?"

Stella shook her head. "Oh, I get these thoughts." She squeezed Isobel's hand and sighed. "I miss Mary so much. We had our differences, but we were still close until Montana. I had these odd feelings, though, like something wasn't quite right. The tone of her letters changed, but I couldn't pull it out of her. Ah, well."

Stella waved her hand towards an antique wardrobe. The door creaked open, and a package wrapped in blue velvet floated out, unwrapping itself in mid-air before the book inside landed on Isobel's lap. Boots, the cat, watched with mild interest before settling back into a comfortable position.

"This was your mother's grimoire," Stella explained, releasing a sigh. "She left it here by mistake. It's time you had it."

Isobel opened the red leather-bound book with gold embossed lettering. As she touched the pages, she felt an inexplicable connection to her mother, a bridge across time and space. Her mother's death haunted her, as if there was something behind a veil she couldn't see. This trip might pull back that veil.

"I will keep it safe." She held the book to her chest. "Thank you, Aunt Stella."

"I ask only one favor from you, Isobel. My sister left with family heirlooms that we must get back. Your grandmother's grimoire and her cursed necklace. Find them. The necklace is silver with a trinity knot pendant encrusted with ruby, emerald, and amethyst gemstones. On the back are ancient rune engravings. I worry everyday someone will find them. If they tried to use them, it would be the end. Dangerous black magick."

Isobel assured her aunt, holding the grimoire close, "I promise, Aunt Stella. I'll find them."

As they embraced, Stella's eyes filled with a mix of pride and concern, shimmering with unshed tears. "Stay safe, Isobel. We can't lose you too."

"Good night, Aunt Stella. I love you." Isobel, feeling the weight of her aunt's expectations and the legacy of her mother's magick, left the room with a heavy heart. Her mind raced with thoughts of the journey ahead and the mysteries she might uncover in Montana.

Chapter Three

Isobel gazed out the window of the Pullman car, entranced by the rhythmic motion of the tall grasses undulating in the breeze, creating waves of green and amber on the rolling hills. The gentle rocking of the train car, coupled with the mesmerizing view, lulled her into a contemplative state, quieting the tumult of her thoughts about the uncertain future and the loved ones she would leave behind in Chicago.

Lost in this tranquil reverie, Isobel barely noticed when a light touch on her shoulder jerked her back to reality. She jolted, her heart skipping a beat.

"Sorry, Miss. I didn't mean to alarm you," a voice said, gentle yet apologetic.

Isobel tilted her head to find a tall, young man with blond thick, curly hair standing beside her, his presence unexpected but not unwelcomed. She stood, a gesture of polite acknowledgment.

"Oh, no. You needn't get up. I only wanted to ask you if you'd mind...," the young man said, pointing to the opposite upholstered high-backed sofa bench. "The porter told me you're traveling to Tin Creek, and I wanted to make your acquaintance since I'm from there."

Opening her mind, Isobel scanned his aura, seeking a glimpse into his intentions. A lemony hue of serenity and goodwill greeted her, reassuring her of his benign nature. "You are welcome to sit and enjoy the scenery. It is a long trip, and it would be nice to know someone from Tin Creek before I get there."

"I'm John Carlyle." He settled onto the bench, extending a hand toward her.

Isobel reached out, her fingers meeting his in a gentle handshake. A sudden spark startled her, causing her to withdraw her hand quickly, her cheeks warming at the unexpected sensation. "Sorry. I'm Isobel. Isobel Perkins. You might know my father, George."

John's smile grew wide and his mouth fell open. "Isobel Perkins! We used to play together. Our mothers were good friends. Until... uh, sorry. I'm sorry. I don't mean to upset you or anything."

She shook her head. "Don't worry. It was a long time ago. I don't have any recollections of Tin Creek." She closed her book, setting it beside her.

"If your trip brings back any memories, I hope they are good ones. We used to have a wonderful time playing." John leaned forward, elbows on knees, clasping his hands under his chin, smiling. "Mother will be so excited to see you. You'll have to come for dinner."

Isobel fiddled with a loose tendril of hair, her mind drifting to the possibilities of rekindling old connections in Tin Creek. "If you still live there, what are you doing here, on this train?"

"I've been at Iowa State University, studying modern cattle ranching techniques. I'm coming home for the summer." His eyes sparkled. "And what brings you back to Tin Creek?"

Her mood shifted as she delved into the reason for her journey. "My father is sick. Someone wrote that he needed help." She hoped to steer the conversation away from her father, a topic that stirred a mix of emotions she wasn't ready to confront. "Do you have any idea who wrote the letter?"

John's expression softened. "I'm sorry George is ill. It was probably Jane from the hotel next door." He ran a hand through his curls, eliciting an unexpected sigh of contentment from Isobel.

"You used to tease me about my curls. Are you sure you remember nothing?" John's chuckle was light-hearted.

"Your curls are nice. Delightful," Isobel replied, her cheeks flushing. "Tell me about Tin Creek." Isobel slipped her book in her reticule, as she had no desire to read now.

"Tin Creek is a regular small town that's growing since mining is still profitable and a new mill opened. Right next to your father's store is a hotel run by Fred and Jane Shaw. They're real friendly folks, and Jane is wonderful." John used his sizable hands to show where each building was. "Across the street is Jack Logan's saloon. I've never been in there, but Jack is a good guy. There's a bakery next to the hotel."

"A bakery! I thought I would have to give up fresh pastries. Thank goodness. I have a sweet tooth. Oh, sorry to interrupt," Isobel said, her hand over her mouth.

John smiled and continued laying out the town in front of her. "It's alright. There's a dress shop, a barber, a bank, a cafe, and the usual business of livery, assayer's office, church, and school. But the roads are dirt, not paved." He raised his index finger. "Oh, there are two saloons now. One of Jack's girls, Marisol, opened her own several years after a freak fire destroyed the first one."

"Tin Creek doesn't sound too bad. I'm afraid the change will be hard, having lived in Chicago most of my life, but it's only for the summer." Isobel tried to decide if John had blue or green eyes, but settled on hazel.

"The summer?" John asked.

"I'm attending nursing school in the fall. Then my uncle received news about my father being ill." Isobel kept smoothing out her blue dress. Every conversation about her father made her anxious, and she didn't know why. "Here I am, traveling to Tin Creek to help him get back on his feet." She reached to stroke the textured fabric on her seat to relieve her anxiety from talking to this young man.

A shabbily dressed couple passing by interrupted their conversation, and John nodded to them. John waited until they walked to the other end of the car and turned to Isobel. "Be careful. They are looking for investors for their new silver mine. It turns out they haven't even seen the mine. They bought it on the word that it's a moneymaker. Lots of folks out here looking to make lots of money overnight and will clean you out with their big claims."

Isobel said, "Uncle Henry warned me about the charlatans. Even in the big city, there are those who think you should help them get rich without lifting a finger themselves."

"So true. Your uncle sounds like a smart man."

"He is." Isobel turned her gaze to the couple, her eyes narrowing as she sought to unravel the truth for herself. The young lady, barely more than a girl, radiated an aura clouded by conflicting emotions. Love, anxiety, and sadness wrestled within her, manifesting as pink and lime swirls entwined with spinning blue orbs.

The young man strutted with an air of unearned arrogance, yet the worn, faded fabric of his attire belied his pretensions. His aura seethed with dark, brooding colors—red and purple swirling together like blood clotting in slow motion, radiating fury and contempt. Above his head hovered a white haze, incongruous with his demeanor, prompting Isobel to stifle a laugh. She pondered the source of his inflated self-regard. Surely, if he had purchased a silver mine without so much as a glance, his judgment in matters of intellect and appearance was questionable. Could he possess some latent talent hidden beneath that malevolent aura? Isobel doubted it; such a sinister energy seemed unlikely to bring any good, especially to the young lady enamored with him.

Isobel wrestled with the moral dilemma of knowing others' emotions and intentions. The responsibility of her gift weighed on her. The line between helping and intruding always blurred.

"Are you all right?" John's concern pulled her back from her thoughts.

Isobel forced a smile. "Just amazed at the trouble people put themselves in."

"Would you eat dinner with me? I think they are serving in the dining car now." John rose and offered to take her hand.

John's offer to join him for dinner in the dining car presented a welcome distraction. As she accepted his hand, feeling the familiar spark again, Isobel giggled, thinking it caused by the carpet. "Yes, he is. I would love to have dinner with you. I want to hear about your family and the cattle ranch."

Walking alongside John to the dining car, Isobel felt a surge of excitement for the journey ahead. Despite the uncertainties and the complex emotions surrounding her return to Tin Creek, the prospect of new experiences and rediscovering her past held a certain allure. This train ride was not just a physical journey, but a passage to a new chapter in her life.

After bidding goodnight to Isobel and retreating to his sleeping compartment, John found himself overwhelmed by the unexpected turn of events. The shock of reuniting with Isobel, his childhood best friend who had captured a piece of his heart, left him reeling. He paced the confined space between the dresser and the bench seat, the bed still tucked away in its daytime arrangement. His heart pounded, a tumult of emotions and memories flooding his mind.

He longed to share this momentous encounter with his parents, but home was still days away. At university, his classmates often teased him for his lack of romantic pursuits. None of the girls there had sparked that special feeling in him, that indescribable catch in his heart or the fluttering in his stomach. He bore their teasing with good humor, unwilling to feign interest in someone just for appearances' sake.

The porter, who inquired, "Sir, are you ready to have your bed turned down?" interrupted his thoughts.

Stepping into the aisle to make room, John responded, "Yes. Thank you." He watched in mild fascination as the porter manipulated a lever, transforming the bench into a bed with practiced ease. The simple yet ingenious design of the Pullman car bed never ceased to amaze him. The porter, completing his task, left a small wrapped candy on the pillow - a thoughtful touch that John barely registered in his preoccupied state.

"Good night, sir," the porter said, offering a polite nod.

"Good night," John replied.

Once alone, he drew the heavy velvet curtain, enclosing himself in a cocoon of privacy. Yet, the solitude did little to calm his racing thoughts. Sleep seemed an impossible feat, his mind buzzing with questions about the next day. Would spending more time with Isobel seem too presumptuous? He didn't want to appear foolish or risk pushing her away. Seated on the edge of the bed, John rubbed his temples, bracing himself for a night of restless contemplation. The chance encounter had stirred something deep within him, and now, more than ever, he felt the weight of uncertainty about what the morrow might bring.

CHAPTER FOUR

ISOBEL LEANED IN, HER curiosity piqued, as John gestured towards the rugged landscape outside the stagecoach window. "That cliff there is called Castle Crag. When we pass it, we will be an hour out of Hamilton where we will stay overnight," he explained, his voice nostalgic.

Isobel, jostled by the relentless bumping of the coach on the uneven roads, sighed in discomfort. "Good. I'm ready to get out of this bouncing box. My stomach has had enough," she muttered, thinking of the peppermint tucked away in her trunk, a small remedy for her queasiness.

"The roads are not the best. It was not something I realized until I went to school," John remarked, his tone reflective.

Elsie, seated across from Isobel and traveling with her attorney husband Jeffery, chimed in, "I'm ready for a break, too. Glad we're nearing Hamilton." Her voice carried a weariness common to long journeys.

Isobel nodded in agreement. "It wouldn't be so bad if there was a breeze."

Elsie raised her eyebrows, a wry smile playing on her lips. "Wouldn't that just make the dust worse? I'm constantly brushing it off."

Isobel glanced at her skirt, now indistinguishable under a layer of dust. Turning to John, she inquired, "Is Tin Creek dusty, too?"

"Don't worry. Travel through town is slow, so it's not dusty," John reassured her, his chuckle lightening the mood. "You're beautiful, no matter what."

A blush warmed Isobel's cheeks, and she averted her gaze to the window. The growing connection between her and John was both exciting and unsettling. As she brushed off another layer of dust from her skirt, her thoughts drifted to the complexities of a serious relationship. Being different, possessing magickal abilities, made the prospect of opening up to someone daunting.

She recalled Aunt Stella's story of finding love with Albert, a man fascinated rather than frightened by her magickal gifts. Could John be as accepting, or would he recoil in disbelief? This uncertainty, coupled with nursing school attendance, had kept Isobel from exploring matters of the heart.

The growing apprehension of seeing her father added to her uneasy stomach.

The stagecoach swerved and lurched, shattering her contemplative reverie. Isobel heard a cracking sound as the coach tilted precariously to one side. Panic ensued inside as the passengers struggled to maintain their balance. Isobel found herself in an awkward, close embrace with John, her face flushed as she scrambled to right herself.

Once outside, they assessed the damage. The wheel lay dislodged on the ground, its hub cracked.

The driver said to John and Jeffrey, "There's a log across the road. I need some help to fix this. We might be in for some trouble, cause a log don't appear out of nowhere."

As Isobel and Elsie chatted while the men worked on the hub, Isobel had an eerie sensation of being watched. "John, I think someone is coming." Her warning was timely as three men on horseback emerged from the trees, charging towards them.

Fear gripped Isobel as she and Elsie sought cover behind the coach. The men drew their guns, but Isobel's heart pounded with dread. She longed to reach for John, but found solace in holding Elsie's trembling hands.

Thoughts of her untimely end in this remote place haunted her. She envisioned a grim scene of their abandoned belongings scattered among the brush. A chill coursed through her as the reality of their perilous situation sank in.

Tension crackled in the air as one horseman, a man with a gruff voice and an imposing stance, shouted, "Drop the guns! It's not three to three. I have two more coming. If you want to live, drop the guns." His words cut through the silence like a knife, sending a shiver down Isobel's spine.

John, his face set in a defiant scowl, retorted, "Hey, Jimmy. Better living robbing? My father was right to run you off." With a reluctant sigh, he let his gun fall to the dusty ground, a gesture mirrored by the driver and Jeffery.

Recognition dawned on the face of the man called Jimmy. "Well, if it ain't little Johnny all grown up and thinking he's a big man now. Yah, the living suits me fine." Joined by the other men, his laugh pierced the air, carrying a chilling and mocking tone.

The leader, imposing and unrelenting, issued his next command. "Give me your valuables! Make it easy and you live. Make it hard and ya don't."

Isobel's hands trembled as she unclasped her cameo necklace, a gift from Uncle Henry. With a heavy heart, she tossed it onto the ground. Beside her, Elsie removed her jewelry in silence, her movements mechanical. Jeffery surrendered his pocket watch and the money in his wallet.

"Open the trunks," the leader demanded, his gaze fixed on the luggage atop the wagon.

John and the driver hastened to comply, unloading the trunks from the back of the coach. Jeffrey added more items to the stash, his actions fueled by fear. Elsie wept while Isobel, her heart aching, offered what comfort she could.

When the driver opened Isobel's trunk, she stated, "There're only clothes and books." John's arms cradled her, his whisper urgent. "Shh. These men are dangerous."

Jimmy, now on foot, approached Isobel's trunk with a sneer. "I'm sure a well-dressed lady has more than that. Dig it out. Daddy must buy you lovely things or is it little Johnny buying you pretties."

His insinuations about her father and John stung, fueling Isobel's rising anger. "George Perkins of Perkins Dry Goods in Tin Creek is my father, and he has never bought me a thing!" Isobel retorted, hands on her hips, her glare fierce. "Look for yourself."

Isobel's confidence in her magical enchantment grew as she watched Jimmy disrespectfully kick her clothes aside while he searched through her belongings. His proximity was suffocating, his red and orange evil aura enveloping her like a scorching wave. "I do nothing nice. So don't push it."

Then Jimmy walked over to John and stood chest to chest. "I know you have nothing cause a tightwad raised you."

Jimmy came back to Isobel and towered so uncomfortably close she felt his breath on her face. "Your father is one of the vilest men in Montana. He uses that store to make people think he is an upstanding person in town, but he cheats, lies, and steals. I almost feel sorry for you."

As Jimmy's grip tightened on her wrist, twisting it, Isobel winced. "Be careful. If I don't hurt you now, I can hurt you later. I know where to find you."

Isobel longed to unleash her magick, to defend herself, but Aunt Stella's teachings echoed in her mind: do no harm. Restricting her powers was a curse at this moment of peril.

Jimmy shoved her, and John's quick reflexes prevented her from tumbling to the ground. Isobel's heart pounded in her chest, the rapid beats echoing in her ears as fear and frustration waged war inside her. Aunt Stella's warnings about her temper rang true; now these bandits knew where to find her.

Finally, Jimmy stepped over to the couple. "It was a pleasure doing business with you. Because of you, you all get to live. At least someone had something worthwhile." He bowed as he backed up to his horse with the bag of stolen items.

The leader said, "Come on, Jimmy. Let's go."

As the outlaws retreated, Jimmy became the target of a hawk's wrath. The sound of the bird's claws tearing into him filled Isobel with a grim satisfaction, knowing that justice was being served in some small way.

As the danger faded away and the stagecoach was being fixed, Jimmy's unsettling comments about her father plagued Isobel's mind.

Was George Perkins as vile as Jimmy claimed? John's silence on the matter only deepened her unease.

Standing there, amidst the aftermath of the robbery, Isobel wrapped her arms around herself, seeking comfort in the self-embrace. The vast unknowns and potential dangers of the West weighed heavily on her thoughts. How would she navigate this harsh, unpredictable world? The thought left her vulnerable, a stranger in a land where danger lurked everywhere.

As the stagecoach neared a small, rustic town nestled in the Montana landscape, Isobel leaned forward, her eyes scanning the horizon for any sign of their destination. "Are we there yet?" she asked, her voice tinged with both anticipation and weariness from the long journey.

John, stretching within the cramped confines of the coach, nodded. "Yes, that's Tin Creek. My family's ranch is just over that hill," he said, pointing westward where rolling hills, dotted with Ponderosa pines and Douglas firs, met the sky. Beyond, majestic snow-capped mountains stood tall, their cliffs a tapestry of pale sand and rustic orange.

Isobel's gaze lingered on the picturesque scene, the natural beauty a stark contrast to the town's simple layout. A single dirt road, flanked by modest buildings, formed the backbone of Tin Creek. As the coach trundled past a church, bank, and various shops, Isobel's eyes fell upon her father's general store. The modesty of the town belied the grandeur George's letters had painted, leaving her doing a double-take in utter disbelief.

Peering out at the sparse population, Isobel wondered about the viability of her father's business. John's family, living outside the town, hinted at a larger community that perhaps frequented these streets on busier days.

The coach halted beside a three-story brick hotel next to the general store. A woman in pants, a sight that shocked Isobel, swept the boardwalk, her thick brown hair pulled back under a bandana. She stopped to wave at the driver and yelled inside, "Stagecoach is here!"

John stepped out first, extending his hand to assist Isobel. The woman jumped in to greet him. "I haven't seen you in ages! Welcome home. And who is this? Did you get married?" Jane's rapid-fire questions left little room for reply. "Boy, is she a catch? Your daddy is gonna be proud of you! Dang!"

John made sure Isobel was on solid ground and whirled around to the woman. "Shh! Jane, I'm not married. This is Isobel Perkins, George's daughter. She's come all the way from Chicago to help him while he is sick." He turned back to Isobel, "Hope our journey is not over."

Isobel, feeling a flush of embarrassment, wondered how to navigate this unexpected attention. She nodded, hoping that was enough for now, and walked over to Jane, who she noticed wore a holster with an ornate gun. She extended her hand to Jane, only to be enveloped in a warm, unexpected hug. "I don't shake hands, I hug. Everyone needs a hug," Jane declared. Her aura of yellow and green eased Isobel's initial discomfort with the trusting woman.

"So glad to meet you, Jane."

Jane led Isobel onto the boardwalk before she returned to talk to the coach driver.

As Isobel stood on the boardwalk, the reality of her new surroundings sank in. Turning towards her father's store, she peered through the grimy windowpanes, her reflection interrupted by the approach of a disheveled man from across the street.

The man, with long, unkempt hair and a handlebar mustache, exuded an air of roughness as he grabbed Isobel's arm once he reached the boardwalk and pulled her into the street. "Get your hands off my girl! She has to be my new entertainer, right? I get only the best girls. I was told she was coming any day. Boy, what a beauty you are!"

Isobel's instinctive reaction was to pull away, repulsed by his intrusive touch and the dark, coal-like aura that surrounded him. She took several steps back. "I am not an entertainer. That was rude of you."

Jane intervened. "No, Tom. She is not one of your girls."

John ran over to Isobel. "Who do you think you are, accosting young ladies off the coach?"

"I beg your pardon. How would you know?" Tom said. He tried to step around John. "I have a girl coming and I was told she was beautiful." He twirled the end of his mustache while looking Isobel over. "And this one is beautiful. Must be her. Few pretty women come to Tin Creek."

Jane held her arms out. "This is George's daughter. Show some respect for once."

Tom stepped back, eyes widening. "Oh, so this is George's little girl. He said she couldn't talk after her mother died." Tom scratched his jaw and lifted one eyebrow. He held his hands out, showing his palms. "He sent you away. Why come back? Are you here to take the store once he's dead?"

"I came to help my father," Isobel said, grabbing her bag. She had a bad feeling about Tom and his odor. A cross of sour milk, sweat, and alcohol was making her sick. *More dangerous people.* Leaving her trunk still sitting in the dirt road behind the coach, she hastily headed back to the boardwalk. She needed a protection spell soon. How in the world did her mother live here?

Tom said, "You'll make good money working for me. I'm much nicer than your cranky father, too."

Jane replied with a sneer, "Both points are debatable."

A black man came out of the livery and yelled, "Tom, leave those folks alone or we'll have a talk."

Tom stopped for a moment, looking at the man, and then headed back to the saloon. He looked over at Isobel and said, "You know where to find me if you have a change of heart. You can work there in a dusty, boring store or you can make a name for yourself while having the time of your life with me." His smile made Isobel cringe.

A blond woman leaning in the saloon's doorway yelled across the street, "You don't want to work here! Tom is an awful boss, an awful man. I wished I didn't work here."

Tom ran over and grabbed the busty woman and shoved her in the saloon's door. "Get in there and shut up. Like I need any help from you."

Isobel imagined a vine coming through the cracks of the boardwalk to trip Tom, allowing the woman to get away from him. But alas, she could do no harm. Her mouth turned down, and she forced a deep exhale.

Jane waved to the black man. "Thanks, Bernard. I guess he doesn't want to have that talk."

Bernard said, "I guess not. I would like to though. He needs it. Need any help?"

She shook her head. "All good."

Bernard returned to the livery.

"I'll help you get your things, Isobel." John picked up her trunk and walked to the door of the store.

Isobel tried the door, but found it locked.

John shouted to Jane. "The door's locked. And who is that man? Where's Jack?"

"Oh shoot! Let me get the key. It's in the hotel. Be right back and fill you in." Jane trotted into the hotel.

As John carried her trunk to the store, Isobel marveled at his strength, her thoughts wandering to the growing connection between them. His defense against Tom's advances had not gone unnoticed, and she felt a surge of gratitude. "Thank you for defending me," she said, her voice revealing her uncertainty about life in Montana. "Are things like this all the time here?"

John reassured her, setting down the trunk as they awaited Jane's return with the key. "No," he said, his tone hopeful. "Tin Creek is usually very quiet. There are good people here. I don't know where that man came from. Jack was the owner when I was home last time. He would give the shirt off his back. Bernard is the man from the livery. Super nice and has a way with horses...and Tom."

Isobel, standing beside John, felt a mix of apprehension and curiosity about her surroundings. The rawness of the West was both daunting and intriguing. As she took in the quiet streets of Tin Creek, she wondered how she would adapt to this new chapter of her life, far from the familiar comforts of Chicago.

CHAPTER FIVE

ISOBEL STEPPED BACK ON the weathered boardwalk, her eyes surveying her father's store. The facade, marred by peeling paint and cracked trim, spoke volumes of neglect. Two front windows, each divided into sixteen dusty panes, offered a murky view inside. The store, much like her father's letters, painted a picture far removed from reality. It stood there, an unmissable eyesore amidst the modest buildings of Tin Creek.

Jane reappeared, key in hand, interrupting Isobel's inspection. "Now I can tell you about Jack," she began, unlocking the stubborn door with a jangle of the skeleton key. "He traveled to Missoula to find saloon girls and never came back. Tom claimed he won the saloon in a poker game." The rattling doorknob punctuated Jane's words and creaking hinges as she nudged the door open.

John shook his head. "Doesn't sound like Jack, does it?"

"No, it don't. Nobody believes it."

Isobel stepped inside, the stale air and dimness greeting her. The grimy windows filtered the scant light, casting long shadows across the cluttered interior. The store, like its exterior, was a testament to years of disregard. Isobel ran a finger along the dusty counter, leaving a clean streak in her wake. She sighed, envisioning the daunting task of breathing life back into this forgotten space.

Startled by the thud of the trunk hitting the floor, Isobel spun around.

Jane asked, "John, do you have time to take that upstairs before you head home?"

"Be glad to. Unless Isobel wants to carry it herself." John winked at Isobel. She smiled weakly at John's jest about her carrying the trunk, noticing the tension in the air that surrounded them. John and Jane's yellow and green orbs, jittery and vibrant, made her wonder about their unspoken anxieties.

Isobel followed Jane to the staircase, its old wood groaning under their weight. Jane's sudden pause caught her off guard.

"I have to tell you something first. And don't hate me, okay?" Jane's nervousness was palpable, the bouncing orbs around her almost distracting.

Isobel reassured Jane, forming a steeple with her hands and pressing them to her lips. "It's fine. I won't be mad."

"Good. So first, I wrote that letter to your uncle. Second, ah... I didn't tell George." Jane placed her hand on her hip and her other hand on the wall along the stairs. "He's a cranky man, and being sick made him worse." She looked at her feet. "I take a lot of crap from just trying to feed him. So don't be scared if he yells. Won't last long 'cause he gets a coughing fit. So just warning ya."

Isobel said, "I'm glad you wrote to my uncle and I'm sorry my father treats you so poorly."

Jane turned back up the stairs and stopped again on the next step. "I hope you won't be mad at me. Can't have that. Just can't."

Isobel smiled at Jane. "It's fine. I won't be mad."

"Good. I've been sweating bullets over it." Jane continued, steps creaking, to the door at the top of the stairs and opened it quietly.

Jane led the way upstairs, the steps creaking with each footfall. The living quarters were even more dismal than the store below. Torn curtains, chipped dishware, and a pervasive musty odor painted a picture of utter desolation. Isobel's heart sank at the sight, her mind racing with questions about her father's lifestyle and the trust fund from Uncle Henry.

John set the trunk down and whispered to Isobel, "Is this okay? I'm going to head home now. I'll come and visit you soon. Good luck."

"Yes, and thank you." John's departure left Isobel feeling alone in this foreign environment. His discomfort was almost tangible, a cloud of nervous energy enveloping him.

Jane's cautious approach to George's bedroom was a forewarning of the confrontation to come. She whispered, "George, are you awake?"

George grumbled, "I am now. What do you want? Can't a man die in peace?"

Isobel stepped closer to the door, but she could only see part of the bed.

Jane opened the door all the way. "You are going to be so surprised. You have a visitor all the way from Chicago." She sounded upbeat, but with caution in her voice.

The orbs became darker and circled Jane's neck, compelling Isobel to place her hand on Jane's arm to comfort her.

"Who the hell would come see me on my deathbed? Nobody comes when I'm well. Must want all this wealth."

"George, Isobel is here!" Jane announced with a forced cheerfulness.

"No, no, no. I don't want her here." George coughed. "She's like her mother." He struggled to get on one elbow and leaned over to glare at Isobel.

To Isobel's surprised, he had blond hair whereas her Uncle Henry had reddish brown hair like her own. His appearance, unkempt and aged beyond his years, was a stark contrast to his older brother, whether by illness, a harsher life, or both.

Isobel said, "Father, I'm here to help you." She tried to keep her bearings. Her own father had black oozing from his body with sharp red daggers shooting out towards her. It was not the reunion she played in her head during her travels. Ignoring her instinct to retreat, she mustered the courage to approach his bed.

"Get out. I sent you away for a reason." George's coughing shook the bed. "You're not my daughter. Get back on the stagecoach and go."

"Father, please. I came to take care of you until you're better." Isobel kneeled beside him. She tried to hold his hand, but he pulled away. "Would you like some tea?"

"I don't..." He coughed up some blood into an already bloody handkerchief. "want your tea."

Jane brought a tablespoon of dark syrup. "Time for the doctor's tonic to settle your cough. You don't want to cough up any more blood."

George opened his mouth and took the medicine. Jane took out a fresh handkerchief from her pocket and handed it to him, taking the bloody one.

Retreating from the bedroom, tears brimmed in Isobel's eyes. Rejected by her own father, compounded by his acceptance of Jane's care, was a harsh blow. She resolved to face the challenge, her determination steeling her against the pain of his words.

Jane went over, gave Isobel a hug, and led her out of the bedroom. She whispered, "It's going to be okay. He is a grouchy man who is deathly ill with consumption. Men are the worst when they're sick. Just big babies. I'm sure it will take a couple of days and he will be thankful you came."

"I hope you're right." Isobel pointed to a closed door. "Is that another bedroom?"

Jane said, "That's your old room. The bed is small, but I guess it will work for now. If not, we'll round up another bed somewheres."

Isobel smiled. "Thank you for your kindness."

"I don't know if it is kindness to bring you here, but it is the last chance you get to see your pa." Jane crossed her arms and cocked her head. "Do you want something to eat? I can fix you something. We have a dining room. If you ever want to eat, you just come on over."

"Jane, get her out of here now!" George said.

Isobel frowned while staring at George's bedroom door. "I am hungry. And this place is a little depressing."

"Let's go, then. You'll eat some grub and feel better about everything." Jane looked around. "The place needs a woman's touch. I think he threw everything away when your mother died. I was told he was a little crazy then." Jane chuckled. "He says your mother was a witch, a real one."

Isobel smiled. If she only knew, she was standing next to one. George had discovered her mother's secret gifts, like her Aunt Stella had feared.

Stepping out of the dreary store and into the fading light of Tin Creek, Isobel felt the weight of her new reality settling upon her. The challenges of adjusting to life in this rugged town, of dealing with a father who was a stranger to her, loomed large. Yet, within her, a spark of resolve flickered, ready to face whatever Tin Creek had in store.

Tom, his face contorted in anger and frustration, dragged Shelley through the saloon. His rough grip tightened as they passed the bar to the left, where the usual clamor of clinking glasses and rowdy banter hushed. Shelley resisted using all her might, her protests echoing through the room. "Damn you! Interfering in my business in front of the entire town. I want that girl in my establishment. I require that girl because you are worthless. Can't make any money with a yammering biddy like you, can I?"

As the scene unfolded, the rest of the saloon's inhabitants ceased their activities and stared with a mix of curiosity and unease.

Shelley, her spirit unbroken, resisted, her voice cutting through the tense air. "Damn you, Tom! Why would a girl like that even want to be near you? You reek like cat piss and skunk mist. You're unbearable, a complete windbag!"

Reaching the top of the stairs, Shelley wrenched herself free from Tom's iron grip. To reassert his dominance, Tom seized the neckline of her dress, tearing it and exposing her. Shelley, mortified, clutched at the tattered fabric, her back turned to the watching crowd below as tears welled in her eyes.

"I hate you, Tom. I hate being here," she sobbed. "You've ruined Jack's place. Everyone goes to Marisol's now. How am I supposed to make money?"

Tom, his face flushed red, shouted back, his words echoing off the walls, "I know I told all of you'ns not to utter that name. This is my saloon, fair and square."

Shelley, her anguish turning to defiance, spat back, "Look at this place! Two customers! Two!"

Tom's anger boiled over as he spat out his retort. "I don't see you entertaining them. You should be there sitting on one of um's lap and giggling your tits for the other one instead of having a conniption." He could feel his control slipping away, a familiar rage consuming him. "That's how you keep customers and make money, you dumb wench. I'm not even a painted lady, and I can do it better than you. What, I have to send you to Calico Queen school now?"

"Shut up!" Shelley, turning away in disgust, was met with Tom's unrelenting grip.

He shook her. "Stay out of my face today, Shelley. Don't push me."

"Yeah, what are you going to do? I'm not afraid of you! You're just a windbag who thinks he's the biggest toad in the puddle. You never shut up." Shelley attempted to tug from Tom's grip while holding her top. "On and on about nothing." She stood her ground, her tears now mixing with a fierce resolve. "You think you are so important, but you're just a nobody like us. That's how we all ended up here."

Tom, his anger reaching a boiling point, acted without thinking. In a fit of blind fury, he pushed Shelley over the balcony. As she plummeted, his heart raced with a toxic mix of triumph and dread. "Let's see you talk back now," he muttered under his breath.

The saloon fell silent except for Shelley's scream, the patrons' expressions a mix of shock and disbelief. Tom stood at the balcony, his chest heaving, the gravity of his actions dawning on him.

The other saloon girls who stayed out of the way upstairs screamed. The customer sitting below ran as Shelley hit the table he was at, breaking it in half, her head striking the back of a chair, splintering it. One of the broken legs impaled itself into the wall. Blood flowed out of Shelley's contorted body, a haunting testament to Tom's unbridled wrath.

No one moved. They stared at Tom, who was looking down calmly with his hands resting on the unbroken part of the balcony railing. "Well, someone get that cleaned up. Girls, in your rooms." He turned and came downstairs nonchalantly.

"Shit! What are we gonna do now?" Walter, an older man who worked at the saloon, asked Matt, the bartender, behind the bar.

"I don't know. I've never had to clean up after a killing. A bar fight, ya but, but never a killing. We gotta do what the boss says." Matt started grabbing rags while Walter grabbed the mop. "Al, are you going to help or just stand there?"

"I guess I might just stand here and watch." Al chuckled.

Walter mopped on one side of Shelley.

Matt was on his knees on the other side, his rags soaked. "Why don't we take her body into the storeroom until we figure out what to do with her? That way, we can clean up the rest of the blood. Don't want anybody coming in asking questions."

Tom blocked two customers, trying to sneak out. "If you know what's good for you, you won't say a word about what you just saw to no one. I won't take too kindly to talk. You don't want to cross me. And the next time you come in, it'll be free drinks for ya."

One customer said, "Oh, no. I don't want you mad at me. No way."

Tom stepped aside and watched them leave. He gestured to Walter and Matt. "You're gonna dig a hole right out the back door and shove her in it tonight when it's too dark for anyone to see what you're doing."

Walter tipped his head and mumbled, "I didn't sign up for this. I didn't want to see no more blood after the war."

Tom said, "What did you say? Do you have problems with how I run this place? You want to join Shelley? Maybe Al can take care of your problems. He don't like you, you know?"

Matt looked at Tom. "He said it's a lot of blood."

Tom replied as he walked away, "Yes, women always do bleed too much."

Matt and Walter wrapped Shelley in old bed sheets to contain the blood. Matt grabbed Shelley on one end while Walter had the other and took her out, blood continuing to drip.

Tom said, "You gonna clean that, too."

Matt groaned.

When they returned from removing Shelley, Walter said, "We'll take turns tonight, so no one will question if one of us is missing for a bit."

"Sounds good. We need to get rid of the broken table and chair, but at least that looks like another bar fight. No big deal." Matt added.

Tom, his heart as black as the night outside, prowled upstairs, a sneer etched on his face. He snarled, "None of this is a big deal. Shelley had to run her mouth and make a scene like always." The burden of resolving the chaos Shelley had left in her wake irked him, fueling his already seething temper. "Al, I hired you to be the box herder here, but what I'm hearing is not good," he growled as he passed Al, shooting him a withering glance.

Tom approached the young girls, his presence looming like a dark cloud. "You need to keep your mouths shut. Not a word to anyone," he barked, his finger jabbing into one girl's chest, forcing her to retreat. "And a new rule. You girls have to stay inside. No going outside embarrassing me anymore. Got that?" His command was absolute, his tone brooking no dissent.

"Get in your rooms!" Al's shout echoed Tom's stern directive, his smile a sycophantic echo of Tom's dark mood.

Downstairs, Matt and Walter scrambled to erase the remnants of the evening's horror. Walter lamented, his hands jammed into his armpits, "I'm not sure we can get it all. There'll be a stain."

Tom, his mind churning with anger and opportunism, snapped, "Throw some paint on it." He stomped downstairs, his boots thudding against the wooden steps.

With Tom's watchful eye on him, Walter hurriedly grabbed paint and a brush, his movements unsteady and his hands trembling.

Standing over the bloodstained floor, Tom envisioned a new future for the saloon. "Paint a square right here. Put a table and chairs," he instructed, a twisted smile creeping across his face. "I'll have it for high-roller poker, where all the action is. The only saloon in town with gambling." The prospect of profits from his new scheme seemed to lift his spirits. In his deranged mind, Shelley's tragic end had become a stepping stone to greater riches.

Tom declared in a booming voice, "I'll be in my room. Don't bother me unless you have a good idea to get the new girl in my saloon. I'm short a girl."

With a final, callous command, "Get me some fixings, too," he retreated to his room, slamming the door behind him. In the solitude
of his quarters, sinister thoughts of his plans, his schemes, and the
power he held over his corrupt domain consumed Tom's mind. The
night's events were but a mere inconvenience in his grand design, the
loss of life a trivial matter in his pursuit of power and profit.

CHAPTER SIX

JOHN EASED OFF THE borrowed mare with a practiced fluidity, his boots thudding against the stable floor. He led the horse to a stall with a gentle hand, removing the saddle with efficient motions. The familiar scent of hay and leather enveloped him as he tended to the horse, providing fresh hay and water before giving her a quick brush down. His movements were automatic, a comforting routine that grounded him in the familiar rhythms of ranch life.

Eager to see his family after months of absence, John hurried toward the house, his heart swelling with anticipation. The sprawling ranch landscape, with its endless fences and open skies, was a stark contrast to the confined classrooms and textbooks. He noted the worn fences that would soon need his attention, a task he welcomed after the long months of academic rigor.

As he expected, he found his mother, Anna, in the kitchen, the aroma of freshly baked cookies filling the air. John crept up behind her, unable to resist the opportunity for a playful surprise. "I'm home. Your cub is back," he announced, wrapping her in a bear hug.

Anna's startled scream turned into a joyous embrace. "My God, you scared me," she exclaimed. "But it's the best scare. I'm so happy you're home."

"Guess who else is back?" John asked, his eyes twinkling with mischief as he reached for a cookie.

Anna's patience with his guessing games was thin. "No. Just tell me. And put that cookie back," she demanded, hands on her hips.

John couldn't resist dragging out the moment. "You loved her like your own daughter," he said, knowing full well the impact of his words.

Anna's reaction was priceless as hands dropped off her hips and chin and mouth dropped to her chest. She placed her hands over her mouth. "Isobel?" she gasped, tears glistening in her eyes.

It was the response he hoped for. All he could do was nod.

Anna bounced from foot to foot and the warmth of his mother's hug enveloped him, her excitement mirroring his own. "Heavens above. How? Why?"

John led his mother to the living room and sat on a stool in front of her. "She was on the train, in the same car as me. And I know this sounds bizarre, but she's the one. I can't get her out of my head. I've been walking on clouds since I found her sitting in a chair with a book looking out the window. Isobel's beautiful."

Anna listened intently, her hands clasping his. "Not any more bizarre than me thinking you two would make a perfect pair when you played together as young tots."

John recalled picking flowers for Isobel, and his mother's scolding that turned into praise for his kindness. But now, Isobel's plans to attend nursing school hung over him like a cloud. "Well, she's here to take care of George since he is so sick with consumption. I don't know how long she will be here. She mentioned going to nursing school in September. So..."

Anna's advice was gentle yet firm. "Enjoy the time she is here. If it's meant to be, it will."

John grimaced. "Easy for you to say. It's not your heart in play."

Anna tilted her head, her response tender. "It is if it is your heart. I'm only telling you that you can't change the future for someone else. This maybe a lifelong dream of hers. Did you invite her for dinner?"

"No. I figured I needed to talk to you first."

Anna gave him a side eye and shook her head. "Never when it comes to Isobel. You go to town tomorrow and ask her. You hear?"

"Yes, ma'am. I better unpack and find father. I'm sure he needs some help."

Chuckling, Anna headed back to the kitchen. "He's going to be happy to see you and not because of your help."

Ascending the stairs to his room, bag in hand, John felt a surge of purpose. He now had a reason to return to town, to see Isobel again. In the privacy of his room, he allowed himself to daydream about the days ahead, each one an opportunity to be near her. The challenge of balancing his longing with respect for her dreams weighed on him, but he was determined to make the most of whatever time they had.

Isobel stepped into her childhood room, a space defined by its stark simplicity. The bed and dresser stood as unadorned reminders of a utilitarian past. She surveyed the room, noting the peeling wallpaper and the musty air that made the space confining. Approaching the window, she attempted to pry it open, only to find it immovable. Her fingers traced around the frame, searching for any obstruction.

She stood in front of the window, closed her eyes to clear her mind, and focus her intention.

"Great goddess Danu, Release the binds that hold this pane, let this window open without strain. So mote it be!"

The power of her words seemed to vibrate in the air, causing the window to rattle and give way, inviting a gentle breeze to waft inside. This breeze carried with it the delightful aromas of the evening, refreshing both the room and her spirit.

As she looked around, Isobel hoped for a spark of recognition, a fragment of memory from her early years. Yet, the room remained alien to her, devoid of any connection to her past. Frustration welled up inside her. She was four when she left this place—shouldn't some remembrance of her home, her play, or her mother linger in the corners of her mind?

Unpacking her travel bag, she laid out her nightgown and then approached the dresser, only to encounter another immovable object—the top drawer. Despite repeating her earlier spell, the drawer remained shut. Leaning down, she inspected the underside, finding no physical reason for its resistance. A realization dawned on her; perhaps her mother had enchanted the drawer to keep it private. The grimoire that Aunt Stella had urged her to find—could it be concealed there?

Exhausted but undeterred, Isobel unpacked her belongings into the other drawers. Settling on her bed, she opened her book, *The Story of a Modern Woman*, and lit the lantern with a breath, a small act of magick in the privacy of her room.

But her mind refused to settle, wandering instead to the mystery of her mother's hidden grimoire. She searched under the bed, feeling along the floorboards for any sign of a hidden compartment. Even after moving the dresser, her search yielded no clues.

George's irritated voice echoed through the thin walls, "Give me peace, dammit!"

Isobel's soft apology did little to quell her determination. She left the dresser askew, continuing her quest in silence. She checked under the mattress, probed the walls for hidden nooks, but found nothing.

The puzzle of the stuck drawer consumed her thoughts. She lay on the bed, her mind racing with possibilities. Where would one hide a grimoire? In plain sight or concealed within the mundane? The question nagged at her, refusing to let her rest.

As the night deepened, Isobel's exhaustion overtook her curiosity. Her last thoughts before drifting into sleep were of hidden compartments, secret spells, and the elusive grimoire that linked her to her mother's mysterious past.

CHAPTER SEVEN

ISOBEL COUGHED, HER THROAT irritated by the clouds of dust billowing up from the long-neglected shelves behind the counter. Years, perhaps over a decade, of accumulated grime coated everything, making her task daunting. After two hours of relentless cleaning, the temptation to use magick for a quick fix gnawed at her. But it wouldn't do; a suddenly pristine shop would raise eyebrows. It was a cruel irony, having the power to make things easier yet bound by discretion.

Isobel's heart sank as she spotted Tom from the saloon making his way across the street through the grimy windows behind the counter. Her previous encounter had been unsettling enough, and she wasn't keen on a repeat. She hesitated, weighing her options. The door was unlocked for Jane's convenience, but Tom's unpredictable nature from the day before loomed in her mind.

No, no, no, don't come in here. Isobel watched with a growing sense of dread as Tom approached the boardwalk and headed straight for her door.

Pushing the door open, Tom stepped in, his presence filling the room with an unwelcomed black aura, flowing and bubbling around him. "Sorry about yesterday," he began, his apology sounding hollow to Isobel. "Thought I had a new saloon girl, and you would be a fine one at that. I hope you will forgive my despicable behavior; I am ashamed of myself." His slight bow did little to soften his rough exterior.

"You caused me quite a fright. But I can forgive you." Isobel nodded, her mind racing for a way to end the interaction. Tom's unkempt appearance and the stench that clung to him only reinforced her desire to keep him at arm's length. His dark aura, swirling ominously, was a visual echo of his malevolence.

"I am Tom McCall. I did not catch your name, only that you are George's daughter." His exaggerated bow, coupled with his greasy hair and soiled clothing, painted a pathetic picture.

"My name is Isobel Perkins," she replied, forcing a smile while her mind screamed for him to leave.

"I didn't realize George had two daughters. Only heard about the mute one."

"I am his only daughter and I can speak very well." Isobel replied while rolling her eyes.

"George talked about how you saw the robbers kill your mother right in front of you."

"That's all he knows about me," Isobel said. His prying only deepened her desire to see him gone.

Wandering around the store, Tom approached the wood stove. He asked, "Do you need your tea refreshed? I see you have water boiling on the wood stove." He grabbed the kettle and walked to the counter where her teacup was sitting.

Isobel turned away, focusing on her cleaning, signaling her disinterest in further conversation. "I have a lot of cleaning to do." *Please, leave. Why me?*

"Here you go. Nice hot tea for the hard-working lady."

Isobel turned back around and picked up the cup. Isobel sniffed the cup warily, detecting a hint of alcohol amid the mint. She set the cup down with a smirk, feigning gratitude. "I will let it cool a bit. Thank you."

"Nothing better than a cup of tea. My mother swore by her tea and liked it piping hot." Tom's lingering presence at the counter, leaning in with an unsettling closeness, left Isobel grappling for a solution.

Great, now what should I do? Isobel caught sight of a gun under the counter. Though unfamiliar with firearms, she had to project confidence. With a shaky hand, she lifted the pistol and directed it towards Tom, the weight of the weapon sending a chill along her spine. "You put something in my tea," she accused, her voice steady despite her racing heart. "My uncle taught me to smell anything before I drink it because men will take advantage."

Laudanum was in the Chicago papers every day. The stories were always the same. Isobel did not intend on falling victim. Tom erred, assuming she was naïve.

Tom shook his head. "I beg your pardon. You are mistaken." His shifting aura, a growing mass of blackness, betrayed his lie.

"I know by your behavior yesterday. Do you keep the women in your saloon there by addicting them with laudanum?" Isobel walked around the counter, the gun still pointing at Tom. "I want you to leave the store and never return. I don't want you to speak to me. Stay the hell away from me." She choke on the crude word as it came out of her mouth. She tried to keep her hand steady, to not betray her fear. It was difficult, if not impossible.

Tom started for the door, his black mass growing larger than him. He stopped in the doorway. Tom hesitated at the door, his hand hovering over his own gun. After a tense moment, he muttered, "Fine. If that's the way you want to be. Just know you are messing with the wrong person in this town."

"Get out! Now!" Isobel's heart was beating fast and her mouth was dry.

Tom's back was to her, but she was hoping he wouldn't turn around and shoot her. Would she, could she, use magick to stop a bullet? Probably not. Too fast for her skill. Did time just stop?

Tom stormed out, slamming the door behind him, causing the entire front of the building to shake. He disappeared into his saloon.

Isobel dropped her arm and let out a heavy sigh. She retrieved her teacup from the counter and threw it out the door.

Isobel sagged against the counter, the pistol slipping from her grasp as relief washed over her. She tossed the tainted tea out the door, her body still quivering from the encounter. Questions swirled in her mind. Why had she come to this forsaken place? Was it worth staying in a town where her father rejected her and where men like Tom roamed free?

The door opened again, and Isobel raised the gun, only to find Jane standing there, her arms raised in alarm. "Whoa! It's me, Jane."

Relieved, yet still shaken, Isobel lowered the gun. "I'm sorry. I thought Tom came back. Oh, my."

Jane's concern was obvious as she stepped closer, her arm wrapping around Isobel. "Are you alright? I saw him leaving the saloon and was sure he was up to no good. Do you want to come over to the hotel for a bit? I'll make you some tea."

Grateful for the offer, Isobel nodded, her hands trembling. "Yes, that sounds good. I'm so shaken." Isobel moved toward the door, accompanied by Jane. "Look at my hands shaking," she uttered, her voice unsteady. "Tom put laudanum in my tea, and I'm sure he would have dragged me across the street. I'm so mad... and scared."

Jane's gaze drifted to the pistol abandoned on the counter, a silent witness to the recent confrontation. "Do you know how to shoot?" she asked, eyebrow lifted.

"No," Isobel replied, her voice still quivering. Her helplessness in handling the weapon added to her growing sense of unease.

Jane's response was immediate and decisive. "I guess I better teach ya." Her words carried a mix of resolve and protective urgency.

Isobel, her hands still quivering, struggled to steady them as she locked the store's door. The lock clicked into place, but her heart continued to pound against her ribcage, echoing the turmoil within. She paused for a moment, her gaze fixed on the saloon across the street, the source of her current distress. Her eyes narrowed, reflecting a mix of anger and repulsion as she replayed the recent encounter with Tom in her mind—his deceitful act, the threat hidden beneath his words.

A deep yearning to seek guidance from Aunt Stella welled up inside her. Stella's wisdom, her comforting presence, felt like a distant solace amid the chaos swirling around Isobel. Isobel longed for the sage advice that had always helped navigate her through troubled waters. The intensity of her emotions—fear, anger, helplessness—felt overwhelming, leaving her grappling for a sense of control in the unpredictability of Tin Creek.

Chapter Eight

Isobel, taking a temporary respite from her tumultuous morning, sat at a table by the front window in the hotel's dining room. The crisp, starched tablecloth and the tastefully draped curtains were a stark contrast to her father's rustic store and the dusty roads of Tin Creek. This unexpected touch of elegance, reminiscent of her home in Chicago, offered her a moment of comfort in an otherwise unfamiliar world.

Isobel exhaled a long, slow breath, the tension draining from her neck and shoulders, her hands steadying after the unnerving encounter with Tom

When Jane entered the dining room, Isobel inquired, "Where is the post office?"

Jane gestured towards the front desk. "Right here," she explained. "Our town is too small for its own post office, so my husband, Fred, handles all the postal duties." She leaned against a nearby chair, her demeanor casual yet attentive. "Do you have a letter to mail?"

Isobel's gaze drifted, a wistful look on her face. "Not yet, but I have so much to tell Aunt Stella," she replied with sarcasm. "Especially about how thrilled my father was to see me." Her thoughts flickered to the strained meeting with her father, a shadow of disappointment crossing her features. She took a deep inhale of her tea, seeking solace in its familiar aroma. "I also need to send a telegram to let Uncle Henry know I've arrived. Where's the telegraph office?"

Jane walked to the window, pointing down the street. "You can send a telegram at the bank over there," she said, directing Isobel's gaze to a modest building on the other side of the wide dusty road. The bank's unassuming exterior stood in stark contrast to the grandeur of the big-city banks Isobel was accustomed to, a subtle reminder of the vast differences between her past life and her current reality in Tin Creek.

Isobel's eyes locked onto the sight of John as he rode past the hotel. Her heart fluttered with a surge of anticipation, a mix of excitement and nervousness tangling in her stomach. She observed him as he maneuvered his horse to a stop, hitching it with practiced ease in front of the store. A magnetic pull drew Isobel towards the window, her body moving against her will, but Jane's hand came to rest on her shoulder, a silent, reassuring message to stay put.

"Don't worry. I'll let him know you're here." With swift strides, Jane disappeared from the dining room, her voice carrying back as she called out to John, "She's over here!"

Isobel could only listen, her heart pounding in her chest as Jane's footsteps faded away. She returned, her presence a brief comfort. "I have to finish some work upstairs. I'll see you in a little while when it's time for George's medicine," Jane's voice was light, her smile fleeting as she glanced at John entering the room.

Isobel's heart danced in a rapid, uneven rhythm, a mix of anticipation and anxiety swirling within her as the room grew warmer, almost stifling. A tentative smile played at the corners of her lips, barely containing the whirlwind of emotions. "Do you need something in the store?" she asked, her voice not quiet above a whisper.

John, oblivious to the storm inside her, took a seat across from Isobel. "Oh, no. I came to see if you've settled in and if you need anything." He placed his tan, wide-brimmed hat on the table, the action so mundane yet so significant in that moment.

Isobel's fleeting smile faltered, turning into a frown as memories of her earlier encounter rushed back. "I'm was trying to clean the store, but I had to come over here to calm down after Tom came in," she confessed, her voice revealing the turmoil that lay beneath her composed exterior.

John's gaze shifted out the window, his eyes narrowing as he peered out towards the saloon, his brows knitting together in a display of concern and confusion. "Why was Tom at the store?" he asked, his voice carrying a note of apprehension.

"That crazy man came in to apologize for yesterday and then snuck some laudanum into my tea." Isobel's heart raced once more, a tempest of fear and anger swirling within as she recounted the harrowing encounter. She took a deep, steadying breath, trying to calm the storm inside her. "I didn't drink it, but he waited for me to. I saw a handgun under the counter, pointed it at him, and told him to leave." Her voice quivered, betraying the lingering fear. "Jane came over after he left and suggested I come here."

John's expression turned grim. "Tom's a problem. Do you want me to go talk to him?"

Isobel shook her head, the tension creeping from her throat to her shoulders, her muscles tightening. "No. I don't think that would help much. He's not a reasonable man."

John picked up a spoon, turning it over and over. "Let me know if you change your mind," he offered. He then shifted the topic, perhaps to lighten the mood. "Well, my mother wanted me to ask you to dinner tomorrow if you can. She's excited to see you."

Isobel's face lit up, her smile broad and genuine, a brief respite from the tension. "Yes, I would love to meet your family," she replied, her spirits lifted.

A blonde young woman rushing in shattered the tranquility of the dining room. Clad in a dress that seemed to cling a bit too snugly to her form, her tightly laced corset only accentuated her pronounced curves. She moved with a bold, predatory grace, her gaze locked on John. A blend of excitement and a sense of ownership colored her approach. "John! You're back! My love is here!" she declared loudly, launching herself at him in a display of affection that was as enthusiastic as it was public. Her aura was a vibrant mix of deep reds and purples, a testament to her dominant and confrontational character. She dominated the room like a tempest, her presence demanding attention, each gesture exuding an unapologetic self-assurance and formidable strength.

From her vantage point, Isobel observed the dynamic between the woman and John. The way she held onto him spoke of a deep-seated familiarity, a relationship with roots and history. Isobel mentally prepared herself to maintain a careful distance, recognizing that any interaction with this woman would require a delicate touch. Her commanding aura and outward appearance marked her as someone not easily swayed or ignored, and crossing paths with her might be more trouble than it was worth.

Isobel felt a rising discomfort as John restrained Betsy with a firm but gentle hold, standing to address her. "I'm back, Betsy," he announced, his voice a mixture of resignation and politeness.

At the sight of the intruder's overt display of affection, Isobel's instinct was to shield herself from the intimacy too private for such a public setting. She attempted to rise from her chair, but the furniture caught on an uneven floor plank. Pushing back with more force, the chair's legs screeched against the hardwood floor, drawing unwanted attention. Isobel cringed, her cheeks burning with embarrassment. "Sorry. I will leave you two to your reunion," she murmured.

Betsy, with a swift, predatory movement, twirled to give Isobel a thorough, scrutinizing look, her gaze traveling from head to toe in a blatant assessment. "Who are you?" she demanded, her tone sharp and challenging.

As Isobel stood, trying to regain her composure, John extended his hand in a gesture of introduction. "I didn't get the chance to introduce you to Isobel, George Perkins' daughter. We traveled on the train together from Chicago." His voice was calm, attempting to bridge the tension.

Betsy's reaction was immediate and marked by shock. Her mouth fell open in disbelief. "You did." She then pivoted to Isobel, planting her hands firmly on her hips, embodying defiance and territoriality. "Do you think you can steal John from me? You might as well go back to Chicago." Her words were sharp and hostile as she returned her full attention to John, standing so close to him that there was a whisker of space between them.

"Why didn't you tell me you were back?" Betsy's voice was a mix of coquettishness and demand as she began stroking John's chest, a possessive gesture. "Mummy and Daddy will be so happy. They're ready to make plans, you know."

John, visibly uncomfortable, edged away, his eyes flicking between Betsy and Isobel. "What plans?" he asked, his tone reflecting his unease.

Betsy's voice rose, oblivious to John's discomfort. "Our wedding. Everyone knows you proposed to me. There's no reason to wait to get married." Her assertion rang through the room, her excitement contrasting with John's obvious reluctance.

Isobel, feeling like a bystander in a play, noticed that she wasn't alone in her observation. Two men at a nearby table in the dining room were eavesdropping, their eyes flicking between the unfolding drama and their meals, a mix of curiosity and entertainment on their faces.

John, displaying a quiet resolve, grabbed his hat and stepped back from Betsy's imposing presence. "I never proposed," he stated. "You're putting words in my mouth. We were friends, that's all." His denial was clear, setting a boundary with a calm yet assertive tone.

Isobel watched, her mouth agape, a bystander caught in the whirlwind of emotions swirling around her. The scene unfolded like nothing she had ever witnessed, leaving her questioning the world she had known. *Do people really act like this? Is this normal?*

John, perhaps sensing her discomfort, crossed the room to join Isobel. "Let me walk you back to the store. I have some errands to run before I return home." His voice was gentle, a stark contrast to the tension in the air. He glanced back at Betsy, adding with a hint of reassurance, "My mother is excited to see you tomorrow."

They left the dining room, leaving Betsy standing alone, her face contorted with fury. "You and your family will regret this and Bell, whoever you are, your father owes my daddy's bank a lot of money." Her voice rose to a shout, ensuring her words reached every corner of the room. "I'm sure I can convince Daddy to take the store and leave you and your pathetic father homeless and penniless."

As they walked away, John leaned in to whisper to Isobel, "Sorry you had to witness a Betsy tirade. She has no self-control, and she imagines a lot."

Isobel, still processing the scene, replied, "I don't think I have ever seen such a spectacle. I'm wondering why you didn't mention her on the train." She shook her head. "But I would have kept that one a secret, I guess." Her words carried a tone of empathy, understanding why John might have withheld Betsy's existence from their earlier conversations.

Isobel fumbled with the lock, her hands still trembling from the earlier encounter as she finally unlocked the store door. "Thank you for walking me back. And that lovely entertainment," she said with a touch of sarcasm, her laugh a mix of genuine amusement and a hint of lingering shock.

John responded with a chuckle, a light-hearted sound that eased some of the tension. "I'm glad we can laugh about it. We can tell my family about it over dinner tomorrow. My parents are not Betsy fans," he admitted, his smile fading into a more serious expression. He paused, his brows knitting together in concern. "How's your father?"

Isobel's gaze dropped to her feet, her shoes suddenly very interesting as she grappled with the reality of her father's condition. "He's not good at all. Jane said the doctor doesn't think he will last long," she murmured, her voice soft.

John's frown deepened, and he tilted his head. "Sorry to hear that. Do you know anything about what she said about your father owing the bank money?"

"I'll ask about the loan at the bank. I don't want to bother my father about it. See you tomorrow. Goodbye." Isobel's voice was steady, but there was an underlying note of worry as she contemplated the financial uncertainties awaiting her.

"Bye, Isobel," John said.

After John left, Isobel secured the door, the click of the lock echoing in the now-quiet store. She needed her reticule before heading to the bank, her mind racing with the events of the day and the tasks that lay ahead. As she prepared to confront the possible financial realities that threatened the store, she felt a mix of apprehension tightening her chest and determination fueling her resolve.

Isobel stepped into the dimly lit, small wooden structure that served as the town's bank. The rickety door, barely more substantial than the one at her store, creaked on its hinges as she entered. Pausing just inside, she allowed her eyes a moment to adjust from the glaring brightness of the sun-drenched street to the dark, dusty interior of the bank. The sparse room boasted little more than a tall counter, barricaded with bars, reminiscent of a fortress designed to keep the world at bay. A placard displayed the name of Mr. Johnson.

After Isobel approached the counter, she stood silently for a moment, taking in the musty smell of old wood and ink. She rapped her knuckles against the wood; the sound echoing in the quiet room, summoning someone to attend to her.

A haze of green appeared followed by a short, stocky man, round glasses perched on his nose. His lips were a thin, tight line, and his eyebrow arched as he peered at her. "May I help you?" he asked, his tone curt.

"I would like to send a telegram," Isobel responded with a practiced smile, though a knot of apprehension in her stomach twisted. This man was Betsy's father, and she wondered if he would be as confrontational as his daughter. The greedy green aura swirled with angry red concerned her since he was the banker handling everyone's money.

"Yes, yes. I can help you with that," he replied, waddling over to the counter, his movements betraying a sense of self-importance. Mr. Johnson slid a piece of paper in front of himself and picked up a pen. "Who and where are you sending the telegram to?"

"Mr. Henry Perkins in Chicago," Isobel answered.

"Any relation to George Perkins?" The banker peered over his glasses with a hint of suspicion.

"Yes, his brother. I'm Isobel Perkins," she replied, keeping her explanation brief. "The message is 'Arrived safely.'"

The man's demeanor shifted, his expression hardening. "Your father's loan is past due. I will. I mean, the bank will have to take possession of the building if he doesn't pay soon." The delivery bristled with hostility.

Isobel straightened her posture, her tone firm yet controlled. "How much is past due? My father is seriously ill."

"I need $100 by the end of the week. There's a gentleman in town interested in the building and has stated he would pay the loan in full to acquire it. I need to keep the bank's interest in the matter," he replied, his grin taking on an unpleasant, almost predatory quality, mirroring his daughter's assertiveness.

Betsy's father added with a sneer, "You met my daughter earlier. She came here right before you, very distraught, my only child, my angel. She said you are ruining her life by stealing her fiancée."

Isobel struggled to maintain her composure, fighting the urge to laugh at the absurdity of his statement. Keeping her face neutral, she replied, "John wasn't aware they were engaged."

Mr. Johnson's face flushed with anger. "Maybe he forgot while he was at school, but they are. She came home one day and told us."

Isobel tilted her head, her voice laced with a hint of skepticism. "In Chicago, the man asks the bride's father for his blessing before he asks the lady. Do they not do the same here?"

Mr. Johnson's response was curt and businesslike. "The telegram for two words is 20 cents."

Isobel retrieved a quarter from her purse and slid it across the counter, a small act of defiance. "You may keep the change or put it toward the loan however you see fit. I want the balance of the loan on paper, please."

"Certainly. You don't have to be impolite," he retorted before disappearing into the back room.

Returning, he slapped the loan document on the counter. "Do you need anything else?"

"No, thank you. I will be back with a payment soon, so you can tell the interested gentleman he will have to look elsewhere for property," Isobel replied with poise, folding the paper and slipping it into her reticule. She resolved to examine it later, away from Mr. Johnson's prying eyes.

As she turned to leave, his voice, sharp and cold, followed her. "Pleasure doing business with you."

Stepping out into the sunlight, the sight of John greeted Isobel riding down the street on his horse. His face broke into a radiant grin upon seeing her, his aura bursting with warmth and friendliness. It was a welcome sight, a moment of joy amid her challenges.

"See you tomorrow," John called out as he approached her.

"Oh, yes. I am looking forward to it," Isobel replied, waving goodbye as he rode off. As she realized their exchange had taken place right in front of the bank, a chuckle escaped her lips. The small, defiant act of friendliness in the face of Mr. Johnson's hostility was a minor victory. She crossed the street, her mind already turning to the problem of the loan, but bolstered by the support she had in this new and challenging environment.

CHAPTER NINE

As ISOBEL AND JOHN arrived at the Carlyle ranch, the breathtaking view of the Bitterroot Mountains captivated her. The vibrant, colored bands etched into the jagged rocks were far more striking here than from the town. Perched atop a hill, the Carlyle family home commanded a spectacular view, with the meandering Tin Creek visible in the distance.

Greeted at the stable by John's father, Peter, Isobel felt a sense of calm emanating from him, his pale blue aura soothing as it ebbed and flowed. "Isobel, how are you? I'm Peter. You probably don't remember me," he said.

"I'm fine, Mr. Carlyle. How are you?" Isobel replied, politeness laced in her tone.

"Good. I'll be better if you call me Peter," he responded, taking the horse's bridle and turning to John. "I'll take care of Beau. Go on and take Isobel up to the house."

Peter's help was tender and nurturing, like a father helping his daughter dismount. "Anna is excited to see you. She's been cooking all afternoon," he added.

As they walked towards the house, Isobel was drawn to the lush vegetable and flower garden. Glancing around, she flicked her fingers at her side, bestowing a little boost to the plants. The action brought back memories of her own garden, stirring a longing within her.

Upon entering the log home, the enticing aromas of rosemary, thyme, and fresh bread filled the air, awakening Isobel's senses. John led her to the kitchen to find his mother, Anna, engrossed in cooking.

"Mom, I'm back with Isobel," John announced.

Anna whirled around and enveloped Isobel in a smothering hug. "I'm so glad you're back. I've missed you," she exclaimed. The warmth of Anna's embrace and her radiant, sunny aura were overwhelming to Isobel, whose family was more reserved.

"It has been a long time, Mrs. Carlyle. Thank you for inviting me," Isobel responded, touched by the affection.

"Dinner will be ready soon. Make yourself at home and call me Anna," John's mother insisted.

Isobel trailed Anna to the warm, bustling stove, the heart of the kitchen. "Do you need any help? I enjoy cooking," she volunteered.

Anna, however, waved off her offer and chuckled. "Dear, I don't make company work. I invited you here to spend time with you, not to put you to work." She then added with a nostalgic twinkle in her eye, "Your mother was a wonderful cook. Oh, speaking of Mary, I have something for you, something she wanted you to have when you were older." Anna's words were a torrent of warmth and affection, leaving no room for Isobel to interject. Isobel watched, intrigued and overwhelmed, as Anna bustled out of the room to retrieve the mysterious item.

John, observing the exchange, offered a lighthearted comment. "Don't mind her. When she's excited, she talks a lot." His words were affectionate, a son's loving acknowledgement of his mother's quirks.

"Your mother has a positive energy. I like her," Isobel replied, her gaze drifting to some medicinal dried herbs hanging in the kitchen. She wondered how Anna knew to use them.

Anna soon returned, cradling a piece of silver jewelry wrapped in a tea towel. "John, why don't you help Isobel put on this necklace?" Anna suggested. "Mary never said much about it, except it's been passed down in the family for centuries, and you were the next to receive it. I always figured it was why I sensed she was still with us."

As John reached to fasten the pendant around Isobel's neck, an electric sensation tingled on her skin where his fingers brushed against her. The pendant itself was a marvel—a trinity knot, intricately designed and encrusted with sparkling ruby, emerald, and amethyst gemstones. The sight of it brought tears to Isobel's eyes, not for its beauty, but for its significance. "Thank you. This is so extraordinary," she whispered, her voice choked with emotion. This was the very necklace her Aunt Stella had spoken of, the missing link to her past.

Anna's eyes mirrored Isobel's tearfulness. "Don't thank me, dear. Your mother entrusted this necklace to me to keep safe for you." Her voice broke as she reminisced, "Oh, I miss her. She was like a sister to me, which meant so much since I only had brothers growing up." Reaching into her apron pocket, Anna produced a handkerchief and handed it to Isobel with maternal care. "Don't cry, dear. I'm a softie myself—I blubber, and trust me, it's not a pretty sight."

In this moment, surrounded by the warmth of the kitchen and the Carlyles' kindness, Isobel experienced a profound connection to her mother. The necklace was not only a piece of jewelry; it was a tangible link to her heritage, a symbol of the enduring bond between her mother and generations of witches.

Peter's entrance into the kitchen was like a gust of fresh air, his voice booming with hearty cheerfulness filled the room. "It smells great! Are we eating soon? I don't think I can wait." His gaze swept over the group. "Hang on, did I miss something? You ladies are all teary. John, what did you do?"

Anna, her eyes glistening, dabbed at them with a kitchen towel. "I gave Isobel Mary's necklace," she explained, her voice a soft mixture of laughter and tears. "She started, and then I started. You know how I am."

Guiding Isobel out of the kitchen, John led her to the dining room, a gentle hand on her back, offering support and comfort. "Isobel, you can sit by Mom," he suggested, pulling out a chair for her. He took his place across the table from her.

Peter chimed in. "John, is it okay if I remain in my usual place?" The lightness of his words brought normalcy back to the emotionally charged atmosphere.

"Sure, Dad. I thought Mom and Isobel have a lot to talk about," John replied, winking at his father, the corners of his mouth twitching into a knowing smile. "Do you want me to be closer to you? Did you miss me? Don't worry, a few more days and you'll be ready to send me back." Isobel's smile was nostalgic as John and Peter's playful banter reminded her of her uncle back home. A pang of homesickness washed over her, mixed with a twinge of guilt for not having written to him. She had only managed a brief two-word telegram since her arrival. Resolving to pen a heartfelt letter to him and Aunt Stella that very night, she noted the things she wanted to share, the comfort of connecting with her family despite the distance.

Peter interrupted her reminiscing. "How is your father doing?"

Isobel's smile faded into a frown, her brow creased. "My father's condition is not stable. I have not spoken to the doctor myself, but Jane says the prognosis is not good. He has a difficult time breathing and is not interested in eating." Her voice trailed off as a troubling thought surfaced—what if her father passed away while she was away? The notion that she should be with him, not visiting, weighed on her heart, casting a shadow over the warm atmosphere.

"Sorry to hear that, Isobel. It's great you came. No one should see the end of their life alone, without family. We're delighted you are here. Isn't that right, John?" His gaze shifted to John, seeking affirmation.

John blushed at his father's directness. His cheeks tinged pink, he managed a shy yet sincere response, "Yes, we are, Dad." The laughter that followed from Peter lightened the mood.

Peter's tone turned serious as he broached the subject of Isobel's recent troubles. "John tells me you've had some problems with Tom. John doesn't know him since Tom came a few months ago, but everyone in town except for a few are ready to chase him out."

Isobel let out a heavy sigh, the weight of the ordeal clouding her expression. "First, he tried to drag me to the saloon as soon as I got off the stagecoach and then attempted to drug me yesterday." Her voice trembled, betraying the fear and frustration she bore recounting the events.

Anna gasped, her hands flying to her mouth. "Oh, my goodness," she exclaimed, her eyes wide.

Gathering her courage, Isobel continued, her voice steadier now. "I saw a gun under the counter, so I pointed it at him. I must confess I don't know how to shoot it, but I was desperate to get Tom out of the store."

Peter put down his fork, his expression turning thoughtful. "Isobel, you need to learn how to protect yourself. John can take you out and practice. Did you notice if the revolver was loaded?"

Isobel shrugged, tilting her head. "I think it was. There was something in the holes."

This elicited a round of laughter from everyone at the table, a moment of levity in an otherwise tense conversation. Even Isobel chuckled, her nerves eased by the family's warm response.

Anna reached out, placing her hand over Isobel's in a comforting gesture. "Peter taught me to shoot when we first met. Young ladies need to protect themselves here on the frontier," she said.

Isobel nodded in agreement, feeling a surge of determination. "That would be a good thing."

John chimed in, "It's not only Tom. You might come face to face with a wild animal. I'd be glad to give you some lessons."

Isobel had a mix of appreciation and resolve stir within her. The idea of learning to shoot, while daunting, also empowered her with a sense of taking control over her own safety.

Anna asked, "Have you met anyone else in town other than Jane and Tom?"

Isobel hesitated, her mind replaying the encounters. "Let's see. I met Betsy and then her father. Betsy claims she's marrying John, and her father is threatening to take my father's store if I don't pay him $100 by the end of the week."

John paused, his knife hovering mid-air over his bread. "Ah, sorry about Betsy. She has this idea that we are a couple, which is certainly not true. I was being friendly because no one else would befriend her when we were kids. And now, this is the thanks I get."

Isobel continued, her voice growing firmer. "Her father accused me of ruining his daughter's life. He's a truly disagreeable man. He even claimed someone was ready to pay off the loan for the store."

At this, Anna turned to Peter, a mischievous grin playing on her lips. "Dear, there's something we've been meaning to get, something we really need before winter. It's still a way off, but it's better to be prepared. You know what I'm talking about, right?"

Peter's face brightened. "Ah, good idea. I can get it installed and we'll be ahead of the game, especially now that John's back. It'll save my old bones some trouble sending John on the roof." He shot a playful grin at his son.

John, now intrigued and puzzled, asked, "So what are we getting, and why am I going on the roof?"

In perfect harmony, John's parents smiled and responded, "A pot belly stove!"

Isobel's mind calculated the cost of a potbelly stove and the additional expense for the piping. The numbers surpassed a hundred dollars, and she had a pang of guilt at the thought of the Carlyles incurring such an expense on her behalf. "Oh, I don't expect you to do anything you weren't planning on until later," she said.

Peter said, "Oh no. Better to get ahead on preparations for winter. We expanded the house last year when John was home from school. The old fireplace couldn't keep up, and it got quite chilly in here last winter." He rubbed his hands together.

Anna, ever the gracious hostess, transitioned the conversation. "Well, that's settled. Who's ready for dessert? I baked an apple pie." She gave John a meaningful look. "Why don't you get some apple cider out of the cellar?"

As John left to fetch the cider, Peter said, "I'm worried about you being in town by yourself. It's a shame how some of the townsfolk are treating you. Jane will surely let you stay at the hotel. It's unfortunate that a pretty young lady like you is a target."

"I appreciate that, really. But for now, my father is my priority, so I'm going to stay with him."

In that moment, surrounded by the warmth of the Carlyle home and the kindness of its inhabitants, Isobel felt a deep sense of belonging. Had she found a surrogate family here, far from her own? The thought brought a comforting sense of connection, a feeling she had been yearning for since her arrival in this new and challenging place.

As the quiet of the night settled in, Isobel tiptoed to her father's room, her movements cautious and silent. Standing at the doorway, she watched, almost holding her breath, waiting for the subtle rise and fall of his chest. In that moment, her earlier fears about his passing were unnecessary. He had lived fourteen years without her presence, and she realized that being there at his end might not mean much to him. And truth be told, she acknowledged to herself; it changed little for her either.

Turning away, Isobel entered her own modest bedroom, a stark contrast to the warmth and liveliness of the Carlyle home. She approached her dresser to wrestle with the top drawer, which had been jammed for days. To her surprise, it gave way, sliding open with a creak. Inside, she found an old cigar box. She carried it to her bed, sitting with the box resting in her lap, a mix of curiosity and apprehension coursing through her.

When she lifted the lid, she discovered a thick, green leather grimoire and a smaller brown leather grimoire inside. A shudder ran along her spine as her fingers brushed over the covers, but she hesitated to open them. Isobel wanted to be alert and rested, to delve into the magick and history they held—the legacies of her mother and her grandmother.

Aunt Stella's recent request echoed in her mind: to find her grandmother's grimoire and necklace, and a warning about the perils of reckless use of magick. Aunt Stella had feared this might have caused her sister's death, a constant reminder of the dangers that witches faced. One misstep could lead to dire consequences.

Her fingers delicately traced the intricate patterns of the necklace, a cherished heirloom that had been handed down through generations of powerful witches in her family. She marveled at the thought of so much magick, lost in a Montana valley. As she touched the necklace, a realization dawned on her—it was the key that had unlocked the jammed drawer, a testament to her mother's ingenuity and foresight.

Leaving the pendant with Anna was a calculated decision; the necklace and the cigar box couldn't be together, a secret safeguard her mother had cleverly put in place.

Ready for bed, Isobel changed into her nightgown and climbed under the covers. Rest eluded her, thoughts swirling around the revelations of the day. With a resigned sigh, she rose and opened the newer grimoire. The scent of exotic herbs wafted from its pages, a tangible connection to her mother. It was too dark to read and too late to delve into its mysteries, so she slid the book beneath her pillow, a symbolic gesture of keeping her mother's legacy close.

The moment Isobel settled back into bed, she realized the necklace's gentle pressure on her neck, its weight a comforting reassurance of the duties she must fulfill. Exhausted, she lacked the energy to delve into the mysterious connection between the pendant and the book. That would have to wait until tomorrow.

With the grimoire tucked beneath her pillow and the enchanted necklace resting against her skin, Isobel drifted towards sleep, her mind filled with thoughts of magick, legacy, and the unexplored secrets of her family's past. Tomorrow would be a day of discovery, but for now, she allowed herself to be enveloped by the night's embrace, the mysteries of her heritage waiting for the light of day.

Chapter Ten

THE GROWLING OF HER empty stomach jolted four-year-old Isobel awake. Rising in her small bed, her head bumped against the underside of the frame with a soft thud. Confusion clouded her mind. How did I get here? She wriggled out, rolling onto her belly and crawling into the sunlit room. The light streaming through her window beckoned her outside to play under the willow tree, a thought that lightened her heart.

As she opened her bedroom door, a jarring sight stopped her in her tracks. Her mother lay motionless on the floor beside the table. Isobel's heart raced as she dashed over, her small voice filled with urgency. "Mama, wake up!" She kneeled beside her, shaking her. "Mama, it's morning. Why are you sleeping on the floor?" As she laid her head against her mother's chest, she noticed an unsettling stillness—it lacked the comforting rise and fall of breath she was used to.

"Why won't you wake up?" Isobel's voice cracked as she shook her mother again, noticing the red stain on the floor and her mother's clothes.

Isobel wanted to hide, overwhelmed by the thought of her father returning. She retreated to her room, closed the door behind her, and crawled into the corner under her bed, her small body trembling.

Isolated and scared, Isobel felt helpless. Aunt Anna and Uncle Peter's ranch seemed far. Maybe Doc would help? But what if her father was downstairs? Her body shivered. Tears streamed down her cheeks as she cried herself to sleep.

Loud, persistent knocking later awakened Isobel. She slapped her hand over her mouth to silence her uncontrolled whimpering. It might be Father. She curled up as small as possible, hoping to be invisible if her bedroom door opened. The pounding went on and on, and she wanted it to end. She pictured her father ripping something to shreds out of rage. She might be his next victim. Would her mother, as always, protect her? She wanted to vanish into the wall or fly away through the window.

Footsteps on the stairs quickened Isobel's heartbeat. She held her breath as long as she was able, then covered her mouth when she exhaled.

"Oh, no!" a man's voice exclaimed. "Mary!"

It sounded like Jack from across the street.

"George," he called out. "Isobel. Are you here?" Isobel was sure it was Jack now, the man who might hand her over to her father. Despite Jack's kindness to her mother, Isobel didn't trust him.

More footsteps followed, accompanied by a woman's voice. "Oh, Mary!" she wept. "Who would do this?" It was Marisol, her mother's friend, but Isobel doubted her trustworthiness. The fear of being handed over to her father was so intense she wet herself while her racing heart caused pains in her chest.

"Isobel," Marisol called out.

The door to Isobel's room creaked open, revealing Marisol's fancy shoes with fluffy feathers Isobel would put on and, try to walk in, were visible. Marisol took a step towards the bed. Then Isobel noticed Marisol staring at her sideways.

"This is where I would hide, too," Marisol said. "Will you come out?"

Isobel shook her head, tears brimming in her eyes. She longed for her mother's comforting embrace.

"I promise I'll keep you safe," Marisol assured her.

Isobel wanted to believe her. "I'll pack some of your things. You can stay with me," Marisol said, struggling with the jammed drawer. "Will you come out when I'm done?"

Once the drawers were emptied, Marisol asked, "Are you ready to go?"

Isobel emerged from her hiding place, pulling her dress back to hide the wetness.

Marisol leaned in, examining Isobel's neck. "We better have Doc check that."

Isobel felt puzzled. Why did Doc need to check her neck? Marisol's once vibrant chartreuse aura, which had fluttered out of her like a fan, now seemed drained, puddling at her feet.

"Is it okay to bring her out?" Marisol called.

"Yes," Doc's voice responded. Isobel hoped Doc would help her mother. She remembered how he had cured her of an illness, and he never liked her father.

Marisol scooped Isobel up, startling her. She was four years old and walked just fine by herself.

CHAPTER ELEVEN

ISOBEL TOOK HER LEAVE from Doc, promising to return soon. He had expressed a keen interest in sharing his plans for expanding his medical practice after learning about her imminent departure for nursing school at the end of the summer.

Isobel knew she would find Marisol at the Sapphire Saloon, which stood out next door. Bathed in hues of purple and blue, it featured a striking leaded glass pane in the door with a sapphire design at its center. Marisol's flair for extravagance was obvious, and her establishment was a beacon of sophistication in the otherwise modest town. Isobel hesitated outside the saloon, searching for a sign of its openness, before trying the door. It opened to her touch, and she stepped inside, unsure of what to expect from a saloon in the middle of the day.

The interior of the Sapphire was a testament to Marisol's lavish taste, adorned with paisley brocade wallpaper in continuing shades of purple and blue. The dark gold-accented wood furniture created an atmosphere of opulent comfort. If Marisol was indeed the designer, her penchant for luxury was unmistakable.

A young lady dressed in a flamboyant red lacy corset and skirt lounging on an upholstered settee watched Isobel's entrance. The woman's attire, short in the front and trailing behind, was both alluring and impractical. "Hmph. It's a bit early to search for your husband, unless maybe he didn't come home," she remarked with a hint of sarcasm.

Isobel, unfazed, replied, "I came to see Marisol. I'm smart enough not to have a husband."

"Good for you," the saloon girl said, a flicker of respect in her tone. "Are you looking for work?"

"I'm not," Isobel replied. "Marisol knows me. Tell her Isobel Perkins is here to see her." Isobel wondered what Marisol's reaction to this unexpected visit would be, especially after her conversation with Doc.

The woman disappeared through a draped doorway, her skirt swishing as she moved. Moments later, Marisol herself emerged, the drape pulled back to reveal a stylish, middle-aged woman dressed entirely in purple. Her unchanged aura enhanced her striking appearance. Marisol's mouth fell open in disbelief. "I don't believe my eyes."

Isobel greeted her, smiling widely, extending her hand. "Nice to see you, Marisol. You still have incredible shoes." Though Isobel couldn't imagine herself in such extravagant footwear, they suited Marisol.

"Oh, Isobel! Look at you, all grown up." Marisol's response was warm as she took Isobel's hand and kissed her cheek.

Marisol glanced at the woman, who had relayed the message. "I hope Carmen didn't sass you. Aunt Flo is visiting every girl today, and it's making them scrappy." She signaled for Carmen to leave, who did so with a smirk and a curtsy. "Your mother made a tea that worked wonders. It tamed them. Oh, how I missed her... and you."

"She's fine," Isobel said, shrugging her shoulders. "I can help you with the tea. I made it for my friends."

"Good! Let's sit and have a drink. Come." Marisol led the way through the draped doorway. She explained the draperies served as a signal for opening time.

Isobel hadn't expected the saloon's interior to be so inviting. Instead of the typical setup, upholstered furniture arrangements with small tables scattered about. The bar, polished and grand, spanned one wall, and a staircase led to an upper level.

As they settled on a sofa, Marisol asked Carmen to bring them lemonade. Turning to Isobel, she said in a low voice, "I can't believe you're here. Did your father die?"

Isobel sighed, a familiar frustration surfacing every time someone mentioned her father. "Jane wrote to my uncle, asking for help. She didn't say why. I agreed to come, since I had nothing pressing over the summer."

Marisol's expression hardened. "After what that monster did to you and your mother, we should dig a hole and dump him in it." She twisted a handkerchief in her hands. "Can you tell I'm still angry?" She threw her head back, laughter mingling with her rage. "He knows better than to come in here."

Isobel leaned forward and asked, "Is there any proof?" The thought of discovering the truth about her mother's death was daunting, yet essential.

Marisol smoothed the fabric on her lap, her demeanor shifting. "You tell a lie often enough, it becomes the truth. That's what he did. Claimed he was in Hamilton buying supplies, but Peter Carlyle checked. No one could confirm his story. He certainly did not buy supplies."

Isobel wished she could remember more. "This town seems to have its share of despicable men."

"Oh, have you met Tom yet? He's the worst," Marisol said, finishing her lemonade.

"Unfortunately, as soon as I got off the stagecoach," Isobel replied with a roll of her eyes.

Marisol, her expression serious, signaled for another drink. Carmen, with an efficiency born of routine, poured it and hurried to place it before her boss. "Watch yourself. The varmint's dangerous," Marisol warned.

Isobel responded with a small, wry smile. "I pointed a gun at him when he came into the store." The memory of her bold action brought a sense of empowerment, albeit tinged with the reality of danger.

Marisol's expression shifted to one of disapproval, her lips forming a tight line. "Figures you'd have problems. A pretty young lady like you," she said, her posture straightening as she prepared to share a cautionary tale. "Let me tell you about a young miner, the very first day Tom set foot in town and took over the Bitterroot Saloon. The place bustled that night, everyone merry and buying drinks, except this one young man. Tom insisted he buy a round, but he refused. Tom was adamant, or so he claimed. The man left in a hurry. The next day, Tom and Al, his henchman, visited his cabin. When the miner wouldn't pay up, they ransacked the place, taking everything, even the food. They beat him so badly, he was bedridden for weeks. He still walks with a limp."

Isobel felt a tight knot in her throat as she listened, horrified. "That's terrible," she said, her voice barely above a whisper.

Marisol nodded, a pensive look crossing her face. "Lately, I haven't seen Tom's girls around town. It's unusual; they're often out shopping, keeping the local dress shop in business."

Isobel, her curiosity piqued, asked, "How many girls work for Tom?" She had been trying to push Tom out of her thoughts but now found herself drawn into his dark orbit. "I saw a blond woman the day I arrived. Tom was furious with her for yelling when he grabbed me."

"That's Shelley. Can't keep her mouth shut, that one. She's playing a dangerous game with her outspokenness. There are two others, Daisy and Cathy. They're living in a world of denial, waiting for Jack to return and set everything right." Marisol's voice trailed off as she shrugged. "Tom's a loose cannon, and so is Al, the man who arrived with him."

Isobel wondered if there were any secrets in town that escaped Marisol's notice. Their conversation turned to the topic of women owning businesses, a subject that intrigued Isobel. Finishing her lemonade, she excused herself, promising to return soon for another visit.

As Isobel walked back, her mind was a whirlwind of thoughts. She pondered how she could unlock her suppressed memories of the day her mother died. The weight of the possibility that her father might have been responsible hung on her. What would she do if the truth turned out to be as dark as she feared? The journey back was not just physical but also a deep introspection into the shadows of her past, seeking answers to questions that might alter her understanding of her family forever.

Henry twisted the key of the doorbell at Stella's front door. Then he twisted it again. Not like him to be impatient, but he had let himself get in a state. Lack of sleep and not eating led to crankiness and now impatience. *Where is Stella?*

Albert answered, eyes narrowed, but his eyebrows raised when he saw Henry. "Hello, Henry. Is there an urgent problem?"

"I need to talk to Stella. I think I have made a grave error."

Albert opened the door. "Come in, come in. Stella is in the garden out back and I was upstairs." He waved Henry to enter the parlor. "I'll go get her if you want to make yourself at home."

"Yes, that would be great. Thank you." Henry entered the parlor and looked around as always to find the newest item Albert found on one of his buying trips. Albert's business seemed more interesting than textiles. Maybe he should take a business trip abroad instead of sending someone else? And take Isobel with him.

"Are you alright? Is something wrong with Isobel? Albert said you are beside yourself." Stella rushed in and cupped Henry's elbow and craned around to peer at him.

"I am sorry to barge in unannounced like this, but I had to talk to you." Henry plopped down on an upholstered chair and placed his elbows on his knees with palms up. "How could I send Isobel to take care of my brother in some desolate place out west? I fear for her safety every minute of every day."

"I wasn't a fan of the idea. George never inquired about her in any of his letters. Like she didn't exist. At least we know she arrived safe."

Stella sat on the end of the settee, close to Henry's chair. Then she stood. "Do you want some tea?"

Henry nodded. "Yes. That would be nice."

Albert entered and sat across from Henry. "You know I take long trips and miss Stella terribly. I write all the things I want to tell her every day and then when I get back, I read them to her."

A long sigh escaped, and Henry put his head in his hands. "I can't sleep, can't eat, and can't stop worrying. I'll try anything." If anything happened to Isobel, it would be his fault and he would never forgive himself.

Stella returned with the tea and held it for Henry until he brought himself upright.

Henry took the teacup and sipped, since he had burned his mouth on Stella's tea before. But he found it was the right temperature. "All this feels like when Mary left. Like déjà vu. I think I am losing my mind."

Stella sat on the settee again, leaning forward. "Is the tea okay?"

"Yes. Very good." He felt better already. He kept sipping it until it was gone.

"Dear, we all miss her so much. She's a grown woman now and could leave for whatever parts. That is the nature of it. You raise them only to see them off in the world." Henry noticed tremors in Stella's hands as she talked and brushed invisible bits from her skirt.

"This is exactly why I came here. You have the finest outlook on life of anyone I've ever known. And this tea is wonderful. Where did you get it?" Henry sat upright, relaxed. "You have done a fabulous job of raising Isobel, and I should have faith in her."

Albert said, "I agree."

Stella blushed and waved her hands. "Thank you. But it was a group effort, the three of us. And the tea is one I make. I will send some home with you. It's good for those moments when you lose all hope." She touched an index finger to her cheek. "I think I gave it to you when Mary left."

Henry remembered how distraught he was and how helpful the tea was. "Yes, I remember. Excellent tea for me. I guess I get pretty uptight when it involves affairs of the heart."

Albert stretched his legs out in front of him. "We should plan a welcome home party so we have something positive to look forward to when Isobel comes back. It's not really that far in the future."

Stella's face brightened. "A party. Good idea. I could invite Isobel's friends. And have it in the garden."

Henry rose. "That sounds wonderful. Thank you for the hospitality and not booting me for being rude, arriving like I did." He turned to Stella. "And thank you so much for your tea. It turned everything around for me. Like magic."

Stella grinned and winked. "Like magick."

Chapter Twelve

After leaving Marisol, the rhythmic clunking of her heels against the wooden boardwalk accompanied Isobel's walk home. At the end of the walkway, she paused and turned to inspect the back of her father's store, a place she hadn't yet explored. The boarded-up back door was a stark reminder of the neglect the building had endured. Along the side, four rose bushes, long forgotten, had scraped away patches of paint in broad arcs, a testament to the harsh winds that frequented the area.

The backyard was an overgrown wilderness. Tall grass tangled with enormous, thorny thistle plants, their pale purple flowers a sharp contrast to the surrounding greenery. Thorny vines snaked chaotically through the underbrush. Finding no clear path, Isobel extended her index finger, channeling her energy to create a trail of clover, the lush green leaves suffocating the invasive weeds. She knew it wouldn't be long before bees would flock to the clover's white blossoms, drawn by their sweet nectar.

At the lot's end stood a willow tree, its beauty marred by fire-scarred bark and crimson leaves. The tree's poor condition weighed on Isobel; she had never attempted to heal something so damaged. The willow, a tree sacred to witches, must have been her mother's doing. What darkness inflicted such wounds upon it?

The remnants of a garden behind the store, now overrun by those thorny vines and their dominating flowers, caught Isobel's attention. She started her restoration here, away from prying eyes. Isobel took a moment to center herself, inhaling and clearing her mind to focus her energy. Arms raised, her fingers became conduits for a shower of sparkles, each one carrying a vibrant rainbow hue. The magick spread across the ground, dissolving weeds and transforming the vines to bear fruit before they withered away, leaving their bounty on the earth.

Satisfied with her work, Isobel turned her attention to the willow. The closer she got to the tree, the more she realized its leaves were unlike any she had ever seen before—each one had a distinct, menacing serration. She prepared to establish a stronger connection with the earth's energy by removing her shoes and stockings. The moment her bare feet touched the ground, a tingling shot through her body, the earth's power flowing into her like a live current.

Eyes closed, Isobel drew the energy further, concentrating it in her arms. The power built within her, straining her capacity to hold it, when suddenly, she felt the unnerving sensation of being watched. Fighting to maintain her focus, she succumbed to the distraction.

With her feet planted on the ground, she twisted around and her eyes locked onto Tom, leering from the side of the saloon. The shock of his presence caused her to release the energy. Drained and empty, Isobel's frustration and anger boiled over. She snatched her shoes and stockings and stomped back to the store's rear.

Isobel knocked over a wooden bucket, plopping herself down, fuming. She chastised herself for not being more vigilant, but was even more infuriated by Tom's intrusion. Touching her trinity necklace, she decided it was time for retribution—time to use her magick without restraint.

Determined, Isobel circled back to the front of the building. There, Tom leaned against a railing, his arms crossed. Locking eyes with him, she muttered a spell under her breath.

Great Goddess Morrigan, Use your power to annoy this rake,
Lay down thorns for every step he takes.
So mote it be!

She envisioned him suffering with each step he took, a fitting punishment for his intrusion.

Unlocking the store door, a grin spread across Isobel's face. She didn't heal the willow, but she prepared the garden for planting and enacted a small measure of justice against the man who was stalking her. Her actions were a balance of caring for the land and asserting her power, a dance of light and shadow that defined her path as a witch.

Tom stood outside the saloon, his gaze fixated on Isobel, the striking redhead with the sun illuminating her hair like a fiery halo. She was stretching in front of the withered willow tree behind the store, a picture of grace and beauty against the backdrop of decay. But as she turned and caught sight of him, she scowled. In an instant, she ceased her activity and stormed off. When she came around the building, she glared at him until she disappeared inside. With a frustrated sigh, Tom turned to retreat into the saloon.

As he stepped inside, a sudden, excruciating pain shot through the soles of his feet, as if he were stepping on a bed of prickly pear cacti. He winced with each step, gritting his teeth and cursing under his breath, tip-toeing to ease the agony. His eyes, adjusting to the dimmer light of the saloon, scanned the room until they landed on Walter, wiping down a table.

"Walter! Get me a chair!" Tom barked, his voice laced with pain and irritation.

Walter, startled by the urgency in Tom's voice, scurried around the tables and grabbed the nearest chair. His expression was one of confusion and concern as he approached his boss.

"Well? Bring it here, you dunderhead," Tom snapped, in distress.

The chair let out a grating squawk as Walter dragged it across the floor to Tom. "Here you go, boss," he said, still puzzled.

Tom collapsed into the chair, pulling off his shoes and then peeling off his socks by the toes. He struggled to inspect the bottoms of his feet, desperate to find the source of his torment. "Do you see anything?" he demanded, his tone a mix of pain and desperation.

Walter bent over, examining Tom's feet. "Looks alright to me?" he said, straightening up with a shrug. "What's the matter?"

"You better look again! There has to be something there. My feet feel like I'm walking on spikes. I can't walk, dammit!" Tom exclaimed, his frustration mounting. He racked his brain for a solution to ease the pain. "Drag my chair over to that table and get me a drink," he ordered, resigned to his immobility.

Walter grunted as he dragged the chair across the saloon to the designated table, positioning it so that Tom faced the right direction. When Tom slammed his fist on the tabletop, rocking it, Walter jumped. Matt, having already poured a drink, watched from the bar as Walter fetched it and placed it on the table in front of Tom.

Tom lifted his foot again, scrutinizing it. Rubbing it caused no discomfort, but the moment he attempted to put weight on it, unbearable stabbing pains caused sweat on his brow. The realization that he might have to sit all day dawned on him, a mix of anger and helplessness washing over him.

"What are you staring at? Can't a man have any peace without a gawker?" Tom lashed out at a man sitting at the next table, nursing a beer. The man spun his attention to a window on the side of the building.

With nothing visible on his feet and no logical explanation for his affliction, he knew even a visit to Doc would be futile. Trapped in his own saloon, he pondered his next move. "Walter! Drag my chair outside," he commanded, hoping the open air might offer some respite from his inexplicable ordeal. Perhaps some fresh air would help him plan a way to get that redhead across the road into his saloon for his own satisfaction. He pulled on the ends of his mustache, while a sly grin spread across his face.

Chapter Thirteen

Isobel awoke with the first light of dawn, her mind set on a singular task—to heal the willow tree without prying eyes. She hoped the late-night revelries at the saloon would keep Tom, and others, in bed, allowing her the privacy she needed for her work.

As she stepped outside, a spectacular sunrise greeted her, casting the Sapphire Mountains in a breathtaking array of oranges and pinks against the backdrop of purples and blues. For a moment, she was captivated, almost forgetting her mission in the face of nature's grandeur.

Isobel made her way along the clover carpeted path towards the willow. She reasoned that focusing her energies on the drooping branches first would be more manageable. She would heal the trunk, hidden under the canopy at another private moment.

Despite the early hour, Isobel scanned her surroundings, including the windows of nearby buildings. The quiet of the dawn provided a tranquil setting, her favorite time for such delicate work.

Isobel slipped off her boots, having foregone stockings, and let her bare feet connect with the cool, damp earth. Her shoulders rose and fell with a deep, grounding sigh.

After several deep breaths, Isobel cleared her mind of any negativity and focused on the ground beneath her. The vitality of the earth traveled up through her soles, filling her feet, ankles, and calves with its potent energy. She concentrated, ensuring not a single stray thought could disrupt the flow. Sweat beaded on her brow, trickling down her nose, but she ignored it, drawing in more power.

Now brimming with energy, Isobel turned her attention to the willow. Its red leaves hung like drops of blood—a stark contrast to the beauty of the morning. She visualized the tree restored to its former glory, a beacon of life and vitality.

With a sudden movement, she extended her arms towards the tree and released the stored energy. Two powerful beams of light shot from her fingertips, enveloping the tree in a shimmering glow. The willow absorbed the energy, its leaves transforming from crimson to a vibrant green, their edges softening and becoming supple. Only the trunk remained scarred, a reminder of the work still to be done.

Exhausted, Isobel doubled over, hands on her knees, as she caught her breath. Her dress clung to her sweat-drenched body, and she was drained, emptied of all her strength.

After a moment, she approached the tree to caress the newly green leaves, embracing the branches. A sense of contentment and peace washed over her. Stepping beneath the canopy, she placed her hands on the still-damaged trunk. "You're next," she whispered, "when I recover my strength."

As she lingered, reminiscing about her childhood days spent under the willow, a sudden whoosh caught her attention. Looking up, she saw a hawk perched atop the tree, its head tilted as if appraising her. Perhaps her healing efforts had made the tree a haven for birds once more. The thought brought a smile to her face.

Satisfied with her morning's work, Isobel headed back upstairs to clean up and rest. She knew questions would arise about the tree's miraculous recovery, but touching her mother's necklace, she found herself unconcerned about others' opinions—a new feeling for her, one she hadn't felt before.

Under the blazing morning sun, John tugged at his collar, the heat making his church suit feel like a constricting shell. He longed for the freedom of his usual denims and boots, finding the stiff formality of Sunday attire more a show for others than an expression of faith.

As Peter steered their wagon to park beside the DeJong's, he noted with surprise, "We must be later than usual if Henrich is here."

Anna, looking over, replied, "No, Elsie is in charge of refreshments this week."

Walking into the church, John trailed behind his parents. They made their way to their usual row in front of the Johnsons. But today was different. The Johnsons, with a show of disdain, stood and moved to the opposite side of the aisle.

Mr. Johnson's voice, loud and contemptible, cut through the murmuring congregation. "I can't bear looking at them."

Mrs. Johnson, theatrically drawing a handkerchief to her eyes, added to the spectacle. "He broke my poor, poor daughter's heart," she whimpered, her act of despair not going unnoticed.

Betsy, their daughter, let out an exaggerated huff. "How could he show up for church with his goings-on with that hussy?" Her words were sharp, intended for everyone, especially John, to hear.

Another family, sitting in the same row as John and his parents, rose and moved to join the Johnsons, their actions an obvious gesture of solidarity. The tension in the church thickened, the air heavy with judgment and whispers.

John leaned towards his mother, his voice low. "I'd rather go visit Isobel than sit here with this nonsense."

Anna, her expression stern yet resolute, shook her head. "Then they win. Stay and listen to the sermon. You'll see Isobel soon enough."

Resigned, John's family remained seated, enduring the barrage of dirty looks and glares from their fellow parishioners. It was another instance where the truth mattered little to the community. The Johnsons had woven their tale of woe, spreading it like wildfire through the parish, and now they had turned their drama towards John's family, setting the stage for a simmering conflict that went beyond mere words and glares.

The rhythmic knocking downstairs jolted Isobel from her thoughts, prompting her to dash down the stairs. She reached the door to see John's family waiting outside, their faces a mixture of expectation and hesitation.

"Good morning! Thank you for dinner on Friday night. I had a good time," Isobel exclaimed, her words tumbling out as Anna embraced her in a warm hug.

Peter, following behind, tipped his hat in a gesture of polite acknowledgment. "Mornin'. We came to get that potbelly stove.

Ready to make a sale, Isobel?" He didn't wait for an answer, striding towards the back wall where three stove models were displayed. "Which one do you want, Anna? It's your idea."

Anna meandered between the stoves, her gaze lingering on the nickel-plated model. She admired her reflection on its polished surface, trailing her fingers over the intricate designs. "You know, I do like those shiny pieces with the pretty designs on them. Will they get dirty fast and need lots of cleaning? I'd rather be cooking than cleaning." Her eyes sought Isobel's approval.

Isobel, hands on her hips, appraised the stove. "When I cleaned them, the nickel pieces cleaned easier than the cast iron."

Anna's attention turned to the store itself as she spun around. "I meant to say when we came in, the store looks wonderful. It must've been a lot of work."

Isobel nodded, a laugh escaping her lips. "Thank you. I wouldn't want to do it again."

Peter chimed in with a smile. "Well, it costs a little more for the shiny bits, but you like it, so that's the one we'll get. Sold. Oh, can't forget—I figure I need twelve feet of piping."

John and Peter grappled with the hefty stove, each taking a side. They moved it only a few feet before having to set it back on the floor, their faces betraying a wish that Anna had chosen a lighter model. Eventually, they maneuvered it outside, while Peter collected some piping and placed it on the counter, all business in his dealings, much like Isobel's Uncle Henry.

Anna pointed to the boarded-up back door with a hint of sadness. "Guess Fred broke in through that door to get to George when he took sick. George never repaired it after Jack broke in when your mother... ah... well, when they found you." She fiddled with a loose thread on her dress shirt and fluffed out her tan calico skirt before changing the subject. "Have you looked at your mother's garden? Maybe you could fix it up and plant something?"

Isobel replied, "I already cleared it and plan on planting some herbs and vegetables."

Anna, admiring her new stove, suggested, "Would you show me while they load this in the wagon?"

Isobel, pulling out a receipt book to calculate the balance due, agreed. "I would love to as soon as I total this. I worked out there this morning as I watched the sunrise. So beautiful."

Meanwhile, John paced between the door and the stove, his silence and agitated aura betraying troubled thoughts. Isobel, still tired from her early morning endeavors, rubbed her neck, trying to focus as she miscalculated the cost of the pipe. With a deep breath, she announced, "It comes to one hundred and forty dollars."

Peter paid her with crisp twenties, turning to John. "Are you ready?" he asked before leaning towards Isobel. "He wants a moment of your time before we leave."

John's face flushed a deep red as he avoided Isobel's gaze and headed towards the door.

Anna held the door open for the men and accompanied Isobel around the building. "Your mother had planted flowers all along this wall," she observed.

Isobel, feeling the weight of her mother's legacy, replied, "I hope I can live up to her. Marisol and Doc had nothing but good things to say about her."

They stopped in the garden, now ready for planting. Anna gazed towards the back of the lot, her eyes widening in surprise. "My goodness, the tree is so different now. What happened? It's not red anymore. What a gorgeous green."

Isobel shrugged. "I do not know." A heaviness weighed on her chest and her palms became sweaty. Marisol had said repeating a lie often enough it becomes the truth. It didn't sit well with Isobel's conscience, but she had no other choice. She eyed the hawk at the top of the tree again. "I'm sure Peter and John loaded the stove by now."

Anna nodded and said, "You're right and they're hungry, too. Better get going."

Upon returning to the front, John escorted his mother to the wagon. Taking Isobel's hand, he pulled her to the side of the building, out of his parents' view. "Isobel, I wonder... I mean I would like... um... would you go to my favorite fishing spot for a picnic Saturday afternoon?"

Isobel's heart leaped. "I would love to," she replied, gazing into his eyes, which were filled with relief and anticipation.

John, his face still flushed, said, "Good."

Isobel watched him exhale, realizing he had been holding his breath. She pondered how life in Tin Creek might change for the better. Maybe, just maybe, things were turning around.

CHAPTER FOURTEEN

ISOBEL'S MORNING BEGAN WITH a sense of purpose, as she counted out one hundred dollars from the cash box. The crisp bills felt heavy in her hands, each one representing a small victory in her struggle. She marked the withdrawal as 'loan payment' in her ledger, the words a stark reminder of the burden she carried for her father. Stuffing the money into her reticule, she set out with determination, her steps echoing her resolve.

As she locked the door behind her, she glanced across the street where Tom's saloon loomed. She shuddered, knowing his untrustworthy nature all too well.

The wind kicked up, sending swirls of dust dancing around her. Isobel covered her nose and mouth with her scarf, the gritty particles stinging her eyes. The oppressive heat of the day coupled with her anxiety made her skin prickle with sweat. She thought of her friends back in Chicago, their laughter and the carefree days in the park. The idea of hosting a grand party upon her return brought a temporary escape from her current predicament.

A rough hand seized her arm mid-crossing, shattering her daydream. Whirled around, she found herself face-to-face with Tom.

His grip was like a vise, causing a sharp pain to shoot up her arm. She tugged and pulled, trying to free herself, but his hold only tightened.

"Let go of me! I told you already I don't want you talking to me," Isobel shouted. She looked around for help, but the nearby townsfolk averted their eyes, offering no help.

Tom pulled her closer, his breath foul and his words slimy. "No one in their right mind will help you. I'm trying to help if you would listen. Instead of doing back-breaking work for an unappreciative father, you can spend time with me and make a name for yourself. Men will come from miles around."

Isobel's hand flew to her necklace, an unconscious effort to seek strength. "No. There is no way I would ever work for you. You are disgusting. Ugh!" She recoiled from his rancid breath, her heart pounding in her ears.

Gathering her composure, Isobel focused her energy, whispering an incantation under her breath.

Spirits of wind and dust, twirl and spin,
Gather your might, let the whirlwind begin.
Rise and twist, to my will you'll be,
Form a dust devil, so mote it be!

The surrounding wind intensified, whipping into a fierce dust devil in the street. Tom's grip loosened in the chaos, and Isobel pushed the swirling mass of dust and debris towards him.

Tom, caught in the maelstrom, tumbled down the street as he yelled for help. The townspeople retreated indoors, leaving him to his fate. Isobel watched, a mix of satisfaction and disgust washing over her.

Brushing off her dress, Isobel continued to the bank, her appearance now disheveled. She imagined the judgmental stares she would receive, but pushed the thought aside, focusing on her goal.

Isobel found Mr. Johnson gazing out the window when she entered the bank. "I see you met the gentleman who wants your father's store and experienced one of our dust devils. That one was pretty big."

Isobel bristled at his indifference to her safety. "You can't mean Tom," she replied.

"Yes, an accomplished proprietor with many successes," Mr. Johnson said, accepting the folded bills with raised eyebrows.

Isobel requested a receipt, her tone sharp. "You seem disappointed by the payment. What did Tom promise you?"

Mr. Johnson sneered. "Nothing. Full payment of the loan. Customary bank dealing. I hope you're not accusing me of anything nefarious. I'm an upstanding businessman and you should be careful with your words. When this town gets its charter, I'm running for mayor."

Isobel took the receipt, pursing her lips. "Tom tried drugging me, so anyone who trusts him is naïve. Take that as a caution, Mr. Johnson. Maybe you don't know him as well as you think you do. I would keep him away from your daughter for her safety." She turned to leave. "Thank you for the receipt. Please have a good day."

As she reached the door, Mr. Johnson's voice rose. "I doubt you care about my daughter at all. I understand you had dinner at the Carlyle's house. You're working hard to take her future husband."

Isobel didn't pause as she closed the door behind her, only to bump into Mrs. Johnson, dressed in green silk topped off by a hat adorned with peacock feathers. "Pardon me. Sorry," she muttered, opening the door for the woman and overhearing the banker's words to his wife.

Quickening her pace, Isobel hurried back to the store, eager to escape any further confrontation and the ever-tightening web of conflict and suspicion that seemed to envelop Tin Creek.

Jane was sweeping the boardwalk, a thick layer of dirt testament to the recent dust devil's passage, as Isobel returned from the bank. The air was still heavy with the aftermath, dust settling on every surface. "Did ya see that big dust devil that came through town? I seen nothing like it. Now I got lots to sweep. Do you want me to sweep in front of your place?"

Isobel, feeling a twinge of guilt for her role in the chaos but unable to suppress a grin at the memory of Tom's misfortune, declined the offer. "Oh no. Can I borrow your broom though? I don't think my father has one." She chuckled, her laughter tinged with irony.

"He probably doesn't. I usually sweep it. I don't mind. But that dust devil took all the dirt in the street onto the boardwalk." Jane paused in her sweeping as she reached the store. "I keep forgetting to ask how dinner was at the Carlyles? Aren't they the nicest folks you ever did meet?"

With a warm smile, Isobel recounted her visit. "Yes, they are pretty nice. They came by and bought a potbelly stove. So I went to the bank and paid on my father's loan." She scrunched her nose in distaste. "Then I ran into Mrs. Johnson when I headed out, but escaped before I got berated for stealing Betsy's sweetheart."

Jane, offering the broom, nodded in understanding. "Here ya go. Have at it. Definitely avoid Mrs. Johnson, a busybody for sure. John and Betsy been friends since the Johnsons moved here. None of the children liked Betsy, so I guess John was sympathetic for her. Kind soul, that one."

"I wondered about that. He had plenty of opportunity to mention her on the train or stagecoach." Isobel choked on the dust stirred by her sweeping. She glanced up to find Tom, his face twisted in annoyance, watching them through a saloon window. "That man is despicable. I have hated no one until I met him." Touching her necklace, she smiled, remembering her magical retribution for Tom. Oh, what a wicked little witch she was becoming. Aunt Stella would be rattled if she knew.

"If you're talking about Tom, you have lots of company. We wished he would leave as suddenly as he came to town." Jane's expression grew serious. "Have you ever shot a gun before? Real important here. Not only for varmints of Tom persuasion, but also varmints who wander around your back door. No fun going to the outhouse and there're eyeballs staring at you in the dark. Hate that. Makes you change your mind of going at all. The best gift Fred ever gave me is a mother-of-pearl inlay Derringer. Named her Susie. I can teach ya out back."

"Mr. Carlyle mentioned learning, too. I better learn how to shoot instead of just pointing a gun at someone." Isobel returned the broom, grateful for Jane's help and camaraderie. "Thanks for letting me use your broom. Would you let people know I am running the store? Hopefully, they will be inclined to give me a chance."

"My broom is your broom. We can target practice later. I already talked to people about you being here when they checked for their mail. Best place to spread news." Jane winked and headed back to the hotel.

A hawk landed on the railing, cocking its head. Isobel sensed a connection, realizing she had an unexpected ally. "Good morning, friend." She watched it soar away, planning to save some food for it in the future.

Back inside the store, Isobel glanced out the window to see Tom still staring from the saloon. She pondered the harsh realities of frontier life, wondering what it would be like to shoot someone. The thought of Tom and Jimmy, the stagecoach robber, deserving a bullet, unsettled her. Never had she harbored such thoughts. A pit formed in her stomach, making her question how much the frontier would change her.

CHAPTER FIFTEEN

AS THE SUN DIPPED behind the Bitterroot Mountains, casting long shadows across Tin Creek, the weight of loneliness and boredom pressed on Isobel. The slow pace of life in the frontier town was a stark contrast to the hustle and bustle of Chicago, leaving her with too much time to dwell on the past. She had already exhausted her small collection of books, leaving her longing for the familiar comforts of home.

Through the dusty window, she noticed Jane outside, sweeping away the remnants of the day. Isobel waved, but her heart wasn't in it. Jane pushed open the door, nodding her head, grinning. "Are you ready for some target practicing? I set up some targets after lunch when I threw out my dish water."

The prospect of doing something different, something that reminded her of the strength she needed to survive here, sparked a glimmer of excitement in Isobel. "Oh, yeah. I'm ready." She rushed to the door with a newfound purpose.

"Wait! You need your pistol," Jane called out, halting Isobel in her tracks.

Isobel dashed back, retrieving the revolver from its hiding spot and tucking it into her apron pocket. She then hurried to lock the front door, securing the store with a final click of the lock.

Following Jane through the hotel, Isobel noticed the everyday struggles of frontier life. The backend of the hotel showed a lifestyle of barely making ends meet. "I got dinner done early. Fred can serve, but still leaves me dishes as always. We have a little time for some practice," Jane said.

Isobel said, "I can help you."

Jane replied, "Criminy, no one has ever offered to do dishes with me. Thanks."

Outside, they approached a makeshift shooting range. Tin cans perched on a log served as their targets. Jane's enthusiasm was infectious, and Isobel found herself enthralled at the moment.

Jane's tone turned serious as she pointed to the willow tree behind Isobel's store. "That tree has been a sad sight since we came here. But now, it's changed. It's beautiful. What happened?"

Isobel averted her gaze as the pang of guilt caused a tightness in her chest. "I don't know." She wondered if lying would ever become easier, but she vowed to herself that this would be the only lie she would allow herself to tell.

"I'm gonna tell the rules of shooting. First, shoot first. Second, well, out here there is only one rule. Don't hesitate. You'll be dead. Aim for the middle of the body if you have to shoot someone. Bigger target." Jane caressed her mother-of-pearl inlaid Derringer as she spoke of its significance to her. "Did I tell you I love this gun? Fred gave it to me for our first anniversary. I better be careful or I get all misty-eyed and I can't shoot misty-eyed."

"How long have you been married?" Isobel asked, looking at her father's handgun, still wondering how to load it or even if she needed to.

"Almost ten years. I'm surprised Fred stays, though. I haven't given him a child. Men want children. I want children. I'm cursed. Oh, now I'm for sure gonna get misty-eyed. Dammit." Jane walked in circles, fanning her eyes.

"Not at all? Not even a miscarriage?" Isobel came over and put her arm around Jane's shoulders.

"Nope. nothing. I'm barren." Jane bowed her head, a tear streaked her cheek, and her aura flooded by baby blue sadness.

"Would you be willing to try one of my teas? There are herbs useful for fertility. It is worth a shot." Isobel smoothed Jane's hair, trying to calm her.

"I'll try anything. You can do that for me? I'd really appreciate it." Jane wiped her eyes on her sleeves and straightened. "First, let's hit some targets. Is your gun loaded?"

Isobel shrugged, eyes wide. "I don't know. I didn't know when I pointed it at Tom. Would have been bad if I had to shoot?" Isobel laughed, but she knew with Tom across the street, it was no laughing matter.

As they prepared to shoot, Jane noticed Isobel's uncertainty. "Let me help you. This spins and the bullets go in here. You look here and you have bullets in the holes. Let me pull this one out. You can see what it looks like without a bullet." Jane tipped the Colt until the bullet slid out. She pulled on it and held it for Isobel. "See? It's easy to load, too." Jane replaced it in the chamber. "That's why I like a handgun instead of a rifle."

"When you want to shoot, you place your pointer finger on here, the trigger. Pull back this to cock it. Then press the trigger." Jane showed Isobel on her gun while Isobel repeated the actions on her father's gun.

"There is a way to sight. Put the notch on the end of the barrel between these notches and it should hit the target if you aimed right." Jane fired at some cans she had on top of a log. She hit the can, and it flew off. "Just like that."

"You hit it! My turn." Isobel imagined telling her friends in Chicago about shooting guns and chuckled. She aimed like Jane explained and pulled the trigger. She missed the target and hit the log. "Oh!" The disappointment stung.

"Most people hit high the first time because they close their eyes or something. You aimed low. Now aim higher. You almost hit it." Jane paced around.

"I am going to hit it this time for sure." Isobel took her time aiming not wanting to miss. She wanted to master anything she tried. She pulled the trigger and heard the bullet hit tin instead of wood. "Yes, I did it!"

"Yeppers. See, it ain't hard." Jane gave Isobel a hug, and they danced around.

"This is the best thing I've done since I got here. Thank you." Isobel returned the hug. She had forgotten all her problems and worries until she saw Tom step out from behind the hotel shed to stand behind Jane. He must have heard the gunshots.

Tom said, sneering, "Hello, ladies. Don't you realize women shouldn't have guns? It's dangerous. Your minds are too delicate and you're too emotional."

Before they could react, Tom grabbed Jane, twisting her arm behind her back. "What if I did this?" Jane's scream pierced the air. Isobel, her heart pounding, pointed the gun at Tom. "Let her go, or I'll shoot!"

"Fred, help. Help me, Fred." Jane yelled toward the hotel.

Isobel wanted to use magick, but couldn't think of what to do. She never learned much past herbs and garden magick. It left her to protect herself and Jane with the means of a gun that she had only shot twice.

Tom laughed and pulled harder on Jane's arm, eliciting another scream from Jane.

Isobel muttered a quick protection spell under her breath, hoping it would be enough.

Goddess Morrigan, Use your shield to protect me and mine.
Use your sword to strike those who attack me and mine.
So mote it be!

The large hawk appeared out of nowhere and swooped down, its sharp talons attacking Tom. He raised his hands to shield his face, releasing Jane. He shot off around the building, the hawk in quick pursuit.

"Are you okay?" Isobel rushed to Jane.

Fred came out the rear door of the hotel. Isobel observed his dark green and blood-red spotty aura showing a low self-esteem and a tendency towards anger. "What's the matter, Jane?"

"Tom attacked me, holding my arm behind my back." Jane ran to her husband, but doubled back to retrieve her gun from where she had dropped it.

"A sheriff is coming in the next few days, which may make Tom think twice. We're going to have a town charter, too. Time to end the lawlessness here." Fred hugged Jane and nodded to Isobel, still holding the gun in her hand. "Were you planning on shooting Tom? You could have shot my wife."

Jane defended Isobel. "I trust her."

While leading Jane back into the hotel, Fred said, "That remains to be seen. The apple doesn't fall far from the tree."

Tom's continued harassment and Fred's mistrust had hardened her resolve. Isobel would no longer be the naïve girl from Chicago. Time to embrace the harsh realities of frontier life and learn to protect herself.

The hawk landed on the shed and cocked his head at Isobel, its yellow eye inquiring. It fluffed its mahogany wings against a streaked white and brown chest.

Isobel bowed to it. "Thank you, noble bird. I am in your debt." *Is this my familiar?*

The raptor flew to the willow tree, landing on top, the branches bouncing from its weight.

As she walked back to her store, her hand settled on the trinity pendant, giving her a newfound determination. To hell with everyone's opinions. Who can be rescued by a bird of prey? Isobel would study her mother's grimoire, learn more about her own powers, and no longer rely on the kindness of others. The frontier had changed her, and she was ready to meet its challenges head-on.

As the morning light filtered through the freshly hung curtains, Isobel attained a sense of accomplishment. The delicate fabric not only beautified the store but also shielded her evening rituals from prying eyes, particularly those of Tom, whose curiosity was as unwelcome as it was intrusive.

Despite her father's worsening condition, Isobel's concern lingered that he might stumble upon her practicing her craft. Opting for the potency of spoken spells, she used the store's counter as her makeshift altar, a space where her voice wouldn't carry to her father's quarters. Once her rites were complete, she could conceal her sacred tools in her satchel, away from any unsuspecting gaze.

Determined to aid her friend Jane with a delicate matter of fertility, Isobel refused to let Fred's dismissive views deter her. Jane's unwavering kindness since Isobel's arrival in Tin Creek had forged a bond she was eager to honor.

Both her own and her mother's grimoires were open for guidance as Isobel laid out her green altar cloth. Stella's handiwork, a gold triple moon and bordered by intricate leaf patterns and Celtic knots, gave her a tangible connection to her cherished aunt.

Centered on the cloth, Isobel placed an oak plaque, its pentagram a family heirloom carved by her great-uncle for her grandmother. Touching the carved lines, she regarded the weight of her heritage, a lineage rich with mystical tradition.

To the left, she positioned a white candle to embody the feminine, and to the right, a red candle to signify the masculine.

Isobel removed four small vials, each a miniature representation of the four elements she created for travel, a testament to Isobel's ingenuity and respect for her craft. At the top of the pentagram, she set a vial containing dirt from her garden back home. To the right, she placed a tiny bundle of sage incense in a vial representing air. To the left, a small vial of water and below, a vial of tiny coal pieces for fire.

Her grandmother's six-inch, double-bladed rose-quartz athame, a tool steeped in history and imbued with energies both dark and light, took its place beside the altar. Aunt Stella couldn't bring herself to use it, and Isobel had asked if she could several years ago.

With her mortar and pestle, Isobel prepared the herbal concoction, handpicking chaste tree, wintergreen, black cohosh, and unicorn root from her compact herb valise. As she ground the herbs, she focused on their purpose, despite the pungent aroma of the black cohosh clouding the air.

Once the mixture was ready, Isobel transferred it to the parchment, setting it upon the pentagram. She lit the candles with her breath while raising her hands, channeling her intent through the whispered incantation:

Great Goddess Anu, fountain of life so true,
Bless this brew for fertility's due.
Grant health and joy, a lineage to see,
Fulfill this plea, so mote it be!

A golden mist, delicate and ethereal, emerged from her palms, enveloping the herbs in a gentle embrace, a sign her spell was cast.

After extinguishing the candles, Isobel wrapped the herbal tea with care and a satin ribbon, its energy pulsating, a promise of hope for Jane.

This is what her craft should be about, not stirring up a dust devil to enable her to traverse a street without being accosted. As she packed away her tools and herbs, Isobel found a renewed sense of purpose. Her actions today transcended the petty conflicts of Tin Creek, aligning her with her true path of healing and service.

Securing her satchel far back on the bottom shelf behind the counter, Isobel opened the store to the promise of a new day. The curtains, now tied back, welcomed the sunlight, symbolizing her readiness to face the world on her own terms, her craft her ally, and her resolve unshaken.

Chapter Sixteen

Perched on the edge of her bed, Isobel poured her heart into letters under the flickering candlelight. The first, addressed to Uncle Henry, detailed the grim reality of George's declining health, the looming debt at the bank, and her unsettling encounters with Tom. The second letter, destined for Aunt Stella, she described how she came to get both the missing necklace and grimoire, her friendships, and her interactions with John, which consumed more ink than she'd expected.

Later, as she delved deeper into her mother's grimoire, Isobel stumbled upon spells for concocting enchanted potions designed to bend others to her will. The discovery troubled her; Aunt Stella had painted Mary as independent and spirited, typical traits of a fire witch, but never hinted at a dalliance with darker arts. Isobel sensed a growing disconnect with her mother's legacy, fearing Mary may have ventured into the shadows of black magick. Despite this, her longing for her mother only intensified, a constant ache in her heart.

Fatigue overtook her, and with the grimoire as her bedside companion, Isobel succumbed to sleep, the charm of her mother's necklace clasped in her hand.

In her dream, a young four-year-old Isobel laid her doll down for a nap. The kitchen was a battleground, the air thick with tension and fear. Isobel's parents' voices clashed, her father's accusations thundering throughout the space. "Witchcraft!" he bellowed, pointing an accusing finger at her mother, who stood defiant, her own voice rising in a desperate incantation that filled the room with a charged energy.

Isobel, her heart pounding, edged closer to her bedroom door, her small frame trembling. The moment her mother's scream pierced the air, Isobel's curiosity turned to horror. She watched, wide-eyed, as her father, consumed by fury, silenced her mother with a rag, his hands then encircling her neck with a terrifying grip.

Driven by instinct, Isobel burst into the kitchen, her tiny voice desperate. "Stop, Daddy! You're hurting Mommy!" But her plea fell on deaf ears, her father's voice booming with condemnation. "Witches are evil," he spat, his grip tightening, his eyes ablaze with madness.

Isobel's mother fought back with fierce determination, her eyes locked on Isobel's, brimming with tears that mirrored the fear and pain etched on her young daughter's face. Isobel, fueled by a rush of primal rage, attacked her father with all the strength her four-year-old body could muster, her small fists pounding against him, driven by a single thought: protect Mommy.

But the struggle was futile. Her mother's resistance waned until she collapsed, a lifeless heap on the floor. Her father, in a fit of blind rage, lashed out with a vicious kick, his grief-stricken howl, "You killed my Pearl!" echoing in the cramped kitchen.

Isobel, propelled by a mix of fear and desperation, threw herself beside her mother, shaking her, willing her to awaken from this nightmare. But her father's hands were upon her again, lifting her from the ground, his grip suffocating, his voice a venomous hiss in her ear.

Panic surged through Isobel as she struggled for air, her small hands clawing at her father's iron grip, her kicks weakening as the room spun, the edges of her vision darkening until there was nothing but the encroaching shadow of unconsciousness.

Jolted awake, Isobel gasped for air, her dream's suffocating grip lingering as she lay in her bed, disoriented and seething with rage. The dark contemplation of vengeance against George flickered in her mind, from the cold finality of a gunshot to the subtlety of poisoned soup. Amidst the turmoil, a single word from her dream resonated with her: Pearl. Who was Pearl?

Clutching her mother's grimoire and the necklace's charm, Isobel sought solace in the remnants of her mother's presence. The book, a tangible link to Mary, offered a whisper of comfort in the depth of her loneliness. Tears streamed down her face as grief and longing overwhelmed her, lulling her back into a fitful sleep.

The Saturday morning sun cast long shadows on the boardwalk as Isobel and Jane observed the steady stream of townsmen converging on Tom's saloon. The air was thick with anticipation, the gathering a symbol of the town's burgeoning sense of community and self-governance. Men from all walks of life, miners with dirt-streaked faces and businessmen in their Sunday best, tethered their horses and joined the growing crowd. Isobel watched, jaw clenched, her gaze lingering on the saloon's swinging doors as each new arrival disappeared inside.

Peter and John were among the last to arrive. Peter, ever the gentleman, greeted the ladies with a polite tip of his hat, exchanging pleasantries about health and well-being. John, however, approached Isobel, his eyes holding a hint of excitement. "Are we still on for a picnic? I don't think this meeting will take long and we can head out."

"Yes. Then you can explain why women are excluded when we are part of the town, too," Isobel retorted, her nose wrinkled. The exclusion grated on her, a stark reminder of society's constraints.

Her thoughts darkened as she recalled the strong desire to put lethal herbs into her father's soup. A perplexing sensation overcame her, as if there were two Isobels vying for control, leaving her mystified about the underlying cause.

John offered a half-smile, perhaps sensing her unrest, before joining his father across the street.

Isobel crossed her arms, her foot tapping. "So, are we expected to let them take care of business? I am a rational woman." Yet, her recent actions belied that rationality, her mind a battlefield of conflicting desires and vengeful thoughts.

Jane offered a distraction. "Do you want the broom? I sweep when I'm angry and work it out of me that way."

Isobel's laughter rang out, a brief respite from her brooding. "No, but can we sit for a spell?" She joked with a witch pun, her laughter masking the darker thoughts that haunted her.

Jane replied, "Sounds good to me. I need to be available in case a guest needs something, since Fred is out."

As they turned to enter the hotel, Marisol's voice called out to them. "Can I join you? We can commiserate over being snubbed from the town meeting." Both nodded in agreement, united in their exclusion.

Inside the hotel's dining room, Isobel's mood lightened as they sat by the window, keeping an eye on the saloon. "We will organize ourselves, Marisol. Let's plot against them. Hell hath no fury than a group of angry women." The words were light, but the undercurrent of her true intent, the plotting of her father's demise, cast a shadow over her heart again.

Isobel asked, "Are you following anything about the woman's suffrage movement? How terrible to be a business owner and not be able to vote. We need to have a voice in what goes on in our own communities." She wanted to ask Marisol about Pearl. She opted to postpone the conversation until they were alone, away from the hotel dining area and other people.

"We need that, and this town needs a newspaper to expose the truth around here." Marisol said, "Start one in your store." Marisol pointed at Isobel. "People might listen because you're educated."

"I would if I stayed in Tin Creek. Nursing school starts in September. I will bury George soon, sell the store, and go home." Isobel couldn't wait to bury George. Slipping deadly herbs in his soup would remain unproductive as he had been eating very little these days, prompting Isobel to consider an alternative.

Marisol frowned and said, "I thought we had you permanently."

"Doc suggested I come back and work as his nurse." Isobel shrugged.

"You should," both women said.

They laughed, but Isobel gave a distracted nod. The thought of staying in Tin Creek, with its potential for new beginnings and the budding relationship with John, was tempting. The unresolved turmoil surrounding her father's fate clouded her thoughts. She was uncertain about her true path—vengeance or healing.

CHAPTER SEVENTEEN

THE JOURNEY TO JOHN'S secret fishing spot was a serene ride, with the gentle murmur of the Bitterroot river accompanying them. The landscape unfurled into a picturesque scene where the river widened, its rocky banks glistening under the soft touch of the morning sun. Isobel felt the light breeze tease strands of her hair across her face, a tender caress that seemed to connect her to the natural world around her. Her hawk, a vigilant guardian, circled above, adding to the atmosphere of the idyllic setting.

John broke the silence, leaning forward, lowering his head over Isobel's shoulder. "This is where I fish. My best spot. Don't tell anyone. It's a secret." He placed a finger to his lips, "Shh. Every fisher has a special spot they don't want to share." His casual shrug belied the depth of his connection to the place, a sacred legacy from his father now shared with Isobel.

As John dismounted with ease and offered his hand to assist Isobel, she admired his gentle manners. Choosing a spot beneath the quaking aspens, the sight of her hawk perched in the branches captivated Isobel, its presence a comforting sign. The simple act of laying out a blue log cabin quilt and preparing their picnic spoke volumes of his thoughtful nature.

"My mother loves these trees. She calls them musical because when the wind blows, the leaves make a pleasant sound, a soothing rustling." John sat and pulled off his boots. "She didn't like anyone wearing shoes while on her quilt. I hated it because I wanted to come and go. Can't do that if you're taking them off and on again."

"You were an active child? Is that why you are the only one?" Isobel grinned as she appreciated the hint to unhook her boots and slide them off.

"Not an only. I had a brother and sister, but both of them died young. Measles. I recovered, but my parents had to bury two children." John unwrapped a sandwich and handed it to Isobel. "Fresh bread."

"I'm sorry. That must have been hard." John's moment of vulnerability gave her a closer connection. "At least your parents love you. I have a father who hates me. It is uncomfortable to live under the same roof as him." Isobel bit into the bacon, cucumber, and tomato sandwich. "Mmm. Good. But Doc thinks he only has a few weeks left." Another pang of guilt hit her, replaced by anger, which she dispatched to enjoy John's company.

"If I had your circumstances, I would be miserable. I don't relish being around people who don't like me. Yes, my parents love me. They have high expectations since I'm their only living child." John reach over with a napkin and wiped the side of Isobel's mouth.

Isobel laughed. "Oh, am I eating like a savage? Excuse me, I will try harder." She enjoyed being comfortable with John. "My aunt and uncle have high hopes for me, too." Her uncle expected her to marry well while her aunt counted on her to be a good witch that stayed out of trouble. Weren't they going to be disappointed?

"Look!" John pointed. "There's a Red-tailed hawk right above us watching."

Isobel smiled at her hawk. "Ah, it's a Red-tailed. How do I know that from any other hawk?"

John said, "The tail feathers are red on top most of the time, but a sure sign is the wingtips don't come to the tail feathers. If they did, it would be a Swainson's."

"Good to know. Well, I will leave a little food for it. Pay for being a sentry." While some witches had cats or frogs for a familiar, Isobel had a hawk.

John asked, "You like birds?"

"All animals and being out in nature. I enjoyed the parks and shoreline in Chicago." Isobel thought about her walks back home. She walked alone because her friends wanted to walk from shop to shop and she preferred the park. Now she sat surrounded by nature with John, hook, line, and sinker content. "Like this."

"What else do you like?" John scooted closer and handed Isobel his flask for her to drink. "Me?" Tangerine sparks shattered through his normal aura of chartreuse, the color of serenity and acceptance.

Isobel drank too fast, and some spilled down along her chin. "Oops. Being savage again. Where are my manners?" She grabbed the napkin and dabbed her chin.

They laughed. And John placed his hand on Isobel's other hand. A tingle surged along her arm. Warmth enveloped around her.

"I do like you, John. I am comfortable with you. No pretenses. And it's as if we have known each other all our lives. But we haven't. Does that make sense?" Isobel looked at John's hand on hers, wondering if she should move her hand. What was the right thing to do? *Oh, dear.* She wondered if her face flushed since she felt hot.

"Yes, it does. About this morning. Are you wanting to vote? My father asked, and I told him that is all women talk about back East."

"Oh, not just there. There is organization in San Francisco." Isobel sat straight. "And yes, I am a modern woman and proud of it. Does that bother you?" She had many discussions with her uncle about the suffrage movement.

John said, "As more women become educated, it becomes inevitable. And fair. It shows society is becoming more civilized. My father doesn't agree, but that is what he knows. You can't prevent progress."

Isobel relaxed. "Phew, I thought I would be walking home."

Their laughter mingled with the rustling leaves, a sweet harmony that underscored the budding romance between them. John leaned over to kiss Isobel. "I'd never let you walk home." His love-laced aura wrapped around the two of them.

John's gentle kiss, a tender exploration of their newfound connection, left Isobel flushed with excitement and a flurry of emotions. But then she sensed she was doing something wrong. To hide her confusion, she said, "Betsy is going to be mad at you!" *Now why did I say that?*

"I don't care. She has a wild imagination if she thought I would marry her. My mother would skin me alive because she can't stand Betsy, but she loves you."

Isobel's eyes welled, but she held it back. It surprised her that Anna's love was paramount to her. Almost as much as her own mother's love. John and Anna were going to make leaving hard.

Fortunately, a large buck drinking on the other side of the river distracted them. Then they packed up for home.

On the way, Isobel asked, "What happened at the meeting this morning?"

John replied, "Mr. Johnson aspired to be mayor and nothing would stop him. My father put his name in and the banker said only people who live in town can run. Dad protested, as did others who live outside of town, but it didn't matter. Mr. Johnson ran unopposed. Then Tom introduced the new sheriff. Father and I don't trust him because his experience was vague and Tom knew him."

Isobel said, "Your father would be a great mayor. I have a nasty feeling about Mr. Johnson as mayor. A man with money and power to boot." She leaned back into John and enjoyed his warmth.

When they arrived at the store and John helped her off the horse, Isobel found a note on the door. "Like I said, our new mayor is going to be a problem."

"What does it say?" John asked as he looked over her shoulder.

Isobel summarized. "The store requires a coat of paint and un-specified improvements or fines, also unspecified, will be assessed." She turned around. "That was fast. I'm sure he already had that planned."

"I'll help you paint, but where is it stated that the buildings have to be painted?" John said, "Is he going to invent rules as he goes?"

Isobel gazed at John. "Probably. There is no one to stop him, is there?"

"Afraid not."

In that moment, standing close to John, Isobel found solace in his strength and the promise of his support.

John approached the Perkins General Store with a heart full of anticipation and a wagon loaded with cans of paint as the first rays of the Sunday sun kissed the quiet streets of Tin Creek. The thought of Isobel's smile, the memory of their picnic, and the softness of her lips from their stolen kiss lingered in his mind, igniting a flame of longing he couldn't extinguish. This wasn't only another chore; it was a labor of love, a step closer to a future he dared to envision with Isobel by his side.

The closed curtains of the store hinted at the tranquility within, a stark contrast to the turmoil of emotions swirling within John. He knocked on the door, a rhythmic thud that echoed his racing heartbeat, careful yet hopeful, wishing not to wake old cranky Perkins but desperate to see Isobel's face.

Isobel's response was swift, her presence at the door like the dawn breaking through the darkness. Her smile, radiant and welcoming, sent a wave of relief washing over him. "Good morning, John! What a surprise," she greeted, her voice a melody that danced in the morning air.

John, lost in the depths of her eyes, presented the paint with a shy pride. "I hope you like the color," he stuttered, clearing his throat after.

She said with a sideways grin and raised eyebrows, "As long as it's not black...or gray."

Isobel's playful remark about the color choices drew a chuckle from John, easing the tension that clung to his shoulders. John set the can on the boardwalk. "I got light blue and white for the trim.

There's black paint for the sign letters." He returned to the wagon for more paint.

He watched her approach his horse, her gentle touch and kind words to the animal reflecting the warmth of her spirit, a warmth he yearned to be enveloped in. "Perfect choice. That is what I would have gotten."

Isobel stepped back onto the boardwalk and looked at the paint cans. "Did you get this in Hamilton?"

John ran his hand through his hair. "Yes. We went there for some shopping and Father needed to go to the bank."

Isobel furrowed her brows. "I thought you banked here in town."

John pulled the ladder from the back of the wagon and set it on the front porch. "Ah, there are some issues with his account, so he visited the Hamilton branch to see if he could get it fixed there. Mr. Johnson has it all messed up. Either he can't do math or he's doing something fishy. Be sure you keep all your receipts. If there is ever a problem, I can take you to Hamilton."

Isobel rolled her eyes. "Don't get me going about Mr. Johnson. Just think, he could be your father-in-law."

The mention of Betsy and the potential of Mr. Johnson as a father-in-law drew laughter from Isobel, but the humor didn't quite reach her eyes. John felt a surge of protectiveness, a desire to shield her from the pettiness and the gossip that threatened their budding relationship. "And don't get me started with Betsy. She has half the town on my back. My parents hear about it every week at church. I don't go because of her."

John walked over to Isobel, wanting to put his arms around her, but that would get the tongues wagging in town. "Let's think about better things, like getting this done." The simplicity of painting the store together, of working side by side towards a common goal, seemed a perfect escape from the whispers and the watchful eyes of Tin Creek. "I'll do the upper areas and you can do the lower areas."

"Let's start." Isobel grabbed the brushes. "I hope we can get it done in one day. We only need to paint the front, thank goodness." She handed a can of blue paint and a brush to John.

John climbed the ladder, leaning on the building's front furthest from Isobel. "If I paint here and you paint over there, I won't drip on you."

"Is that a promise?" Isobel tilted her head at John at the top of the ladder.

Without glancing down, John said, "No. I won't make a promise I might not be able to keep."

Isobel said, "That's good to know."

In the simple act of painting the store, John found a moment of peace, a shared purpose, and a glimpse of a future filled with possibility.

Chapter Eighteen

The weight of impending nightfall pressed on Isobel's spirit, the looming dread of nightly torment rendering the comfort of her bed a cold, unwelcome sanctuary. The ghastly spectacle of her parents' last argument replayed with torturous clarity—their heated exchange, smelling her mother's cooking, hearing the wind, people riding horses on the street, and a dog barking.

Haunted by fragments of her young life, the days offered no reprieve for Isobel. The store became a canvas of troubling memories, each corner whispering secrets of a childhood spent under its roof. But Dawn's presence now held a comforting familiarity, her once golden locks a testament to passaging time and the enduring nature of memory.

Within the confines of that same building lurked a specter far more sinister than any ghost—her father, a man whose existence was synonymous with betrayal and murder. Isobel's footsteps echoed through the empty store, her fists clenched as tight as her jaw. The teachings of Aunt Stella, a beacon of light in the darkness, seemed distant, overshadowed by the consuming desire for retribution that clawed at her soul.

As night enveloped the world in its inky clasp, Isobel hoped for solace in the ritual of sleep, her hands clutching a satchel of lavender as if it were a lifeline. The fabric of her pillow offered a whisper of comfort as she surrendered to the embrace of exhaustion, her consciousness adrift in the sea of her own turmoil.

But this night was different. Instead of the familiar scene of horror, her dreamscape transformed into a solemn cemetery. Her mother stood, an ethereal figure amidst the tombstones, dress and hair blowing where there was no wind. Her voice, a chilling gust that cut through the stillness. "I want revenge. Avenge my death!"

The words were a dagger to Isobel's soul, a command that defied the essence of her being. "Why are you asking me to do that? I can't. I just can't."

Awakening in a cold sweat, Isobel's heart raced with an urgency that propelled her from bed, her thoughts an uproar of confusion and fear. The increasing heaviness of her mother's pendant served as a constant reminder of her lineage that now demanded a sacrifice she wasn't willing to make.

The weight of the decision crushed Isobel as though it were a physical burden, while her mind became a battlefield for conflicting desires. To hasten death was to play a role she never envisioned for herself. The concept of taking a life, even one as tainted as her father's, was alien to her nurturing spirit. The acid taste of bile rose in her throat as she contemplated the dark path her mother's voice urged her down. Could she cross that line?

The pendant around her neck, once a symbol of her mother's love and protection, now felt like a shackle, pulling her deeper into a moral quagmire. To avenge her mother's death with belladonna, to play the executioner in the dead of night—was this the justice that her mother sought? The notion clashed with every fiber of her being attuned to healing, not harm.

Doubt gnawed at her willpower, the inner turmoil magnified by the stark reality of her father's impending demise. He was already on death's doorstep, his breaths numbered, his suffering clear. Was it her place to speed up the inevitable, to usurp the natural order for the sake of vengeance?

Isobel wrestled with the dichotomy of her desires. The impulse to right the wrongs done to her mother warred with her innate compassion and the ethical boundaries of her craft. Revenge called to her from the shadows, a siren song of retribution, yet her soul recoiled at the thought. This internal strife threatened to tear her apart, leaving her stranded at the crossroads between the darkness of retaliation and the light of her true nature.

Isobel approached her father's door, her hand trembling as she turned the knob. The stench of decay that greeted her was a grim harbinger of the truth that lay within. The silence was deafening, a notable contrast to the labored breaths that had once filled the room.

Isobel moved closer to the bed with apprehension, her hand reaching out to touch her father, the icy chill of his skin a confirmation of his passing. In that moment, the turmoil within her subsided, replaced by an overwhelming sense of peace that washed over her like a cleansing rain.

A cold flush passed over when she realized she didn't have to kill him. No need for dark magick and compromising the family code. The relief took her to her knees, crying with breath catching in her chest.

The revelation came crashing down on Isobel as if it were a tidal wave—she hadn't visited her mother's grave. A sense of urgency propelled her into action, her movements swift and determined as she threw on her clothes. Time was of the essence; she needed to pay her respects under the cloak of night, to stand by her mother's resting place in solitude, before the first light of dawn painted the sky.

With her heart pounding against her chest, Isobel's mind raced with thoughts of her father's silent departure from this world. The question of his burial loomed over her, a shadowy specter of worry. The cost, undoubtedly more than the meager funds she had at her disposal, gnawed at the edges of her resolve. Yet she pushed the concern aside with a steely determination. Somehow, someway, she would find a solution.

The cool night air nipped at her skin as she made her way through the deserted streets, the solemn stillness of Tin Creek enveloping her. On the other side of the church, the looming silhouette of the graveyard gate appeared, a gateway to a childhood buried alongside her mother.

As she blended into the night's shadows, Isobel prepared herself for the inevitable clash with her past and the challenges that awaited her in the aftermath of her father's death.

In the solemn quiet of the cemetery, Isobel navigated through the weathered wooden crosses, casting long shadows in the moonlight. Each one whispered a tale of a life long ended, their story fading like the worn inscription under the moon's melancholy glow.

Isobel ventured to the cemetery's far edge. Her gaze fell upon an angelic statue perched atop a small rise, its sorrowful eyes gazing downward. Beneath it, etched in stone, was her mother's name - Mary Perkins, the letters barely discernible under the moon's silver sheen. Isobel's heart ached as she kneeled before the grave, her fingers tracing the cool, moss-covered engraving. The statue, though adorned with nature's markings, seemed out of place, too grand for the likes of George to have commissioned.

A familiar Irish lullaby floated on the breeze, its haunting melody wrapping around Isobel like a long-lost embrace. She scanned her surroundings, but the cemetery lay empty, the song's source unseen. Yet, she recognized that voice, a comforting presence from her past, her mother's gentle tones.

"Isobel, you came. I've been waiting for you," whispered the voice, ethereal yet distinctly Mary's.

On her stomach, the earth beneath her transform, the once scratchy blades softening and turning a vibrant green. "Mother, I miss you," Isobel confessed, her voice breaking. "I remember now, everything."

"I wanted to save you the pain of losing your mother so young. How is my sister?"

"Aunt Stella is well, but George died tonight," Isobel confessed, her voice trembling. As she spoke, her gaze drifted upwards to her hawk companion, now perched atop the angel statue, as if standing sentinel over the poignant scene.

Mary's response, "Good on both counts," echoed with a mix of vindictiveness and relief, revealing the depth of her hatred for George.

"I am reading your grimoire, and I have some questions." Isobel, enveloped in the ghostly presence of her mother, wrangled with a surge of conflicting emotions. Her outstretched arms towards the grave symbolized her yearning for a connection long lost. But deep inside, she dreaded what her mother might ask of her next.

"We can talk about that another time. I'm going to ask you to do something the night of George's burial. It will give me a connection to him eternally, even as he burns in hell. I have powers in the afterlife to exact my revenge on him. No one should take a mother from her child."

Isobel added, "And send her away."

"I sent you to Stella, to be safe and loved. I compelled him, commanded him. And I had plans for George. Penniless and lonely. Nothing working out right. He deserved a hard life. Every day without you, I made him pay. You will find the spell I want you to perform on the last page of my grimoire."

As dawn painted the sky with the first strokes of pink and orange, Isobel knew she must leave. *What will this spell ask me to do?* "Speaking of, I need to return to make preparations for George's burial. Will I always be able to talk to you here?"

"Only when there is moonlight."

Isobel chuckled at Mary's remark about John being a good husband, but inside she was uncertain about what lay ahead. She rose and brushed the grass from her skirt.

Her mother said, "Wait! Before you go, I need to confess something. Please."

"What is it?"

After a long pause, Mary said, "George is not your father... Henry is." Mary's voice trailed off. Her mother's admission hung in the air, laden with regret and secrets.

Isobel struggled to process the revelation that Henry, the man she adored and respected, was her biological father. Isobel's mouth fell open, unable to form words. Eyes fixated on the headstone, time froze as the news dropped out of the air in a cemetery in the early dawn. When her body functioned again, she cried. Not tears of sorrow, but joy. The man who was always there for her, who she loved like a father, was her father. "Oh, mother! That is certainly good news. I can not believe it. Why did you marry George instead of Henry?"

Mary said, "I am relieved to speak the truth after all these years, but will tell you more next time. Henry doesn't know. There is a letter I wrote him and never sent. I hid it under a floorboard in my bedroom. Right under the bed. Send that to him. Now get some rest."

"Good night, Mother." Isobel walked back to the store. Her steps were lighter, yet her heart was heavy with the enormity of what she had learned. The mysterious circumstances of her mother's marriage to George, the man she despised, loomed in her mind, a puzzle waiting to be solved.

Back at the store, Isobel sat on her bed, the revelation still sinking in. The newfound knowledge of her true parentage with Henry brought both joy and complexity to her life. The store, her burgeoning relationship with John, and the secrets of her mother's life all swirled in her thoughts.

But her heart yearned for Chicago, for the familiar embrace of her aunt and uncle, now known to be her true father. Isobel grappled with the choice, her mind a whirlwind of emotions and possibilities. Could she leave behind the budding connection with John, a bond that had signs of being fated? Or would the call of her family, and the life she had always known, prove stronger?

In the stillness of her room, Isobel wrestled with these thoughts, her future hanging in the balance, a crossroads between two very different paths.

Chapter Nineteen

Isobel's heart pounded as she ensured the curtains were closed and double-checked the locked door while she awaited the undertaker's arrival. The thought of George lying lifeless upstairs, the man she'd always believed to be her father, weighed on her. She busied herself, trying to distract her mind from the grim reality awaiting a floor above her.

The knock on the door made her jump, even though it was expected. Peering through the curtains, she saw Jane and John, their eyebrows drawn together. News spread fast in a small town. A rush of gratitude filled her as she let them in, their presence a comfort in her swirling sea of emotions.

"How are you doing, Isobel? Doc told me this morning, and I rode out to tell the Carlyles." Jane's hug provided a gentle warmth to her soul that melted away the coldness that had settled inside her.

"I'm managing, somehow. It's all surreal," Isobel confessed, her voice barely above a whisper, her thoughts still entangled about her true parentage and the letter hidden beneath the floorboards.

Jane said, "Don't worry. Everything will work out."

John took off his hat and set it on the counter. His gentle hand on hers brought a flicker of warmth to her cold, anxious heart. "We're here for you, Isobel. Anything you need, just say the word."

Isobel smiled at John and Jane, relieved by his love clouded chartreuse and her optimistic fanned daffodil auras she appreciated at the moment. "That's very thoughtful. Both of you. I'm waiting for the undertaker, but what do I do next? I sent a telegram to my... um... uncle, but I'm not expecting him for the burial." She shrugged.

Jane took her hand. "Come eat with us. Don't spend all your time by yourself."

They turned when they heard another knock. When Tom appeared peeking in around the curtain with that familiar, unwelcomed smirk, Isobel's spine stiffened. Her body pressed against the door and her foot braced against the bottom. Isobel opened it a sliver. "Go away."

Tom's presence was invasive, his breath foul with his face shoved against the door's crack. His offensive black aura flowed through the opening. "When are you paying your father's bar and whore tab? He owes me money."

Isobel leaned her head back, nose wrinkled. "How much does he owe, and why didn't you mention it before?" Her voice was steady, but inside, she seethed. The audacity of him to claim a debt from a dead man was appalling.

Tom's hesitation, his eyes darting around as if concocting a figure on the spot, only fueled Isobel's suspicion. "$50," he declared, a sum Isobel was certain was plucked from thin air.

Isobel glance at Jane and John, who both had their mouths open, and back at Tom's mug in the crack, "I will bring it to you after I bury my father. I'm sure you can understand the circumstances."

The moment she closed the door on Tom's smirking face, she thrust her chin out, lip curled. She wouldn't let him, or anyone, bully her into submission. Not now, not ever.

"Good," Tom shouted and returned to his saloon.

Jane looked across the street. "There is no way your father owes him anything. Tom makes everyone pay first, drink later."

"I don't trust Tom," John said. "But how do you prove it with George passed? That's exactly why he waited."

"I'll take care of it after I bury my father. One problem at a time. I will not worry about it now. Tom wants to rile me up." Isobel straightened and put her shoulders back. Tom was at the bottom of her list of worries.

The undertaker's arrival was a grim reminder of the task at hand. Before she could close the door behind the undertaker, Doc arrived. John led the undertaker upstairs.

Doc asked, "Isobel, how are you?" He took her hand and patted it while Isobel saw sad blue streaks in his aura. It made him even more endearing that he would feel sorrowful that cranky George had died.

Isobel replied, "I'm doing fine." That was a lie. She wasn't fine at all with the stress of everything building. She wanted to be alone, to process the revelation of who her father was. Biggest news of her life and she had no one to talk to. And she had a hidden letter to find.

Doc said, "I came by to inform you of what you need to do with George's bedding and clothing. I didn't have time to tell you this morning since I had a patient."

When John and the undertaker brought George downstairs wrapped in his sheet, Jane turned away, hands covering her face. Doc put a hand on her back. "You did a wonderful job of taking care of him. No one else wanted to, but you did it out of the goodness of your heart. Now he is out of pain and misery."

Isobel doubted George's misery was over. It was understandable that no one lifted a finger for the ill-tempered man, and she could vouch for Jane's heart. But George would burn in hell and her mother would make him pay in her own mysterious way.

John came back into the store. "He wanted to know when you wanted the burial. I told him as soon as possible since you weren't waiting for family."

"Thanks, John." Isobel turned to Doc. "What do I need to do?"

"You need to take all of George's clothes, bedding, and mattress out and burn them. I don't want you and anyone to sleep in that bed. We need to do it now." Doc headed for the stairs, waving for her to come.

Isobel followed, along with Jane and John. "Why do we have to burn the mattress? It seems a little extreme. There was a sheet on it. Do hospitals have to do the same thing?"

Doc replied when he opened the door of George's room, "The clothes harbor the germs much like the trains of skirts did in the past and those ridiculous wild beards and mustaches. When you're admitted to a sanitarium with tuberculosis, your clothes are burned."

Isobel said, "Oh, should you and John start with the mattress then, and Jane and I can bring the clothes and bedding? George had little to nothing." She walked to the window and tried to open it to let some air in, but it wouldn't budge.

John said, "Here, let me." He pushed and wiggled the window, breaking it free to slide up. A slight breeze came in, bringing welcome relief.

John then pulled on the mattress. Doc grabbed the other end, and they drugged it to the head of the stairs and took it slow on the stairs, being careful not to stumble. Doc said, "This mattress is pretty heavy for as thin as it is."

It's the weight of the secrets and lies it had borne over the years.

John and Doc dumped the mattress at the back of the lot in an empty area way behind the garden and opposite the willow tree. Isobel and Jane threw the clothes and bedding on top. Isobel returned to the store to get matches and a water pitcher.

When Isobel returned, Doc started the fire. As the flames consumed George's belongings, Isobel let out a huge breath, her arms crossed tight across her body. The smoke, twisting into a grotesque horned beast, as if the essence of George had seeped into the mattress. Behind the fire, the willow appeared to be bending away with its long, drooping branches wrapped around the trunk as if to avoid the smoke. Isobel knew she needed to finish healing the tree, and soon.

"Stay out of the smoke. Let's walk to the garden until it is all burned." With Doc taking Jane by the arm and John taking Isobel, they hurried towards the garden right behind the store.

Jane asked Doc, "How fast do you think they can get ready for the burial? I want to make sure we have enough food in case people want to eat after."

Doc replied, "Oh, I'm sure by tomorrow morning. I asked him to have the casket ready a couple of weeks ago, so it's digging a hole at the cemetery." Doc walked along the garden. "Isobel, what are you growing in your garden? I remember your mother had a green thumb."

"There are carrots, onions, greens, turnips, and lots of herbs. I grow everything I need for my teas. This afternoon I am going to harvest some herbs. It is a pleasant distraction." Isobel rubbed her hands on some lavender and offered it to everyone's nose one by one. "We need some lavender today."

Doc said, "It's good to stay busy, but don't spend too much time alone. Go visit John and his family, Jane, or Marisol. You have support here. Don't be afraid to depend on others. You weren't close to your father, but it is still a loss."

Isobel smiled at Doc, Jane, and John. "Oh, I will. I know I have friends here. That is worth more than anything. I will write to my... uh... uncle and aunt and let them know what is going on, too. Writing is cathartic for me." Isobel inhaled the lavender scent on her hands again. She wanted some chamomile and lavender tea. The day was a trying one, and she couldn't wait to find the letter her mother hid.

Placing her hand to her nose again, Isobel inhaled the aroma of the lavender and let her breath out, wishing her troubles would leave her like her breath.

Once the mattress and George's clothes had burned to ashes, Doc pulled out a sliver of soap from his jacket pocket and said, "We must scrub our hands vigorously." As they scrubbed their hands clean, it gave Isobel a sense of closure, of washing away a part of her past that had always been foreign and oppressive.

Satisfied, Doc returned to his office, Jane to her hotel, and John escorted Isobel back into the store.

"I have to get back to the ranch to finish my chores. Do you want to come with me? Doc said you shouldn't be alone." John grabbed his hat off the counter.

"I would love to visit with your family, but I have things to get done before tomorrow. Will your parents come to the burial? I would like them to." Isobel replied as she grabbed some twine to tie the herbal bundles and set it on the counter.

"Yes." John tilted his head forward and said, "Are you sure you will be alright?"

Isobel said as she walked to the door with John, "I am going to be fine and I will see you tomorrow." She stopped at the door and smiled as she gazed at his handsome face. "Thank you for being here."

John smiled back. "I will always be there for you, Isobel." Then John walked out the door and mounted his horse. He tipped his hat at Isobel and she waved as he headed home. As John rode away, Isobel's mind was already turning to the hidden letter.

Isobel locked the door and raced upstairs. George's bed moved with little effort without a mattress. On hands and knees, the floorboard gave way, revealing the sealed envelope that held the key to her past and her true identity. She slipped out the letter and sat to stare at it. *What did it say?* She held the letter to the light coming in from the window to realize the words were hidden, a final enchantment from her mother, ensuring the truth would only be revealed to Henry. Her mother thought of everything.

Isobel sat there, the letter in her hands, the dawn of a new day casting light on the path ahead. The revelation that Henry was her true father was both a shock and a relief, a piece of the puzzle that made her feel whole. Yet, the mystery of her mother's life, her choices, and the secrets she kept were still unraveling.

Under the cloak of a full moon, Isobel's silhouette melded with the eerie shadows cast by the ancient willow. The night air, thick with the scent of damp earth and the remnants of a brief evening shower, whispered secrets only the initiated could decipher. The tree, a sentinel of sorrow and dark enchantments, stood defiant against the celestial glow, its black twisted form a testament to the malevolent curse it bore.

Isobel's heart raced as she approached, her boots sinking into the soft, moist ground, leaving a trail of determined steps from the back of the store to the cursed tree. The zigzag scar that marred the kitchen floor inside mirrored the sinister line that stretched towards the willow, a dark artery connecting the source of the curse to its manifestation.

Drawing a deep breath, Isobel steeled herself for the task at hand. Her connection to the craft, nurtured by her aunt's teachings, was about to be tested against a darkness that threatened to swallow her whole. She placed her right hand on the gnarled trunk, feeling the cold, almost pulsating malevolence beneath her fingertips. Her other hand, trembling, connected with the earth, seeking the nurturing embrace of the Mother below.

Whispering an invocation, Isobel sought to bridge the chasm between the corrupted and the pure, to channel the life-giving energies from the depths below to the blighted soul of the willow.

In the shadow of the moon's soft glow,
By the whisper of the winds that blow,
From the earth's deep heart, where secrets lie,

Hear my call, hear my heartfelt cry.
Ancient willow, gnarled and bent,
By darkened curse, not by nature sent,
I summon light, I beckon grace,
To cleanse this blight, to heal this place.
Mother's hand, though led astray,
Cast shadows dark upon this day,
I seek to mend, to right the wrong,
With this spell, with this song.
Elements of earth, air, fire, and sea,
Lend your power, set this spirit free,
From root to leaf, let life renew,
Bathe in the moon's silvery hue.
By the power of three times three,
As I will it, so mote it be,
Let this curse be now undone,
By the rising of the sun.
Blessed willow, stand once more,
Proud and strong, as you were before,
A beacon of hope, of life anew,
Blessed by the morning's early dew.

The air around her stirred, a silent orchestra conducted by an unseen force, as the strands of her hair danced to an ancient rhythm, and the willow's branches swayed in a ghostly ballet.

The energy surged, a torrent of raw power that threatened to overwhelm her. Isobel funneled it towards the tree, her entire being a conduit for healing and rebirth. The curse, a shadow woven by her own mother's hand, fought back, a tempest of dark will against the light she offered.

Drained to the brink of collapse, Isobel crumpled to the ground, her forehead kissing the earth in a gesture of surrender. Each breath was a battle, her life force ebbing away as the price of her audacity. Despair wrapped its icy fingers around her heart, tears of failure mingling with the dirt beneath her.

Yet, in her darkest moment, the willow responded. Tender branches moved with a gentle purpose, caressing her with a touch infused with the very essence of life she had sought to give. They wove around her in a delicate embrace, a lattice of energy that breathed vitality back into her depleted spirit.

Lifted by the tree's newfound strength, Isobel's body was cradled in a cocoon of living wood and pulsating energy. The branches, acting with an intelligence born of their shared triumph, unwound their embrace, setting her upright.

Before her stood the willow, transformed. The blackened bark had given way to a healthy, rich brown, its leaves shimmered under the moon's gentle caress, and the air was alive with the promise of new beginnings. Overcome with joy and relief, Isobel wrapped her arms around the trunk, her heart singing in harmony with the healed spirit of the tree.

As she rested in the willow's shade, now a monument to their shared victory, her hawk familiar alighted upon a high branch, its cry a triumphant fanfare that pierced the silence of the dawn.

Burying George loomed in the back of her mind, a shadow on the horizon of her newfound hope. Yet, Isobel felt fortified, empowered by the impossible made possible. The weight of her mother's request, a tether to the darkness she had fought so hard to banish, seemed less daunting now. She had faced the abyss and emerged not only unscathed but stronger.

With the first light of dawn painting the sky in hues of gold and rose, Isobel knew it was time face the duties that awaited her. The willow, her guardian and ally, rustled in the gentle morning breeze, a whisper of encouragement and a reminder of the strength that lay within her. The hawk, her vigilant sentinel, took flight, its shadow fleeting across the ground as Isobel made her way back into the store, ready to confront what lay ahead with the resilience of the earth and the fierceness of the sky in her heart.

CHAPTER TWENTY

UNDER THE VEIL OF a looming thunderstorm, the dark, swollen clouds mirrored Isobel's tumultuous emotions as she gazed out her window. The somber ambiance was a fitting backdrop for the grim task ahead. With a heavy heart, she turned away from the window, her mind fraught with the impending finality of George's funeral. The green dress she chose, once a symbol of hope and new beginnings on her journey to Tin Creek, now felt like an ironic twist of fate—worn to impress a father who was now a mere memory.

With a heavy sigh, Isobel turned from the window, the weight of the day pressing on her. She dressed slowly, each movement deliberate, her thoughts a whirlwind of emotions. She wished for Henry and Aunt Stella's comforting presence, their absence a sharp pang amidst the already overwhelming sorrow.

Jane's presence at the hotel was a beacon in the gloom, her words a gentle nudge back to reality. "If you didn't come soon, I was going to drag you over. Doc's orders." Jane's voice pulled Isobel from her reverie.

"I hope no one chastises me for not wearing black. It would be hard to get a black dress on short notice."

Jane waved her hand. "Folks around here don't worry about such things. No extra money for fancy stuff."

Over coffee, Fred's staunch dismissal of Tom's dubious claim against George's estate was a small victory in the sea of Isobel's worries.

The procession to the cemetery was a silent, somber affair. John, his parents, and Marisol, along with a handful of townsfolk, formed a small, tight-knit group, their presence a testament to the communal bonds of Tin Creek. The air was thick with unspoken words, each step a shared burden as they made their way to the undertaker's.

Jane broke the silence. "Fred and I invite you to the hotel for a meal after the burial, so we can eat together."

Isobel put her hands to her mouth. "I cannot believe how kind you are when my father did not treat you well. Unfortunately, I do not know why he was such an angry man. I hope I can repay the kindness you have shown me."

Jane blushed and dipped her head. "Don't. You are like a sister to me."

While smiling to Isobel, Fred took Jane's hand. Perhaps he was changing his opinion of her.

John's arm was a steady presence as he escorted Isobel down the worn path to the cemetery, the overcast sky casting a somber shadow over their procession. His voice, empathic, asked, "How are you feeling, Isobel?"

Isobel's response was automatic. "I'm fine." Yet her mind was far from it, tangled in the complex web of her plans for the evening. The full moon's glow that night would be her ally, casting its ancient light on the intricate spells she intended to weave, spells that delved deeper into the arcane than any herbal concoction her mother had penned in her grimoire.

Their footsteps were the only sound, aside from the distant rumble of thunder, as they approached the cemetery's edge where the undertaker stood, his cart a stark reminder of the day's purpose. The air was charged, heavy with the promise of rain, mirroring the tumult in Isobel's heart.

At the gravesite, Isobel took her place, the earth beneath her feet cold and unyielding. John's hands found her shoulders, a gesture meant to comfort, yet it only reminded her of the chasm between her current reality and the peaceful life she once envisioned. She glanced at the plot chosen for George, isolated on the cemetery's fringe, a stark contrast to the communal resting places of the others. "Why is my father being buried so far from my mother's grave?" The words escaped her before she could stop them.

Anna's arrival brought a small measure of solace, her embrace warm in the chill air. "She wrote a letter to the undertaker a month before she died, asking not to be buried next to him. I thought it was a strange coincidence, but Mary did strange things sometimes." Her words, meant to comfort, only deepened the mystery of Mary's actions, leaving Isobel to ponder the enigmatic legacy her mother had left behind.

Isobel's heart skipped as Anna's words sank in, a mix of disbelief and dread pooling in her gut. "She knew?" she whispered, more to herself than to Anna. The notion that her mother had foreseen her own demise was unsettling, to say the least. "I need to see her grave... before I leave," Isobel said, her voice barely above a murmur. "Would you come with me?" she asked, seeking some semblance of comfort in Anna's presence.

Anna's response was immediate, her grip on Isobel's arm both reassuring and firm. "Of course, let's go together," she said, her voice steady and warm.

The undertaker's voice broke through Isobel's swirling thoughts, his words blending into the somber ambiance of the cemetery. Isobel realized she hadn't absorbed a single word he'd said until he posed a question to the gathered mourners. "Does anyone here have anything to say?" The silence that followed was thick, heavy with unsaid words everyone was too polite to say.

The abrupt and clumsy arrival of Tom, his disheveled appearance and drunken gait sending a jolt of tension through the small crowd, shattered that silence. "I want to give my last respects to one of my best customers," he slurred, his attempt to navigate around the grave more of a stagger than a walk. His presence was like a dark cloud, casting a shadow over the solemn proceedings.

"You are all a sorry bunch," Tom declared, swaying as he tried to maintain his balance. His arms flailed for emphasis, causing him to teeter even more. "Burying someone you don't even like. Trying to look all high and mighty. I was his only friend." His scornful words sliced through the mournful air.

Fred's response, a raspberry, punctuated the absurdity of Tom's claims. "You're no friend to anyone," he retorted.

Undeterred, Tom's grimace turned into a sneer as he continued his tirade. "I supported him even when he was at his worst." With a dramatic flourish, he produced a bottle, raising it in a mock toast before taking a swig. "...to a good man," he proclaimed, before staggering off, leaving a trail of his thick, black aura.

Jane's exasperated outburst echoed the sentiments of all present, "Good god, can't we get rid of him?"

Laughter rippled through the somber air, a brief respite from the weight of the day's events. Marisol's voice, tinged with determination, cut through, "Jane, I'll help you, dear. Any other takers?" Her offer, a beacon of solidarity in the dreary atmosphere of the cemetery, sparked a flicker of hope in Isobel's heart.

Fred's response came with a hint of bitterness, "The entire town except the sheriff, the mayor, and Tom's buddy, Al." The words hung heavy, a reminder of the alliances that shielded Tom from the consequences of his actions. The realization of the power he wielded through his connections tempered Isobel's relief at not being alone in her disdain for Tom.

As the men assisted the undertaker in the solemn task of lowering the coffin, Isobel's thoughts drifted to the mysteries surrounding her mother. How had Mary, with all her peculiarities and secrets, come to marry George and settle in the dusty confines of Tin Creek? The enigma of her mother's life, a puzzle she longed to solve, seemed as distant as the storm clouds gathering overhead.

The sharp sound of a shovel slicing through the earth interrupted Isobel's thoughts. Isobel's spine shivered as she watched the undertaker cast dirt into the open grave, the sound echoing with a chilling finality. She stared into the abyss, expecting to feel a surge of emotion, a connection to the man who had been a constant, albeit turbulent, presence in her life. But the void returned nothing, leaving her to question the depths of her own empathy. Was she heartless, devoid of the capacity to mourn the man she had known as her father?

The hypothetical dread of losing Henry or her aunt, the true anchors of her existence, clawed at her insides. The acute pain that accompanied the thought served as a stark contrast to her indifference towards George's passing. It was a reassurance, however painful, that her capacity for love and loss remained intact, untouched by the complexities of her tangled lineage.

As the last echoes of the funeral rites faded, the attendees dispersed, each lost in their own reflections. The cemetery, a quiet expanse under the gray, brooding sky, seemed to hold its breath. Isobel's gaze wandered, searching for a familiar face amidst the departing crowd. She spotted Anna, John's mother, moving with purpose toward a secluded part of the cemetery.

Drawn by an invisible thread, Isobel followed, her footsteps muted against the soft earth. They arrived at Mary's grave, where Anna placed a bundle of flowers at the base of the angel statue. The serenity of the moment was stark against the backdrop of the day's somber events.

Isobel's voice broke the silence. "I can't remember her funeral. Was I there?" The question hung in the air, heavy with unspoken emotions.

Anna's response was gentle, tinged with sorrow. "No. You were in shock. Doc watched you during the funeral and burial. We all wondered if you had seen her die because you refused to say a word. Do you have any memories?" Her eyes searched Isobel's face, seeking a glimpse into her hidden thoughts.

Isobel's denial came quickly, too quickly. "No." The lie was a shield, protecting her from the torrent of memories threatening to surface.

Anna's empathy enveloped Isobel like a warm embrace. "You poor dear." Her arm around Isobel was a lifeline, anchoring her in the present amidst the swirling questions of the past.

The conversation turned to the angel statue, its origins shrouded in mystery. "Who paid to have the angel statue on her grave?"

Anna's reply offered no answers, only deepening the enigma. "Another mystery. It showed up on the stagecoach for the undertaker. No one knows who shipped it here or where it came from." The mystery of the statue, like many aspects of Mary's life, remained unsolved, a puzzle piece missing from the jigsaw of Isobel's past.

Isobel's mind raced, Henry the only possible link to the statue's origins. The thought of confronting him with such a question was daunting, adding another layer of complexity in the intricate web of her family's secrets.

Anna's voice, pulling Isobel back from the precipice of her thoughts, was a reminder of life's simpler pleasures. "Time to think of better things. Things I am grateful for. Good food is always on the top of that list." Her words were a balm, easing the tension that had knotted within Isobel.

Together, they turned away from the grave, leaving behind the angel's silent vigil. The promise of a shared meal awaited, a brief respite from the day's sorrows and the shadows of unanswered questions that lingered in Isobel's heart.

The hotel dining room buzzed with the clatter of cutlery and muted conversations, a stark contrast to the solemnity of the morning's events. The light-hearted banter served as a collective attempt to steer away from the day's somber undertones. But Isobel's thoughts lingered on the unresolved, her spirit tethered to the weight of recent revelations and the specter of impending nighttime confrontations.

Outside, an unsettling tableau unfolded. Tom's three henchmen, a trio of intimidating figures, loomed across the street in front of the saloon. Their presence was a silent challenge, a reminder of the simmering tensions that lay just beneath the surface of Tin Creek's daily life. Isobel's discomfort was palpable, a knot of anxiety tightening in her stomach. She understood all too well that Tom's minions were pawns in his game of intimidation, their watchful eyes meant to unsettle her.

Seeking to reclaim some measure of control and inject a moment of levity into the oppressive atmosphere, Isobel approached the window. Her gaze fixed on the three stoic figures, a mischievous glint sparked in her eyes. She leaned in, her lips barely moving as she whispered an incantation, drawing on the whimsical magick of her youth.

Great Goddesses, Fand and Li Ban.
Press the waters of these three, so they may run to go wee.
So mote it be!

The spell, simple yet potent in its intent, was a playful retaliation, a means to turn the tables on her adversaries. As the magick took hold, the men shifted uncomfortably, their stoic postures crumbling under an invisible, pressing urgency. One by one, with growing desperation, they dashed behind the saloon, their composure undone by an unseen force.

From her vantage point, Isobel's laughter bubbled up, a rare sound of genuine amusement that lifted the heaviness from her heart. The spell, a relic from her school days, had transformed her tormentors into the butt of a joke, offering her a fleeting sense of triumph over the oppressive shadow Tom cast over her life.

In that moment, the dining room's atmosphere lightened, the laughter a beacon of resilience in the face of adversity. Yet, as the laughter faded, the reality of her situation settled back in, a reminder of the battles that lay ahead and the uncertain path she must navigate in the wake of her father's death and the dark heritage left in her mother's grimoire.

Chapter Twenty One

UNDER A VELVET SKY pierced by the luminous gaze of the full moon, Isobel treaded the now familiar path to the cemetery, her silhouette a blend of determination and trepidation. Laden with her magikal arsenal and the enigmatic bundle of enchanted rope, she moved with a purpose that belied the inner turmoil swirling within her. The spells she intended to cast tonight ventured far beyond the comforting realms of her usual herbal concoctions and benign garden charms. Tonight, Isobel would step into the shadowy depths of her power, into realms she had never dared to traverse.

The celestial glow cast an ethereal radiance upon her mother's monument, the angelic figure standing as a silent sentinel in the night. Isobel paused, her eyes tracing the divine form bathed in moonlight, before steeling herself for the task at hand. George's grave lay ahead, a dark maw in the earth that awaited her invocation.

The urgency of the moment was a tangible weight that constricted her chest and muddied her thoughts with doubt. The leap from theoretical knowledge to practical application of such potent spells was a chasm she had yet to bridge. With each step towards the grave, the reality of her undertaking became more daunting.

Armed with a branch cut from a birch, Isobel etched a sacred circle into the earth around the grave, her movements deliberate, tracing the boundary between the worlds. White and black candles, symbols of purity and the void, were placed at the head and foot of the grave, their flames flickering like the hesitant beats of her heart.

The mortar received its somber ingredients: wormwood for opening the gates to the spirit world, bay laurel to summon the dead, and mugwort to compel honesty. The addition of nightshade, a perilous ally, was an acknowledgment of the grave risks she was about to undertake.

Then came the moment of blood magick, a rite so personal and profound that it anchored her very essence into the spell. The bite of the athame's blade against her palm was a stark reminder of the spell's gravity, a physical pain that mirrored the emotional tumult of invoking her father's spirit. The sage and vervain tea, her safeguard against malevolent forces, was a bitter draught that fortified her resolve.

Encircled by the protective barrier, Isobel began her ritualistic dance around the grave, her voice steady as she invoked George Perkins on each pass. The air thickened with anticipation, the boundary between realms blurring as she kneeled, pressing her forehead to the cold earth. The words of the spell, a haunting litany, poured from her lips, reaching into the depths for answers only the dead could provide.

Mighty Diana, keeper of the silent dead,
Lend me the voice from the realm's shadowed bed.
Summon forth George Perkins from the night's deep veil,
At the tolling hour, let his spirit sail.
To stand before me 'neath the moon's soft glow,

And reveal the truths I seek to know.
Bound by your will, let him not deceive
In this sacred hour, his truths we'll receive.
By the power that moves in leaf, in land, and sea,
As I will it, so mote it be!

The moment Isobel completed the chant, a sudden tempest appeared to emerge from the earth beneath her feet. Both candles extinguished with a hiss as an invisible maelstrom whipped her hair and dress into a frenzied dance, the force of it almost uprooting her from her position. The ground trembled, fissures webbing out from the grave like dark veins, and Isobel's heart skipped in alarm, her wide eyes reflecting the chaotic sway of shadows around her.

A thunderous voice erupted from the void, the air vibrating. "What do you want from me? Why do you not leave me be?" It was George, his tone bitter.

Regaining her composure, Isobel straightened, her resolve hardening. "I have questions, George Perkins, and you're bound to truth by the spell." She brushed the clinging earth from her attire and face as she rose, her movements deliberate.

George's spectral voice hissed through clenched ethereal teeth, "I am bound, yes, but know this, my torment continues beyond the grave."

Isobel let loose a bitter chuckle. "I'm sure you're reaping what you sowed. Now, tell me, do you owe Tom anything?"

The air trembled with George's incorporeal fury. "No! That cur has not a penny from me! I settled every tab upon order, and never laid hands on his women after he took over. He's a vile creature, indulging in his own filth." His voice, though disembodied, carried the weight of his vehement denial, echoing around the silent tomb-stones.

As George's spectral remark hung in the air, Isobel could almost visualize the venomous spittle that would have accompanied such vitriol in life. She cocked her head, a wry smile playing on her lips despite the gravity of the situation. "Fascinating, isn't it? We're having our most meaningful conversation ever, and it's only possible through the veil of death and magick," she remarked, her stance defiant with hands firmly on her hips.

Her next inquiry was loaded with years of buried anguish. "Why, George? Why did you murder my mother?" She steeled herself, uncertain of the volatility of a spirit's wrath.

His response was chilling in its detachment. "She was a witch, and witches are a blight upon the earth. I had to silence her incantations." George sounded composed as he justified his heinous act. "I figured it out from everything going on. Too many 'miracles'. Then I saw your mother light a candle without a match. She's the one who started the saloon fire and killed the only woman I ever loved, Pearl."

Isobel's hands clenched into fists, her nails digging into her palms. The accusation that her mother was responsible for another's death ignited a storm within her.

Isobel pressed on, struggling to maintain her composure. "And what of your assault on me? I was but a child, George. Unlearned in the ways of witchcraft you so despised." She was eager to conclude this unearthly dialogue, mindful of the night's waning hours and the critical tasks that lay ahead.

His confession was a whisper of shadows, a murmur of regret. "Fury, a momentary loss of control blinded me. But I spared you, didn't I?"

Her voice was steely, her patience spent. "Sparing me doesn't absolve you. What kind of monster lays hands on a child in such a manner?" With that, Isobel resolved to close this chapter, turning her back on George's spirit and the darkness it represented.

Isobel's fingers clawed into the soft, damp earth of George's grave, each handful of soil a testament to her resolve. The rope, heavy with enchantments and the weight of her intentions, lay coiled like a dark serpent at her side. She buried one end deep within the grave, the moist dirt clinging to her hands as she solidified its place. "Farewell, Uncle George," she whispered.

His retort, a venomous sneer from the beyond, "Ha! So you know. Didn't appreciate having to raise my brother's spawn," only fueled her determination to sever this toxic connection.

Horrible father, horrible uncle. Good riddance.

Isobel stood, her silhouette a stark contrast against the luminous backdrop of the night sky, where the stars winked and the moon bathed the world in a ghostly glow. The perfect stage for her craft, yet the weight of doubt left a light quiver in her stomach.

Dragging the rope, she traced a spectral path through the cemetery, the line between life and death blurring with each step towards her mother's resting place. The monument to Mary Perkins loomed ahead, an angelic sentinel in stone, under which she knelt with reverent purpose. Her athame, gleaming under the moonlight, carved into the earth as she secured the rope's other end, binding her parents with an unbreakable magical tether.

A sudden rustle shattered the night's calm, sending a jolt of adrenaline through Isobel's veins. Her heart raced as she scanned the shadowy expanse of the cemetery, half-expecting the emergence of some unknown threat from the darkness. But it was her hawk, perched atop the angel statue, that caught her eye, its presence a comforting reminder of their connection. With a deep, steadying breath, Isobel let the tension drain from her body, her gaze lingering on her feathered guardian as she prepared for the final act of her spell.

Isobel rose, her figure casting a long shadow under the moon's ethereal light. She stretched her arms wide, embracing the celestial power above. But as if mocking her efforts, a sudden rush of dark clouds veiled the moon, plunging her into an unexpected darkness. She stood there, defeated, her arms falling limply to her sides.

The darkness seemed to press in on her, a tangible force of tension and thwarted intentions. But as quickly as they had come, the clouds drifted away, and the moon emerged once more, its light a beacon of renewed hope. Reinvigorated by the lunar energy now bathing her once again, Isobel spun on her heels, her cloak billowing around her. Each turn was a defiance against the darkness, a dance of resilience and determination under the watchful eye of the moon.

Mighty Morrighan, battle crow, protector of those who've passed.
Link Mary Perkins to her foe at last,
Let her haunt his spirit to her heart's content,
As justice demands and her spirit consents.
So mote it be!

Under the cloak of night, Isobel stood still for a moment, the weight of her task heavy on her shoulders. Her mother's spirit was now entwined in a spectral dance of vengeance, the rope between the two graves pulsating with an ethereal light, shrouded in a ghostly mist. The ground around the rope seemed to thrum with energy, the air charged with anticipation of the unearthly bond that was forming beneath the soil. This connection, once forged, would be indissoluble, a perpetual chain binding the avenger to her quarry.

Relieved of the physical and metaphysical load of the rope, Isobel's steps quickened as she made her way back to the well-trodden path leading to the heart of Tin Creek. The night's embrace was less suffocating now, her passage illuminated by the intermittent glow of the moon peeking through scudding clouds. Her lone sentinel, the hawk, sliced through the air above, its keen eyes cutting through the darkness, a silent guardian on her solitary journey.

The town lay in slumber, unaware of the nocturnal rites that had unfolded at its fringes. Isobel's mind was already racing ahead to the morrow, plotting the last act of this drama. The debt, a fabrication of greed and malice, demanded a resolution befitting its deceitful origins. Her preparations would need to be meticulous, a concoction brewed not just from herbs and whispers but from the essence of justice and retribution.

With the dawn's light still a whisper away, Isobel's shadow stretched long before her, cast by the moon's silver luminescence. The quiet of the night was a stark contrast to the storm of emotions and plans raging within her. Tomorrow, she would face the architect of her recent tribulations, her determination hardened by the trials she had endured. The payment would be delivered, oh yes, but it would carry with it the sting of her rebuke.

Chapter Twenty Two

In the dim light of dawn, Tom jolted awake, finding himself sprawled across a table in the saloon, clad only in his undergarments. His head throbbed with the remnants of last night's indulgence, a dull ache pulsating behind his eyes. He glanced around the deserted saloon, a wave of relief washing over him at the absence of witnesses to his undignified state. Still, the pressing need to visit the privy overshadowed his embarrassment. The mystery of his scant attire and how he landed in such a compromising position would have to wait; nature's call was urgent.

After addressing his immediate needs, Tom's only desire was to seek refuge in his bed, to escape into the oblivion of sleep, and shake off the vestiges of his hangover. But as he staggered to the stairs, poised to ascend to his private quarters, the entrance swung open, and Isobel Perkins stood framed in the doorway, her presence ethereal, casting a soft glow into the dimly lit saloon.

Tom froze, caught in the throes of a dilemma. He yearned for her to marvel at the splendor of his establishment, to become ensnared by its allure. He fantasized about her becoming the jewel of his saloon, a magnet for patrons whose lavish spending would line his pockets. Isobel, the embodiment of grace and beauty, was the key to his grand schemes, the final piece in his vision of prosperity and desire.

As Isobel's gaze finally settled on him, a surge of panic sent his heart racing. Tom glanced down in horror at his disheveled appearance, his undergarments stained and frayed, a stark contrast to the image of sophistication he wished to project. In a reflexive, almost comical gesture, his hand darted down to scratch an itch, a common mannerism among men, but one he profoundly regretted in that moment.

Mortified, Tom cursed his luck. Of all the ways to present himself to Isobel, this was the worst imaginable. His mind raced with damage control strategies, but the damage was done. The impression he had made was far from the grandeur he envisioned, reduced to a figure of ridicule in his own saloon.

Isobel turned her back to Tom, a clear signal of dismissal as she delivered her parting words, the cool detachment in her voice slicing through the saloon's silence. "I will pay you at the sheriff's office, provided you can get dressed." She exited, leaving no room for rebuttal, her footsteps a final punctuation to the encounter. Tom grappled with the sting of her indifference, his mind racing to plan a response that never came. Cursing under his breath, he knew he had to act.

In a frenzy, Tom bounded the stairs, two at a time, to his quarters. The scene that greeted him was one of chaos: garments flung across the room, a testament to a night's revelry now regretted. He snatched his trousers, shirt, socks, and boots from the floor, fumbling with each piece of clothing to regain some semblance of decency. His fingers trembled as he buttoned his shirt, cursing the complexity of dressing when every second counted.

A hurried glance at the small, smudged mirror on the wall confirmed his disheveled state. With hasty strokes, he smoothed his hair and attempted to tame his mustache into something resembling respectability. Tom's heart pounded as he thundered back down the stairs, each step resonating through the deserted saloon, a stark reminder of the urgency of the moment.

Bursting through the saloon doors, Tom was propelled by a singular obsession: to intercept Isobel before she reached the sheriff's office. His mind was ablaze with schemes, not only to claim the fabricated debt he had brewed but to entice her into his employ. The thought of leveraging George's non-existent debt for his gain was a gamble, but Tom was a man who thrived on separating a fool from his gold.

As he sprinted towards the sheriff's office, his breaths came in sharp, ragged gasps. The office loomed ahead, a beacon of authority and, in his case, an opportunity. Tom had played his cards well in securing the sheriff's position for Paul, a man as unacquainted with this side of law enforcement as Tom was with honesty. The townsfolk's naivety was their Achilles' heel, one that Tom exploited without remorse. If they only knew the true nature of Paul's past, or his own for that matter, the calls for their expulsion would be swift and merciless. But for now, Tom had a more immediate concern: to weave his web of persuasion around Isobel and secure his advantage by any means necessary.

Tom barreled into the sheriff's office, a modest single-room structure that Paul had taken over as Tin Creek's symbol of law and order. The room was sparse, with a desk that seemed too large for it, sitting in the middle, a testament to Paul's attempt at authority. In the back, a lonely, unused jail cell cast long shadows across the wooden floor, hinting at the quiet nature of the town's crime rate.

Tom's entrance was like a storm, disrupting the stillness. There, to his chagrin, stood not only Isobel, his intended quarry but also Jane, whose presence was an unwelcome complication. His gaze flitted to Paul, who was maintaining his rifle, with an air of disinterest about him despite the unfolding drama.

Paul peered at Tom with a hint of amusement dancing in his eyes. "Morning, Tom. You are worse for wear. I'm surprised you're upright after last night," he remarked, the corners of his mouth twitching with suppressed laughter.

Tom's irritation was palpable as he shot Paul a withering look. "I want to know why in the world I gotta come here to get what's owed to me?" His voice was laced with annoyance, his gaze drifting to Isobel, imagining her not in the modest attire she wore but in something far more flattering and less... proper.

Isobel's retort was sharp, her disdain for Tom's lack of decorum clear. "You should try wearing clothes when you run your business. I went to the saloon, and you stood there in your dirty, stained underwear scratching yourself. What is a respectable woman supposed to do?"

Jane couldn't contain her mirth, her laughter echoing through the room. "Oh, you don't say! Did you run out of clean underwear, Tom?"

Even Paul couldn't hold back, his laughter joining Jane's, filling the room with a chorus of mockery directed at Tom.

Isobel cut through the laughter with a tone that brooked no nonsense. "Now I have the money here and I will count it out on Paul's desk. I want you to sign this paper that you received payment in full. Then you can take your money and work naked all day for all I care."

The tension in the room was palpable, a mix of amusement at Tom's expense, and the serious undertone of a transaction that was anything but ordinary. Tom, caught between indignation and the need to secure what he claimed was owed, found himself under the scrutinizing gaze of those who held the upper hand.

Tom's strides were deliberate and heavy as he approached the desk, a stark contrast to the debonair image he usually projected. His well-tailored clothes and polished boots were a testament to his vanity. The insults hurled at him for his earlier undignified state rankled him. "Fine. Fine. Just count the money," he grumbled, his voice thick with irritation. He shot a disdainful look towards Jane, his lip curling in contempt. "I got laundry to do."

Isobel counted the bills, laying them out on Paul's desk for all to see, her movements precise and deliberate. "Ten. Twenty. Thirty. Forty. Fifty. There is your money." She pushed a piece of paper towards Tom with a firm gesture. "Sign here and George's debt is paid in full."

Tom, attempting to regain some semblance of control, turned to Isobel with what he imagined was a compelling gaze. "Why not work it off in my saloon? I'm short a girl."

Jane's reaction was immediate and fierce. "Watch your tongue, Tom. She's a lady, not a whore," she spat, her body tensing as she took a menacing step towards him, ready to defend Isobel's honor.

Isobel intervened, her hand clasping Jane's arm with a reassuring grip. "Because I own a shop. I'm not destitute," she stated firmly, her voice laced with resolve.

Tom, undeterred by the rebuff and the palpable tension, shrugged. "You want to do it this way? Your loss." He scribbled his signature on the paper with a dismissive flick of his wrist, not bothering to read the contents.

Isobel wasted no time in securing the document. "Come on, Jane. Thank you, Sheriff," she said, her tone brisk as she pulled Jane towards the door, eager to leave the stifling atmosphere and Tom's unseemly proposition behind.

Tom's ears pricked up at Isobel's remark, 'No need to poke the bear.' His face flushed with anger, and he whirled on Paul, his voice rising in indignation. "I am not a bear! Do I look like a bear?" His hands flailed in the air, emphasizing his frustration.

Paul shook his head, his shoulders shaking with silent laughter.

Pacing like a caged animal, Tom's thoughts raced. He hadn't expected Isobel's resolve or her resources. His scheme to ensnare her in his saloon's web had crumbled. Stopping, he fixed Paul with a steely gaze. "You need to work with me here. We're on the same side, and there's no way we're going to run this town if you chuckle and heehaw with those two women." His voice was a low growl, laced with barely contained fury.

Paul leaned back in his chair, his expression one of mock seriousness. "Humph. You have no sense of humor. This town is boring, so it's entertaining." His lips curled into a mischievous smirk.

Tom's patience snapped. "Be it as it may." He spun on his heel, his hand grasping the doorknob with such force it seemed he might rip it from its hinges. "You're going to come to my way of thinking. Believe me." His parting words were a threat, echoing in the small office as he yanked the door open and stormed out, leaving it to slam shut with a resounding bang that echoed off the walls, a testament to his simmering rage.

Tom's stride was heavy as he navigated the wooden boards of the boardwalk, his boots sending up small puffs of dust as he descended onto the hard-packed earth of the livery. A scowl creased his brow, his thoughts a turbulent storm. "This ain't my day. What I want I didn't get. How hard can it be to score a girl when I got a business and looks to boot? At least, I got some money. Maybe I gotta buy her something. Some girls go for that." His monologue was so consuming that he almost tripped while stepping back onto the boardwalk, his foot catching the edge in a clumsy dance.

Steadying himself, Tom's gaze drifted across to the Perkins Hardware. The curtained windows were a barrier to his prying eyes, a symbol of his failure. Yet the thought of Isobel bending to his will under his roof sparked a sinister grin across his face. Surrender was not in his vocabulary.

With renewed determination, Tom swaggered into his saloon, the doors swinging behind him with a thud. Inside, the usual suspects were attending to their duties: Matt was arranging the new whiskey shipment behind the bar, Walter was sweeping the sawdust-covered floors, and Al lounged against the wall, the picture of idleness.

"Howdy boys," Tom announced with a flourish, his voice echoing through the half-empty saloon. "I made some money today off of Isobel Perkins, the pretty little lass." He slapped the envelope on the bar with a triumphant thud, drawing the attention of his employees.

"Open it, Matt. Count it out for everyone." He beckoned Al and Walter closer with a grandiose sweep of his arm, like a ringmaster heralding the spectacle to come.

Al rose and strolled over while Walter abandoned his broom against the staircase, both drawn to the promise of drama at the bar.

Matt, with an air of skepticism, tore open the envelope and laid out its contents. "One, two, three, four, five...maple leaves." The bar was now adorned with a quintet of bright green, Big Leaf Maple leaves, each one mocking Tom's earlier confidence.

Al burst into laughter, the sound booming in the saloon. "Have you hit the sauce too hard already this morning?" he jeered, amusement casting light on his dark eyes.

Matt and Walter exchanged glances, their expressions a mix of confusion and irritation. Tom's grand reveal had fallen flat, turning him into the punchline of a joke he hadn't intended to tell. The tension in the room was palpable, a mix of amusement and disbelief at Tom's expense for the second time today.

Frustration boiled within Tom as he jabbed the envelope with his index finger. "No. There were five bills in there," he insisted, his voice laced with disbelief. Mimicking the act of counting out money, his hand hovered over the bar, each imaginary bill slapped down with increasing force. "And I walked straight here," he declared, tracing an invisible line from the sheriff's office to the saloon, his movements punctuated by agitation.

Pacing like a caged animal, Tom's hands fluttered in the air, a physical manifestation of his growing distress. "How can that be? How? A clever trick?" he muttered to himself, the words escaping through gritted teeth.

Walter shrugged, his indifference fueling Tom's ire. "Of course, you don't know. You never know nothing," Tom sneered, his words dripping with contempt.

Matt, concerned, furrowed his brows in confusion. "Did anyone see her pay you?" he inquired, hoping to shed light on the perplexing situation.

"Yeah, yeah! Paul did. And Jane, too," Tom exclaimed, his arm sweeping towards the door in a grand gesture, recounting the humiliating encounter. "Isobel paid me over at Paul's office 'cause she came over here and caught me in my knickers. She turned and ran right outta here."

Al, seizing the opportunity for humor, quipped, "Your knickers? It was probably all the holes that had her running. Ya might consider some new ones so you don't scare the ladies off."

Tom, unamused, retorted, "Al, if it covers my ass, it's good enough for me. Damn it!" His frustration reached a boiling point, and with a thunderous slam of his fist on the bar, he declared, "I'm trying to get her here, right here." His finger jabbed at the bar with vehemence, marking his territory.

Turning to Matt with a sense of resignation, Tom demanded, "Give me one of those," his gaze fixed on the new whiskey stock. "I'm going to my room. Don't bother me."

Matt complied, placing a bottle of whiskey before Tom, who snatched it with a gruff, "Here you go, boss."

Al shot Matt and Walter disdainful glares, ensuring Tom's solitude. "I'll make sure no one bothers you, Tom."

With a storm brewing within, Tom ascended the stairs, his final command echoing through the saloon. "I want everyone to hatch a plan to close that damn store and get Isobel working here. And not any stupid ideas, Walter." The door to his room slammed shut, a testament to his fury. "I've been had by that damn woman!" His voice, filled with venom, reverberated off the walls.

From the seclusion of his room, Tom peered out the window, his gaze fixating on Isobel's store, now bustling with activity. He watched, seething, as Isobel attended to a customer with ease. Shaking his head, he muttered a dark promise, "It's dangerous to cross me. You have no idea. When I want something, I get it by whatever means." The determination in his voice was chilling, a harbinger of the lengths he would go to achieve his desires.

Chapter Twenty Three

Isobel jolted awake, not to the gentle chirping of robins, but to the thunderous boom-boom-boom that rattled her windows like an angry fist. Panic clawed at her throat as she flung open the curtains, her heart leaping into her chest at the sight of Bernard, the livery owner, his face contorted in rage as he bellowed, "Stop this madness!"

Scrambling out of bed, Isobel threw on clothes with trembling hands, each frantic tug mirroring the frantic hammering against her shop door. Adrenaline coursed through her veins, propelling her down the stairs, the pounding growing louder with each step. She flung the door open, wooden planks being affixed across the entrance blocking her way. Panic and confusion swirling within her, she darted through the back, grateful for the repaired exit.

As she rounded the corner of the store, the culprit came into view: Al, Tom's minion, was the architect of this morning's chaos, hammer in hand and feet in a wide stance. His aura of black with red streaks matched the angry countenance on his face. Across the street stood Tom, the orchestrator of this siege, his smirk a silent taunt. "He does a fine job, don't you think?" Tom mocked.

Fueled by indignation, Isobel charged at Al, shoving him with all her might. "Stop what you're doing. You have no right. Go back across the street. This is my property and you are trespassing," she asserted.

Al, unyielding, shrugged off her assault and resumed his task, the hammer echoing her escalating frustration. Isobel yelled at Tom, "You can't do this! This is my store."

"I can because you still owe me fifty dollars. When you pay me for real, the boards come down. Of course, you could remove them yourself," he taunted.

Paul's arrival offered a glimmer of hope. His presence on the boardwalk exuded authority, but his unsettling aura clashed with justice, mirroring Tom's ominous aura. "I heard there was a commotion here. Why are you boarding up your store?" he asked.

"I am not! Al is because Tom told him to. He is trespassing," Isobel protested, her stance defiant, hands planted on her hips. Her stomach fluttered and her chest tightened. *Is Paul who he says he is?* She hadn't noticed the contradiction yesterday when he was behind his desk.

Paul's voice boomed across the street, seeking confirmation. "Tom, is that true?"

Tom's casual, arrogant dismissal as he sauntered into the street was infuriating. "She hasn't paid me my money."

Paul scratched his jaw. "Come on, Tom. I watched her count out the money in my office."

The air crackled with anticipation as the townsfolk, drawn by the commotion, spilled into the street from adjacent establishments, their curiosity piqued by the unfolding drama. They formed a makeshift audience, witnessing the standoff between Isobel and Tom.

Tom, with a flourish of feigned innocence, proclaimed, "It was an amazing sleight of hand. When I counted it out in my saloon, it was maple leaves. You can ask my bartender." His gaze dropped to his hands, as if questioning their own complicity.

Paul, the sheriff, pointed his index finger at Tom. "I asked you if you were satisfied before you left, and you fanned it out to me and said yeah, satisfied. Now you're not. Remove the boards. The debt was paid."

Tom, undeterred and defiant, planted himself beside Al. "No. It stays. I'm serious. I did not get my fifty dollars." His stance was an obvious challenge as he spoke to Al. "Don't you take it down unless you want to cross me."

Isobel, seizing the moment, shifted her gaze to the assembled crowd. "Who believes Tom?" A tense silence followed; not a single hand raised in Tom's defense.

Carmen, known to all from Marisol's establishment, couldn't contain her disdain. From her elevated position on the hotel board-walk, she declared, "Tom is a ratbag scoundrel." Her words, sharp and condemning, echoed through the crowd, finding resonance in many nodding heads.

Isobel, emboldened by the support, posed another question. "Who believes I paid Tom?" In a show of solidarity, every hand in the crowd soared into the air, with Jane and Carmen raising both.

Dawn, the beloved baker, couldn't hold back either. "Who wouldn't believe it? Isobel is a good woman. Can't say anything good about Tom." Her words, simple yet powerful, underscored the community's trust in Isobel.

Facing Tom, Isobel raised her eyebrows and gave an icy stare as she jutted her head forward. "No one believes you because Paul and Jane were witnesses. Maybe you hid the money and picked up some leaves, so it appears I tricked you and now you're playing the poor victim." The accusation hung in the air, a damning indictment of Tom's character, leaving him exposed before the judgmental gaze of the entire town.

Tom crossed his arms over his chest, his voice rising above the murmuring crowd. "They didn't witness your trickery, that's all. Why don't you show us how you did it? Sleight of hand tricks, that's what it is." His gaze swept over the gathered townsfolk, searching for a hint of sympathy. "What did I ever do to any of you?"

From the fringes of the crowd, a young man, his leg dragging with a pronounced limp, bellowed with raw emotion, "You kicked me out because I wouldn't buy a round for everyone, then beat me up, leaving me for dead." His accusation, heavy with the weight of injustice, resonated through the tense air.

Tom's reaction was dismissive, a sneer twisting his features as he waved away the young man's grievance as if swatting an annoying fly.

Paul said, "Take the boards down or I'm throwing you in jail. And that goes for you too, Tom." His finger, unwavering, pointed at Tom, leaving no room for negotiation.

Bernard, a respected figure from the livery, started a chant that became a unified demand. "Take it down!" The rhythmic call echoed through the street, a vocal manifestation of the community's unrest.

Al, caught in a moral quandary, glanced towards Tom for direction. Tom gave a reluctant nod, signaling defeat, before he made his way back to the saloon, shoulders drooped, his figure diminishing with each heavy step.

Paul, seizing the moment to disperse the onlookers, announced, "Well, there's nothing more to see. Let the man do his job in peace." His voice, steady and commanding, urged the crowd to disband.

Al, with a begrudging sense of duty, removed the wooden barricade from Isobel's door, his arms laden with the remnants of his misguided task.

Isobel, seizing the moment for accountability, confronted Al. "What made you think this was the right thing to do?" Her tone sought to pierce through his misguided loyalty.

Al's lip curled as he looked down at her. "I was just toeing the mark. Ya don't have to have a high falutin conniption fit." His stare lacked any warmth.

Paul joined in the cleanup, his actions speaking of solidarity with Isobel as they cleared the aftermath of Tom's rash decision.

Isobel, her gratitude genuine, acknowledged Paul's intervention. "Thank you, Paul." Her smile, a beacon of warmth amidst the tension, conveyed her appreciation. *Why is his aura like that?*

"No problem, Isobel. Have a good day." Paul's parting words, simple yet sincere, marked the end of the confrontation as he retreated across the street, the embodiment of law and order in their small town.

Jane handed Isobel her broom. "Time to work that anger out."

Isobel, her resolve firm, accepted the broom, shoulders back, chin high. "Oh, I'm going to work it out alright." Her words, though light, carried the promise of retribution and the unspoken resolve to stand her ground, come what may.

As Al's subtle nod redirected Tom's attention towards the entrance, the saloon's atmosphere thickened with anticipation. Tom's boots clicked against the wooden floor, each step echoing in the dimly lit room adorned with oil lamps, casting long shadows as he approached the door.

"What's up, Paul? You got a long face. Come in for a drink?" Tom's voice, infused with feigned nonchalance to conceal his underlying tension.

Paul, removing his hat to reveal the sweat-stained band, replied with a gravity that filled the room, "We need to talk."

Tom gestured with a grand sweep of his arm towards the newly established poker table, its surface gleaming under the flickering light, surrounded by mismatched chairs bearing signs of brawls. "Why don't you sit at my new poker table? The hottest spot in town." He then called out to Matt, the bartender, whose wary eyes met Tom's before complying, "Matt, pour Paul a drink. Our sheriff needs something to loosen him up."

As Paul settled into a chair, his gaze fell to the floor, where a sinister stain peeked from the fresh paint. "Decorating the floor with someone's blood again?" The accusation was dense with implications of past misdeeds.

Tom, carrying Paul's drink, noticed the scrutiny of the bloodstain, a grim reminder of Tom's violent temper. With a resigned sigh, Tom admitted as he sat, "What can I say? I like blood." He leaned towards Paul. "I've been meaning to talk to you, too. You know, we have history." His last word came out like a hiss.

Paul took a swig with furrowed brows. "Yeah, we do."

"It would be a shame if it came out your past is not exactly what you say it is." Tom sneered as he side-eyed his friend.

Paul scowled, his foot tapping. "What are you getting at, Tom? Make your point. I'm not in the mood."

Tom put on his best fake smile. "I think we should stick together. Then this town would truly be ours. Right now, you aren't too helpful for my...our cause. I'm here to make money. That's why I brought you here, in case you forgot." *Sometimes Paul is such an infernal idiot, he would swim across the river to get a drink.*

Paul, pointing with his index finger, countered, "I'm doing my job. I don't see how I'm stopping you from making money. You have always been your worst enemy. This 'sheriff' business is not to my liking. Sweeten the pot before I find something better for myself."

"I want that girl, Isobel, working for me. You stood there and defended her. You stay out of my way." The offer that followed was a desperate bid, leveraging Paul's vices. "I'll pay you in booze and women. How's that for you? Or do I need to bring up Carson City?"

The moment of truth arrived as Paul weighed his options, his gaze drifting towards the upstairs. "Sure, Tom. Sounds like a deal to me." His conditions, however, came with a warning: "Don't go killing anyone in town. Too hard to let that pass without raising questions."

A clink of glasses sealed their pact, a sinister echo of their shared past, "Just like old times," Tom declared, an evil grin spread across his face.

Paul's departure on the creaky wooden staircase with a blond woman in tow, marked culminating their agreement.

"That's better. Now I can get what I want." Tom grabbed the empty glasses and set them on the bar.

Chapter Twenty Four

THE MORNING SUN BARELY pierced the gloom of Isobel's shop as she slid the heavy curtains aside, only to be greeted by the unwelcome sight of Al and Walter, looming like sentinels on her doorstep. The boardwalk under their feet creaked as they shifted their weight, an implicit threat in their stance. Isobel's heart raced as she unlocked the door, confronting the blockade head-on. "If you are not here to purchase something, please leave," she stated firmly, her voice steady despite the adrenaline coursing through her veins.

Al sneered, brandishing a rifle with an ease that spoke of too many confrontations. His aura, a swirling mass of black and red, pulsed with malevolence. "Tom told us to make sure no one comes in. What are you gonna do about it?" he challenged.

Beside him, Walter, looking more uncomfortable with the situation, tipped his hat in a feeble gesture of apology. "Sorry, gotta do what the boss says," he muttered, his sage-colored aura tinged with submission and unease.

Al turned his disdainful gaze to his companion. "Where's your gun? Can't figure why Tom keeps you around. And don't apologize. Just do your job." He then fixed his stony stare back on Isobel. "You ain't gonna make any money today."

Walter remained silent, his head bowed, the very picture of reluctance.

Isobel met Al's gaze. "We shall see," she retorted. Surprised that she spoke with a calm that belied the storm brewing within her, she locked the door with a decisive click and drew the curtains shut, plunging the shop back into shadow.

Behind the safety of her closed door, Isobel's mind raced. If these men were determined to stand in her way, she would ensure this was the last time they dared to defy her. She recalled a spell from her grandmother's grimoire, one that could turn the tide in her favor. The challenge, however, lay in gathering the correct ingredients.

Isobel ascended the creaky stairs, her heart pounding in rhythm with her hurried steps. The musty scent of aged paper greeted her as she entered the dimly lit kitchen, where the grimoire lay open on the worn wooden table, its pages yellowed with time and use. She marveled at the meticulous illustrations that adorned the pages - detailed sketches of herbs in all their forms, alongside breathtaking landscapes that whispered tales of her ancestral homeland, Ireland. A wave of relief washed over her as she discovered the spell required herbs she already possessed in her shop.

With urgency propelling her movements, Isobel dashed back downstairs. The jars on the shelf behind the counter blurred together as she searched for the ingredients. Her hands, trembling, selected the herbs with precision, her mind already weaving the threads of the spell.

Back at the top of the stairs, Isobel paused, her chest heaving with exertion. She knew well that magick was no trivial task; it demanded a calm, focused mind. Rushing through the motions would only invite failure. Closing her eyes, she inhaled, allowing the stillness to envelop her, grounding her scattered thoughts.

Returning to the table, Isobel began her work. The herbs crumbled under her deft fingers, releasing their potent scents into the air. The room filled with the earthy aroma of the crushed botanicals, each one a vital component of the intricate tapestry of her spell.

Then came the most challenging part - summoning the tears. Isobel sank into a chair, her mind casting back to the darkest day of her life. The vivid memory of her mother's lifeless form on the cold floor surged forward, the anguish as raw and piercing as it had been years ago. Her breaths became shallow, her chest tight with sorrow. Tears welled up in her eyes, spilling over and trailing down her cheeks. She held a small crucible beneath her chin, capturing the droplets - each one a testament to her pain, a vital ingredient in her magical brew.

For a moment, Isobel allowed herself to feel the full weight of her grief, considering the catharsis of a good cry. Yet, even in her vulnerability, she maintained control, channeling her emotions into the spell. With a heavy sigh and a determined press of her lips, she blended her tears with the herbs, each drop infusing the mixture with the depth of her sorrow and the strength of her resolve.

Isobel snatched a simple dress from her room, the urgency of the situation lending her movements a frenetic edge. Clutching the ancient grimoire and the mortar filled with her prepared concoction, she added two swathes of fabric from the latest shipment intended for sale. The ensemble of items pressed against her created a comical figure as she navigated the narrow staircase back to the shop floor, a soft chuckle eluding her lips despite the gravity of her task.

Upon reaching the counter, she realized her oversight - a candle, an essential component of the ritual. With a muttered curse for the lapse, she dashed upstairs once more, her frustration mounting with each step. Descending with a white candle in hand, she placed it on the counter, gathering her wares once again. A sharp exhale from her lips sparked the candle to life, casting flickering shadows across the walls.

Isobel steadied herself, the weight of the grimoire pressing against her arm, the fabrics draped over her other arm, and the mortar and dress balanced between. Peering through the curtain, she saw Al and Walter still blocking her entrance, their presence a stark reminder of the conflict at hand.

With a deep breath, she centered her focus on the two men outside, envisioning the transformation she sought to invoke. The words of the spell, imbued with her intent and desperation, flowed from her lips:

Mighty Goddess Caillech, wielder of transformation and change,

Cast upon these men a garb strange.

Clothe them in fabric, in dress, let their minds reel in distress.

Confound their senses, twist their sight,

Bind them in attire tight.

So mote it be!

Isobel darted to the curtain, her heart racing with anticipation. Her spell had taken effect, she could feel it. Pulling the fabric aside, her eyes confirmed the chaos she had unleashed. Outside, Al and Walter stood, attired in dresses that clung to their masculine frames. She couldn't contain herself; laughter erupted from her, vibrant and unbridled.

Jane's laughter soon joined hers from next door, a hearty sound that could infect a crowd. "Fred, you must see this! Hurry!" she called, her voice bubbling with mirth.

A mischievous boy in the street, seizing the moment, lobbed a rock towards Al, then scampered away with the agility only youth could afford. "Despicable urchins!" Al cursed, his frustration palpable. "What purpose do they serve? Nothing but nuisances!"

Walter, ever the gentle soul, countered, "I've always been fond of them. Dreamed of having my own, if only I'd had the chance to marry."

Bernard, busy with his daily chores at the livery, paused, his attention caught by the peculiar sight. A deep chuckle escaped him as he beheld the spectacle. "Well, I'll be damned. Al, I thought you were made of tougher stuff. What's this? A new fashion from the dress shop?" His laughter was hearty, echoing through the street.

Isobel's laughter mingled with the growing chorus of amusement, drawing a scowl from Al. The hotel's boardwalk bore witness to Fred's amusement as he observed the scene, his laughter restrained by his crossed arms.

Walter, bewildered, inquired, "What's the joke, Al? Why's everyone in stitches?"

Al, glimpsing Walter's attire, burst into laughter. "You're the one in a frock, prancing about like a dame!" he jeered, his own attire momentarily forgotten.

Walter's face twisted in confusion and hurt. "I'm not the one dressed for a tea party, Al. Your outfit's sprouting daisies, hardly flattering for that belly."

Al's patience snapped, his hand tightening around his rifle. "Watch your tongue, or you'll regret it. You're the one in flowers, not me."

Walter, defiant yet wounded, suggested, "Then take a good look at your own reflection, if you dare."

The tension between them crackled, a volatile mix of confusion, denial, and the dawning realization of their ridiculous predicament.

The bewildered pair staggered towards a shop window, their steps halting and uncertain. As they peered into the glass, the reflection that greeted them was nothing short of astonishing. There they stood, two burly men clad in floral-printed shirt dresses, the fabric clinging to their rugged frames. Their jaws hung open in disbelief, their rugged features contrasting with the delicate patterns adorning them.

The mischievous boy who had started the chaos returned, his reinforcements in tow. A chorus of youthful laughter echoed through the streets, each giggle a piercing arrow to Al and Walter's pride.

"Look, it's a bearded lady!" one bold child proclaimed, pointing at Al. In a vain attempt to salvage some dignity, Al ran his fingers through his beard, only to incite further glee among the young audience.

Tom, drawn by the commotion, stormed out of his establishment, his eyes widening at the spectacle before him. The sight of the entire town's youth assembled, their laughter uncontained, was too much. "What circus is this?" he bellowed, his voice laced with fury. "A mission turned mockery! Get back in here, and for heaven's sake, get properly dressed!" With that, he stomped into the shadows of his saloon.

The journey back across the street was a gauntlet for Al and Walter. Encircled by jeering children, they navigated through the sea of mockery, each step a trial under the weight of ridicule.

Once the spectacle had dispersed, Isobel turned to the gathered children, her voice warm and inviting. "How about a sweet reward for such splendid entertainment?" she offered. The promise of candy drew an enthusiastic response, and soon the shop was abuzz with eager chatter as each child made their selection.

The eldest among them, a lanky boy with a mischievous glint in his eye, turned to Isobel with a grin. "Thanks, Miz Perkins. We can laugh at them anytime you want," he declared, his companions nodding in agreement before scampering off with their sugary spoils.

Watching them go, Isobel mused on the day's events. The spell had worked wonders on Al and Walter, but she knew it was only a matter of time before Tom regrouped. The next move would have to be bolder, more direct. Tom had yet to feel the true sting of her magick, but that was about to change. The necklace around her neck grew warmer.

The moment widow Marsh's silhouette vanished from view, Isobel's eyes narrowed as she caught sight of Al's menacing form looming over the frail woman. His voice, laced with veiled threats, sliced through the quiet street, warning her against setting foot in Isobel's store again. Heat flushed through Isobel; she couldn't stand by and watch her patrons terrorized.

With a burst of energy, she thrust the door open, stepping onto the boardwalk with a force that made the wood beneath her feet creak in protest. "Enough, Al!" she bellowed, her voice carrying across the street. "You will not intimidate my customers. Leave at once!"

Al's response was a derisive sneer, his bulky frame almost swelling with defiance. He tilted his massive head, his belly protruding as he jeered, "And what will you do about it?" His feet shifted, planting themselves more firmly on the ground in a deliberate challenge.

The door slammed shut with a resounding thud behind Isobel, the sound echoing her mounting resolve. She was at her breaking point, the cumulative weight of the daily harassments by Al, orchestrated by Tom, pressing down on her. The time for passive resistance had passed.

With swift steps, Isobel ascended the stairs, fists tight, straight to her mother's grimoire. Clutching the ancient tome, she descended, her movements a whirlwind of purpose. The book thudded onto the counter, its pages fluttering as she searched for the perfect retribution.

Her mother's clever manipulation of spirits, turning whiskey into water, sparked an idea in Isobel's mind. Perhaps it was a silent battle against George's own demons. But now, the battle was hers, and she needed whiskey—an ingredient George had in abundance.

Illusion spells held a tantalizing allure, yet they came with their complexities. She had toyed with casting one to refresh the store's facade, to spare herself the laborious task of painting. But the spell's transient nature, its inability to withstand scrutiny, forced her to abandon the idea in favor of manual labor, with John's invaluable help. Stakes were different now, and the spell she sought to perform after she closed for the day would strike at the very heart of Tom's arrogance.

The "Closed" sign clinked against the glass as Isobel turned it with a resolute flick of her wrist. The store, now shrouded in the dimming light of dusk, echoed with the finality of the day's end. Upstairs, she transformed the kitchen into a sacred space, the table cleared of all but her magickal intentions.

Isobel's movements were methodical, each step imbued with purpose. She unfurled her altar cloth across the table's surface. Atop this, she placed her altar items with deliberate care: candles to represent the elemental fire, a chalice of water to mirror the fluidity of change, a feather for air's elusive touch, and a sturdy stone to ground her intentions in the earth's unwavering resolve.

The gathering shadows in the room seemed to lean in, as if drawn by the gravity of her undertaking. Isobel's heart drummed in a steady rhythm, her resolve steeling against the weight of the task before her. She retrieved an amber bottle from a hidden nook, its contents distilled for temptation and vice that she sought to transform.

With a deep, steadying breath, Isobel lit the candles, their flickering light casting a warm, golden glow that pushed back against the encroaching darkness. She poured the whiskey into the chalice, the liquid's rich aroma filling the air before she whispered the ancient words of transformation.

The incantation was a melody of power, each syllable a thread in the tapestry of change she wove. Her voice, firm yet imbued with reverence, danced with the candlelight, intertwining with the elements she called to witness and aid her spell.

Mighty Goddess Bec, guardian of the sacred spring,
Let only water flow where spirits once did sing.

Transform the saloon's brew across the way so neat,
Into nothing but pure water, every bottle, every seat.
So mote it be!

As the last word left her lips, a hush fell over the room. The whiskey, once a symbol of ruin and despair, shimmered under the candlelight. Isobel watched, her breath held in anticipation, as the transformation unfolded, the spirit of the liquid bending to her will, reshaping itself into the pure, life-giving essence of water.

Isobel retreated to the sanctuary of her bedroom, where the world outside seemed both distant and much too close. She nudged the curtain aside, allowing herself a sliver of a view of the saloon across the street, its raucous energy barely contained within its walls. The window creaked as she cracked it open, the night air carrying the saloon's din into her otherwise serene room. Settling onto her bed, she opened a book, a gift from Aunt Stella, its pages whispering promises of escape.

But the words blurred before her eyes, her thoughts ensnared by the complexities of Tin Creek. The town, with its tight-knit community and simple pleasures, could have been a haven if not for the shadow cast by Tom and his relentless antagonism. The banker, a mere obstacle she was determined to overcome with pragmatism. And then there was Doc, who saw a future for her here, and John, whose presence stirred something deep within her. Yet, Tom loomed over these budding possibilities like a storm cloud, threatening to unleash chaos at a whim.

A sudden uproar from the street shattered her musings. A man's voice, laced with indignation, cut through the night, his accusations of "cheat" and "swindle" piercing the usual hum of the saloon. Another voice joined the fray, its owner stumbling out into the night, his protestations painting a picture of betrayal. "I'm no sucker! You pulled a fast one on me. I paid for a drink. Not water!" he bellowed, his voice a mixture of confusion and anger.

Tom appeared at the saloon's entrance, his figure framed by the dim light spilling out onto the street. "You got what you paid for. If you don't like it, go somewhere else," he retorted, his words slicing through the tension like a knife.

Isobel watched, a small smile playing on her lips as the scene unfolded. Her spell had woven its magick, turning Tom's liquor into nothing more than water, sowing seeds of discontent among his patrons. This was more than a mere inconvenience for Tom; it was a blow to his reputation, one that could steer his customers into the welcoming arms of Marisol's Sapphire Saloon. With any luck, this debacle would force Tom to turn his gaze inward, to deal with the fallout and leave her to live her life in peace.

CHAPTER TWENTY FIVE

HENRY'S GAZE DRIFTED THROUGH the carriage window as the familiar silhouette of Prairie Avenue homes glided past, their grandeur a stark contrast to the turmoil churning within him. The unsettling visit with Stella had left a heavy cloud over his spirits. As his carriage drew to a halt, he barely acknowledged Charlie, his loyal driver, before disembarking with a heavy heart.

His feet moved almost mechanically along the cobblestone path leading to the imposing three-story limestone mansion he called home. A symbol of prosperity and legacy, the house was a testament to the affluent life he and George, his estranged younger brother, were born into. But tonight, its opulence bore hollow.

The grand door swung open, leading Henry into the echoing stillness of the expansive foyer, a stark reminder of the void Isobel's absence had left. Her vibrant presence, once a staple at his dinner table, now lingered only in the pages of her letters, amplifying the distance between them.

With each step deeper into the house, Henry's mind replayed Isobel's latest correspondence. George's death, although a closure to a chapter marred by rivalry and betrayal, wasn't the source of the gnawing anxiety within him. It was Isobel's situation in Tin Creek that unsettled him, her safety a constant shadow in his thoughts, magnified by the knowledge that he had sent her into uncertainty.

Henry's conversation with Stella had only fanned the flames of his worry. Stella's maternal instincts echoed his own fears, both dreading that Isobel's newfound connections in Montana, especially the mention of a young man, might sever her ties to Chicago forever.

Henry couldn't shake off the disappointment that Isobel hadn't confided in him about this young man, the silence a growing chasm. In an era where communication was bound by letters and the rare luxury of a telephone, the distance to Montana struck him as insurmountable.

As Henry draped his coat over the weathered oak of the hall tree, Estelle glided towards him with the quiet efficiency that had always characterized her movements. The soft rustle of her skirt whispering against the polished marble floor of the grand foyer. In her hands, she clasped a small folded note, the crispness of the paper contrasting with the soft, worn lines of her hands.

"Sir," Estelle began, her voice carrying the gentle, unobtrusive authority honed by years of service, "you received two calls from Mr. Steyer during your absence." She extended the note towards him, her gaze steady and expectant. "He expressed a need to speak with you on a matter he described as urgent. 'Urgent' was his precise word."

Henry's hand paused mid-air, the motion of hanging his hat forgotten as he turned to face her. The weight of the word 'urgent' hung between them, heavy with unspoken possibilities. He accepted the note with a nod, his fingers brushing against hers in the exchange.

"Fine. Thank you, Estelle," he replied, his voice carrying a mix of appreciation and the underlying tension that the message had stirred within him. The echo of his steps was a solitary sound in the expansive foyer, carrying him towards the unseen burdens that awaited.

Surrounded by the rich mahogany and leather of his study, a room that had witnessed countless decisions and contemplations, Henry reached for the silver candlestick phone with a sense of resignation. The familiar weight of the receiver was little comfort as he dialed "Central 596," bracing himself for a conversation that might increase his turmoil for Isobel's well-being.

Henry's grip on the receiver tightened as Aldus's voice, usually a balm of reassurance, now carried ominous news through the line. The scratch of his fountain pen punctuated the stately silence of his office as he took meticulous notes, the ink flowing like the mounting dread within him. "So my gut feeling was right. Tom McCall is even worse than I thought. My niece could be in danger." The mention of Isobel's potential peril sent a shiver along his spine, prompting an urgent, "Are you available to go to Montana with me?"

The pause before Aldus's affirmation was a chasm of anticipation. Henry exhaled a sigh of relief, a plan forming in his mind. "Great. Tomorrow. I'll make the plans and call you right back," he declared, a determined edge to his voice.

The moment he set the receiver down, Henry was in motion, his mind racing ahead to the logistics of their journey. He dialed the train company, each ring echoing in the hushed ambiance of his office, adorned with the weight of his family's legacy. Booking their passage, he pondered Isobel's courage, her lone venture a testament to her resilience. Guilt gnawed at him for insisting she face such risks alone. The specter of Mary, and what might have been, haunted him anew, intertwining his past regrets with present fears.

Estelle's tentative interruption, the door ajar only a crack, her voice soft yet clear, "Dinner is ready, sir," grounded him back to the present. He acknowledged her with a raised hand, his thoughts still ensnared in the web of what awaited them in Montana.

With a final note penned, Henry made one last call to Aldus. "We leave tomorrow at 8:30 in the morning. We will arrive in Missoula in four days," he briefed with military precision. "I imagine we will be there for a few days. Once we conclude our business, you can return, and then I'll travel on to visit my niece before I come back."

After he hung up, Henry allowed himself a moment of respite. Tomorrow, he would embark on a journey fraught with uncertainty, driven by the unwavering commitment to protect Isobel, the closest thing to a daughter he had ever known.

As Henry's gaze settled on the painting of Isobel, a wave of nostalgia washed over him. There she stood, her youthful innocence captured beside the Irish setter she adored, a testament to the summers filled with laughter and joy she spent under his roof. Those days, he would shelve away some demands of his textile empire to relish in her company, in the warmth she brought to his stately, often too quiet, home. She was more than a niece to him; she was the beacon of light in his otherwise reserved existence, the child he cherished as his own.

The resolve settled in him like a stone in still waters. Henry would finance Isobel's nursing education, a silent rebellion against his own antiquated expectations of matrimony he once harbored for her. How could he, a man who lived in the shadow of an unrequited love for Mary, Isobel's mother, dare encumber Isobel with the chains of an unwanted union?

With a methodical grace, Henry tidied his desk, aligning papers into neat stacks, the act a soothing ritual that brought order to his thoughts as much as it did to his workspace. His meticulous nature found comfort in the predictability of an organized environment, a stark contrast to the turmoil of his inner world.

Rising from his desk, he made his way to the dining room, a grand space adorned with intricate cornices that danced like lace along the high ceiling, the rich woodwork framing the windows casting long shadows in the evening light. Here, in the heart of his vast abode, the echo of his solitude was most pronounced. He took his place not at the head of the grand table, designed to host a multitude, but at the seat nearest the kitchen. It was a practical choice, sparing his staff the needless length of steps, yet it was also a poignant reflection of his loneliness. Surrounded by the grandeur of his dining room, the table set for one was a silent testament to the life he led—a life of quiet order, absent of the chaos and warmth of a family he longed for but never had.

Henry's pallor deepened under the flickering candlelight, his thoughts a tumultuous storm as Estelle's concerned voice broke through his reverie. "Sir, is everything OK? You look pale. Do you want me to send for the doctor?" Her words echoed in the grand dining room, amplifying the gravity of his worry.

With a weary wave of his hand, Henry attempted to assuage her fears. "Estelle, I'm fine. It's just... I'm troubled about Isobel. I must leave for Montana first thing tomorrow. Ensure everything is ready for an early departure. And please, inform Charlie about the carriage," he instructed, his voice a blend of fatigue and determination.

Estelle's brows furrowed in concern, her affection for Isobel clear. "Yes, sir. I do hope Isobel is alright. She's such a delightful young lady." Her words were a balm, yet they couldn't quell the unease gnawing at Henry's heart.

Shaking his head, Henry replied, "Isobel is fine, as far as I know. But that might not last unless I intervene. This isn't something I can resolve from here." His voice trailed off, the weight of his impending journey settling over him.

Dinner lay before him, a feast that mocked considering the turmoil within. He moved his fork through the meal, each bite a reminder of the looming threat to Isobel. The situation with Tom McCall loomed over him like a dark cloud, his appetite vanishing with each thought of the peril she might face.

CHAPTER TWENTY SIX

TOM'S FURY WAS A tempest, his heavy boots thundering against the saloon's wooden floors as he expelled the last of the disgruntled patrons. "What the hell is going on?" he bellowed, his voice ricocheting off the walls. "All of 'em claimed we served them water. They think they can swindle me? The whole lot are cheats and liars!" His stride was a storm's path to the bar. "Matt, pour me a glass."

Apprehensive, Matt complied, sliding a glass of whiskey across the polished counter with the care of handling dynamite.

Tom seized the glass, the liquid's clarity mocking him, and downed it in one defiant gulp. But the expected burn of whiskey was absent, replaced by the traitorous smoothness of water. "What the hell is this shit?" Infuriated, he launched the glass like a missile, aiming for the grand mirror behind the bar, its gold-etched 'Bitterroot Saloon' insignia now a target for his wrath.

The glass struck with a violence that echoed through the silence, fracturing the mirror's surface. Cracks sprawled across the reflective expanse like lightning, a web of betrayal and deceit.

Matt, having ducked, rose to survey the aftermath. The bar, once a place of camaraderie and laughter under Jack Logan, now bore the scars of Tom's tempest. The fractured mirror, a once-proud guardian of the saloon's soul, now wept shards of glass, its fragmented surface a testament to Tom's impotent rage.

With the mirror's demise, the upper balcony, usually alive with the soft whispers and rustles of the girls, fell quiet, their hurried retreat a silent rebuke.

Tom's reflection, now a broken mosaic of his fury, stared back at him—a grimace of realization and defeat. "What happened to the whiskey that's supposed to be in that bottle?" he demanded. "Matt, you better not be pulling one over on me. Open another one. Check it!" His fist pounded the bar with a finality that echoed the break of his resolve.

As more fragments of the mirror succumbed to gravity, the saloon was enveloped in a hush, the only sound the sinister tinkle of falling glass—a requiem for Tom's shattered illusions.

"Walter! Clean up this mess!" Tom's command cut through the tension, but before Walter could move, a burst of laughter erupted from Al, uncontrollable and mocking.

Tom whirled around, his glare a weapon aimed at Al. But Al's laughter only grew, a raucous sound that filled the room, mocking Tom's unraveling with every chuckle. In that moment, the saloon had become a stage for his folly, witnessed by the very man sworn to follow him.

Tom's gaze was an eagle's, sharp and unyielding, as he monitored Matt's every move behind the bar. Trust was a currency devalued in Tom's realm, where loyalty was as fleeting as shadows at dusk. The saloon now felt like a ship adrift in a storm, with Tom as its beleaguered captain.

Matt, with hands that betrayed a tremor of fear, uncorked another bottle, the sound echoing in the tension-laden air. "I swear, I have nothing to do with it. I just pour drinks," he professed.

Tom's patience was a dam breached. "Yeah, yeah, yeah, you just pour drinks. Tired of hearing it." The whiskey, if it could be called that, disappeared down his throat, its passage unmarked by the familiar fiery trail. The glass hit the bar with the finality of a judge's gavel, its sound a punctuation to Tom's growing fury.

Matt recoiled as if struck, the muscles in his neck taut with anticipation of a storm's break. Walter, sensing the impending maelstrom, retreated from the bar's front line, seeking the relative safety of distance.

"Dammit. This is freaking water." Tom's voice was a low growl, his pacing a predator's cagey tread. His eyes, seeking a target for his wrath, found none on the empty balcony. The girls, wiser to the winds of Tom's temper, had vanished like smoke.

Halting his restless march, Tom demanded, "When did we get this whiskey?" His question hung in the air.

"We got it two days ago," Matt replied. "I poured this same whiskey last night. I don't understand." His head shake was a silent plea for reason in a world gone mad.

Al, roused from his bemused observation, heaved himself upright with the deliberation of a bear disturbed from slumber. "You send me along all the time 'cause you don't trust these knuckleheads. And there was no funny business that I saw." His words were a gruff defense, his jutted lip a challenge to refute. Sinking back into his chair, he added with a sneer, "But then I wasn't wearing no dress either." His arms folded over his expansive belly, a barrier against the world's absurdities.

Tom's agitation was a storm brewing within the confines of the Bitterroot Saloon. Each step he took along the worn wooden floorboards echoed his inner turmoil. His fury was a dark cloud that hung over the room, threatening to burst. "I'm sending you guys back with this joke of a whiskey tomorrow morning, and you're bringing back the real deal. I can't afford to lose my customers over this."

He prowled back and forth like a caged animal, his mind a whirlwind of thoughts and schemes. Every so often, his piercing gaze would land on Walter, who froze in place, caught in the eye of Tom's storm. "What are you gawking at? Can't a man think?" Tom barked, his voice cutting through the tense silence. "Get back to cleaning! That's what you're paid for, isn't it?"

Walter, jolted into action, scrambled back to his broom, sweeping the lingering debris of the shattered mirror with a fervor borne of fear. Matt, meanwhile, cleared the bar of glass shards, his movements careful and deliberate, a stark contrast to Tom's erratic pacing.

Al sat slumped in his chair, a grumbling statue of discontent. But Tom's patience had worn thin. He loomed over Al, his hands planted on his hips, his shadow engulfing the disgruntled man. "And you, what's eating you? You pushing a butt nugget?"

Al surged to his feet, closing the gap between them, his frustration mirroring Tom's. "It's been one mess after another since that Perkins girl showed up," he spat. "I didn't sign up for dresses and humiliation. You promised easy money, not this circus."

Their faces were mere inches apart, two storms colliding. Tom's nostrils flared with each breath, his mind racing. Al's outburst was the last straw. "If you think you can do better, then go!" Tom hissed, his voice venomous.

Al's retort was swift, his body pressing forward in defiance. "I'm going to Virginia City, where the girls are easy and the dice rolls freely. Let's see how you fare without me, chasing a dream that'll never be yours."

With that, Al shoved past Tom and stormed out. Tom watched him go, a part of him envious of Al's freedom. But Virginia City, with its lawmen on the prowl, was no sanctuary.

Alone now, Tom mulled over his dwindling options. The whiskey fiasco was a pressing issue, but Isobel Perkins remained his ultimate prize. His resolve hardened; he would not be deterred. With or without Al, with or without the town's approval, Tom McCall always got what he wanted. And Isobel would be no exception. He needed to tighten his grip on Paul, ensure his loyalty. The game was far from over, and Tom was ready to play his hand.

The atmosphere in the Perkins Hardware Store shifted as Marisol stormed in, her presence slicing through the calm like a blade, her aura a fiery crimson trail in her wake. The door banged against the wall, left ajar in her haste, as she marched straight to the counter where Isobel was working on her inventory.

Isobel looked up, startled by the sudden intrusion, her eyes widening as she took in Marisol's livid expression. The air seemed to crackle around them, charged with Marisol's fury.

"Wait until you hear what that scoundrel did now!" Marisol glared out the window at Tom's saloon with her lips tight and her fists tighter.

"I can't even fathom what Tom has concocted now," Isobel said, her voice laced with resignation. She had enjoyed a brief respite from Tom's machinations, but now it appeared things were back to normal as customers entered the saloon and stayed.

With a slam of her fists on the counter, Marisol's outrage caused Isobel to flinch. It was a side of Marisol she hadn't seen before, a storm raging within the usually composed saloon owner.

"Tom's slander knows no bounds," Marisol seethed, her gaze piercing through the window towards the Bitterroot Saloon. "He's spreading vile lies that your father contracted tuberculosis at my establishment. A blatant falsehood, considering George's loyalty was always to Tom's den of iniquity."

A knot of anxiety tightened in Isobel's stomach, her hands coming to rest on the scattered papers before her. "But how do you disprove such baseless accusations?" she asked, her mind racing. Had Tom thought Marisol had something to do with his whiskey problem? *This is my fault.*

Marisol's fists clenched and unclenched as she grappled with the injustice. "The mayor's siding with Tom, demanding I close the Sapphire until I can clear my name. It's a witch hunt, orchestrated by Tom to cripple me."

Marisol exhaled. "Doc had to give everyone a clean bill of health, and naturally, I footed the bill. It's not right for the girls to pay for this slander." Her voice carried a mix of resolve and frustration. "None of us are ill, yet the mayor's blind allegiance to Tom's lies is infuriating. I'm withdrawing every dime from his bank as a start. And I'd advise you to steer clear of it too, especially after he strong-armed you into that unnecessary expense of painting your store, right on the heels of your father's death."

Isobel nodded, her thoughts adrift amidst the turmoil of her own dilemmas. "I still have the loan to pay off. Several more payments. And I'm considering selling the store, anyway." She began tidying the scattered order forms, a tangible symbol of the interruption to her daily routine. Sliding the order book back beneath the counter, she added, "Nursing school starts soon. I want to stay to see how things go with John, but I aspire to be a nurse. I can't let that dream go." The inner conflict was palpable, a tug-of-war between her burgeoning affections for John and her lifelong aspirations, further complicated by the newfound connection with Henry.

Marisol's inquiry was gentle, laced with genuine interest. "How long is nursing school? I'm curious. Doesn't Doc want you to come back?" Her smile was a beacon of warmth in the chilly room. "He's not the only one, you know."

"The basic program is two years, ending in June of the following year," Isobel responded, her mind already weaving through the implications of Marisol's inquiry. "What exactly are you proposing?" she asked, a flicker of hope igniting within her. Perhaps Marisol had a solution, a means to mitigate the unforeseen consequences of her spell, a chance to right the wrongs cast upon those around her.

Marisol paced the room, her energy a whirlwind of determination and distress. "I think I've come across a solution," she began, her voice tinged with a hint of excitement. "In Missoula, I stumbled upon this sweet young girl, lost and alone. It didn't feel right to leave her to fend for herself, so I brought her here. She's not cut out for saloon life at all, but she has a knack for numbers, managing my accounts with ease. I believe she could oversee the store in your absence."

As they were talking, Doc entered, the door closing behind him. His presence brought a sense of authority and comfort. "Heard you were here," he said, moving towards Marisol with a gentle demeanor, taking her hand in his. "I've finished with the girls. Rest assured, there's no tuberculosis or any other public health concern among them."

A sigh of relief escaped Marisol's lips. "Could I get that in writing?" she asked, hope flickering in her eyes.

"Of course," Doc assured her, his voice steady and reassuring.

Marisol's frustration found a new target. "And while you're at it, could you enlighten Mr. Johnson at the bank? Tom's deceit shouldn't carry weight." Her annoyance bubbled over. "And another thing—my accounts are a mess. Gemma's caught many discrepancies. It's hard not to suspect foul play." Her voice crescendoed with each grievance, her agitation clear.

Isobel intervened with a calming solution, pouring chamomile and lavender tea, its aroma promising tranquility.

"You're getting worked up, Marisol," Doc observed, patting his pockets in vain. "I can't believe I don't have some smelling salts with me."

Isobel reassured them, "This tea should do the trick." She kept her voice soothing to temper the heated room.

Doc, with a physician's keen eye, scrutinized Isobel, his gaze probing beyond the superficial. "You are right, young lady. Just like your mother. How are you doing? I haven't talked to you much since your father died. Are you getting enough sleep? You look tired, a little peaked."

Isobel mustered a smile. "I'm fine, Doc. Marisol has an idea for the store while I'm gone to nursing school." Her gaze shifted to Marisol, seeking reassurance in the shared plan, yet the shadow of uncertainty lingered. Especially now that she has a father back in Chicago. She felt like the rope in a rope pulling contest.

Marisol, now somewhat soothed by the tea, clutched the cup with both hands, her movements less erratic but still laced with residual agitation. "It's the new girl, Gemma. I thought Isobel could hire her to run the store while she's gone." Her pacing, though slowed, underscored the urgency of her proposal.

Doc's eyes brightened. "Excellent idea! She's a lovely young lady."

Isobel, her interest piqued yet cautious, leaned forward. "I want to meet her first and have her work a day or two to see how she would do. I need someone I can trust."

Marisol nodded. "I trust her with my books, so I'm sure you can trust her. When do you want me to send her over?" Her voice, steadier now, carried a note of optimism, painting a picture of a potential solution that could bridge Isobel's diverging paths.

Doc cut through the burgeoning plans with a decisive intervention. "While you two plot out Isobel's life, I'm going to write a letter for you that you can post in your window for the public. I'll talk to Mr. Johnson, too. And whatever you can do to bring Isobel back is fine by me."

Marisol's face glowed, her earlier tension dissolving into a relieved smile. "Thank you!" she exclaimed, her voice echoing in the store.

Isobel, however, felt a pang of frustration. "Bye, Doc." The words were polite, but her mind raced with the unwelcome realization that everyone seemed eager to steer the course of her life. The weight of their expectations pressed on her, mingling with her own uncertainty. She needed clarity, and she needed it soon.

Doc nodded, a knowing look in his eye. "Bye, ladies." With that, he left, the bell above the door jingling behind him.

Seizing the moment to lighten the mood, Isobel quipped, "Why not bring her now? At least I know I won't catch anything from her," her words laced with a playful edge.

Marisol set her teacup down with a gentle clink. "I'll be right back," she declared, her determination clear. The door swung shut behind her, leaving Isobel in a pool of silence that filled the room.

Alone with her thoughts, Isobel's mood sobered. She berated herself for the unforeseen ripple effects of her spell casting. The interconnectedness of life in Tin Creek was a complex web, and her actions had ensnared Marisol. It was a sobering reminder of the responsibility that came with wielding magick. She had to be more cautious, more aware of the potential consequences. It was a lesson learned the hard way, and one she would not soon forget.

Chapter Twenty Seven

ISOBEL LET OUT A soft chuckle as Marisol and Gemma entered, the former adjusting Gemma's hair with a maternal fussiness. Gemma's youth was evident, her features carrying the freshness of someone a year or two younger than Isobel.

"Well?" Marisol prompted, nudging Gemma towards Isobel.

With a modest dip of her head, Gemma approached, her voice carrying a distinct Irish lilt. "My name is Gemma. Pleased to meet you." She then retreated, seeking the familiar comfort of Marisol's proximity.

Observing Gemma's reticence, Isobel extended a welcoming hand. "I'm Isobel Perkins. Pleased to meet you, Gemma."

As their hands met, the unexpected surge of energy, a palpable vibration that resonated between them, bewildered Isobel. Gemma's eyes, a mirror to Isobel's own with their shared hue and golden specks, held her gaze. The moment was fleeting, yet the jolt of connection prompted Isobel to withdraw her hand. "Oh, sorry," she stammered, unnerved by the encounter.

Gemma shifted, her foot drawing circles on the floor. "It's alright. People don't know what to make of me. I'm used to it," she murmured, her voice barely above a whisper.

Isobel, attempting to regain her composure, smiled. "Marisol tells me you're good with numbers," she ventured, changing the subject. Her head tilted as she added, "That's important, but customer interaction is key. Can you manage that? Trust is crucial here; it drives sales."

Gemma hesitated at first, but met Isobel's gaze once more. "I can do it. Talk to the customers. Make them comfortable. Can I work for you? Please?" The earnest plea, accompanied by a radiant smile, transformed her youthful features and cast a glow of sincerity and eagerness.

Isobel's expression softened into a warm smile, her voice carrying a note of optimism. "Let's give it a week, see how we fare. I'm hopeful you'll find this place more agreeable." She crinkled her nose, adding, "This job's bound to suit you better than the saloon." Her gaze shifted to Marisol, her tone apologetic, "No slight to your establishment, but she's quite young."

Marisol's response was nonchalant, a gentle shrug of her shoulders conveying her understanding. She then placed a reassuring hand on each of Gemma's shoulders, her voice tinged with a protective undertone. "I took her in to look out for her after finding her alone. She'll be better off here." Her head tilted towards Gemma, her eyes reflecting a mix of hope and concern, akin to a mother's watchful gaze over her fledgling. "If she's ready to give it her all."

Gemma smoothed her dress and straightened her posture while nodding to Marisol. "I am." Turning back to Isobel, her eyes sparkled with excitement, "So, you're really hiring me?"

"Yes, I am," Isobel confirmed, her mind racing through the numbers, pondering what she could afford to offer. "Why not start right away?" She inquired about Gemma's current living situation, already thinking ahead about the girl's well-being.

Marisol chimed in before Gemma could utter a word. "She was at the boarding house, but she's been with me lately because of some unwelcome attention from a couple of young men."

Isobel's stance shifted, her hands landing on her hips as she processed this new information. "Well, that problem will soon be solved," she declared, a hint of resolve in her voice. "I ordered a new mattress to replace my father's. You'll have a place in the spare room upstairs." Isobel understood all too well the distress caused by harassment.

Gemma's response, "I would like that very much," carried a hint of eagerness, her glance flitting to Marisol, seeking a silent affirmation. Marisol's lack of dissent brought a wide smile as she faced Isobel again.

"Well, it seems we have our course set," Isobel declared, ushering Gemma towards the counter with a gesture that signaled training had begun. "You've got a bit to learn. How well do you know herbs?"

"Have fun, girls!" Marisol left with a wave.

Isobel watched Gemma's fingers trail across the array of jars lining the shelves, her curiosity piqued by each label she scrutinized. "My mother taught me some back in Ireland when I was a wee lass. My Grandma taught me more."

Isobel's eyes twinkled. "Ireland, you say? I never would've guessed," she teased, before her tone softened with genuine curiosity, "And your mother? Grandmother? Where might they be now?"

The shadow that fell over Gemma's features was stark; her lips pressed into a thin line, sealing away words unspoken.

Isobel sensed the shift. "I understand, truly. My mother passed away when I was young. Raised in Chicago by my aunt, she's the one who passed on her herbal wisdom to me. I've continued making teas, much like my mother did. You'll find the town abuzz with tales of her healing hands." She noted Gemma's distant gaze, attempting to reel her back. "When did you leave Ireland? My family, too, has roots there, carried over by my mother and aunt in their youth."

Gemma withdrew, her interest in the store's contents a shield against further inquiry. "Maybe another time," she murmured, a soft finality in her voice.

Isobel respected the boundary. "Of course, we'll talk when you're ready." She guided Gemma through the store's practical spaces, ending their tour upstairs. As they entered the living quarters, Isobel's eyes darted to her mother's and grandmother's grimoires left open on the kitchen table. With a swift, protective motion, she gathered them into her embrace, then ushered Gemma into what would soon be her bedroom. "It's simple, but it's home." The room, though modest, held promise, and as Gemma ventured further in, Isobel could only hope this new beginning would bring them both the peace they sought.

Gemma's sudden twirl in the center of the room, arms outstretched, brought a fleeting moment of joy to the otherwise tense atmosphere. Her abrupt halt and the grave assertion that followed, however, sent a shiver down Isobel's spine. "This is big compared to any place I've lived before... Someone died in here. And out there." Her finger pointed towards the kitchen, her voice dropping to a somber note. "Choked to death."

Isobel felt a chill as if a shadow had passed through her, her voice barely a whisper, her pulse racing, "How do you know that?"

Gemma's casual shrug in response as she returned to the kitchen did little to ease the growing unease swirling within Isobel.

The memory of the peculiar sensation when their hands met resurfaced in Isobel's mind, her gaze scrutinizing Gemma, searching for an aura that wasn't there. Her thoughts raced--was Gemma gifted with the witch's hindsight, able to perceive echoes of the past? The implications were staggering. Could Gemma be a witch, unbeknownst even to herself?

Gemma gasped. "Oh no! I forgot to tell you and Marisol said nothing either, but I have a pet raccoon. He won't leave me." Her eyes were wide, imploring, "I can build a cage out back if it's a problem."

Grateful for the distraction from the whirlwind of concerning thoughts, Isobel stashed her precious tomes in her room, her movements brisk and determined. Returning to face Gemma, she closed the door with a soft click, her mind working to accommodate this new, unexpected element of their arrangement. "Hmm. I think we can manage. Is he a problem inside, like breaking things and being... ah... messy?" Her inquiry was cautious as she navigated the complexities of their budding relationship and the mysteries that Gemma brought with her.

Gemma's smile widened, her excitement palpable as she spoke of Shadow. "Shadow's clever, you know. He even has his favorite toy, a little cloth doll I stitched together for him. He never tears it apart; just carries it around, cuddling it when he sleeps." Her voice carried a tender warmth, illustrating a deep bond between them.

Isobel, intrigued and somewhat apprehensive about the dynamics between a raccoon and a hawk as familiars, inquired, "And where does Shadow spend his time currently?"

"Oh, he's having the time of his life back at Marisol's, surrounded by his playthings. Shadow's a charmer, you'll see." Gemma's eyes sparkled with fondness for her unusual companion.

Nodding, Isobel mulled over the logistics. "Well, we'll have to make some adjustments, but I'm sure we can accommodate Shadow. Why don't you bring him over tomorrow? It'll give him a chance to get used to his new surroundings."

Gemma's response was a squeal of delight. "Truly? Oh, Isobel, you're as wonderful as Marisol said!" Her gratitude was effusive, almost childlike in its purity.

As they made their way back downstairs, Isobel reflected on the serendipity of Gemma's arrival. Her own life had been a tapestry of unexpected turns, and Gemma's sudden appearance felt like another intriguing thread woven into the pattern. Yet, the mystery of Gemma's past and her potential gifts lingered in Isobel's mind, a puzzle awaiting its solution.

Chapter Twenty Eight

As Isobel turned at the sound of the door opening, her heart skipped a beat at the sight of John standing in the doorway, bathed in the warm glow of the setting sun that filtered through the windows. The rugged rancher, with his hat in one hand and a small, mysterious box in the other, brought an air of anticipation that tingled along Isobel's spine. The box, innocuous, sparked curiosity, a silent question lingering in the air between them.

John, catching Isobel's gaze, offered a gentle smile that softened his weathered features. "Isobel, would you join me for dinner?" The invitation caused Isobel's heart to flutter, her feelings for the rancher deepening despite her attempts to keep them at bay.

Isobel's response was a radiant smile, her voice tinged with genuine delight. "Yes, I would love to." As she called out to Gemma, her new employee, "Gemma, are you finished?"

John, placing his hat on the counter with a gesture of respect, inquired with a nod towards the back room, "Great. How's she doing?"

Isobel replied, "Good." Her mind, however, was a whirlwind of thoughts about Gemma. The young girl's mysterious past and potential magical abilities weighed on Isobel, casting a shadow of concern. In the world of witchcraft, one's history could be a beacon of light or a darkened path, and Isobel felt the burden of unraveling Gemma's story.

Gemma emerged from the back, her arms laden with boxes, her expression a pained look. She glanced at Isobel and then at John. "Did I do something wrong?"

Isobel's smile was reassuring, a beacon of kindness in the dimming light of the store. "Oh no. Just time to lock up. You're doing great."

Gemma let out a huge breath as she set the boxes down with a quiet thud. "Oh good. I don't want to get fired from another job."

Isobel shook her head. Gemma wobbled on the uncertain grounds of her new employment. "You didn't get fired by Marisol. I stole you because you had skills I wanted." Isobel hoped to instill a sense of worth in the young girl, whose talents in mathematics shone as brightly as the stars in the night sky.

Gemma tilted her head, her brows knitting in a silent query. "But I wasn't looking for another job. It's unusual, that's all. See you tomorrow, Isobel. Hi, John. Bye, John." With a swift motion, Gemma scooped up Shadow, her raccoon companion, and exited, leaving a trail of unspoken questions in her wake.

"Isn't it strange for a raccoon to follow Gemma around like a dog?" His question hung in the air.

Isobel's laughter was a melodious sound that filled the room, her amusement clear. "Why? The raccoon loves her." But her laughter masked a deeper, more complex web of thoughts. How could she unravel the tapestry of her life to John, a tapestry woven with threads of magick, familiars, and a legacy stretching back to her mother and beyond? The mental image of a family portrait featuring her and her mother, each accompanied by their unusual companions, presented a fantastical tableau compared to the conventional family scenes John might be accustomed to. In that moment, Isobel stood at the crossroads of her past and her potential future, wondering how to bridge the worlds she inhabited.

Isobel's anticipation and nerves were obvious as she fiddled with the doorknob before pausing, her actions deliberate as she drew the curtains across the windows to shroud the store in privacy. "Alright. I'm ready." Her voice was a soft declaration as she secured the lock, turning to John with a smile that barely masked the tumult of emotions swirling within her.

John's hand found the crook of her elbow, a reassuring warmth that guided her towards the hotel dining room. Each step they took was charged with an electric energy that Isobel found both exhilarating and daunting. Was it love that pulsed between them, or the thrill of new companionship? The question loomed in her mind, a shadow that danced at the edges of her joy. *Don't imagine something that might not be there. Enjoy his company and let what happens happen.*

The dining room, with its ambient lighting and hushed tones, offered a cocoon of intimacy as Jane ushered them to a secluded table. The centerpiece, a vase brimming with vibrant flowers, expressed a silent testament to John's thoughtfulness, possibly plucked from his mother's cherished garden. Jane's conspiratorial wink at John didn't go unnoticed by Isobel, igniting a flicker of curiosity and, perhaps, hope.

As John attended to her with a chivalrous gesture, pulling out her chair, Isobel found herself enveloped in the comforting familiarity of their conversation. "How's your mother doing? I'm sorry she was ill. Did the tea I sent help her?" Her inquiry, genuine and concerned,

bridged the gap between polite small talk and the deeper connections forged by shared experiences and mutual care.

John's response, infused with gratitude, resonated with Isobel.
"She is much better and said it was the tea that did it. She improved
the next day." His words were a balm to Isobel's soul, affirming her
place in the intricate tapestry of his life.

"That's good. Your mother is incredibly nice. I'm glad I could help
her. Those are her flowers, are they not?" Isobel's observation, tinged
with a sense of belonging, wove her further into the fabric of John's
world, a world she was both eager and hesitant to fully embrace.

John's hands betrayed a hint of nervous energy as they smoothed
the fabric of the tablecloth before he repositioned the vase, making
room for the small, enigmatic box that had signs of being more
than its physical contents. The flowers, a vibrant testament to his
mother's garden, stood as silent witnesses to the unfolding scene. "I
know you love my mother's garden, so I brought some. Jane is fixing
us a special meal tonight."

Isobel's playful suspicion was laced with an undercurrent of
hope, her head tilting as she probed for the hidden significance of
the evening. "Something's up. What are you two scheming? It's not
my birthday, and it's not yours." Her heart was aflutter with the
possibilities, each beat a question mark echoing her inner turmoil.

John's explanation was simple, yet profound. "I met you, well
we reunited a month ago. It's our one-month anniversary. And I
wanted to make it special. We can do this every month to show how
special you make every day." The pink streaks in his aura wove a
tapestry of affection and intent.

The impact of his words was like a gentle wave, washing over
Isobel and leaving her adrift in a sea of emotion. Signifying their time

together, juxtaposed against the looming separation, cast a shadow over the momentary joy. Monthly celebrations, charming in their simplicity, were now a poignant reminder of the impending distance between them when she left for nursing school.

Isobel grappled with the dichotomy of her feelings and the reality of her situation. The specter of Betsy's past involvement with John lingered, a nagging doubt that clouded her ability to embrace the moment. Could their nascent bond weather the challenges of time and distance? The uncertainty was a heavy cloak, dampening the light of the occasion with shades of apprehension.

Yet, amidst the turmoil, the undeniable connection between them—evident in John's aura, the warmth of his touch, and the sincerity in his eyes—offered a beacon of hope. It was a delicate dance of heart and mind, each step forward matched by a hesitant glance backward, as Isobel navigated the complex terrain of her heart's desires and her fears.

The evening had been progressing with a quiet intimacy, underlined by Jane's efficient service. Her movements were graceful and practiced as she poured wine into the glasses, the liquid shimmering under the dim lighting of the dining hall. The arrival of the steaks, perfectly cooked and accompanied by creamy mashed potatoes and vibrant carrots, should have been the centerpiece of the evening. Instead, an unsettling quiet loomed over the room.

Isobel's observation broke the calm. "Why is there no one else eating here today? Isn't that strange?" Her voice carried a note of curiosity mingled with unease.

John's response, a simple affirmation with a knowing grin, was abruptly cut short. His expression transformed from relaxed contentment to alarm. The utensils clattered against the plate, a discordant sound that shattered the tranquility. He rose, his body taut with urgency. "Leave," he commanded, his eyes wide with a mixture of concern and resolve.

A sharp, excruciating tug at her hair as if it was being torn from her scalp, propelling her from the sanctity of her chair to the unforgiving floor below. To preserve some semblance of modesty, she grappled with her skirt, trying to smooth it around her legs as she extricated herself from the tangled embrace of the chair. The sight above her sent a chill along her spine. Betsy towered over her, a menacing figure bathed in a dark purple aura of jealousy, her fists clenched in anger.

"Stop seeing my fiancée! Do you hear me? How about a kick to your head?" Betsy's voice was venomous, her leg drawn back in a threatening gesture, poised to strike.

In a swift motion, John intervened, pushing Betsy back with a firm hand. "Betsy, you need to stop," he asserted, as he helped Isobel to her feet. His words severed any perceived connection with Betsy, clarifying that he had no romantic interest in her.

Jane, hearing the commotion, dashed out from the kitchen, her eyebrows raising. "What's going on here?" she demanded, taking in the chaotic scene.

Isobel, shaken and rattled, hurried out of the dining room into the lobby. She almost tripped over a sign that read 'Closed. Private event,' her heart pounding in her chest.

Jane, eyebrows drawn together, reached out and grasped Isobel's arm. "Wait. Isobel, don't leave yet. We have a sheriff now. He told me if anyone gets out of hand to get him." Doggedly in her stride, Jane's skirt billowed as she hurried out the door.

Betsy's taunting voice echoed through the lobby, "You can't do anything to me. My daddy is the mayor, and the sheriff works for him." She strutted towards the door of the dining room.

As Betsy made a sudden move in Isobel's direction, Isobel retreated, her back pressed against the wall, her eyes wide with apprehension. The tension in the air was thick, a charged atmosphere that threatened to erupt at any moment.

John's movements were like a caged animal, pacing back and forth with a protective ferocity to shield Isobel from Betsy's venom. His voice thundered in the tense air, "That's the problem with you. You get your way all the time. You're a spoiled brat." His finger jabbed towards Betsy in accusation. "I don't want you in my life, you hear?"

Isobel, feeling dismantled and exposed, fumbled with her hair to regain some control. Turning away from the toxic spectacle, she faced the wall, her shoulders trembling. The once quaint town of Tin Creek now felt like a prison from which escape was her only solace. A single tear betrayed her stoic facade, trailing down her cheek. She brushed it away, unwilling to grant Betsy any semblance of victory.

Visions of home flooded her mind, each evoking a pang of longing. Aunt Stella's comforting presence, her nurturing teas that mended more than physical ailments. Henry, with his well-meaning awkwardness, always tried to shield her from the harshness of the world.

The sound of the door swinging open heralded Jane's return, this time with Paul in tow. His approach was direct, his voice carrying the weight of his badge. "Jane tells me someone assaulted you. Knocked you out of your chair? Where is the assailant?"

Overwhelmed, Isobel could only muster a weak gesture towards Betsy, her tears now flowing, a silent testament to her turmoil.

Jane led Paul into the fray. "Betsy is over there."

Isobel trailed behind them, each step heavy with hesitation. Her mind was a battlefield, dark thoughts of retribution clashing with her inherent goodness. The thought of succumbing to the darker aspects of her powers chilled her to the core. Was this the precipice upon which all witches stood, teetering between the light and the shadow? The very notion sent a shiver along her spine, a warning of the thin line she tread. Her trinity pendant warmed against her chest.

John dashed to Isobel's side, his hands finding her trembling shoulders with urgency. "Are you alright?"

Isobel could only muster a fragile nod, her lip betraying the tremor of her emotions.

Paul, with a raised eyebrow, glanced at Jane. "Betsy. You're telling me that Betsy attacked Isobel? Did you see it?"

John said, "I did. Betsy attacked her! She pulled her out of her chair and was about to kick her!"

Betsy, with a veneer of confidence masking her malice, retorted with a sneer, "Both of them are lying. I walked by and she fell out of her chair by herself." She gestured towards the wine bottle, her voice dripping with condescension. "Too much wine." Her face contorted into a smug grin, oblivious to the unflattering comparison it drew to a petulant swine. "Isobel doesn't like me, wants my fiancée, and starts trouble with everyone. She spread rumors that Tom tried to drug her and make her work in his saloon." She caressed her figure, relishing in her own perceived allure with a self-indulgent flair. "Now, why would Tom want a skinny little thing like her?"

John recoiled as if slapped. "You're lying, Betsy, and you know it." His accusation was sharp, a knife through the tense silence.

Paul, swayed by the town's social hierarchies, his head shaking with resignation. "I know Betsy and her family are upstanding citizens in this town. And Tom is a smarter businessman than that." He turned to Betsy, his actions deferential, a knight offering his shield. "Miss Johnson, would you like me to accompany you home to ensure no harm comes to you?"

John's voice thundered through the room, "What? Betsy assaulted my girlfriend, and you make it like she's the innocent one." His protest was a storm breaking against the unjust calm Paul and Betsy presented.

With a haughty tilt of her head, Betsy said, "I believe I need an escort. I feel threatened." Her words dripped with feigned vulnerability, a stark contrast to her earlier aggression.

Paul, embodying the authority he wielded, stepped close to John, their faces mere inches apart. "Don't make trouble. Not wise for an out-of-towner." His warning was a clear line drawn in the sand, marking John as the outsider, the other.

Turning his attention to Isobel, Paul's demeanor shifted as he paraded Betsy by his side, her smug satisfaction radiating like a beacon of injustice. "I'm keeping an eye on you. You've caused enough problems in this peaceful town. Keep going and you'll be the first occupant of the new jail." His words were an icy blade, threatening to sever Isobel's ties to the community she was becoming a part of.

In that moment, the roar of Isobel's indignation drowned Aunt Stella's sage advice to take the high road out. Her gaze locked onto Betsy with the intensity of a brewing storm, and beneath her breath, she whispered a subtle incantation, a spell she'd used to unravel stitches. The air between them crackled with unspoken conflict, the battle lines drawn not with swords but with wills and words.

Goddess Cerridwen, hear my plea,
Unravel these binds, set the fabric free.
As the cauldron stirs, let the threads untie.
Undo the stitches under your watchful eye.
With wisdom and transformation, guide this task,
In your power and grace, I humbly ask.
Release these stitches, so mote it be!

As Betsy and the sheriff made their way into the street, Isobel watched the fruits of her clandestine magick. Hidden from view by the doorway, her eyes locked onto Betsy's form. The dress betrayed her, starting from the critical junction where the waist and back seams converged, coming undone.

Betsy's hand flew to her back, feeling the unexpected draft and the gaping maw of fabric that no longer served its purpose. She attempted to gather the fabric, a futile gesture against the relentless unraveling. Isobel's heart raced with a dark satisfaction, imagining the dress disintegrating thread by thread until Betsy was disrobed.

Realizing the sheriff was just another puppet in Tom's grand scheme was a bitter pill to swallow. The corruption seemed to seep into the very foundations of Tin Creek, leaving Isobel feeling isolated and besieged. The quick spread of news about her private dinner with John only added to her frustration. How did Betsy find out so fast? The town's grapevine was more efficient and venomous than she'd expected.

Fueled by indignation, Isobel retreated to her sanctuary, locking the door behind her. She reached for George's old whiskey bottle, her hands shaking, ignoring the persistent knocking echoing from below.

John's public acknowledgment of their relationship had been a beacon of hope in the murky waters of town politics and personal vendettas. Yet, the relentless tide of small-town intrigue and malice threatened to wash it all away. The thought of leaving it all behind, of handing the reins over to Henry and escaping to Chicago, became a siren call as she struggled to resist.

The whiskey offered a temporary reprieve, dulling the edges of her reality and blunting the sharpness of her predicament. John's gift, once a symbol of burgeoning affection, now lay forgotten in the whirlwind of her turmoil.

In her whiskey-induced haze, Isobel's thoughts drifted back to the spectacle of Betsy's unraveling dress. A bubble of laughter burst forth, unchecked and wild, tears streaming down her face in a cathartic release. It was a simple spell, yet effective in its execution. Did it bring harm? Perhaps. But in that moment, Isobel found it hard to care. The thought of exposing the town's figurative emperors in their naked deceit was tantalizing. Tomorrow, Tin Creek could witness the true colors of its so-called leaders, laid bare for all to see.

Chapter Twenty Nine

As the afternoon waned, the sight of Marisol battling the relentless wind to shut the shop door captured Isobel's attention. Dark, ominous clouds, like outstretched fingers, crept over the Bitterroot Mountains, a prelude to the impending storm's wrath. Isobel remembered the last tempest that had turned the streets into impassable rivers of mud, paralyzing the town under its sudden ferocity.

Because of her busy schedule and the immense popularity of Isobel's herbal teas at the Sapphire Saloon, Marisol rarely found the time to make purchases herself, often delegating such tasks to her employees. Marisol's presence hinted at matters more pressing than business.

With effort, Marisol secured the door against the wind's howl and turned, her expression a mix of determination and purpose. A mixture of curiosity and apprehension bubbled up inside Isobel, leaving her with an intriguing sense of anticipation. "What are you doing braving that wind? Is there something wrong?"

Adjusting her hat with a dramatic gesture, Marisol brushed off the question with a charismatic flair. "Why can't I simply check in on my favorite merchant in these turbulent times?" Her tone was light, but her eyes hinted at deeper intentions. She mentioned Jane's account of the recent altercation with Betsy, her face contorting with a knowing grimace.

A wave of discomfort crashed over Isobel at the mention of the incident, her emotions still raw from the confrontation and the town's unsettling response. "I am doing as well as I can." She busied herself with a basket of fabric remnants to distract herself from the turmoil that brewed not only in the skies above, but within her own heart. The thought of leaving Tin Creek, coupled with the unresolved feelings for John, cast a shadow over her spirit, much like the storm clouds that now threatened to engulf the town.

Marisol's dramatic flair was clear as she sifted through the pile of fabric remnants on the counter, discarding one after another with expressive gestures and a scowl. "Oh, this won't do," she muttered, her dissatisfaction apparent in her every move.

Marisol's eyes lit with a twinkle of mischief. "A miner told me a juicy bit," she began, her voice bubbling with barely contained glee. "His neighbor saw Sheriff Paul escorting Betsy home, and she was practically in her birthday suit!" Marisol's laughter rang through the store, infectious and unrestrained. "The neighbor called her a strumpet, tossed a blanket at her, and told her to cover up until she got home to strip for Paul." She doubled over, clutching her sides, her laughter echoing around the room.

Isobel joined in, her laughter a release from the tension and the bruise on her hip, a reminder of her recent altercation with Betsy. "Maybe she has a thing for Paul. They're perfect for each other," Isobel quipped, a hand flying to her mouth in surprise at her own candor. What was happening to her? Since when did she make such bold remarks?

Marisol, seizing the moment to shift the conversation, leaned in closer, her voice dropping to a conspiratorial whisper. "Well...maybe I can get your mind off of that spoiled brat with a little intrigue." She paused, taking a deep breath as if to emphasize the gravity of what she was about to reveal. "I received a telegram inquiring about Jack, the man who used to own the Bitterroot Saloon. He traveled to Missoula and vanished without a trace." Her eyes narrowed as she glanced towards the saloon across the street. "Then that scoundrel Tom showed up." She slapped her beaded gloves on the counter, her expression a mix of suspicion and determination. "I never believed that tale about Tom winning the saloon in a poker game. Jack didn't gamble." Her voice was firm, underscored with a conviction that suggested she was onto something significant.

Isobel's curiosity piqued as she placed another folded fabric square back into the basket, her movements slow and deliberate, a contrast to the whirlwind of thoughts in her mind. "Why would someone be looking for him now? Hasn't Tom been here for a while?" she mused.

Marisol's expression darkened for a moment, her lips twisting into a grimace as she contemplated the question. "Tom got here about six months before you did. He hasn't been here long but made a terrible impression real quick," she responded.

Isobel smoothed out another piece of fabric, her fingers tracing the patterns as she pondered Marisol's words. "Did the telegram give you any other information?" she inquired, her curiosity growing with each passing second.

Marisol's eyes sparkled as she continued the prospect of unraveling a mystery. "Oh, that's the interesting thing. The telegram originated in Chicago. And you're from Chicago and have family there," she declared, her grin widening.

A knot formed in Isobel's stomach as she wondered what connection her past in Chicago could have with the events unfolding in Tin Creek. "Yes. I am from Chicago. It *is* a big city."

Marisol leaned forward, her eyes locked on Isobel's, searching for any clue that might lead to a scandalous revelation. "So, is there something going on from your end and you're not telling anyone? Is there a big secret? Why in the world would the telegram come from Chicago? Who in the hell cares about Tin Creek there?" she pressed.

Isobel could sense the intensity of Marisol's stare, realizing her friend's eagerness to hear a compelling narrative. "I cannot think of anything. I wrote to my uncle that George passed and spelled out his debts. Oh..." she trailed off, a sudden realization dawning on her.

Marisol leaned in even closer, her breath quickening in anticipation. "What?" she whispered, her voice barely audible over the sound of the wind howling outside, a storm brewing not only in the skies above, but in the conversation unfolding before her.

Isobel's fingers lingered on the folded fabric remnants as she considered her words, her brow furrowing with the weight of realization. "I listed his debts. Tom claimed George owed him money. I added a remark that Tom required everyone to pay in advance. My Uncle probably agreed the debt was dubious and checked into it. He's meticulous in his financial dealings and has a lot of connections. It could be my uncle starting this. He would follow a mouse down a hole if he thought the mouse had something important." She sighed, the air heavy with unspoken questions and longing. What mysteries are you unraveling now, Uncle Henry? The thought of seeing him again stirred a mix of comfort and yearning within her.

With deliberate movements, Isobel transferred the folded remnants into a basket adorned with a 'Sale' sign, her actions soothing yet distracted. "If you hear anything, let me know. And I will do the same," she said.

The creak of the stairs drew their gaze as Gemma descended with careful, measured steps, a teapot cradled in her hands. Shadow, her ever-playful raccoon companion, treated the staircase like his personal playground, bounding with youthful abandon. Isobel observed Gemma's cautious descent, her hand grazing the wall for support. The idea of installing railings had been on Isobel's mind, a small comfort to ease Gemma's trepidation and a new adventure for Shadow.

Gemma's arrival brightened the room, her smile a beacon of warmth as she recognized Marisol. Setting the teapot down, she enveloped Marisol in an eager embrace, a gesture of pure affection.

Marisol reciprocated with a gentle hug, her hands comforting on Gemma's back. "How are you doing, Sunshine? And how's Shadow?" she asked.

"Good. I miss you. But I love it here, too. Is that possible?" Gemma's query was innocent, her eyes flitting between Marisol and Isobel, seeking affirmation.

In unison, Isobel and Marisol reassured her, "Yes, it is." Their shared glance conveyed a silent understanding, a moment of silent communication amidst the unfolding stories around them.

Isobel marveled at the unique lens through which Gemma viewed the world, suggesting an unconventional background. Unraveling the mysteries of Gemma's character was like peeling back the layers of an onion. Without the tears.

Marisol made her way to the door with a determined stride, casting a parting instruction over her shoulder. "I'm off to Missoula tomorrow to meet with Mr. Steyer, the investigator. I'll be out for a few days, but I'll fill you in upon my return. And Isobel, darling, could we perhaps see a bit more flair in your fabric selections? Something with a touch of allure for me and my ladies?" She offered a conspiratorial wink to Isobel, then shifted her focus to Gemma. "Take care, dear. I'll catch up with you once I'm back."

As Marisol wrestled with the stubborn door, Gemma sprang into action, bracing against the wind's fury to ensure the door clamped shut with a satisfying thud.

Isobel reflected on Marisol's vibrant presence in Tin Creek, acknowledging the void her absence would create. She cast a contemplative gaze towards her fabric inventory, acknowledging the utilitarian nature of her stock—functional cottons and wools that catered to the practical needs of the townsfolk, a far cry from the luxurious textures Marisol sought. Scribbling a mental note, Isobel resolved to scout for fabrics with a touch of opulence, something that would resonate with the tastes of Marisol and her entourage.

Meanwhile, thoughts of Henry flickered through her mind, trusting in his diligence to unravel any mysteries that might threaten her well-being. Despite his questionable decision to send her to Tin Creek to deal with George, she found solace in the thought of soon departing this town, leaving its complexities and troubles behind.

CHAPTER THIRTY

As DUSK SETTLED OVER the shop, casting long shadows across the floor, Isobel's attention turned to the imposing burlap sack resting on a wooden cart. With determined hands, she delved into its contents, scooping a cascade of beans that whispered secrets of distant lands as they tumbled into the bin, their journey ending with a hushed rustle.

The cart, a relic of necessity and craftsmanship, protested with a chorus of squeaks as Isobel guided it back into the storeroom's embrace, a shadowy realm where the day's toils were put to rest. Her thoughts meandered back to an incident that had etched itself into the fabric of her new life here—the day the burlap had betrayed its seams, spilling pinto beans in a tumultuous wave across the floor, coinciding with Ben's unwitting entrance. The local carpenter, his boots skidding on the sea of beans, had joined her in a dance of chaos and laughter, later building the cart that now bore the weight of her labor, a silent guardian crafted from kindness and refusal of payment.

In the tranquility that followed the day's activities, Gemma's voice pierced the silence. "Can you put these boxes on the top shelf? I can't reach." Isobel's intervention, a simple change of the ladder, was a beacon of guidance. "How's this? Try turning the ladder so the steps lead up to the shelves," she suggested.

But peace was a fleeting visitor, banished by a trio of ominous knocks—THWACK! THWACK! THWACK!—that resonated through the store. The sound sent a surge of adrenaline coursing through Isobel. Her fingers found solace in the icy embrace of the pistol hidden beneath the counter, a silent vow of protection sheathed within her apron.

The back door became the epicenter of an impending storm as the glint of an ax blade tore through the wood. Isobel's protective instincts flared as she ushered Gemma to safety, her voice a clarion call amidst the chaos. "Get help. Go next door."

With resolve steeling her spine, Isobel confronted the breach, her defiance echoing in the cramped space. "Stop... Stop!" This was her domain, her sanctuary, not a prize to be claimed by force.

The door yielded with a resounding crack, surrendering to the relentless assault. Tom forced his way through the splintered remains, his presence a dark cloud looming over Isobel's resolve. "I'm tired of waiting. Today is the day. You're coming with me," he announced, his voice laced with ominous intent.

Isobel's flight towards the front, a desperate bid for escape, was thwarted by Tom's iron grasp, her freedom slipping through her fingers like grains of sand.

Summoning the remnants of her will, Isobel retaliated with a fierce heel strike. The pistol, an extension of her turmoil as she closed her eyes, found its mark in the silence that followed. The gunshot, a thunderous roar in the confines of her world, marked a turning point in their confrontation. A line crossed from which there was no return.

Tom's scream tore through the charged air of the shop, a raw, guttural sound of agony that resonated off the walls. He stumbled backwards, his form collapsing against the counter with a force that shook the foundations of the room. "My foot. You shot me in the foot, you damn whore," he howled. Clutching at his foot, he watched as his blood seeped through his fingers, painting the wooden floor a stark crimson.

Isobel's spirit flared at the venom spewing from Tom's lips, the insult igniting a blaze within her. With a fluid motion born of anger and defiance, her hand struck out, connecting with his face in a resounding slap that echoed like a gunshot in the quiet aftermath. She retreated, putting space between her and the source of her turmoil, seeking refuge near the front door, her heart a tumult of emotions.

Tom, his features twisted in a grimace of pain, reached out to regain control, to pull her back into his sphere of influence. But his grasp found only emptiness, his balance precarious as he leaned on the counter for support, his injured foot hovering above the pool of his blood.

Isobel, revolver in hand, stood at the crossroads of her conscience, the simplicity of ending Tom's threat forever a seductive whisper in her mind. Yet her moral compass, usually so steadfast, wavered under the weight of her rage, the pendant at her chest pulsing as if alive with her inner turmoil. Jane, John, and Gemma interrupted her moral struggle as they burst into the room, their faces a tapestry of shock, concern, and disbelief.

John's expression morphed into one of pure fury as he took in the chaos before him. "Isobel, are you alright?" he demanded.

Seeking solace, Isobel leaned into John's embrace, the warmth of his concern a balm to her frayed nerves. "Yes," she managed, her voice barely a whisper, the acknowledgment of his protection a weight on her heart as she pondered the complexities of her impending departure from Tin Creek.

Tom, from his diminished position against the counter, cast a pitiful look their way. "Well, I'm not. I'm the victim. The whore shot me. I'm just here, bleeding out. I need Doc," he whined, his plea a stark contrast to the violence he had wrought.

Isobel, pulling away from the safety of John's arms, stood her ground with hands planted on her hips. "You broke in! You deserve to bleed every drop of blood," she declared, the words fueling the tempest within her. Thoughts of dark retribution danced at the edges of her mind, spells of vengeance and pain whispering sweet promises of justice. But the tenet of "do no harm" held her back, a beacon in the darkness of her desires.

"What happened?" Jane asked, her gaze darting between the protagonists of the unfolding drama.

Isobel drew a shaky breath, her account rapid and laced with the adrenaline of survival. "Tom broke in through the back door with an ax. He said he was taking me and then assaulted me. I fired in self-defense," she recounted, the words a testament to her ordeal.

Tom slammed his hand against the counter, drawing attention to his self-proclaimed victimhood. "You can't recognize I'm the victim, the one who got shot here, bleeding," he protested, his arrogance undimmed even in defeat. "When is someone going to get Doc?" he demanded.

Jane's laughter was a retort in itself as she prodded Tom's shin. "You still have your other foot. You could hop over to Doc's," she suggested.

Gemma's soft giggle joined Jane's, a moment of levity in the tension that filled the room.

Jane's tone shifted, a stern warning to Tom. "Maybe if you stay out of here and away from Isobel, you wouldn't get shot," she advised, her actions speaking louder than her words as she secured the revolver within her skirt's waistband.

Tom's surrender to gravity, his form collapsing onto the floor with a muted thud, was a declaration of his defeat. "Not going anywhere," he conceded.

John advanced towards Tom with measured, determined strides, the air between them charged with an unspoken challenge. He positioned his foot over Tom's injured one. "Does it hurt?" he asked, his voice low and dangerous.

Tom's face contorted in a grimace of agony, the pain obvious in his sharp intake of breath. "Ya, that hurts! I ain't done nothing to you." His words were a desperate plea, muffled by the pressure of John's boot. He fought against the unyielding weight, a futile struggle that highlighted his sudden vulnerability. John held his ground, the pressure constant before he relented, stepping back and granting Tom a momentary reprieve.

Isobel watched, her emotions a whirlwind of conflict and dark fascination. Tom's pain, a visible manifestation of his defeat, stirred within her a fierce, almost primal desire for vengeance. The allure of wielding her hidden magick to inflict further agony was tempting, the thought of his bones cracking under the might of her will sent a shiver of anticipation along her spine. Yet, the echo of her solemn oath, "do no harm," resonated within her again, a steadfast reminder of the path she had chosen, a path that now seemed strewn with the shadows of her darkest impulses.

John's boot made a definitive thud against the wooden counter, a clear, unyielding statement of his intent. "Stay away from Isobel." The words rumbled from his throat, not only a warning, but a primal declaration of protection, his presence as immovable and formidable as the mountains that bordered their town.

Jane, with a fluid grace that belied the steely resolve beneath, turned on her heel towards the door. "I'm going to get the sheriff. Paul needs to know Tom attacked a woman again." Her parting glance at Tom was laden with scorn, a verbal slap that resonated in the tense silence that followed. "You can nurse your foot in jail." With those final words, she departed, the door slamming behind her with a force that echoed like a shot.

Gemma followed in Jane's wake.

John's embrace enveloped Isobel, a sanctuary amidst the storm of emotions that raged within her. "I can't bear anything happening to you." His words were a soothing balm, a tender apology for the tempests they had weathered together.

Tom, his figure slumped in defeat against the counter, could not mask the pain that seeped into his voice, a sneer tinged with suffering. "Oh puleeze, save me from the lovey-dovey." His attempt at disdain fell flat, lost in the gravity of his defeat.

Isobel, caught between the solace of John's embrace and the urge to escape Tom's venomous barbs, stood her ground, her resolve fortified by John's unwavering support.

John's boot edged closer to Tom once more, a silent but potent threat. "Do you want me to test your pain again?"

Tom whined, "I wish to be left alone with the hole in my foot. Better than watching love birds pecking all over each other."

Their standoff was interrupted as Paul and Jane re-entered the fray. Paul's approach was swift as he pushed past John to confront Isobel. "I have to place you under arrest." His words, a cold decree, cut through the tension.

Jane flung her hands skyward, as if to ward off an impending storm. "Wait! I told you Tom attacked her." Her arm, extended like a blade, pointed towards the ravaged door, its splintered remains a silent witness to the violence that had breached the sanctum of the store. "Look at what he did to that door. The ax is right there." The evidence lay bare, the ax still gleaming in the fading light.

Gemma's voice, small but fierce, cut through the thick air, her form wrapped in a self-embrace that spoke volumes of the fear she'd endured. "It was scary. I ran to get help," she confessed, her voice a whisper.

Isobel leaned into John's unwavering presence. "He used an ax. I had to shoot in self-defense." Her admission, trembling like the leaf of a willow in the storm, sought ground in the tumultuous landscape of justice and retribution that Paul was shaping with his decrees.

Paul laid down his edict like a hammer to anvil. "I can't let people going around shooting in town."

Gemma wrapped her arms around Paul's arm, a visual plea, her voice a murmur against the gale of impending judgment. "You can't take her." But her plea was met with a brusque gesture, a storm's gust that sent her reeling, saved from the fall only by Jane's timely intervention.

Paul's interrogation, as sharp and cold as a winter's night, sought to pierce the key aspect. "Did you shoot Tom?" His gaze, fixed upon Isobel, awaited her testament.

Isobel, her resolve a fortress against the siege, declared her innocence with the fire of a thousand suns. "I told him to stop! Tom grabbed me and threatened to kidnap me. What was I supposed to do, for pity's sake?"

Tom brandished his wound like a banner on the battlefield. "She didn't give me time to stop. She shot me."

Paul pronounced his verdict with the gravity of an avalanche. "Isobel, you need to come with me. I am arresting you for attempted murder." The world seemed to fracture at his words, the air charged with the thunder of a storm unleashed.

A chorus of disbelief rose from the assembly that echoed off the walls. "What?" they cried.

Paul's grasp sought to lead Isobel away. "Isobel, are you going to come willingly?" His question, a demand cloaked in the guise of choice, bore down upon her like a mountain's weight.

Isobel's spirit, fractured by the injustice, cried out against the storm. "This isn't right." Her words, a lamentation for the truth and fairness, were swept away in the maelstrom of accusations and deceit.

Tom's laughter, cruel and jagged as a shard of ice, sought to wound her further. "Now you're a murderer. Another title after whore." His taunt, a venomous dart aimed at her heart, sought to poison the well of her spirit.

Jane's retort struck back. "You're not dead yet." Her words, a beacon of defiance in the darkening gloom, rallied the forces of righteousness.

John towered over the proceedings, his fury a tempest that threatened to break. "You can't be serious. You are going to arrest a woman for self-defense and charge her with attempted murder for a flesh wound." His gaze, turning to Tom, promised a reckoning that the dawn might yet bring.

Paul's shove set the stage for a battle yet to come. "If you interfere, I can lock you up too." His threat propelled Isobel towards the gathering clouds.

In the waning light, Jane's grasp on John's arm was not merely a touch but a call to arms amidst the chaos. She whispered with the urgency of a battle plan, "Wait. You can help her better outside of a jail cell. We can come up with something. Look, I'll send a telegraph to her uncle..." The words were like a spell, casting a possibility of salvation. With a deft motion, she passed the pistol to Gemma. "Put it back where it belongs."

John became the anchor in the tempest that raged around Isobel. "Isobel, we will get you out. I promise."

Isobel was a figure of tragedy drawn across the canvas of the town's main thoroughfare. Each step under Paul's firm guidance was a dirge, the dust beneath her feet a testament to the path she was forced upon. The world seemed to press upon her, a suffocating cloak woven from strands of despair and disbelief. What would the whispering winds carry back to her family? The shadow of her thoughts swirled with the dangerous allure of dark spells and retribution. The dreams she harbored, of healing and helping, lay in ruins at her feet; her life, once a tapestry of ambition and hope, now frayed and torn, dragged through the dust of a path she never chose.

Isobel's vision blurred through the veil of tears as she found herself ensnared in the iron grip of her new, grim reality: a cold, unforgiving jail cell. Paul, with deliberate motions that mocked her despair, unlocked the cell with a key that glinted in the dim light. With a rough push that sent a jolt through her body, he thrust her inside the barren cell and secured the door with a finality that echoed off the wooden walls.

Regaining her balance, Isobel watched through the window of the sheriff's as Paul's retreating figure made its way towards the malevolent glow of Tom's saloon, a beacon of her tormentor's triumph. She moved to the wooden bench that was more a plank of judgment than a seat, the rough grain of the wood pressing into her as she sought some solace in its solidity.

Isobel's journey to this moment—a spectacle for the onlookers at the livery and behind the obscured windows of the hotel and bakery—was a march of shame. Innocence bore no weight on the scales of Tin Creek's justice; her reputation lay in tatters, trampled underfoot by the very people she sought to serve.

Trapped in this cell, Isobel grappled with the cruel twist of fate that had transformed her from a defender of her own dignity into a prisoner of circumstances. The walls of the cell closed in, each wood plank a testament to her isolation. Her thoughts turned to Henry, a distant beacon of hope in this mire of despair. Yet even his influence was a mere whisper against the clamor of her immediate peril.

As tears continued their relentless descent, staining the fabric of her blue skirt with sorrow, an unexpected phenomenon caught her weary eye. Amidst the dance of dust motes in the slanted beams of sunlight, an ethereal aura of shifting colors materialized. Isobel's heart skipped a beat, her breath caught in her throat. Even in her despair, the sight was a stark anomaly in the drabness of her sur-roundings. She rose, driven by a mix of fear and wonder, her tears forgotten. The spectral colors swirled with an intensity almost alive, a silent witness to her plight, unyielding in its presence.

In the dim confines of the cell, Isobel's reality fractured as the familiar voice of her mother, long silenced by death, echoed in the air, infusing the space with a surreal energy. "Daughter, I am here to help you. You have power without the need for herbs or books. I have learned this myself; I have the power of the old ways, and as do you."

Isobel's heart raced, a tumult of emotions clashing within her. "Oh, Mother! What do you speak of? I read nothing in your gri-moire about what you are talking about." The words tumbled out.

Before her, the aura pulsed like a living thing, its movements syncing with the cadence of her mother's voice. "My spell book is just a bunch of herbal recipes. You can't write about genuine power. It has to be felt. I want you to focus on the candle over on the desk and will it to light. Don't blow breath or motion with your hands, use only your mind. Do it, Isobel. This is your first lesson."

Drawing a deep breath, Isobel locked her gaze on the solitary candle across the room, its wick an unlit beacon in the gloom. She willed herself to stillness, her mind reaching out to the inert wax and thread. A silent command, a plea for light without spark or flame. The initial attempt faltered, the connection slipping like sand through fingers.

With a renewed resolve, she closed her eyes, diving into the depths of her being where a nascent power stirred. A warmth blossomed within her, a beacon in the dark expanse of her soul. The flicker of light danced against her closed lids, a sign of success in the silent chamber. But the flame extinguished, leaving her in darkness again.

"You felt that power. But be careful, no one knows. Look at what happened to me. They have persecuted witches through the ages thinking we are evil when it is others who are." The aura intensified, its crimson swirls a storm of emotion and warning. "You and I will right the wrongs and do good to those who deserve it."

A chill traced Isobel's spine as she recalled the fiery tragedy tied to her mother's legacy. Doubt whispered in the shadows of her mind. "I don't know what lighting a candle does to help me or anyone else unless they need light in darkness."

Her mother's voice bore into her. "You must take the first step on any journey to get where you want to go. Now how can you cause Tom misery, day and night? Make him pay. Focus on that."

Isobel stood at the precipice of a path veiled in shadows, the potential of her newfound power a siren call in the cell's silence. The choice lay before her: to embrace the legacy of the old ways or to tread a path of her own making.

Isobel's resolve anchored her to the cold, hard bench within the confines of her bleak cell. She clasped the trinity pendant, its edges biting into her palm as she delved into the depths of her quandary. "A man who cannot urinate becomes sick, and it happens quickly for those who drink alcohol. So that is how I can inflict discomfort." The words echoed in her mind like a distant storm brewing with the potential to unleash chaos. She envisioned Tom, the root of her turmoil, his body a vessel for accumulating toxins, a prison for his own vices.

"Word will get to you. You have many here who are on your side. John loves you, Jane feeds your soul and your stomach, and Marisol tells you the truth always. What can you do to Paul?" The maternal voice, woven with the fabric of the aura, offered both solace and a directive. But when thoughts of retribution turned towards Paul, Isobel hesitated. He was but a shadow under Tom's looming presence, a figure swayed by the winds of influence rather than malice.

Isobel's resolve wavered as the cell's oppressive gloom deepened with the night's advance. The dim moonlight filtering through the small barred window only stressed the stark shadows, casting long, dark fingers across the cold wooden floor. Isobel shifted, the unforgiving bench beneath her offering little in the way of comfort or warmth. She wrapped her arms around herself, seeking solace in the scant heat her body could muster, her thoughts a turbulent sea churning with doubt and fear.

In this moment of vulnerability, the words of her mother echoed once more. "I am with you always." The assurance, though comforting, also bore the weight of an unspoken challenge. It was a call to embrace the latent power that coursed through her veins, a legacy of her lineage, yet untamed and wild.

Isobel's gaze drifted to the extinguished candle on Paul's desk, its wick a charred testament to her fledgling attempts at harnessing the arcane. She pondered the nature of her abilities, the raw energy that ebbed and flowed at the edge of her consciousness. It was a force that demanded respect, a servant to neither will nor whim, but a partner in a delicate dance of intent and consequence.

The silence of the cell was a canvas, upon which the whispers of her own doubts painted scenes of uncertainty. But a spark of defiance flickered to life within her. Isobel closed her eyes, centering herself amidst the storm of her emotions, reaching inward to the wellspring of her power. She envisioned the candle's flame, not as a mere flicker of light, but as a beacon of her will, a symbol of her determination to bend the world to her desires.

With a breath that was part prayer, part command, Isobel focused on the essence of a flame, willing it to life with the full might of her burgeoning power. The air in the cell grew thick with anticipation as Isobel's will collided with the immutable laws of nature.

And then, with a suddenness that stole her breath away, a soft glow illuminated the cell. Isobel's eyes snapped open, and she beheld the candle, reborn from the ashes of her doubt, its light a small but defiant star in the darkness of her cell. In that moment, Isobel understood the true nature of her power. It was not a force to be wielded like a weapon, but a gift to be nurtured, a companion on the long and winding road of her destiny.

The candle's light cast long shadows across the cell, but to Isobel, they were no longer symbols of fear or confinement. They were the dancing partners of her light, a reminder that even in the deepest darkness, her spirit could not be caged.

Isobel's focus sharpened on Tom, envisioning his discomfort as a tangible force. Her hands clenched the pendant tighter, the gems imprinting their will upon her flesh. A sheen of perspiration veiled her brow as she summoned the full extent of her burgeoning power, her breaths becoming shallow drafts in her persistent efforts.

With a newfound sense of purpose, Isobel lay down on the bench, the candle's glow a silent sentinel in the night. As sleep claimed her, she knew that whatever trials lay ahead, she would face them with the strength of her ancestors and the light of her own indomitable will.

Chapter Thirty One

Henry and Aldus, stepping off the train in Missoula, found themselves engulfed in the bustling frontier chaos. The wide, dusty street before them teemed with life, a veritable river of wagons and riders, each moving with the urgency of a storm. With the sun beating down, casting long shadows that danced between the obstacles, they dodged their way to the imposing structure of the Montana Hotel.

The elevator, a creaking contraption of wood and metal, became their momentary refuge. "I'll meet you in the lobby after we settle in, then we can walk to the police department," Henry declared, his voice echoing in the confined space. "Agreed," Aldus responded.

Reunited in the lobby, Henry noted Aldus's punctuality with a nod. Their path to City Hall was an odyssey in itself, a brief journey marked by the unpredictable ebb and flow of life in Missoula. A wayward dog launched itself at Henry, leaving dusty paw prints on his trousers—a stark reminder of the unpredictable nature of the frontier. The fireman's call returned the dog to its post, but the encounter left Henry rattled, his thoughts derailed by his dirty pant legs.

The brick edifice of City Hall stood as a testament to the town's aspirations, its steps leading them to an office too small for the burgeoning chaos it sought to contain. Inside, the world narrowed to the confines of a room where law and order hung in the balance.

They held back as the blond, bearded policeman directed a young man with a telegram, the energy of the office a microcosm of the town's pulse. When the path cleared, they approached, their intent as solid as the desk that separated them from the lawman.

"What can I assist you with?" the policeman inquired.

Henry, flanked by the stoic figure of Aldus, laid bare their quest with a clarity born of urgency. "My name is Henry Perkins, and this is Aldus Steyer, a private investigator. We wish to speak with Jack Logan, a man in your jail, and the witness who testified against him," Henry said.

The lawman regarded them with a mix of curiosity and skepticism. "I'm Dan Hundt, chief of police. What do you need to talk to Jack about?" His voice was steady, yet the slight twist of his mouth and the rhythmic tapping of his finger on the aged wood of the front desk betrayed an undercurrent of apprehension.

Undeterred by the chief's stoic demeanor, Henry pressed on. "I want to know if Jack is acquainted with Tom McCall, wanted for multiple murders, a train robbery, and kidnapping for ransom, who took over his bar. Or if the witness knows this man. I have a hunch she does. She might have lied for whatever reason to frame Jack." The room contracted around them, the weight of the accusation hanging like a storm cloud ready to burst.

Chief Hundt's response was a weary exhalation, the burden of his office clear in the lines etched into his weathered face. "The witness gave testimony under oath. Are you suggesting she lied?" His simple question carried the weight of navigating the intricate web of justice in a land where moral boundaries were as hazy as the fading dusk.

Henry's retort was sharp. "You believe a woman of ill-repute?" he challenged.

Chief Hundt's reply was a testament to his character, a man shaped by the harsh realities of his environment. "I don't judge any woman by how she supports herself," he stated, a firm rebuke to Henry's insinuation. "It's a rough world here."

In that moment, Henry felt the ground shift beneath him, the foundations of his beliefs challenged by the stark truth of Chief Hundt's words. This journey to the heart of the untamed West was more than a mission to save his niece; it confronted his own preconceptions, a realization that the world was far more complex than the black-and-white morality of his sheltered existence. The chief's simple statement echoed in Henry's mind, a reminder that in this land of endless skies and insurmountable challenges, survival was the ultimate virtue, and judgment a luxury few could afford.

Henry's gaze shifted. "What if someone paid her to say what she said?" He turned to Aldus. "She might have needed the money bad enough to agree. I want Mr. Steyer here to talk to Jack and the witness. He's skilled at getting the truth out."

Chief Hundt, a man seasoned by the trials of frontier justice, responded with a gruff acquiescence that echoed off the sparse walls. "Fine. I'll have her and Jack here, but I'll be overseeing the questioning." His voice carried the weight of authority, yet as he leaned back, arms stretching towards the heavens as if seeking guidance, there was a hint of resignation. "I'm not sure how fair of a trial he got since he was assigned an inexperienced young lawyer fresh out of law school. But we'll sort this out."

Henry's plea was heartfelt, a desperate entreaty from a man standing at the crossroads of family loyalty and the inexorable march of justice. "Great. This is important to me since it impacts a family member. You understand, don't you?" His hand extended, a bridge across the chasm of their disparate worlds.

Dan, rising to meet the gesture, inquired with a hint of curiosity that cracked his stoic facade. "Are you related to Jack Logan?"

"No. But Tom McCall showed up and claimed Jack's saloon and now is harassing my niece." His declaration was a beacon, casting light on the tangled web of connections that bound them all. "See you tomorrow. Oh, Jack's attorney will be with me."

Dan's eyebrows arched, a silent testament to the shock that coursed through him. "Jack doesn't have a lawyer."

Henry's smile was a harbinger of the storm to come, a promise of upheaval in the established order. "He does today. My belief is that Jack Logan is innocent, framed. So I hired one. You may be familiar with John Quinn."

At the mention of John Quinn, Dan's head recoiled as if struck. "Um... yeah, I know John. Everyone does." Sinking back into his chair, the chief of police's hands splayed in a gesture of resignation. "I guess I'll see you tomorrow."

Henry's gaze lingered on the chief's face, probing for the slightest shift, the barest crack in the facade at the mention of John Quinn. In Aldus's words, Quinn was a titan of the legal field, his reputation a beacon that cut through the murk of Montana's justice system. Henry held fast to the belief that the right allies, the kind who could turn the tide of fate, were crucial in any endeavor. Quinn was such an ally, a key to unlock the doors barred by bureaucracy and obfuscation.

The air in the room shifted as a figure staggered in, his entrance a dissonant note. Collapsing against the desk, the man's blood painted a stark trail across the wood, pooling on the floor. His words, a desperate plea, "I've been stabbed. In the Midway. She took all my money," hung in the air like a specter before he crumpled to the ground.

Dan sprung into action, his duty as a keeper of peace overshadowing the matters at hand. Henry could only offer a silent wave, his departure marked by the urgency that now consumed the office.

Outside, the streets of Missoula whispered secrets of their own. Henry and Aldus sought refuge in a modest eatery, a stark contrast to the violence that had just unfolded. The hotel manager's words echoed in Henry's mind, a cautionary tale of the Midway Plaisance's shadowed alleys and the dangers that lurked within. The incident in the police station was a grim testament to those warnings, and Henry's thoughts spiraled to Isobel. What kind of world had he sent her into?

Dinner was a quiet affair, the day's revelations casting long shadows over their meal. Together, they forged a plan, questions for Quinn that would illuminate the path forward. And there was Marisol, the unexpected piece in this intricate puzzle. Henry had reservations about involving her, her profession clouding his judgment. But in this tangled web, every thread had potential, and Marisol's insight into Isobel's circumstances, however slim, was a chance Henry would take.

As night wrapped its cloak around Missoula, Henry and Aldus retreated to heir rooms. Tomorrow's promise shone in the darkness, giving hope for justice for Jack Logan and exposing the evil hidden in Tin Creek, possibly closer to Isobel than anyone imagined.

Chapter Thirty Two

Isobel Perkins awoke with a start, her eyes opening to a cold, unwelcoming world of iron bars and thick wood walls. The reality of her confinement struck her with a brutal force. Her once bright future, filled with dreams of nursing school, was now as distant and unreachable as the stars themselves. She lay there, a caged animal, her fate in the hands of those who sought to bind her freedom.

The silence of the morning was broken by Paul, the sheriff. He settled into his chair with a nonchalance that stung Isobel. He didn't utter a word to her, his indifference to her plight as sharp as a blade. Soon after, Jane burst into the room like a ray of hope piercing through the gloom. She carried a plate heaped with eggs and bacon; the aroma filling the cell and igniting a hunger in Isobel she hadn't realized was there. Despite her situation, her body yearned for sustenance.

"Good morning, my little beauty in the pokey. I brought you something to eat," Jane announced, her eyes flashing with disapproval at Paul. "I wanted to bring you dinner last night, but someone didn't want to do his job. Too busy drinking and carousing."

Paul shrugged. "Yesterday was a busy day for me. A man has to take care of his needs."

As Jane approached the bars, Isobel reached out, her fingers brushing against cold metal, a cruel reminder of her captivity. Jane slid the plate under the small gap at the bottom of the cell, and Isobel devoured the food with a fervor born of uncertainty and fear. Each bite was a small rebellion against her fate. "Thank you. You are a genuine friend. I don't deserve you."

"You are my best friend. You are like a sister to me," Jane whispered, leaning in close. "I sent a telegram to your uncle."

Isobel paused, her heart heavy with worry. "I don't know what he could do for me. He's going to be worried. But thank you. Who knows? Maybe he can use his connections."

John appeared in the doorway. His smile warmed her heart, but the reality of her situation, of being seen in such a state, made her want to dissolve into the floorboards.

John approached her cell with a determination that spoke of a sleepless night and a resolve as unyielding as steel. "I couldn't sleep knowing you're here. My father and I are going to Hamilton today, then all the way to Missoula if we have to. We're going for the US Marshall." He spoke in hushed tones, mindful of prying ears.

Jane reassured John with a gentle pat on his arm. "I telegraphed her uncle. We'll get her out, don't worry. I have to get back to the hotel. I'll see you later. Bye."

As Jane departed, John reached through the bars, his hand seeking Isobel's. "How are you holding up? Since this is so hard for me, I can't imagine what you are going through. My mother is worried sick. She'll come see you when she can."

Isobel's heart was a maelstrom of fear and uncertainty. The possibility of a grim future loomed over her like a dark cloud. "I'm afraid I have ruined my life."

But John's hands cradled her elbows, pulling her as close as the bars would allow. His voice was a blend of vulnerability and conviction. "I need to tell you something. It's on my mind all the time. I don't want to spend my life without you. I love you, Isobel. When we get you out of here, will you marry me?"

The proposal hung in the air, a stark contrast to the bleak surroundings of the jail cell. Isobel's heart raced, torn between the love she felt for John and the fear of the unknown future that lay before her.

Isobel's heart was a tumult of emotions as Doc stormed into the sheriff's office, his presence like a sudden gust of wind that stirred the stagnant air. She watched, torn between the hope John's proposal offered and the bleak reality of her confinement. The bars of her cell grew colder, more imposing, as she grappled with her choices.

Paul rose from his chair, frowning, tilting his head while making eye contact with Doc. "This is getting ridiculous. I haven't had this many people here since this place was built. What do you want, Doc?"

Doc stood his ground with the steadiness of a mountain. "I came to talk to you. Am I to talk to you somewhere else? Is it unreasonable that I come to the sheriff's office to talk to the sheriff?" His gaze met Isobel's and John's, offering a nod of solidarity before turning back to confront Paul.

Isobel's mind raced as she considered her response to John. The weight of her decision bore down on her, causing her shoulders to slump. The cold iron bars, rigid and unforgiving, served as a constant reminder of the divide between her desires and the harsh reality.

Paul's sneer cut through the tension. "Well, I'm here, ain't I? State your business." His stance was defiant, rooted in the belief in his authority.

Doc's response was a tempest, his words lashing out with the force of a storm. "What I want to know is why you have this young lady locked up when all Tom has is a flesh wound? I saw what he did to that door to get to her." He clapped his hands together, a sound that echoed like thunder in the small office. "He had ill intentions, and she was protecting herself. It looks fishy. Very fishy."

Paul leaned forward, his hands pressed against the desk as if bracing against the gale of Doc's argument. "She shot Tom. Flesh wound or not, we can't have people settling problems with guns. I'm here to enforce the law. That's why I'm here. I don't tell you how to do your job, so don't tell me how to do mine." His words were a bulwark, an attempt to shield his actions behind the mantle of the law.

Doc's retort was a blade, sharp and unyielding. "Tom has bigger problems than his minor flesh wound. That accusation of attempted murder is ridiculous. If he dies, it will be from his plumbing problems poisoning him." With that, he turned on his heel, his departure as dramatic as his entrance, the door slamming shut in his wake like the last note of a symphony.

In the aftermath of Doc's exit, John drew Isobel close once more, his embrace a haven in the storm. "Back to what I said. Isobel, will you marry me?" His kiss was a flame that seared through the cold metal, igniting a warmth that enveloped them both.

Paul's outcry shattered the moment. "Stop that! You will not do that in my office with my prisoner." His command was a cold splash of reality. "If you can't, then leave." His words were a reminder of the chains that bound her, not just the iron of her cell, but the expectations and laws of a world determined to keep her from the life she now yearned for with John.

A buoyant energy marked John's step back with arms opened, his smile a beacon in the dim confines of the sheriff's office. "Well?" he asked.

Isobel's cheeks glowed with a warmth that rivaled the setting sun. "I will marry you if I get out of here soon. I want to be your wife. But. Big but. If I go to prison, I want you to move on with your life," she declared, her words carrying the heavy weight of reality.

John's reaction was electric, his joy erupting like a geyser. "Yes! She said yes!" he exclaimed, his voice echoing off the walls, a stark contrast to the somber bars that caged Isobel.

Paul's response was a dark cloud looming over their moment of joy. "Might be a long wait. Prison time. And why would you want to marry a jailbird? I guarantee you she won't be the same sweet, innocent girl you think she is," he jeered, his words like venom.

Isobel's heart skipped at the jab, her mind racing. "How do you know I would change?" she said. "You said innocent. You know I'm innocent."

Paul's glare was a blade, sharp and unwelcome. "I told you I don't want to hear a peep out of you. John, get out. I have things to do," he barked. Rising from his seat, he moved with the certainty of a man used to wielding power, his steps carrying him to the door, which he held open with a finality that brooked no argument.

"Isobel, I will be back. My mother is going to be happy you said yes. I love you," John's parting words lingered in the air, a balm to Isobel's tumultuous heart. His wave, as he retreated through the door, was a last flicker of hope in the dim cell.

Paul, following in John's wake, shook his head in disbelief, or perhaps disdain. Isobel watched through the barred window as he made his way towards Tom's saloon, his steps heavy on the boardwalk.

The sheriff's office was silent in their absence, leaving Isobel alone with her racing thoughts and the warmth that flushed her cheeks—the heat of a newfound commitment mingling with the fire of uncertainty. She smiled despite herself, her heart torn between the love she had just embraced and the dreams she feared slipping away.

Through the front window, Gemma's figure appeared, her hand waving energetically. Isobel bit her lip. How was Gemma managing without her?

Suddenly, a voice echoed in Isobel's mind, clear and unmistakable. "I'm doing okay." Isobel's eyes widened in shock, her gaze fixed on Gemma, who nodded in confirmation outside the window. The revelation that Gemma possessed a gift beyond the ordinary, a connection that transcended physical barriers, left Isobel reeling.

"Why didn't you reveal this before?" Isobel thought, her mind racing with questions and possibilities.

Gemma's response was a silent yet poignant admission of her fears and loneliness. "I was afraid you wouldn't want me around. Now I'm afraid you won't be around. Jane tells me they will get you out. I miss you so much."

Isobel's heart ached for the girl, her own sense of helplessness magnified by Gemma's solitude and strength. "I'm sorry. Marisol and I are not there for you right now. This must be hard, but you are strong. Stay safe, Gemma."

With a promise to return, Gemma's presence faded from Isobel's mind, leaving her alone once again in her cell.

The weight of the day's revelations—a proposal, Doc's fierce defense, and Gemma's extraordinary ability—swirled in Isobel's mind, distracting her from the grim reality of her confinement. She rose, pacing within the limited confines of her cell, each step a restless echo of her caged spirit.

In the dim light of her cell, the corner opposite Isobel became a canvas for the extraordinary. A multi-colored aura shimmered into existence, a spectral presence that Isobel recognized as the ethereal manifestation of her mother. This was her mother's unique way of reaching across the veil to communicate, a constant reminder of the unseen bond they shared.

Isobel's voice was a hushed murmur, a thread of connection in the cell's stillness. "Hello, mother."

The aura pulsed, its colors swirling as if stirred by a gentle breeze. The response came, a voice in her mind, both familiar and distant. "Hello, Isobel. Congratulations! I'm so happy for you. It will be even better when they free you from this wretched box."

Isobel's expression flickered with uncertainty. "Thank you. I'm glad you believe that. One moment, I'm sure that will be true, and the next, I wonder what prison will be like."

The aura glowed brighter. "I expect you will walk away to live your life as you want."

Isobel, her doubts casting shadows in her heart, confided, "I'm hoping you perceive something I am not privy to. I don't share your confidence. With Mr. Johnson as mayor, Paul as sheriff, and Tom in both their ears, I don't see how I'm getting out of here." She reached out towards the aura, her hand passing through the shimmering light, the sensation causing the hairs on her arm to stand on end.

Her sigh echoed in the cell, a tangible manifestation of her longing for a physical connection with her mother.

"Don't fret. Think about the wonderful people in your life. I will talk to you later," came the comforting assurance.

As the aura faded, leaving Isobel alone with the stark reality of her surroundings, her thoughts turned to those who had touched her life in Tin Creek. Each face, each memory, was a precious jewel in the tapestry of her experiences. Despite the grimness of her current situation, she felt a deep gratitude for these connections, a resolve to carry them in her heart regardless of what the future held. The cell, with its cold, unyielding bars, could not imprison the warmth and richness of the relationships she had forged.

CHAPTER THIRTY THREE

THE FIRST PEEK OF sunshine made its way through the grimy windows of Tom's room above the saloon, casting a weak glow on the chaos of the night before. Tom's awakening was a battle, his head echoing with the pounding drums of his own heartbeat, a painful reminder of last night's excess. The throbbing in his foot, a stark souvenir from a bullet's kiss, mocked him as he swung his legs off the bed. Doc had shrugged it off as a flesh wound. But Tom's grumbled thoughts dismissed the doctor's optimism with a sneer. What did Doc know?

With a grimace, Tom reached for the piss pot. The mere thought of making Walter deal with it later brought a twisted smirk to his face. As he positioned himself, an unexpected challenge presented itself. No relief came, only a growing frustration as he realized his body was betraying him. "What the hell is wrong with you?" he snarled at his disobedience, shaking his head in disbelief. The morning ritual he took for granted had turned into an inexplicable ordeal.

"Well, to hell with that." Abandoning his futile attempt, Tom dressed with a mix of anger and desperation, his movements hindered by the pain shooting through his foot. He descended the stairs, each step a reminder of his vulnerability, into the saloon that served as both his kingdom and his cage.

"Hey, get me breakfast. Do you think getting shot makes you not pee?" he barked at Matt, who was restocking for the day's inevitable debauchery.

"Hell if I know. Never heard of it. Isobel didn't shoot you there." Matt disappeared into the back room of the saloon.

After Tom ate his breakfast, the visit to the outhouse was a disaster. The simple act of relieving himself had become a Herculean task, leaving him cursing his fate and the bullet that had started this whole mess. Panic set in, a feeling foreign and detestable to him.

Pacing the ground with the desperation of a caged animal, Tom yelled, "For God's sake, I can't drain my dragon. Anybody got any ideas? Should I drink more to overcome the pressure to its breaking point? What do I do? Come on, help me!"

Walter stopped sweeping and leaned on the broom. "My momma always put my brother's hand in warm water to make him go before bed. You could try that."

Tom threw his hands up and looked at Walter with disgust. "What? That sounds ridiculous. Go back to sweeping!"

"Want me to get Doc, boss?" Matt asked. "If you drink more, you'll have to pee more. Might get worse. Though, I don't know. I'm not a doctor, I just pour drinks."

"Not yet. I got an idea." With those words, he embarked on a laborious ascent. The staircase, once a mundane architectural detail, had now become a stage for his relentless battle. Every step he took was a testament to his unwavering resolve, with the railing serving as an ever-present partner in his dance of determination and agony.

Reaching the top, he posed a question to the silent hallway, a gambit that laid bare his reliance on the loyalty—or fear—of those under his employ. "Which one of my girls will help me? A or B? Who's it gonna be?" With a brash movement, he announced his choice by flinging open a door, an intrusion met with immediate resistance.

The woman's voice, sharp with defiance, pierced the tension. "Go away!" But Tom, driven by a mixture of need and the intoxicating power he wielded, refused to retreat. His next actions were those of a man unaccustomed to denial, a figure who used control as both weapon and shield. Retrieving a vial from his pocket, he approached the woman with a predator's confidence, his intention clear in the grim set of his jaw.

"Oh, you only need a little sauce to make you feel better," Tom proclaimed. The struggle that ensued was brief yet intense, a physical manifestation of the conflict between power and resistance. Tom's grip was unyielding, the vial's contents a tool of subjugation as he forced the woman to consume the liquid. Her subsequent collapse, a silent testament to the imbalance of power, left a lingering echo of discord in the room.

In the shadow-laden bedchamber, Tom found himself locked in battle with his own flesh. Each futile attempt to stir life into his unyielding body served only to deepen the chasm of his frustration, echoing the hollow void of his diminishing control. He was a man accustomed to bending the will of others to his own, yet here and now, he was a captive to his own rebellious nature.

With every unsuccessful endeavor to awaken his desire, the stark realization of his impotence was like an icy blade against the sinews of his being. This was a new kind of warfare, one not fought with guns or guile but with the betraying silence of his own flesh.

As Tom reassembled his attire, the woman retreated further into the sanctuary of her bed, clutching at her covers as if to shield herself from the world outside her blankets. With a heavy heart and heavier steps, Tom traversed the room to the balcony and yelled, "Get Doc."

Descending the stairs, each step a testament to his waning vigor, Tom's presence filled the room not with his usual commanding air but with a cloud of despondence. He sank into a chair as if it were his throne of despair, elevating his injured foot onto another as a makeshift pedestal for his misery. The saloon around him buzzed with the life that drained from his own essence, every throb of his wound a reminder of battles fought and now, a battle lost within himself.

Matt continued his menial tasks with a diligence that bordered on the mechanical. The silence between them stretched, becoming a chasm filled with Tom's growing frustration and Matt's apparent indifference. Tom's patience, already thin, snapped under the weight of the silence and his own unvoiced expectations. "I'm surrounded by imbeciles," he muttered. "Where the hell is Doc?" he demanded.

Matt replied, "He will be on his way when he finishes. I found him in the hotel dining room having coffee."

Tom cocked his head at Matt and glared at him. "Didn't you tell him it's an emergency?"

Matt shrugged his shoulders and put his hands out, palms up. "Yeah, I told him you couldn't pee."

The revelation of his condition, announced to the public by Matt in a manner so casual, stung Tom with a betrayal more acute than any bullet. It wasn't the physical ailment that tormented him now;

it was the exposure of his weakness, a secret laid bare for all to gossip over. "You said this in front of everyone? Do you think they all need to know I can't pee?" Tom slammed his hand on the table. "That's it. I refuse to sit here with you and that vacant space in your head. I'm going to my room. Send Doc up when he gets here. Sheesh."

Progress up the saloon's timeworn staircase was a trial of endurance for Tom, each motion stirring the tempest within his bladder and the aching pain of his foot. His discontent reverberated through the empty corridor, culminating in the emphatic slam of his door.

When he heard a knock on the door, Tom said, "That better be you, Doc. Anyone else can vamoose." As the door swung open, Doc emerged, his mere presence bringing a sense of relief to Tom's jangled nerves, yet his silent arrival spoke volumes about his own physical decline.

Doc, straightforward and clinical, said, "I'm told you can't urinate this morning, Tom. Is it causing discomfort?"

Tom's declaration was as blunt as it was fraught with frustration, his voice laced with the pain from the bewildering betrayal of one's own body. He gestured toward himself, his movements painting a vivid picture of his plight. "It hurts like a son of a gun. I can't get it up either." His words were an attempt to vocalize the inexplicable, the sudden dysfunction a stark departure from the man he knew himself to be. "It's dead. Isobel must have done something when she shot me." He surrendered to the absurdity of his situation with a helpless lift of his hands, his sigh carrying the weight of a man grappling with the unforeseen consequences of violence. "I was fine before."

Doc approached the matter with the methodical precision of his profession. He placed his bag on the bed, its contents a testament to his readiness to confront whatever ailment lay before him. "Did you urinate last night?" he asked.

Tom's reply came with an edge of desperation, the recollection of his actions the night prior offering no solace to his current predicament. "Ah, yeah. I did. I drank a lot to help me with my trauma yesterday. Pissed twice early in the evening. But nothing since so now my back teeth are floating." His attempt at humor did little to mask the severity of his discomfort. As he curled inward, the cramps seizing him were a cruel reminder of the body's demand for relief, the pressure within him building to an intolerable crescendo.

Doc retrieved his stethoscope and some tubing from his bag, tools of his trade that appeared both benign and invasive. "I need you to take your pants down so I can examine you," he stated, his voice betraying none of the discomfort that the request might induce.

Tom, caught in the grip of his malady, responded with a grimace that twisted his features as he complied. The act of lowering his pants, a simple motion in healthier times, now became an ordeal, fraught with pain and a piercing blow to his dignity. "Boy, you really know how to humiliate a man, Doc. If I wasn't in pain, I wouldn't do this in front of you." His words echoed in the tense air between them.

Doc's response was gentle, yet firm. "I'm sure. Pain makes us do strange things."

Tom's next words were a plea, whispered as he surrendered to the examination. "Everything is between us, okay? I don't want anyone in town knowing about this. It's none of their business." As he laid back, his fear of becoming fodder for the relentless mill of town gossip pressed on him, much like his bladder. In that moment, Tom was aware of the thin veil of privacy that separated his current humiliation from public spectacle, his dignity teetering on the edge of the town's insatiable curiosity.

The physician moved with a deliberate precision that belied the tension threading through the air. He wielded the stethoscope, pressing it against the fabric of Tom's shirt and then his lower abdomen.

Tom, for his part, lay sprawled on the bed, a figure caught between defiance and helplessness. The bed, a silent witness to his discomfort, creaked in empathy with every grip and shift of his body. "Hey, if you don't mind. I already tried that to get something to come out. God almighty. Aww." His voice, a blend of irritation and pain, filled the room, an audible marker of his internal struggle.

The doctor, undeterred by the protest, responded with a gravity that pulled the air tight around them. "Tom, I'm going to catheterize you and that will drain out the urine from your bladder. But I need some help to hold you down. Are Matt and Walter available?" As he spoke, his hand delved into the depths of his medical bag seeking the tools of his trade with an almost ritualistic reverence.

Tom's reaction was swift, a mix of indignation and disbelief coloring his tone. "Like this, you want my men to come in here? Where is the decency? For God's sake." He sat up, his protest a physical manifestation of his internal turmoil, a man grappling not only with his bodily afflictions but with the erosion of his dignity. "I'm tough. You don't need them." His words, steeped in a desperate assertion of strength, expounded a challenge to the unfolding reality of his situation.

As the doctor turned towards the door. "You may think you are tough, but you are already in pain and this will hurt worse." With these words, he opened the door and his call for help pierced the usual din of the establishment. "I need two of you to help me!"

Matt and Walter, upon hearing the summons, ascended the stairs in haste, their footsteps a rapid drumbeat against the old wood. Meanwhile, the two saloon women, drawn by the commotion, tiptoed down the hall, their presence adding to the growing audience at Tom's open doorway.

Tom, from his position of compromised dignity on the bed, viewed the gathering with a mix of frustration and disbelief. "What? I have no privacy in my own room." His gesture, a sweeping motion of his arms, was both a plea and a command. "You two get in here and shut the door!"

The doctor's instructions to Matt and Walter were precise, his tone brooking no argument. "Ok. Matt, hold his upper body and Walter, you hold his legs. Don't let him jerk around." Their response, a smile and a wink, inappropriate with the gravity of the situation, still they positioned themselves with an understanding of the seriousness of their task.

Tom's indignation tinged his response with anger and embarrassment. "Stop smirking! You think you're going to enjoy this? Don't push it." His internal monologue was a whirlwind of frustration. The indignity of the situation was compounded by his two lackeys, now witnesses to his debilitation. "And not a word about this outside that door." With resignation heavy in his voice, he gave the doctor the go-ahead, "Go ahead, Doc. Do your worst."

As shadows playing across the walls as if to underscore the tension of the moment, Doc, with a steadiness born of necessity, grasped Tom's shaft, preparing to breach the natural order for the sake of relief. Tom protested, "Wait! It ain't natural for something to go in, only out. Isn't there another way?"

"Sorry, Tom, but the other option is surgery, and that's not appropriate here. Do you want relief?" Tom's nod, a silent concession to his predicament, granted Doc the permission to proceed despite the unnaturalness of the situation, a stark reminder of how quickly the ordinary can become extraordinary.

While Doc commenced the delicate intrusion, Tom was a study in contradiction; a man braced for battle against an invisible foe, his teeth clenched like a warrior's grip on his sword, yet trying to cloak his screams in silence. The pain, however, was a foe mightier than any Tom had faced, tearing through his defenses and eliciting screams that echoed off the walls, a raw and primal sound that spoke of human fragility.

Matt and Walter, steadfast at their posts, became the anchors in the storm, their grips unyielding as Tom fought against the invasion, a testament to their strength and loyalty. Below, the nightstand's piss pot, now placed between Tom's upper legs, became the receptacle of his torment, filling with the evidence of his body's betrayal.

As the pot accepted the last of his suffering, Tom's body sagged into the bed, the tension washing away in waves of painful relief, leaving behind a man forever changed by the ordeal, his screams now whispers in the air, a testament to the price of relief in the face of nature's defiance.

"Get that tube out of me," Tom's voice cracked, a blend of plea and command as he fought to reclaim control over his body and circumstance, wrenching himself from Matt's hold with a desperation born of deep discomfort. His leg, too, broke free from Walter's grasp, a testament to his resolve.

Doc responded while gathering his tools, his voice steady but not unkind. "If you don't start urinating on your own, I have to do this again. I see no reason you can't urinate. There's no obstruction." His words, meant to reassure, resounded like a veiled threat of repeat discomfort.

Scrambling, Tom fought to clothe himself, to cover his exposure with the fabric of his pants and the remnants of his dignity. "Get out!" The words were a sharp dismissal, flung like darts at Matt and Walter, who, catching the urgency of his tone, retreated with uncharacteristic haste, their exit a clumsy dance of pushing and evasion.

Turning to Doc, Tom's concern was palpable, the fear of repeated indignity shadowing his features. "My pecker better work. Don't wanna go through that every day." It was a statement filled with the hope of normalcy, a plea for the end of this unexpected trial.

Doc, packing away the last of his equipment, offered a parting sentiment, his tone carrying a mix of professional detachment and personal hope. "Let's hope so. I don't enjoy doing it." With that, he opened the door.

"I would hope not," Tom's voice carried a mix of disdain and discomfort, the thought of the procedure making him guard his privacy with a protective hand. "Oh, no," he muttered to himself, a grimace forming as he contemplated the unnaturalness of it all.

Doc, with a hint of amusement in his voice, offered a comparison. "Childbirth is still more painful."

Tom's response was swift, edged with a hint of sarcasm. "Well, good for them." He rose, his movements stiff, as if every step reminded him of the ordeal, and made his way toward the door, eager to distance himself from the memory.

Before departing, Doc offered one last piece of advice, a warning wrapped in concern, "No drinking or you'll be seeing me sooner than later."

Tom, trailing behind Doc with a mix of reluctance and resignation, countered with a question that spoke volumes of his distress. "How's a man to live?"

Later, Tom found himself amidst his men, his posture rigid with indignation, his voice rising in a challenge, "What are you looking at? Don't look at me. Don't bother me." The encounter had stripped him of his dignity, leaving him raw and exposed. His privacy violated not only by the procedure but by the prying eyes of his employees.

But it wasn't the invasion of his privacy that gnawed at him; it was the fear of what might lie ahead. The dread of impotence haunted him, a specter looming over his future. What if he couldn't get it up anymore? The thought alone was an icy shiver along his spine, a nightmare from which he could not awake. "No man should have to live that way," he mumbled to himself, a silent vow to himself to fight against this new affliction, to reclaim every piece of his manhood, no matter the cost.

Chapter Thirty Four

In the stagnant air of her confined space, Isobel succumbed to the doldrums, her only respite being the hum of an aimless tune. The cell, her current abode, felt more like a cage, stifling her with its restrictive embrace. Throughout her life, Isobel had thrived on activity and purpose; thus, this enforced idleness gnawed at her spirit. The brief visitation from Jane, John, and Gemma had been a welcome distraction, yet it barely dented the monotonous stretch of the day.

Any soul at the door sparked a flicker of interest in Isobel, yearning for any reprieve from her banal reality. John's father, Peter, promised such a diversion. He entered with a demeanor that carried the weight of his purpose, doffing his hat in a gesture of respect out of place in the jail's starkness. "Good day, Isobel. How are you doing?" he inquired, his voice carrying a warmth that belied the cold bars between them.

Isobel, with a humor that adversity had not dulled, replied, "Doing alright, considering where I am sitting." Her words floated between them, a testament to her resilience.

Peter's attention then turned to Paul. "Why in the world would you lock up a tiny woman for defending herself? I thought you had better senses than that. At least, I got that impression from all the law experience you stated you had," Peter said, towering over Paul both in stature and in moral ground.

Paul's defense was swift, albeit predictable. "She broke the law. I can't have people shooting someone."

"Are you saying that the women of this town can no longer defend themselves from the men? Men don't always have morals or they get drunk and act badly. There are wild animals to contend with, too. The west is hard for women in the first place and now you make the case that those in Tin Creek should be in peril for their safety and, indeed, their lives." Peter's stature grew, his presence filling the room with an unspoken challenge to Paul's authority.

Paul rose, perhaps feeling the need to reclaim some semblance of control, to stand on equal footing with the man who dared question his judgment. "I uphold the laws that are for men and women. Women don't have to live here if it is too hard for them."

The discussion shifted to Tom, the catalyst of Isobel's predicament. "Why isn't Tom in jail for assaulting Miss Perkins?" Peter's inquiry aimed right at the heart of the matter.

Paul leaned forward, knuckles on his desk. "There is no proof. The only one injured was Tom." Isobel, from her vantage within the confines of her cell, observed the telltale signs of Paul's mounting frustration. His face, a canvas of emotions, betrayed the rising storm within, turning blotchy red. These days, the slightest provocation unsettled the sheriff, a fact Isobel had become all too familiar with, witnessing the transformation unfold with each visitor that dared to challenge him.

"You have two witnesses, Paul, so that's hogwash. I hear you spend all your time at Tom's saloon. It's pretty suspicious that you won't arrest him when he attacks a woman. Sorry, but the town is getting fed up with how you are doing your job. They will run you out of here." His nod towards Isobel was a silent acknowledgment of their shared struggle within the confines of these walls.

"I'm doing my job fine. Do I tell you how to do your cattle ranching? No. I don't need you or anyone else telling me how to enforce the law in this town." Paul's retort was a desperate grasp at authority, a man cornered by his own limitations. His hand, drifting towards his gun, spoke louder than his words, a threatening gesture that hung in the air like a promise of violence. Isobel, caught in the middle, held her breath, the palpable tension threatening to erupt into something far more dangerous.

Peter, unflinching in the face of Paul's thinly veiled threat, met the sheriff's gaze with a calm resolve. His movement was deliberate, placing his hat atop his head as a sign of departure, but not defeat. "We'll see what the Marshal has got to say." With those parting words, he stepped back, leaving the room and its charged atmosphere behind, a gesture that carried the hope of justice beyond the walls of the Tin Creek jail.

In a flurry of motion that was almost too swift to follow, Paul surged from behind his desk, his movements a blur as he hastened to intercept Peter. With strained urgency, he cried out, "Marshal? Wait!" Isobel, her gaze fixed through the window, watched as Peter Carlyle made his way to his horse. Mounted, he trotted off, leaving behind more than the dust his departure kicked up.

The door, subjected to Paul's frustration, slammed with such force it rebounded, a testament to the tempest brewing within him. He braced against it, ensuring its closure, as he muttered a curse under his breath, "Damn! Just what I need." Isobel observed him, pacing like a caged beast, his gaze periodically cutting through the air to fixate on her with an intensity that pulled the very light from the room. "What are you looking at?" he barked with venom.

Retreating, Isobel sought solace in the small comforts available to her, the texture of the wooden bench beneath her fingers a meager distraction from the unfolding drama. Paul, in this moment, was the embodiment of raw, unchecked emotion, akin to a cornered creature ready to lash out at any perceived threat.

The sudden entrance of Tom, however, shattered the tense atmosphere. His arrival was as subtle as a storm, the door withstanding his entrance. "What was Peter Carlyle doing here? Only time he comes to town is for supplies." His gaze lingered on Paul, an unspoken recognition of the storm that had passed through moments before. "Whoa. Not good, huh? Need a drink to calm down?" he offered, a gesture of camaraderie in the face of adversity.

Paul's response was nothing more than a glare, a silent rebuke as he resumed his restless pacing, the weight of his hand on his pistol a constant reminder of the authority he wielded and the burdens that came with it.

Tom positioned himself in front of Paul, his presence as immovable as stone. "Maybe if you tell me why you're worked up, I can help. Keep it in and someone will get killed. That's what it looks like to me," he said, hands out in front of him, attempting to pierce the veil of Paul's mounting frustration.

"The Marshal is coming, that's what is wrong! Dammit. This is your fault. You started all this," Paul retorted, his finger jabbing in the air towards Isobel as if she were the root of a problem far greater than any one person. "All over this damn woman. What's so damn special about her? I don't get it," he continued, his frustration bubbling over as he invaded Tom's personal space. "Now I got problems. I should have stayed in Bannack. The money from gambling was good and what I make doing this ain't," he bellowed, the red in his cheeks deepening with each word, his anger tangible in the spit that flew with his words. "You promised me a good deal, and I got nothing."

"I will not discuss this with an audience. Come to the saloon and we'll talk. And calm your ass down before you get there. You get all perturbed way too easy, like a woman. Gad!" With a forceful yank, he opened the door, the sound of it slamming shut behind him echoing through the room, though it rebelliously swung open once again.

Paul gave the door a sharp kick, pulling it closed with a force that left no question of his intent to seal the room from further intrusion. Isobel watched as Paul strode off in the same direction as Tom, the air still vibrating with the tension of their confrontation.

Isobel exhaled deeply, the silence of the room enveloping her like a cloak, offering a momentary respite yet also a cage for her swirling thoughts. The imminent arrival of the Marshal loomed over her like a storm cloud on the horizon—was it a harbinger of salvation or further turmoil? The walls of her cell closed in as she pondered the uncertain future.

Tom's condition, a puzzle wrapped in an enigma, further complicated her thoughts. Despite Doc's assurances of Tom's suffering, the evidence before her eyes suggested otherwise. Was her attempt at retribution so feeble? Doubt crept into her mind like a vine, entangling her confidence and leaving her questioning her abilities, her choices, her very essence. Her life, once a tapestry of aspirations and dreams, now felt like a tangled mess of yarn—frayed, knotted, and incomplete.

Her gaze drifted to her hands, the sight of her fingernails—a small victory in her long battle against anxiety—serving as a bitter reminder of her current powerlessness. The urge to revert to old habits gnawed at her, a physical manifestation of her inner turmoil, craving release.

Isobel allowed her thoughts to drift like leaves caught in an autumn breeze, each one a silent whisper of rebellion against her captor, Paul. In the solitude of her confinement, a seed of an idea took root, nurtured by the fertile ground of her frustration and the latent power that coursed through her veins. She envisioned a subtle yet relentless curse, a hex that would see Paul stumbling and tripping, a puppet dancing awkwardly on the strings of her will. The corners of her mouth curled upwards in a smile as she pictured him, graceless and floundering, a constant victim to invisible snares at his feet. She dwelled on this fantasy, weaving it with the threads of her focus and intent, until the novelty wore thin, diluted by the passage of time and the dawning realization of her own powerlessness. With a sigh, she let the idea dissipate.

In a desperate bid for distraction from the maelstrom of her thoughts, Isobel turned away from the bars that held her, her attention fixating on an imperfection in the wooden wall. She picked at it, her movements mechanical, each flick of her finger a tiny rebellion against the chaos of her situation. Gradually, exhaustion overcame her, pulling her into a restless sleep, her worries momentarily silenced but lingering beneath the surface, waiting to be awakened.

The sudden, violent entrance of the saloon door jolted Tom, eliciting an involuntary step backward as his heart leaped into his throat. He squinted against the harsh back light of the sun, which rendered the newcomer little more than a silhouette—ominous and threatening. His body coiled, ready for whatever danger this shadow might portend, every sense sharpened by the surge of adrenaline.

Paul, emerging from the blinding glare like a storm front rolling over the plains, met Tom's wary gaze with one of equal intensity. With deliberate motions, he commandeered a chair at a nearby table. Flipping it around with a practiced ease, he straddled it in reverse, a silent testament to his brooding discontent. Resting his head atop clenched fists, he seemed to embody the tempest of his emotions, a man on the brink.

From his dominion behind the bar, Tom raised his voice, a blend of caution and command cutting through the tense atmosphere. "Hey, I hope you plan on cooling off! Leave your gun with Matt. I don't want anyone shot in here. Blood is a pain in the ass to clean up." He approached Matt, the bartender, instructing him with a nod. "Matt, pour him his usual." Claiming the freshly poured glass, Tom navigated the tension-filled room to stand before Paul, the drink placed before him with a definitive clack.

Extending his hand, a silent but unequivocal gesture, Tom reiterated his stance. "I say it again. Give up the gun. I don't let anybody have their gun, so I don't have to worry when they get worked up. How do you think I keep my customers alive?"

Paul's response was terse, his authority unmoved by the whiskey or the plea. "Not giving up my pistol. I'm the law in this town." The whiskey disappeared in a single, defiant swallow, his posture returning to one of resolute isolation, a scowl etched deep upon his features.

In the dimly lit ambiance of the saloon, where every shadow held a story, Tom's attempt at levity was a thin veneer over the tension that crackled between them. "You're the law until the Marshal comes, you mean," he quipped, the jest a risky gambit in their high-stakes dialogue.

Paul, unamused and stony-faced, pushed his empty glass across the table towards Tom, his gaze laden with unspoken threats. "Don't have to keep your secrets if I go down. You better hope the Marshal doesn't come. This is bad news for both of us. How are you planning to stay low while he is here? You're wanted, too." The words hung in the air, a specter of mutual destruction that neither man could afford to ignore.

Tom, his jaw clenched in frustration, managed a terse reply before turning away. "Lower your voice. You want to advertise. I have my head down when I need to. No one suspects anything. They all believe I won this saloon in a poker game." His voice was a low growl, a testament to the tension simmering just beneath the surface.

As Tom retreated to the bar, the brief exchange with Matt highlighted the intricate dance of trust and suspicion that governed their world. "Fill 'er up, Matt." The glass, sent sliding back for a re-fill, fell short of its intended mark. Matt's slight tilt of the head and Tom's resigned shrug were the currency of their communication.

Matt's skillful bartending, the glass spinning to a stop in front of Tom, was a small spectacle of precision. Tom acknowledged the skill but reserved his trust, a commodity as rare and precious as the truth in their line of work. The departure of Al, once a trusted ally, lingered in his mind—a reminder of the transient nature of loyalty in a world where every shadow could be an enemy in disguise.

Seated in proximity that allowed for hushed exchanges, Tom endeavored to impress upon Paul the gravity of their predicament. The imminent arrival of the Marshal peeled back the edges of the reality they had constructed in Tin Creek, exposing them to the peril of recognition. The weight of their bounty pressed more heavily upon Tom as he contemplated the facade beginning to crumble.

As the liquor began its work, tempering Paul's fury into a resigned despondency, he lamented their situation. "Yeah, all is good for you. You had some guy locked up for your murder. Peter Carlyle is no fool. He's right that Isobel shouldn't be there and you should. How soon before he contacts the Marshal?"

Tom, intending to fetch another drink for Paul, paused to impart a piece of strategic counsel, his voice a whisper of conspiracy. "The Marshal sometimes comes out to these parts without a reason. You need an excuse to be out of town."

Upon his return, Tom presented the whiskey to Paul, along with a suggestion, a potential lifeline, in their sea of troubles. "Take your prisoner to Hamilton because I don't know, maybe because the townspeople are creating an uproar about a woman being in jail. Or leave her here and say you are checking on some outlying areas for any problems. See, you have possibilities." The burden of their situation weighed on Tom, discomfort evident in his shifting posture. The thought of enduring another of Doc's invasive procedures was almost as unbearable as the prospect of sobriety in the face of their dilemma.

Tom's strategy unfurled as he watched Paul's descent into inebriation, his head inching ever closer to the table's surface, the weight of their situation pressing down like an invisible force. "But! Do us all a favor and confiscate all the guns from the women in town. You can never trust a woman with a gun. Need to keep them in their place."

Paul, buoyed by the alcohol, voiced his agreement a bit too loudly, lifting his glass in a toast to the notion. The sudden increase in volume caught Matt's attention, who shot a wary glance in their direction. "That's a good idea! Fewer guns to be used on me when everyone finds me out."

Tom hissed a warning into Paul's ear, "Shhh! Damn, you don't know how to keep your voice down, do you?" His eyes darted around the saloon, assessing the potential for eavesdroppers. Matt's gaze had shifted away, but not before Tom had seen him eavesdropping. To his right, patrons averted their eyes, a clear sign they had been listening. Another, utilizing the mirror behind the bar, had been observing their reflection with keen interest. "There's no one here I can trust."

Paul, irritated and unrestrained, retorted, "Don't shush me every damn time I open my mouth. I'm outta here. You're worse than my ex-wife." In his haste and disarray, he upended his chair and fumbled over it, making his erratic exit into the street.

Alone now, Tom pondered the efficacy of their conversation and whether Paul would remember any of their plans. The immediacy of his own discomfort, a reminder of his predicament between dehydration and the dread of another invasive procedure, loomed over him. The dichotomy of his situation, thirst against torment, was a stark reminder of the precarious balance he was forced to navigate.

Chapter Thirty Five

In the wake of their meeting in the saloon, Paul carried the kernel of Tom's advice with him, a strategy as cunning as it was unanticipated. Disarming the women of Tin Creek struck him with the force of revelation, a stratagem so simple that it bordered on brilliance. Tom, for all his bluster and swagger, had a mind that could cut through the Gordian knots of their predicament with surprising acuity. Not that Paul would ever feed that ego of Tom's, already bloated beyond measure by self-importance and vanity.

Paul set forth, his boots kicking up dust as he strode towards his office, plotting his course with the meticulousness of a general marshaling his forces. His mind unfurled a scroll of names and locations, starting with the epicenters of potential resistance—Perkins General Store, the Tin Creek Hotel, and the notorious Sapphire Saloon. These places, havens for the town's most formidable women, would be his primary targets, a starting point from which he would cast his net wider to encompass others like Dawn from the bakery and the ever-prim lady presiding over the dress shop.

Upon crossing the threshold of his office, Paul was quick to interrogate. "Isobel, which women have guns? I need a list."

Isobel, from her confined vantage, met his inquiry with a blend of defiance and incredulity, her arms folded as if to fortify her resolve. "It's not my job to tell you who has a gun and how would I know anyhow."

Undeterred, Paul pressed on, his demands unfurling like a flag in the wind. "And I need the gun you used to shoot Tom for evidence. So, where's the key to your store?"

"I am not giving you permission to enter the store without me. Sorry, I'm not stupid. And I don't want you or Tom anywhere near Gemma, either." In this chess game of wills, Isobel was determined not to yield her queen, guarding the few pieces she had left on the board.

Isobel's sudden act of defiance, a spit in his direction, caught Paul off guard, shattering the illusion of her usual calm demeanor. Her actions, a stark departure from the docility he expected, left a trace of surprise in their wake. Her temper flared, a brief spark of rebellion before she withdrew into silence, smirking as she seated herself on the bench. Paul found himself eager to escape her presence, her unpredictable moods turning her company into something akin to a chore.

"Fine. I'll find the guns myself. Even if I have to lock up more people." His words were a hammer, slamming the final nail into the coffin of their conversation as he secured the door behind him. Each encounter with Isobel became a test of patience, her presence a thorn in his side.

Paul's mission led him to the Sapphire Saloon, a place that awakens even at this early hour, its very existence a challenge to his authority. He loathed the establishment, not only for its feminine touches but for the women it housed—women who, in his eyes, bore an undeserved sense of superiority. Their beauty, though rivaling any others in town, was marred by their pride. To Paul, their allure faded to insignificance when juxtaposed with the vulnerability of their position.

As he reached for the doorknob of Marisol's establishment, an unexpected stumble over the threshold served as a humbling reminder of his own fallibility. The door, unlocked, suggested a confidence on Marisol's part, a testament to her unspoken sway over the townsfolk. Unlike Tom's, her business thrived, a beacon for those wary of crossing her—a woman whose influence extended far beyond the walls of her saloon.

His call echoed up the staircase, a demand cutting through the early morning silence. "Hey, I need to talk to Marisol!"

A melody descended, a female voice weaving notes into words. "She's not here!"

Then, a voice as loud as a thunderclap retorted, "Who the hell wants to know?"

"The sheriff! Where the hell is she?" Paul yelled.

From the depths of the saloon, the thunderous reply came, "Missoula. Get on your horse and look for her there. She left two days ago."

The sing-song voice added, a lyrical afterthought, "No idea when she'll be back."

"Do any of you have a gun?" Paul's inquiry cut through the exchange, sharp and probing.

Laughter cascaded down to him, a duet of defiance. "Like we'd tell you!" they sang, their voices intertwining in mockery.

The laughter, a symphony of scorn, ignited a fire within him. "You might if ya went to jail. I'll throw in some charges to keep you there for a while." His words, a gritted threat, echoed his growing frustration. Women, in their complexity, were proving to be an ever-present thorn in his side.

The melody soured with bitterness. "Charges? You haven't even charged Isobel yet."

The sonorous command followed, an expulsion wrapped in resonance. "Get out!"

With a final shout Paul declared as he stepped towards the door, "I will be back later with handcuffs."

A woman, carrying a tray that bore not only treats from the bakery but also a hint of mischief, maneuvered around Paul with a grace that belied the chaotic energy of the place. She offered a flirtatious bat of her eyelashes and a coo that danced in the air long after she spoke. "Ooh! Handcuffs are my kind of fun. Bring money. Lots of money." The moment hung suspended, a tableau of the everyday meeting the extraordinary, before Paul, with a motion that felt both resigned and defiant, slammed the door shut, the sound a definitive full stop to the encounter.

Driven by a sense of duty that was as much a part of him as his own shadow, Paul made his way to the Tin Creek Hotel. Each step on the boardwalk was a testament to his resolve, though not without its trials—a sudden trip serving as a jarring reminder of the town's neglect. "This town needs to get it together and fix the boardwalks," he said.

The lobby of the Tin Creek Hotel greeted him with a silence that waited with bated breath, an empty stage upon which the day's drama would soon unfold. Paul's investigation led him to the dining room, where the mundane act of serving breakfast became a scene of quiet observation. Another stumble, an inadvertent call for attention, had all eyes on him, a momentary connection in the shared human experience of faltering.

Fred said with a hint of jest, "Can we get you something this morning? You look like you could use some strong coffee. Too much time at Tom's last night?" The words were a light veneer over the undercurrents of tension that had woven themselves into the fabric of their interactions.

Paul scowled, red crept up his neck and face. "What interest is it of yours? And no, I don't need or want any damn coffee. I'm here on official business."

Jane pursed her lips and asked, "So, what's your official business today, Paul? You sure are cranky this morning. What's eating you?"

"Jane, I need you to give me your gun. I know you have one, so don't deny it." Paul stood tall, so she saw he meant what he said. "I'm confiscating guns from the women in town so they can't shoot whenever they want."

With a shake of her head, she said, "Nope. Not giving it to you. My pistol was a gift from Fred. If he thinks I can handle a gun, that's all the permission I need. If you ain't eating or staying in a room, leave. When you're in a better mood, you can return." Fred's nod of silent agreement was a stand against Paul's authority.

In the charged atmosphere, Paul stood his ground. "Fred, she has to give it up today, and I'm not joking. I plan on arresting people for non-compliance. If you want your wife joining Isobel, ignore me." His hand, resting on the gun at his hip, was not just a gesture but a statement, a symbol of the lengths he was prepared to go.

Fred shook his head, showing his palms. "What the hell is going on with you, Paul? You can't just take anyone's gun if they have done nothing wrong. Did a woman spurn you and you gotta take it out on all of them? You have been in a dark mood lately. There has been talk in town. Be careful."

Paul's scowl was a darkening sky, a precursor to the tempest that his heart had become. Fred's accusations, veiled as concern, felt like the first drops of rain heralding a deluge. "I need the gun by the end of the day. Drop it off at my office." His words were the rumble of thunder, a distant yet inevitable storm on the horizon. The subsequent trip, a minor betrayal by his own body, elicited a chuckle from Fred. Paul walked away, a man wrestling with the storm within, each step an effort to steady himself against the tide of his own tumultuous thoughts.

The general store loomed ahead. Peering through the window, he noted the repaired back door, a detail that, under normal circumstances, might have gone unnoticed. Yet, it was a stark reminder of his oversight in the Isobel incident, a lapse that gnawed at the edges of his resolve. The realization that he had not confiscated Isobel's pistol at the crucial moment was a weight, a missed step in the dance of justice he was supposed to lead.

As he turned, Tom's presence, casual yet calculated, was like a mirror reflecting the doubts and fears Paul was struggling to quell. The need to secure Isobel's gun became more than a matter of protocol; it was a test of his resolve, a challenge to prove himself to Tom. Why he even cared was a mystery. Tom had proven to be a thorn in his side more than a few times.

As Paul navigated the confines of the general store, he heard, "Hi, are you wanting to buy something?" The source, Gemma, emerged from the back room doorway, her stature small but her presence undeniably strong.

"No. I came for Isobel's pistol for evidence. Where is it?" Paul crossed his arms while tapping his foot.

Gemma's response was a physical shrug, an embodiment of nonchalance and uncertainty. "I don't know where her gun is," she declared, before pirouetting gracefully around the counter, her glance downwards fleeting yet laden with unspoken words.

Paul, sensing a lead in her evasion, pursued the trail she laid out, his gaze sharp as he surveyed the area behind the counter. But Gemma raised her hand in protest. "No customers behind the counter."

His retort was swift, a growl laced with frustration. "I'm not a customer. I am here on official duty." Gemma retreated as he stumbled in his advance, his glare a silent challenge to her unspoken thoughts and slight smirk.

The shelves yielded nothing but air and the echo of lost possibilities. "Why is there nothing here?"

Paul's inquiry was met with a response as elusive as the item he sought. "Because there is nothing there right now," Gemma replied.

His frustration boiled over, a tempest threatening to unleash upon the store and its keeper. "Find that gun and bring it to me, or you'll find yourself in jail with your boss." Gemma met his warning with a smile from Gemma, cryptic and unsettling, a smile that chilled the very marrow of his bones.

As Paul emerged from the threshold of the general store, a hawk, perched upon the railing, unfurled its wings in a display of primal defiance. The sudden gesture caught him off guard. His hand sought for his pistol, but the bird, as if mocking his readiness, launched itself towards him. With arms raised in defense, Paul braced for impact, only to find the hawk altering its course, skimming the boardwalk before disappearing into the expanse beyond the building. Straightening his posture, Paul forced a breath out in frustration.

The petulant kick of dust beneath his boots, all the while under the scrutinous gaze of Tom, marked his journey back to the office. Tom's eyes traced every step, a silent witness to Paul's simmering discontent. However, instead of the expected solitude of his office, Anna Carlyle and Jane sat on the bench outside like vigilant guardians of the community's morale.

Unlocking the door heralded not the sanctuary of isolation but the entry of these determined women. Their presence was a constant, a revolving door of community concern and feminine intrigue that filled his space with an endless stream of visitations, each carrying the weight of sustenance and societal obligation.

Jane whispered to Isobel about Tom's inability to urinate, causing a sudden silence to fall over the office. Such trivialities of town life, however, served only to deepen Paul's resolve.

A decision crystallized within him, born of the din of female voices and the unyielding responsibilities they represented. These bonds would not shackle him any longer. His declaration was silent but resolute. No more. His claim over the basket of food Anna held punctuated the finality of his decision. "She won't be eating this. I will. Now get out!"

Paul's height and determination thwarted Anna's protest and attempt to retrieve the basket. She said, "Good thing my husband left in search of the Marshall. Tin Creek was more peaceful before you or Tom came to town."

Her mention of the Marshal, a threat to Paul's precarious position, propelled him to push them out, a futile attempt to regain some measure of peace.

Paul contemplated an escape to Virginia City. But Tom's presence remained a constant reminder of the tumultuous and dissatisfying path Paul was on, a path that didn't bring him any closer to freedom but kept him entangled in the dramas of Tin Creek.

Chapter Thirty Six

Henry had not expected the bustling energy of the hotel lobby that morning. As he and Aldus wove through the dense crowd, the air was thick with the murmur of conversations and the clatter of luggage. Their journey to the dining room felt like navigating a complex labyrinth filled with obstacles at every turn. Finally reaching the dining room, they found themselves in yet another queue, this time for a table amid the early morning rush.

Upon reaching the front, Henry said to the host, "Party of three. Mr. John Quinn is meeting us here." He watched as the host's expression shifted from routine to recognition upon the mention of Quinn's name.

"Mr. Quinn is already here. Would you follow me?" came the reply, prompting a nod of approval from Henry. The prospect of meeting the highly recommended Mr. Quinn sparked an interest that the wait had dulled.

As they made their way to the table, Henry observed the crowded dining room, noting the vibrancy and the diverse conversations that filled the air. It was a cross-section of Missoula's morning life, bustling and full of potential.

Upon their approach, a young man with short blond hair rose to greet them. His posture and the readiness in his stance spoke of eagerness and professionalism. "Mr. Perkins? Nice to meet you," he said, extending a hand that Henry found to be both firm and reassuring.

Good, firm handshake. Handsome. A fleeting thought crossed Henry's mind, one that bordered on matchmaking for Isobel, but he quashed it. He had learned his lesson about meddling in such affairs. "Nice to meet you, too, Mr. Quinn. Please call me Henry. No need to be so formal," he replied, hoping to establish a rapport built on mutual respect and less formality.

"Just call me John," Quinn replied, turning to Aldus with the same cordiality. "Mr. Steyer? Nice to meet you."

Aldus, slightly detached, responded without missing a beat. "Nice to meet you. Aldus is fine. No formalities here, either." His gaze lingered on the room for a moment longer, taking in the scene, before settling back on the task at hand.

As they settled into their seats, the server approached, distributing menus and gathering their drink orders with a practiced efficiency before retreating to fulfill them. This brief interlude allowed them to turn their attention to the matter at hand.

John said, "I appreciate you contacting me about this case. I looked over the file to familiarize myself and can understand why you questioned the ultimate outcome. Any reasonable man would." His words were measured, reflecting a deep dive into the nuances of the case at hand.

Aldus picked up his spoon, transforming it into an impromptu mirror to survey the room behind him—a habit that spoke of his constant awareness and the unconventional methods he employed in his investigations. "Jack had no knife or gun when they arrested him. The bodyguards at the brothel held him, after they beat him pretty severely, until the police arrived." He returned the spoon to its place, his arms folding as he leaned into the conversation, signaling a shift to a more serious tone. "So no way to tell if he had blood on him from murdering someone or from the beating. He had little money on him. Not enough for any use at a brothel." His head shake underscored the gravity of the situation and the ambiguity surrounding the evidence.

Henry, observing Aldus's unorthodox use of the spoon, filed away the technique as clever yet peculiar. "The only thing they have is this woman's testimony that she witnessed Jack murder the man. She said he stabbed him multiple times. But he had no knife on him. And they never found one." Henry's analytical mind grappled with the inconsistencies in the evidence, his gesture with his knife highlighting the absurdity of the situation. "I'm assuming they looked for it." He paused, the weight of his skepticism clear. "I don't understand how they can determine he is guilty without the knife. If he didn't leave the brothel, what happened to the knife?" Setting down the knife, he mirrored Aldus's posture of deep thought, the question hanging in the air like a sword of Damocles, challenging the foundation of the case against Jack.

John unfolded his napkin and draped it across his lap. "I'm sure they wanted to lock up someone, anyone, to finish the case. Most of these growing frontier towns do not have the skills and knowledge to investigate pick-pocketing, much less murder. Jack had no lawyer, so they rammed this through. Very unfortunate." His tone conveyed a blend of resignation and critique, a commentary on the justice system on the frontier.

Henry, seizing an opportunity for a lighter moment, turned to Aldus with a proposition laced with camaraderie. "Aldus, you could open a branch office here and expand your business." His smile and wink added a layer of jest. "I don't mean you leaving Chicago because I want to keep you around for myself."

Aldus responded with a raised eyebrow and a chuckle, "I have no intentions of moving my family from Chicago."

John, catching on to the speculative nature of their talk, added his perspective. "A good investigator would be invaluable in these parts. The more money that flows in with the gold and silver prospecting, the more crime."

As their meal was served, Henry reflected on the value of companionship and the missed opportunities for social gatherings back home. The arrival of their food paused their discussions, providing a welcome distraction. As he spread butter on his toast, he said, "Hopefully, this will only take one or two days. I would like to get this settled so I can go on to Tin Creek to visit my niece."

John queried as he lifted his coffee, "What is your niece doing in Tin Creek?" The steam from the cup obscured his face.

Henry, lost in thought, divulged, "She is running my brother's general store. I sent her there when he was ill, but he was sicker than anyone knew and passed. Now she has stayed to keep the shop going, and I'm uncertain why. Sell it and come home."

John, with a knowing smile, offered, "You might have lost her to the magical pull of the west. It happens to the best of us."

A shadow of worry crept over Henry, darkening his animated demeanor. He stuttered, a rare moment of vulnerability, "I hope not." The thought of Isobel choosing the wild expanse of Montana over her family's proximity sent a chill through him. Montana was a long way to visit. He preferred a short carriage ride, not four days of travel on a train and another on stagecoach.

Aldus called out, "Henry!" snapping him back to the present.

Startled, Henry looked up, "What?" His mind had been miles away, with Isobel and the life she was building without him.

"Are you alright? I asked if you were ready to go," Aldus repeated, eyebrows drawn together.

Regaining his composure, Henry placed his napkin on his plate as a sign of finality. "Absolutely. Let's get this done." His resolve hardened; the mission in Missoula was no longer about justice for Jack Logan and going after Tom McCall. It had morphed into a personal crusade to ensure Isobel's return. The sooner he finished in Missoula, the sooner he could see Isobel and bring her home. He steeled himself for the challenge ahead, determined not to let the mystique of the west claim another soul from his family.

As Henry, shadowed by Aldus and John, traversed the threshold of the police station, the man stationed at the front desk met them with a warm greeting, rich in an Irish timbre. His broad smile served as a beacon of hospitality. "What can I do for you on this grand old day?" he asked.

However, before Henry could weave a response, Dan Hundt, the police chief, interjected, closing the distance from his desk with purposeful strides. "I'll attend to this," he announced, extending his hand to John with a camaraderie that spoke of past encounters. "Mr.

Quinn, nice to see you again," he uttered, nodding in acknowledgment towards Henry and Aldus. "Morning."

John reciprocated the gesture, his handshake firm. "Good to see you, too. We are here to speak with that witness and your prisoner, Jack Logan. And there is supposed to be a woman from Tin Creek, too?"

Amidst these formalities, Henry's gaze swept across the room, landing on a figure poised with an air of distinction. He recalled Isobel's vivid descriptions of Marisol as possessing both elegance and unbridled spirit. Henry concurred with Isobel's assessment. Marisol's allure was undeniable, a trait she shared with Isobel's mother, Mary, known for her untamed essence.

Dan, breaking Henry's reverie, said, "Well, the woman from Tin Creek is sitting at my desk and I got her some tea." His gesture towards Marisol was one of subtle pride.

"And the witness?" John pressed, curiosity leading their steps towards Marisol.

Dan's response came with a slight shake of his head. "She hasn't arrived yet. I'll send someone to get her if she does not appear soon. Let's go into the briefing room." His words guided them forward, into the heart of the station.

As Henry advanced towards Marisol, he executed a courteous gesture, removing his hat with a grace indicative of a man who navigated the nuances of etiquette with ease. His movements were deliberate, signaling respect without expectation, as he awaited some signal from Dan for a formal introduction. Noticing Dan's attention was elsewhere, he ventured forth of his own accord. "I'm Henry Perkins. Pleased to meet you, Miss..."

Marisol's response was swift and poised as she rose to her feet, embodying both confidence and an informal charm. "I'm Marisol and only Marisol. No Miss." Extending her hand, a bold move that contradicted societal norms, she bridged the gap between them. "I'm pleased to meet anyone related to sweet Isobel. And such a good-looking one, too."

Henry, taken aback by the unexpected gesture, hesitated before accepting her handshake. "Thank you for responding to my telegram and understanding the urgency." His appraisal of Marisol was both measured and revealing, noting the spark of life that animated her presence. "I'm glad you have a favorable impression of my niece. Isobel means so much to me."

Marisol's smile was a delicate balance of warmth and strategy, her head tilt causing the feather in her hat to dance like a quill in the wind. "You're welcome."

With formal introductions out of the way, Henry presented Aldus and John to Marisol. Their greetings exchanged, Marisol gracefully accepted their acknowledgments before accompanying Henry into the briefing room. Her elegance carried her effortlessly, yet her gaze remained fixed on Henry, an unspoken dialogue hanging in the air as she settled into her chair.

The men arranged themselves in the remaining empty chairs, Aldus preparing their written inquiries for the session ahead. Marisol cast a discerning eye over the notes, her expression clouding. "I hope this isn't an inquisition."

John offered reassurance with a practiced smile. "Oh, not for you." His demeanor was soothing, aimed at dispelling any apprehension. "We are going to get some background information and what you know about Jack Logan. Standard questions."

Marisol's posture softened, her hands resting on her lap. "Jack is a good man. He runs, or rather, he used to run a clean saloon. He treated his workers well. I even worked for him until I went out on my own." Her gaze lifted, sweeping across the faces of the men, an unspoken plea in her eyes. "We're still good friends. I can't believe he lost the saloon and everything he built on a poker bet. He didn't even gamble!"

Aldus made a note before inquiring further, "Who did he lose the saloon to?"

Marisol inhaled, the air heavy with the weight of her words. "That scoundrel, Tom McCall."

Henry's expression twisted with recognition. "The man that my brother owed money to."

A laugh escaped Marisol, but it held no joy. "George didn't owe Tom a dime. Tom makes everyone pay up front, no one having a tab. Then when Isobel paid him with witnesses, mind you, he turned around and accused her of cheating him out of the money." Her gaze locked with Henry's. "Of course, no one believed him."

Aldus, pausing in his note-taking, looked up. "When was the last time you heard from Jack?"

Marisol drew her eyebrows together and lowered her voice. "It was several months ago. He left for Missoula to find some new girls for his saloon, maybe even a singer. All the best saloons have to be on the lookout for new girls. But he never came back. I haven't heard hide nor hair from him." She straightened, her resolve firm. "I hope nothing happened to him. That's why I came. He is like family to me."

Dan's interruption was sudden, drawing all eyes to him. "Jack's alive and well, but someone else isn't. I'm sending someone to get the witness." He stood, his movements swift as he conferred with the Irishman, who dashed out with urgency. Returning to his seat, Dan's impact was felt as he re-joined the conversation with a thud. The room braced for what was to come.

Marisol's hands became a knot of anxiety. Her question came out strained. "What do you mean, someone else isn't alive? What's going on with Jack?"

Henry reached out, his gesture one of comfort, as he took her hand. "Don't worry. That's why we are here to sort this out."

Her eyes met his. "Oh, I hope so." She teetered on the brink of despair. "We need Jack back at his saloon so all can go back to normal."

Henry's thoughts swirled with unanswered questions, but Aldus steered the conversation back to the task at hand. "How long have you known Jack Logan?"

"For almost 24 years," Marisol responded, her gaze shifting to Henry. "Matter of fact, longer than I have known his brother. I came to town to help Jack open the saloon soon after George and Mary moved there."

Aldus continued, his pen a blur across the paper, capturing every word.

The front desk man returned, escorting a woman whose appearance was as chaotic as her reluctance. Her gown billowed around her, makeup smeared, hair in disarray. "I had to interrupt her business and drag her out because she didn't want to come."

Dan rose, his stance authoritative. "I didn't expect she'd come on her own. Otherwise, she would have already shown up." He grasped the woman, her resistance met with his unyielding grip. He deposited her into the chair with a force that left no room for protest. "You're going to answer all the questions these men have for you. Mind you, one of them is a powerful attorney and I ain't going to tell you which one. We're going to skip introductions since I don't have all day." His gaze turned to Aldus, a silent command to begin. "Go ahead with your questions."

Aldus poised his pen above the pad, a silent prelude to inquiry. "What is your full name?"

The room's tension seemed to coalesce around the woman as she scowled in response. "Louisa Marie Pennington."

Impatience gnawed at Henry, prompting him to leap into the fray. "Do you know Tom McCall?" His intrusion into the line of questioning was abrupt, an apology to Aldus already forming in his mind.

Louisa glared. "Yeah, so what if I do?" Her discomfort was apparent, her gaze darting around as if seeking an escape.

Henry pressed on, his curiosity undiminished even as Aldus signaled for restraint, pointing to their prepared questions. "How do you know him?"

Louisa's defiance seemed to deepen, her gaze locking onto Henry. "He's a customer, and he owes me a bunch of money."

Henry leaned in. "Hmm. How much?"

Louisa recoiled, her defensiveness a barrier. "None of your business."

Henry's pursuit was relentless, a determination to peel back the layers of her association with Tom McCall. "Is he such a friend that you owe him any loyalty?"

Her frustration erupted, the slap of her hand against her leg a punctuation. "Look, I don't owe him one damn thing. Tom's a cheat, and he didn't pay me what he said he would."

The atmosphere thickened with tension, Henry pressing for a crack in her facade. "Why don't you get back at him for not paying you what he promised? Here's your opportunity."

Louisa's resolve wavered, her admission hanging in the balance. "I can't. I already testified."

John's intervention was smooth, a calm amid the storm. "What does your testimony have to do with Tom McCall?"

Louisa seemed to fold into herself, a visible retreat. "He told me what to say. I didn't want to, but he promised me a lot of money that would get me out of this hellhole, back home."

The room's air shifted, a collective response to her revelation.

John explained, "Miss Pennington, you can recant any part of your testimony. If you lied under oath, you must recant anything that is not the truth. You'll pay a fine for lying under oath. Are you prepared to tell us the truth?"

Henry's offer was immediate, a pledge of support. "I'll pay the fine." His gesture, hands open and inviting, sought to bridge the chasm of her fear. "Please, we're asking for the truth."

Her resolve crumbled, tears marking her confession. "Okay. Jack Logan did not kill anyone. He was downstairs the whole time."

Marisol, a silent observer until now, reacted with a gasp, her hands covering her mouth as if to hold back her own outcry.

Dan posed the question, slow and steady. "Did you witness who did?"

Louisa, elbows pressed into her sides, making her body as small as possible, nodding through her tears. "If I tell you, lock him up so he can't find me and kill me next."

Dan, his demeanor shifting to one of solemnity, leaned in closer, his shadow falling over her. "Don't you feel any guilt for an innocent man locked up for your lie that you thought would make you money?"

Her sobs grew more frantic as Dan, with a sign of resolve, fetched his keys. "I'll be right back." His departure left a heavy silence in his wake.

Louisa's distress deepened, her sobs becoming a physical manifestation of her fear. "He's gonna kill me."

John repositioned his chair to face her, his eyes seeking hers. "They'll arrest him, he'll stand trial, and you'll testify again. Did anyone else witness the murder?"

Louisa, her face a canvas of streaked makeup and despair, caught her breath, revealing another piece of the puzzle. "Another girl did... but, but she left the... she left the brothel. Had to move... move to another one... down t-the street. She was afraid..."

John extended a handkerchief, a small gesture of comfort amid the chaos.

Louisa clung to it, her lips and chin trembling. "She was afraid Tom... that he would come back and... k-kill her since she saw the... whole thing."

Aldus asked, "You're saying Tom McCall is the murderer?"

Her confirmation was a nod, her tears unyielding. "Yes! I hope I live to see this over with."

The room shifted again; the atmosphere charged with anticipation, as Dan returned, Jack Logan in tow. Marisol's reaction was immediate, a burst of emotion as she embraced Jack as best she could.

Jack, even constrained by handcuffs, conveyed a warmth, his smile slow, eyes shining. "I am so happy to see you!"

Marisol's response was heartfelt. "I've missed you. You've got no idea. You need to come home."

Henry added, "In due time." His nod to Jack carried a weight of unspoken commitment. "We have to get Jack's saloon back." His gaze then shifted to Dan. "She said Tom McCall is the murderer. How quickly can we get him arrested?"

Marisol's input was a bleak reminder of the town's dynamics. "The sheriff lets Tom do whatever he wants."

Dan asked, "I didn't know Tin Creek had a sheriff. Who is he?"

Marisol's answer was a simple statement, yet it echoed. "Paul Burke."

Dan's declaration sliced through the tension in the room, a revelation that sent ripples of shock. "What? The Marshals have an arrest warrant for him. He changed his name after a train robbery and started impersonating a law officer in Bannack, but he is anything but—" His voice boomed across to the Irishman, "Get me the US Marshal!"

"Yes, sir!" The Irishman's response was swift, his departure a blur as he dashed out the door.

Dan's focus returned to Louisa. "I need to keep you close so you don't disappear either by your choice or someone else's. So give me a minute to figure it out."

Aldus asked, "Are we finished, then?"

John, standing, announced, "That sums it up. I will get this taken care of on the court side, and Dan will take care of his side."

Henry, feeling a rush of satisfaction at their progress, prepared to rise. "Almost time for lunch. Marisol, you are welcome to join us." Her nod prompted him to turn towards Dan. "Is Jack free to go? And is there anything you need from us? I will be in town the rest of today and will head to Tin Creek tomorrow." His thoughts danced to Isobel, the anticipation of their reunion mingling with his plans.

Dan, pulling papers from his desk, laid down the next steps. "Paperwork first. Then he can go. Might be best if we know where to find him for a few days."

Henry's response was generous. "I will book him a room at the Montana Hotel where I'm staying at as my guest."

Jack, still bound by the handcuffs, conveyed his gratitude with a gesture. "How do I repay you? I don't even understand why you are doing this."

Henry said, "I would do this for any good man. Now we can ensure Mr. McCall pays for what he did to you and the man he murdered." His thoughts drifted to Isobel, reflecting on the sheltered life they had provided her, wondering if they had done her a disservice.

As they prepared to leave, Henry sought Marisol's insight. "Please fill me in on how my niece is doing over lunch. I would appreciate it."

Marisol gave his hand a squeeze, conveying a shared affection for Isobel. "She's the sweetest, toughest young lady I know. Reminds me of her mother. I would be glad to fill you in, even on the young man who is courting her." Her wink hinted at stories yet untold.

Henry mused, a revelation dawning. "Ah, so that is why she stays."

"Not only him. Isobel has made a place for herself in town, just like Mary did."

Henry, lagging a step behind the others as they exited the stifling confines of the police station, found himself enveloped by the glaring sunshine of the day. His mind was a tumultuous sea, waves of thought crashing against the stark reality Marisol had laid bare. Her words, while filled with pride, echoed in his heart like a dirge. The very notion of Isobel embedding her roots deep into Tin Creek's fabric as her mother had stirred a tempest of emotions within him. It was a bitter draught to swallow. The realization that the ties binding Isobel to this rugged frontier might be stronger than those pulling her back to the safety and comfort of home. As he trailed in the wake of his companions, the cobblestones underfoot seemed to blur, reflecting his turmoil. The ache in his heart burgeoned, a yearning not just to see Isobel but to communicate the depth of his missive, to bridge the gap time and distance had wedged between them. With every step, his resolve hardened; he must reach Tin Creek posthaste, to stand before his niece, to say the unspoken, to affirm the bonds of family that he feared were fraying at the edges.

Chapter Thirty Seven

After lunch, Henry traversed the threshold of the Bank of Missoula, its towering presence a monolith of granite and brick. He navigated through a vestibule adorned with the sheen of copper, each footfall resonating with purpose. Upon reaching the first teller's cage, he said with a calm assertiveness, "Good afternoon. Who would I speak to about some mishandling of accounts at your branch in Tin Creek?"

The teller returned the greeting with equal politeness. "Good afternoon to you, too. I can help you. What account are we talking about?" As he poised himself, pencil and paper at the ready, he seemed prepared to delve into the matter with diligence.

But Henry, sensing the complexity of his predicament, rebuffed the offer. "I don't think so since I suspect it is not only one account but several. Who should I speak to?"

The teller lowered his writing implement. "I believe Mr. Clarkson, our Vice President, can help you." He leaned in, sharing in a conspiratorial whisper, "A woman from Tin Creek came in yesterday afternoon, and Mr. Clarkson looked at the ledger with her. Let me see if he is available."

Henry observed as the teller navigated the labyrinthine depths of the bank. Upon his return, the young man beckoned, a gesture that set Henry on a path through the bank's inner sanctum. The surrounding architecture, an elaborate dance of white oak and marble, spoke of a grandeur and a commitment to excellence that belied the darker undercurrents of his visit.

Henry navigated the sea of chaos that was Mr. Clarkson's office, a landscape dominated by ledgers and papers scattered as if caught in a tempest. Upon reaching the large desk, he said, "Thanks for seeing me," his hand bridging the distance between them. "I am Henry Perkins. My brother has an account with your Tin Creek bank. I have concerns about what is going on with his account."

Mr. Clarkson, with an air of authority tinged with approachability, reciprocated the gesture. "I'm James Clarkson, Vice President. Well, I am sorry you are having issues. Hopefully, we can figure it out. Please, take a seat." As he navigated around the desk, he said, "A woman came to me yesterday about some irregularities with her account and said others had problems, too, so I actually have the ledger on my desk at the moment." He sifted through the chaos. "The branch manager sends the transactions daily to be recorded."

Seated, Henry explained, "My brother owns the Perkins General Store. Well, he did until has passed recently. He had taken a loan out and then fell ill. My niece took over, making the payments until I paid the loan in full. But your bank has insisted she continue making payments or you would auction the store off."

Mr. Clarkson nodded and said, "Sorry about your brother. Such a shame." He delved into the ledger, a tome that held more than numbers—it held the fates of those it accounted for.

Henry, anchored by the hope of resolution, provided the specifics of his intervention. "I sent $700 from my bank in Chicago over three weeks ago. My niece has made 3 more payments of $50 each Friday since then. Is my payment in the ledger?"

Mr. Clarkson said, "Hmmm. I see your payment but not any others. Is your niece getting a receipt each time? Is she sure she is paying for the correct account? I'm sure it's a simple mistake." His finger traced down the page. "I see the loan was in default. Was this when your brother was ill?"

"Yes. My niece brought the loan current. The banker, Mr. Johnson, told her he had another man in town wanting to pay the loan in order to take the business. That is not a good way to do business when a business owner is ill. My niece has made the payments to the right account, as there is only one account. I'm frustrated and I'm sure you would be too. And, yes, my niece has all the receipts. She is a smart young lady with a good head for business." Henry's frustration simmered beneath the surface, a quiet storm brewing against the dismissive stance Mr. Clarkson seemed to take towards Isobel's capabilities.

Undeterred, Henry shifted the conversation towards a solution borne of desperation and determination. "I have an offer that will make your job easier. I am going to Tin Creek to make some investments in town and I want to buy the bank branch. What will it take for that to happen?"

Mr. Clarkson closed the ledger with a finality that echoed through the room. "I'm not sure, as would have to make some calls. Why do you want to buy our branch? These irregularities can be fixed. We need time to investigate."

But Henry saw through the veneer of bureaucratic delay. "These irregularities and simple math problems, as you call them, are embezzling. How do you suppose you are going to fix that? Are you going to have Mr. Johnson arrested and charged? Probably not, as its adverse publicity and not good for business. If I am in control, I will send him to jail." His voice was a blade, sharp and pointed. "You don't take advantage of hard-working people."

Mr. Clarkson recoiled, the surprise etched across his face a stark contrast to the resolve burning in Henry's eyes. The air between them crackled, a battle of wills set against the backdrop of justice and retribution.

Henry leveled a steely gaze at Mr. Clarkson. "You have an employee who is stealing. From your customers and you." Rising from his seat, a gesture not of departure but of declaration, he stood tall, embodying the very essence of determination. "I'll be in Tin Creek at the hotel. Contact me by post there. Don't bother with a telegram, since that goes to your dishonest banker. If I hear nothing in a week, I will send all relevant documentation to my attorney, John Quinn. And I will add anyone else's documentation to make sure there is a solid case against your Tin Creek branch banker and this bank. It was nice meeting you, Mr. Clarkson. I can see myself out." With these words, he turned, his departure not only from the room but from a situation he hoped to rectify.

As he navigated the maze of the bank, his path brought him back to the young teller's cage, where his journey had begun. Henry paused, placing his hand on the counter. "I appreciate your help. What is your name?"

The teller extended his hand in a gesture of camaraderie. "I try my best. My name is Teddy Williams. I hope you have a pleasant day, sir."

With a nod and a handshake, Henry continued on, the melody of his whistle a light counterpoint to the weight of his thoughts. As he stepped out into the open air, the bustling streets of the surrounding city, his mind lingered on Mr. Clarkson, ensconced in his office throne amidst a kingdom of chaos. The messy desk, a battleground of paperwork and problems, stood as a testament to the myriad challenges one faces. Yet, it was Henry's belief that problems, like beasts in the night, were best dealt with while small, lest they grow into monsters too formidable to tame. His whistle faded into the hum of the city as he disappeared into the day, a lone figure set against the backdrop of a world where right and wrong often blurred, but where justice, he hoped, would find its way.

Isobel, draped in a cloak of despair, longed for a reprieve. It was then, amidst the shadows of her confinement, that her mother's presence, a wisp of light and wisdom, materialized before her.

"Cheer up Isobel."

Isobel's spirit, tethered by the walls that encased her, stirred with a reluctant hope. "I can try, but no promises. Being caged like a wild animal is rattling." Her attempt to muster dignity, to lift her head, was an ordeal, each movement a battle against the weight of her gloom.

"Since your attempt to harm Tom was successful, what are you considering for Paul?"

With a thoughtful touch to her cheek, Isobel pondered, her mind weaving through possibilities. "I did think to make him trip, but I haven't seen it work. He spends too much time with Tom in his saloon. What if drinking alcohol made him ill? He wouldn't want to be at Tom's. That is what I'll do. Make him vomit with every drop. That'll help remove two bad influences."

Her mother's voice buoyed her spirits. "That's a good idea. You are very analytical with problems. Time to focus and make it happen."

"Here's to witchcraft like I didn't know existed." Hands clasped around her talisman, she delved into the essence of her intent, her focus sharp as a blade, envisioning the aversion Paul would soon harbor towards any tavern's liquid kiss.

Leaning back, her thoughts meandered to the past, to the choices that shaped their lineage. "Can I ask you why you married my father? I don't know what you saw in him. Wouldn't Henry have been the better choice?"

Her mother's response was a tapestry of regret and reflection. "I was looking for adventure and had a choice of two men. George promised that adventure and Henry promised security. I made an awful, impulsive choice. But would Henry have been right for me or I for him? Who knows what the future would have been? Be careful what you wish for, I guess."

Isobel's heart ached for paths not taken, for dreams deferred. "Hmm. I hope I make the right choice. I have always wanted to go to nursing school, but now I want a life with John, too. Of course, both are gone as long as I'm sitting in jail." The thought of separation from John was a quandary that twisted her soul.

"Nothing says you can't have both. Anything worth having is worth sacrificing for. I'm sure John will support your decision. Doc would be a good doctor to work for. You can do this, daughter. You can do anything you set your heart on."

Isobel, her spirit kindled with newfound resolve, faced the bars that imprisoned her. "If I can do things with only thinking it so, then I can unlock this jail door, right, Mother?" Her hands graced the cold iron, a symbol of her dilemma.

"Yes, but it is against the law to break out of the cell. Just because we can, we shouldn't. You still must abide by the laws. You must be careful to consider your choices, or you will become dark. Stay within the bounds of light magick. Don't make the same mistakes I have."

But as Isobel wrestled with the moral fabric of her actions, the door swung open, revealing Paul, a portrait of misery, his skin a pallid hue of regret. Without words, Isobel acknowledged her hand in his plight, a silent victor in their unseen war.

But victory was a hollow chalice, her triumph tinged with the bitter dregs of guilt. Had she already stepped over the line to dark magick with Tom and Paul?

Chapter Thirty Eight

Isobel's focus wavered, her mind adrift from the pages of "Esther Waters" where the fates of Esther, Fred, and Latch intertwined in literary suspense. Hunger gnawed at her, a relentless reminder of her current predicament, exacerbated by the erratic arrival of food, courtesy of Paul's unpredictable schedule preventing Jane's visits.

The room's monotony shattered with Tom's entrance, his posture bent, his movements betraying pain. His glare fixed on Isobel, accusation thundering in the small office. "You did this to me! You wench! I'm suffering."

Paul asked, "If it's so bad, why are you here?"

Tom roared, "Look, I asked you to charge her and request a trial. I want her to hang, or at least spend the rest of her life behind bars."

Paul's response, laced with a smirk, revealed unexpected news. "Did you know John, Peter's son, proposed to her right here? And she said yes." He smacked his thigh and laughed.

Tom's eyes grew wide, mouth slackening. "No! Young people are foolish. I tried to help her, but she didn't want any part of that. I wanted to make her a star singing in my saloon. Why would she prefer to marry a boring rancher?"

Paul asked, "Can she sing?"

Tom waved his hand, retorting, "How the hell do I know? She's beautiful. She doesn't need to sound good. Men want a pretty face. They ain't gonna listen." He lowered his brows and scowled. "But now she needs to pay for what she did to me. Look at me. I'm a broken man."

Isobel, attempting to drown out their ignorance, pondered the injustice that fueled such men's views, her thoughts touching upon the broader struggle for women's rights. Their disdain for women, a stark contrast to her own aspirations and dignity, sparked an idea of retribution.

With a mischievous determination, she closed her eyes, her touch on the necklace her conduit to mischief. A stifled laugh escaped her as she envisioned Tom's humiliation, a silent testimony to her focus.

Tom's sudden outcry, "Awww. Nooo!" broke the tense air as he toppled his chair, his gaze locked on the floor in a mix of shock and disgust. Isobel, her eyes now open, watched the scene unfold, Tom's embarrassment manifest in a puddle that seeped into the floorboards, leaving a damning trace of his presence.

Paul's mouth fell open, his upper lip curled back as he rose from his chair. "What the hell! Did you piss yourself?" The incident, both grotesque and revealing, left an indelible mark. Tom retreating from the scene of his shame, leaving behind a question of accountability, "Who's gonna clean that up? God, Tom!"

Tom's departure was a spectacle of desperation and discomfort, his movements a chaotic mix of limping and an awkward waddle, hands clutched over his front. "I'll send Walter over to clean it up," he stuttered. His attempt to exit, marred by a collision with the non-swinging door, elicited a curse. "Damn door." Regaining some semblance of composure, he opened it and disappeared into the outside world.

"Damn! The smell!" Paul's face pinched as he swatted the air, his glare landing on Isobel with an unspoken warning. But Isobel's snicker broke free despite Paul's disapproving snap of his head, escalating into full laughter.

Isobel's mind wandered to the prospect of the town learning of Tom's mishap, a scenario that hinged on Jane's next visit. She reinforced her magickal safeguard against Tom, ensuring no relief from his newfound affliction would find him. Soon after, Walter entered, the embodiment of discretion, to erase the physical evidence of Tom's humiliation before making his own quiet exit.

Paul followed Walter out, leaving Isobel to the solitude of her cell and the heaviness of her thoughts. The lock's click was a stark reminder of her isolation and dependence on the whims of those who held the keys to her freedom.

Startled from a light slumber by the unlocking door, Isobel observed Paul's return. His condition deteriorated, a sickly hue to his skin. His actions, likely fueled by an ill-advised visit to the saloon, brought Isobel a perverse sense of satisfaction, wondering when, if ever, he would learn his limits.

As sheriff's door swung open once more, Jane stepped through, her arms laden with a plate that ensnared Isobel's senses. Isobel's gaze, however, drifted to Jane's eyes, which widened at the sight of the large damp stain marring the floor. Leaning closer, Isobel confided in a whisper, "Tom wet his pants and left that enormous spot."

Jane, her astonishment barely contained, slid the plate under the bars with a mixture of sympathy and mirth. "No kidding? I hope you enjoy dinner. There is a piece of pie for you. You've got to be starving." Her gaze swept over to Paul, her nose wrinkling. "It sure stinks in here. Smells like you peed yourself."

Paul protested, "I did not pee in here. Someone else did. Get outta here. I don't want to listen to your crap."

Laughter, light and shared, bubbled between Jane and Isobel. Jane shook her head. "Whole town's gone wild. Even have a hawk on top of the jail the whole time you've been in here. Well, I have work to do. At least my guests don't pee in their rooms. See you later, Isobel."

With Jane's departure, Paul muttered, "I gotta get outta this damn town," his glare directed at Isobel, who met his gaze with a triumphant smile. The plate before her, a feast for the senses, made her forget the confines of her cell. Regrettably, her feathered companion outside remained beyond the reach of her kindness.

In that moment, Isobel reveled in the discomfort of her adversaries, her conscience untroubled by the mischief she had wrought. With each bite, she savored not just the meal but the minor victories it represented. Perhaps, in time, reflection would bring a different perspective. But for now, she indulged in the moment, her spirit unburdened by the shadows of her actions.

In the heart of Missoula, amidst the bustling tapestry of Main Street, John and his father secured a modest room within a local hotel offering two twin beds, a simple dresser, and a solitary table set by the window. John wondered if the noise of urban life, a stark departure from the tranquility of the valley they called home, would keep him awake.

"That was quite the ride, our fastest yet. Now, we still have time to get over to the Marshals before dinner. I have to find a jeweler, too," John remarked, testing the resilience of one bed as he sat.

Peter responded, "I'll go see the Marshal and you go get that ring. Meet you back here. No reason for both of us to talk to the Marshal."

John, wrestling with the constraints of time and the weight of purpose, rummaged through his bag for the currency needed for an engagement ring. "Isobel is my fiancée, so I want to see the Marshal with you, too. This is frustrating. How did Tin Creek change this much while I was at school?"

Peter's hand, a comforting weight on John's shoulder, offered solace. "Change is inevitable. Some good, and some bad. We have some unwelcome changes to deal with, and I will not rest until things get back to normal. I'll meet you back here." With that, father and son embarked on their separate quests, the door's closure behind them a silent testament to their resolve.

John's journey to the jeweler, a venture marked by anticipation and a sense of purpose, culminated in the acquisition of a ring for Isobel. Returning to their room, the wait for his father became a battle against time and anxiety. He opened the box, the ring inside a symbol of unwavering devotion, a promise of eternity to Isobel, whose memory danced through his thoughts, igniting a love that had flourished from their first encounter.

Peter's return brought an end to John's solitary reflections. Depositing his hat on the table by the window, he said, "We are getting back in time for a lot of action. The Marshal tells me that Jack has been in jail all this time, framed for a murder."

John pulled his head back, lifting a single eyebrow. "That's hard to imagine Jack would kill anyone."

Peter, seated, his posture one of earnest contemplation, shared more of the Marshal's revelations. "He said a man from Chicago provided Jack a lawyer and got him released. The Marshal is coming to Tin Creek to arrest someone but wouldn't tell me who. I talked to him at length about Isobel's incarceration. He was hesitant to say anything until he gets to Tin Creek."

John pinched his lips together as he clenched his fist. "But we need to get her free," he declared.

Peter extended his hands in a calming gesture, outlining their plan of action. "We head back early tomorrow. Hopefully, the Marshal will release Isobel, we can chase Tom and Paul out of town, and Jack can get his saloon back. It will make the town much quieter."

John's focus, however, remained on Isobel, his concern for her safety paramount. "The most important thing is Isobel. I want her with me. I want to protect her." Approaching his father, he sought validation for a symbol of his commitment, revealing the ring intended for Isobel. "What do you think of the ring?"

Peter's approval was immediate, his eyes reflecting pride and understanding. "Very nice. I'm sure she will love it." As he reclined, Peter shared news of potential allies and unexpected developments, weaving a narrative of intrigue and hope. "Oh, and I had time to stop at the main branch of the bank. They agree the discrepancies look real, so I have them investigating it. Might actually have the money I thought I had all along. And then they told me a man from Chicago has inquired about buying the Tin Creek bank! Of course, they didn't say who, but it has to be the same man who helped Jack."

John, processing this new information, pondered the connection to Isobel and the mysterious benefactor from Chicago. "Hmm, Isobel is from Chicago. Jane sent her uncle a telegram yesterday, but I don't know if he could do anything this quickly. Maybe it's someone else. But who else from Chicago would have an interest in Tin Creek?"

Peter tipped his head down. "If it is him, I welcome his help. The situation needs to change all around."

The weight of decisions and uncertainties showed on John. "I didn't realize how stressful it is buying a ring and waiting to hear about what the Marshal said."

Peter, rising with an air of readiness, hinted at the challenges yet to come. "There are many more stressful things coming for you. Ready for dinner?"

John jumped up, rubbing his hands together. "Boy, am I! I'm starving. You can tell me more about the bank problems over dinner." He led the way, the promise of a shared meal a temporary respite from their troubles.

Peter said, "My treat."

John laughed at Peter's offer. "Good thing because I'm broke now."

Their laughter, a moment of lightness amidst the gathering storms, echoed in the hallway as they set out together, united in purpose and bound by the trials they faced.

CHAPTER THIRTY NINE

ISOBEL JOLTED AWAKE FROM the sound of the sheriff's office door creaking open. Her heart raced as Paul stepped into the dim light, his presence an ominous harbinger. "Get up!" His voice was terse, keys jangling ominously as he unlocked the cell, the door swinging wide with a harsh clang against the bars. With a rough hand, he clasped her wrists in cuffs, dragging her toward the exit with an urgency that bordered on desperation.

Where is he taking me? Am I being transferred to another jail for a trial?

Isobel stumbled to match Paul's brisk pace, the threat of his temper a tangible shadow looming over her. Outside, the chill of dawn greeted them, a lone horse waiting.

Paul hoisted her onto the saddle before mounting behind her, steering them towards the hidden recesses behind Tom's saloon. Tom appeared, his movements deliberate, his silence a stark contrast to his usual bravado.

As they embarked on their clandestine journey, Isobel's breaths came in sharp, panicked gasps, the realization of their intent to vanish without trace setting her heart pounding against her ribcage. The cool night air bit at her skin, a chilling reminder of her vulnerability.

Breathe in. Breathe out.

Their path led them to the Bitterroot River, its waters parting around an island sentinel amid its flow. The horses crossed with ease, emboldened by the familiarity of the route to the mountain pass beyond. Isobel, despite her mounting dread, could not fathom the reason for their flight or the mysteries that lay beyond the mountains' shadowed peaks.

Along the relentless march of their journey, Isobel's discomfort grew, the harsh rub of the handcuffs against her wrists becoming a maddening distraction. She focused her will inward, seeking a semblance of relief, but her efforts only magnified the pain, fueling her frustration and anger. The irony of her situation was not lost on her: capable of influencing others yet powerless to ease her own suffering. *Can I not help myself?*

Paul said, "Burke Gulch is the fastest way to Virginia City. Otherwise, we have to go south following the river and it takes another day and a half."

Tom's response, shouted over the rhythmic pounding of hooves, echoed his urgency. "Whatever gets us there the fastest! I want away from Tin Creek and whoever might follow us once they figure out we are gone and took her with us."

The journey through Burke Gulch unfolded under the relentless sun, the terrain challenging them with its gradual ascent to steeper slopes. As noon approached, they halted, though remained astride their mounts, allowing the horses a momentary respite and drink.

Paul, in a calculated act of cruelty, divided the food Anna had prepared for Isobel between himself and Tom, intentionally depriving her. "I don't want her to have the energy to think. Did you bring water?"

Tom retorted, "What? You think I'm an idiot? Of course, I brought water. Who goes out here without water? Yeah, we are traveling along water for now but I know farther up that may not be the case. Maybe I shouldn't share any with you since you insult me. I'm still pissed off that I have to leave my beneficial situation."

Their bickering escalated, revealing the fractures in their alliance. "It's your own fault. You wanted me to side with you on everything, and I did. And she is my prisoner now. If you weren't so hung up on her, we wouldn't be riding to Virginia City to start over. Being sheriff was easier before you had to have a 'deal'." Paul's attempt to seize the water bottle from Tom resulted in a petty struggle, a momentary lapse into indignity, before he took a greedy swig and reluctantly returned it to a visibly affronted Tom.

Isobel's throat ached with thirst, a discomfort magnified by her failed attempts to soothe the chafing at her wrists through her latent abilities. Staring longingly at the river, she yearned for the water's cool embrace, envisioning its refreshing touch to no avail. Her frustration boiled over into an involuntary groan.

Paul's stern rebuke cut through the air, "I said not a peep from you," as he urged their horses forward, ascending the rugged path of Burke Gulch once more.

Tom's voice broke the silence. "Don't you wish women couldn't speak at all? I do. Every time they get to talking, it's just nonsense."

Paul, nodding in agreement, lamented, "Better world if they didn't exist. Damn women have caused me grief my whole life. Just because they get with child, they want to chain you down and do what they want."

The banter turned personal as Tom probed, "Well, how many children do you have then? Is this a repeat problem? That's funny."

Paul's glare was met with Tom's laughter, an echo of mockery in the vastness of their escape.

The conversation dwindled to silence, leaving Isobel to stew in her predicament, sandwiched between two men seething with animosity. Her eyes scanned the landscape, memorizing each landmark in the desperate hope of finding her way back should the chance to flee arise. The gulch's singular path offered no immediate escape, and uncertainty clouded her thoughts about what lay beyond.

Doubts swirled within her. Did John realize she was missing? Would she ever reunite with Aunt Stella, Henry, or feel her mother's guiding presence again? *Mother, are you there?* The silence that met her silent pleas to her mother was a stark contrast to the solace those conversations had provided within the confines of her cell. Now, engulfed in the wilderness's vastness, Isobel felt the acute absence of that comforting connection. "Mother, I need you," she whispered into the void, her heart aching for a sign of her mother's presence, a beacon of hope amidst the desolation of her current journey.

The gulch constricted, its waters dwindling to a mere trickle as the towering walls encroached, casting long shadows that melded into an early twilight. Their makeshift camp nestled among youthful maples that dared to reach for the sky amidst the imposing pines. With a roughness that spoke of long days and frayed tempers, Paul dislodged Isobel from her perch atop the horse, her landing a harsh greeting from the unforgiving earth. He then secured her to a nearby tree with a length of rope, ensuring her movements were as restricted as the landscape that enveloped them. "If you have to relieve yourself, you're doing it here. No funny business."

Meanwhile, Tom busied himself with the domestic chore of preparing their campsite. "Remember ol' Jimmy and how he made the worst coffee?"

Paul's laughter cut through the thickening air, a momentary reprieve from their grim undertaking. "Gad! Mud soup is more like it. Can't figure out how he made it so bad. I bet he dumped dirt in it when no one was looking. You ain't planning to beat him at that, are you? It's always a competition with you."

"No. You're making the coffee in the morning," Tom declared, his tone leaving no room for debate as he arranged his bedroll with a finality that mirrored his words.

The banter devolved into a squabble over duties, Paul exasperatedly tossing his blanket to the ground. "No. I have extra stuff taking care of her. You fix coffee. You're so lazy after having everyone say 'yes, sir' 'no, sir' to you all day."

Tom's laughter, a brief echo in the gulch's quiet, carried a note of challenge. "I can fix that problem of yours. I'll take her and you can fix coffee. And it's not being lazy, just smart. If you can get someone else to do the work, it's because you're smarter."

Paul, perhaps seeking solitude or simply a moment to himself, retreated to the creek's edge, leaving Isobel to confront the indignities of captivity. She, too, succumbed to the call of nature, her movements awkward and cautious to preserve what little dignity she could muster under the watchful eyes of the wilderness—and her captors.

The sensation of being observed pierced her solitude, and turning, she confirmed her fears: two sets of eyes bore into her, an unwelcome intrusion that sparked a fierce desire for retribution. Oh, how she wished to wield her newfound abilities not just for escape, but for vengeance. If only she had mastered these gifts sooner, she might have turned the tables on Tom, ensnaring his mind with troubles far removed from any thoughts of her.

Isobel's mind wandered to past grievances, her fingers instinctively seeking the cold comfort of the silver trinity pendant at her neck. She entertained vengeful fantasies where Betsy's malice was silenced, her ability to speak stripped away, and her threat of physical harm curtailed by a sudden deformity. Her imagination even cast Betsy's father as a target, envisioning him cursed with an inability to grasp wealth or wield it. Yet, as her thoughts darkened, a surge of guilt washed over her, a reminder of the path she was venturing down.

This was not the purpose of her power, a gift that Aunt Stella had always insisted was meant for healing, not for harm. Yet, here she was, contemplating acts of malice, veering dangerously close to the shadowed legacy of her grandmother, whose name was synonymous with darkness. Would Aunt Stella view her with disappointment, or would her mother, who had encouraged her subtle revenges against Tom and Paul, understand? The question of her mother's fate, whether darkness had consumed her and led to her tragic end, now haunted Isobel. Perhaps her current plight reflected her own inner turmoil, a manifestation of the darkness she dabbled in.

Adjusting her attire with care, Isobel moved within the confines of her rope-bound world, seeking some semblance of comfort on the unforgiving ground. The night brought no peace, only a series of fitful awakenings, each noise from the wilderness a reminder of her vulnerability. The imagined presence of predators, the stories of the mountain's wildlife she had once dismissed as tall tales, now seemed all too real in the shadow of the trees.

Despite her fears and the discomfort of her surroundings, exhaustion eventually claimed her, dragging Isobel into a restless sleep. The night's chorus, a blend of real and imagined dangers, faded into silence as she succumbed to the weariness that the day's ordeal had wrought upon her. In her dreams, the line between the magick she wielded and the darkness it could summon blurred, a reflection of her struggle to find her place within the legacy of power that was her birthright.

John stirred from his slumber, a silent shadow moving with purpose in the dim light of the early morning. His preparations were quiet, a consideration for his father's rest, until anticipation overcame patience, compelling him to rouse his father from sleep.

Peter, emerging from the depths of rest with a stretch and a hint of humor, commented, "Now, if you would only be this eager to work." His movements were swift, packing his belongings with the efficiency of one accustomed to the road.

"Yeah, I'm keen to get back. Let's go," John declared, his eagerness barely contained as he gathered their bags, casting a playful challenge over his shoulder. "Last one down, pays the bill."

Their journey later intersected with the stagecoach, Peter spurring his horse to meet it with the grace of a seasoned rider. Marisol shouted from the window, "Are you giving me a grand escort?"

"Good day, Marisol! How was your trip?" Peter called out.

Marisol's reply, "Very productive. Jack is coming home soon. Let me introduce you to Henry Perkins, Isobel's uncle," introduced a new chapter to their encounter.

Henry said as he leaned out the window, "Nice to meet you, Peter Carlyle. When we get to Tin Creek, I would like to meet your son."

With a gesture, Peter beckoned John closer, introducing him to Henry. "This is my son, John. John, this is Mr. Perkins, Isobel's uncle."

John, ever mindful of the impression he wished to convey, responded with respect, "Mr. Perkins, I'm pleased to meet you. It's an honor. Isobel talks about you and her aunt frequently."

Henry's face brightened as he tilted his head. "I am looking forward to seeing her and getting to know you."

John, caught between the desire to share his joy and the propriety of letting Isobel share their news, stumbled in his response, "And I look forward to getting to know you, too. We...uh, yeah."

Peter steered the conversation towards a polite conclusion. "We shall see you when you arrive in town. My wife is waiting for us to get home. Goodbye. Safe travels." With that, they parted ways, each expecting reunions and revelations yet to unfold in Tin Creek.

In the wake of their encounter with Marisol and Henry Perkins, a stark realization dawned on John, casting a shadow over their brief interaction. "Father, they have no idea where Isobel is right now!"

Peter gave his son a grave nod. "You're right. I guess they will find out when they get there. Go ride on ahead and check on Isobel. Make sure everything is alright. We have been gone a couple of days already."

With a sense of purpose fueling his actions, John spurred his horse into a frenetic dash, leaving a trail of dust in his wake. His heart raced as he approached the sheriff's office, dismounting in haste, only to find the door barred, the inside revealing an unsettling emptiness that echoed his growing dread.

It was Jane, emerging from the hotel with tears staining her cheeks, who confirmed his worst fears. "John, she's gone. So are Paul and Tom. They were missing early this morning." Her words, though expected, struck John with the force of a physical blow.

Driven by desperation, John sought answers at the Bitterroot Saloon, confronting Matt behind the bar. "Where are Tom and Paul?"

Matt's response was a grim portrait of the reality they faced. "No idea. Tom disappeared before anyone got up. We looked for him and found Paul and Isobel gone, too. I'm sorry, John. I'm sure they took Isobel with them. And that's a scary thing, John. Tom is dangerous. So is Paul. They have history and it's not a good one."

John's resolve hardened as he paced, the weight of his next steps heavy on his shoulders. "I have to go find Isobel. The Marshal is coming, but I'm not about to wait for him. By the way, Jack will be home soon."

Matt sprang into action. "Hey, Walter! We're closing the saloon. Get your gun and we need to get horses at the livery. We are going to help John find Isobel. Hurry!" Turning back to John, he added, "We'll meet you out front."

With a heart burdened by urgency, John retraced his steps to the sheriff's office, grabbed his horse and marched to the livery next door. "Bernard, I need a fresh horse. I have to go after Tom and Paul to rescue Isobel."

"Give me five to get one ready." Bernard grabbed a saddle and ran to a stall.

John spun around and headed towards Isobel's store. As he approached, Gemma emerged, distress visible on her face. "Isobel's in danger, John. I don't know what to do!"

John said, "Don't worry, Gemma. Matt, Walter, and I are going after her. Her uncle is coming. Please assure her I will not let any harm come to her. I swear." His words were a solemn oath, a promise to breach the veil of peril that had ensnared Isobel.

As if on cue, Matt and Walter emerged, their arrival heralded by a whirlwind of dust as they rounded the saloon. "We're ready!" Matt shouted.

John, tipping his hat to Gemma in a gesture of reassurance, declared, "We will be back with Isobel." John ran to the livery and met Bernard in front. He mounted. "Thanks, Bernard." With that, the trio set off, their horses galloping towards the river, the sound of their departure echoing through the town like a drumbeat of impending reckoning.

Chapter Forty

As the small search party neared the river, Matt aligned his horse alongside John's. He said, "Last night, Tom and Paul whispered all night at a table close to the bar and one thing about this job is you learn to read what people are saying because of how loud it can get. So I made out Virginia City and Burke Gulch. But I also overheard Tom saying he wants to start a brothel. We should search for tracks in that direction."

John, spurred by the intelligence, nodded. "Let's get going. Thank you for the help. Jane and Gemma know we are looking for Isobel, so they can tell her uncle when he gets to town. He's going to be upset coming all the way from Chicago to find her arrested and now kidnapped." With a renewed focus, he steered his horse along the river.

At the river's edge, John's eyes discerned the telltale signs of passage—tracks leading across. This confirmation of their course brought a fleeting moment of relief amidst the maelstrom of concern. The rumors of Virginia City loomed large in his mind, a potential haven for Tom to vanish with Isobel.

Walter's unease with the crossing highlighted his inexperience, his horse mirroring his hesitancy. "I don't know. I'm holding you up and I don't want to do that."

Matt reassured him. "You are doing fine and with a little time in the saddle you'll be riding like a pro."

The path through the gulch was easy going at first, allowing them to press forward with urgency. Despite their efforts, the specter of Tom and Paul's lead weighed on John, his mind racing to figure a way to close the gap without taxing their mounts.

Amidst the physical challenge of their pursuit, John's thoughts turned to Isobel. Guilt gnawed at him, pondering if his actions—or lack thereof—had placed her in greater jeopardy. *I should have camped outside the jail as her guard.* Tin Creek's transformation from a town lacking law enforcement to one oppressed by a corrupt sheriff underscored how important their mission was not just for Isobel's sake, but for the community's future.

Walter approached John, leaning in, eyebrows raised. "Matt heard Paul talking about the Marshal. Do you believe he is coming to Tin Creek, and that's why they took off with Isobel? Tom's obsessed with her. That's all he talks about. He's crazy, but that's a whole another level."

John, his gaze fixed on the path ahead, replied, "Yeah, the Marshal is coming. I'm assuming he's coming to arrest Tom, since he had something to do with Jack being framed for murder. That's all I got. Before Tom or Paul hurt her, I have to get to her. I proposed to her and I want her to be my wife." His words, though meant to reassure Walter, also steeled his own resolve. "Jack is coming back, so your life will be better."

Walter tapped his fist to his chest, his eyes softened. "I'm so glad. You have no idea. No idea at all." His voice trailed off as he divulged a heavier truth. "I have to talk to the Marshal. Matt and I have witnessed stuff you don't want to know about." He pulled his horse away, a shadow cast upon his demeanor.

John shouted to bridge the growing distance, offered a rallying cry. "Things will get better soon! I believe it. We have to stay positive." The determination in his words belied the turmoil within as he urged his horse onward.

Matt called out to Walter with concern. "You okay?"

Walter nodded with a small smile.

As dusk enveloped them, rendering the path indiscernible, they conceded to the night, halting their pursuit. Matt retrieved their meager provisions. They gathered, partaking in dried beef and biscuits, a silent communion that spoke volumes of the shared journey, their individual burdens, and the unspoken hope that bonded them in their quest to save Isobel.

As the dust settled on the Main Street of Tin Creek, two strangers at the sheriff's office drew the immediate attention of Jane, who approached them. "Hey, hey, are you looking for the Sheriff?"

The taller of the two, exuding an authority that caused Jane's heart to skip a beat, turned to face her. The glint of a US Marshal badge caught her eye, signaling both trouble and salvation. Removing his hat with a practiced ease, he introduced himself, "I'm Cam

McDouglas, US Marshal. I am looking for Paul Burke and Tom McCall. Do you know where they are?"

Jane's response was staccato. "They left and took our Miss Perkins. She's in danger. We have to find her before something happens. Isobel's fiancée and two of the saloon's men left to search for them." Her breaths came quick and sharp, betraying her effort to maintain composure in the face of looming dread.

Fred raced out of the hotel and moved to Jane's side, offering a silent strength that bolstered her resolve, though her heart ached for the return of her friend, safe from the clutches of peril.

Marshal McDouglas, his demeanor unchanging, acknowledged Fred's gesture with a nod. "Well, I am on official business to arrest Paul and Tom. I have talked to Isobel's uncle and Mr. Carlyle, so that is an additional concern as well. Get as many men as quickly as possible. Does anyone know which direction they went?"

Fred spread his arms in a gesture of readiness. "No, I don't. Hopefully, all five horses headed in the same direction. I'll go find some men. Jane, ask Bernard to get as many horses as he has saddled up." With those words, he sprinted down the street, embodying the urgency of their mission.

Jane, watching Fred's retreating figure, felt a surge of pride and purpose swell within her. With no time to lose, she dashed towards the livery, the weight of their task pressing down upon her.

As Jane rushed into the livery, she found Bernard tending to John's horse, unaware of the chaos unfurling outside. "Bernard! We need horses. The Marshal wants a search party to find Isobel, well, Tom and Paul, too. Fred has gone to find volunteers." Her voice betrayed her desperation—not only for Isobel's safety, but grappling with her own inability to join the search. She was torn between her duties at the hotel and her concern for Isobel, whose plight seemed to grow darker by the moment.

Bernard paused, his expression solemn as he processed Jane's plea. "I can get five more horses. John, Matt, and Walter took three already. Don't worry, I'll get them ready." His reassurance was swift, but the weight of the situation hung in the air as he set to work, the clatter of hooves and the scent of hay a stark contrast to the turmoil outside.

Stepping back into the daylight, Jane scanned the horizon for Fred. Her heart caught in her throat. The sound of approaching horses whipped her around, her pulse racing. It was the Marshal and his deputy, bearing news that kindled a flicker of hope amidst the fear. "We found the tracks. As soon as the men are ready..."

"They're coming. Horses are being saddled. Fred will return soon," Jane responded, her gaze locking onto the Marshal's as if trying to draw certainty from his resolve.

Cam's acknowledgement was curt, his focus already shifting back to the task at hand as Fred and the others rallied behind Jane, a tangible manifestation of the town's resolve. "You're right. They're coming right behind you. This is good, as there's no time to lose to get Ms. Perkins back safe."

The assembly of men, led by Cam, embodied a determination as palpable as the dust they were about to kick up. "Men, I am Cam McDouglas from the US Marshal office. We found tracks heading east toward Burke Gulch. We are in pursuit of Paul Burke and Tom McCall. They abducted Isobel Perkins. Paul and Tom are wanted dead or alive, but foremost is Miss Perkin's safety. No shooting of any kind until she is safe. I am the only authority. We'll ride until nightfall. Ride out double file."

Jane's farewell, though laced with love, was a testament to the conflict raging within her—a mix of hope, fear, and the unbearable thought of loss. "Bring back Isobel!"

Fred's response, a vow laden with the weight of his promise, left no room for doubt. "Not coming back without her just for you. Love you."

"Love you back!" Jane called out, her words trailing off as the riders disappeared into the distance, each hoofbeat a reminder of the perilous journey ahead and the fragile thread upon which Isobel's fate hung.

As the search party disappeared into the distance, merging with the rugged terrain that led toward the gulch, Jane stood motionless, her gaze lingering on the vanishing figures until they were no longer visible. With a heavy heart, she turned back towards the hotel, her shoulders bearing the weight of the myriad emotions that tore at her: fear for Isobel's safety, dread at her husband's departure, and an unsettling personal concern she dared not say aloud.

The stagecoach's arrival, a welcome distraction from her spiraling thoughts, hinted at the return of a familiar face. The sight of a feather dancing in the air inside the coach sparked a flicker of hope—Marisol's return. Jane's pace quickened, a mix of anticipation and anxiety propelling her forward as she greeted Marisol with a warmth that belied the turmoil within. "Marisol, welcome back." The embrace they shared offered Jane a momentary reprieve from her worries, a bear hug that seemed to bolster her spirits.

Marisol asked as she touched Jane's cheek, "Are you alright, Jane? You appear a little peaked. How about a surprise?" Her words, laced with concern and a hint of mischief, further stirring the pot of emotions Jane struggled to contain.

Jane, caught between the need to share her own harrowing news and curiosity about Marisol's surprise, hesitated. "I could be better, but I have bad news." The uncertainty of the situation, compounded by the mystery of the stagecoach's other passenger, left her on edge.

Marisol's gesture towards the coach did nothing to ease Jane's growing apprehension. Who else had arrived with Marisol, and what news did they bring? Could it be Jack, bearing tidings that might lift the pall that had settled over the town?

Gathering her resolve, Jane took a deep breath and unraveled the series of events that had plunged her world into chaos. "Tom broke into the store." She gestured to the building next door, the site of the confrontation that had set their current nightmare into motion. "Isobel shot him in the foot when he attacked her and tried to take her." The recounting of Isobel's ordeal, her subsequent arrest by Paul, and the trio's mysterious disappearance at dawn overwhelmed her, tears breaking free as she laid bare the gravity of their predicament.

Marisol's return, meant to be a beacon of hope, had instead become the backdrop for a tale of betrayal, violence, and loss. As Jane's tears flowed, the silence that followed her confession hung between them.

Marisol approached Jane, her presence a beacon of hope amidst the turmoil. "It will be alright. The Marshal is coming to arrest Tom and Paul." Her words soothed, yet they hung in the air, heavy with the weight of recent events.

Jane, struggling to master her emotions, managed a response. "He's here. Or he was. He left with Fred and several men to follow the tracks. John, Matt, and Walter left earlier." That action was being taken offered little solace, given the uncertainty that lay ahead.

Marisol, grasping Jane's hands with a reassuring grip, prepared to lift the veil of despair. "Time for some good news." She gestured towards the stagecoach, inviting the unknown visitor into their circle of concern. "Isobel's Uncle Henry is here."

The news, intended as a ray of light, only reminded Jane of Isobel's absence, her grief rising again like a tide. "But Isobel isn't. I wish she was because she would be so happy." She embraced Henry, her apology for Isobel's absence, a raw expression of her own longing for her friend's safety.

Henry, responding with a warmth that echoed Isobel's own, reassured her. "No, dear. I'm happy to be here and I trust they will find her. But I would like a room. I plan on staying a few weeks." His determination to remain close, to be part of the effort to bring Isobel home, was a small comfort in the face of overwhelming odds.

Gemma stepped out onto the boardwalk from the store. "Jane, have they found Isobel yet?"

Jane shook her head. "No, not yet. Come meet Isobel's uncle."

Gemma's head ducked down.

Recognizing Gemma's retreat into old habits of timidity encouraged her. "He doesn't bite. I promise." Her words bridged the distance, leading Gemma to a tentative meeting with Henry.

Henry held his hand out to the young girl. "Nice to meet you, Gemma. Isobel has told me you are a good worker and a miracle at math."

Gemma blushed as she gave a timid shake and made a quick departure to Marisol's welcoming embrace.

As Jane led Henry to his room, the logistics of managing the hotel in Fred's absence loomed large, her thoughts a tangle of professional duty and personal fear. Henry's offer to manage his own luggage was a small but significant relief, his demeanor echoing Isobel's grace under pressure.

In this moment, Jane stood at the crossroads of hope and despair, buoyed by the support of those around her yet anchored by the absence of Isobel and Fred. The resolve to maintain the hotel, to hold fast to the belief that Isobel would return, became her beacon in the gathering darkness.

CHAPTER FORTY ONE

DAWN BROUGHT NOT THE light of hope but the shadow of despair for Isobel, as a brutal kick jolted her awake, her body folding into itself as a shield against the assault. Pain, a relentless wave, coursed through her, pulling her into the abyss of fear and suffering. Tom grabbed her, his hands clamping down with a ferocity that robbed her of breath, pinning her against the tree. The rough bark bit into her skin as he loomed over her, a predator claiming his prey. "You're riding with me today. Better get used to my body on you. You're mine now. I always get my way. And I will have my way when we get to Virginia City." His words, vile and menacing, filled the air, his intentions clear as the morning sun.

Isobel, trapped in his grasp, turned her head away, an attempt to escape the reality of her predicament, if only for a moment. His inebriation was a bitter reminder of her dire situation. Tom's poor self-control made him dangerous and unpredictable, but possibly give her an advantage to torment.

As Tom unfastened the rope, his grip unyielding, he dragged her to his horse with a demeaning gesture that left her feeling violated even before the journey resumed. His mockery, a cruel jest at her expense, was a twisted prelude to the torment he promised. "How was that? Was that good?" His laughter, a sound more chilling than any scream, punctuated the dawn. "Hey, Paul! Are you ready to go or do you have to fix your hair?" His contempt for his accomplice hinted at the fractures within their alliance.

Paul retorted with a veiled threat of desertion. "Might leave you on your own once we get over the mountain, so I don't have to listen to your flapping mouth. This was my plan to go to Virginia City."

In a moment of desperation, Isobel whispered to the steed, "Back up." The horse moved away from Tom. But as Tom reached out, Isobel commanded, "Trot." The horse, responding to her plea, quickened its pace, a fleeting taste of freedom on the treacherous path ahead. Paul, quick to quash any hope of escape, seized control.

Paul's frustration with Tom boiled over into an open confrontation, his voice echoing against the mountain air. "Get your ass on your horse and let's get going. I got better things to do than babysit you two." With a swift, contemptuous flick of the reins across Tom's face, Paul veered his horse, taking the lead up the rugged path that carved its way through the mountains.

Isobel, despite the peril of her situation, found a grim satisfaction in the discord she had sown between Paul and Tom. Their mutual animosity was a crack in their alliance she could exploit, a sliver of hope in her desperate bid for time and sabotage.

As they crested the mountain before noon, the journey's strain showed. Paul, relentless in his pace, clashed with Tom's grumbling demands for a respite. "I better be able to pee." Tom's discomfort was clear, his horse equally perturbed by his constant shifting.

The landscape that unfolded before them was a stark reminder of the journey's magnitude—a sprawling valley hemmed in by distant peaks. While Isobel marveled at the vast beauty of the world beyond her immediate plight, her thoughts drifted to John and the life they could have had together. Regret tinged her memories of their last encounter, her acceptance now a source of poignant reflection.

Looking skyward, Isobel found a familiar shape tracing the azure expanse above—her hawk, a silent guardian on her perilous journey. A plan formed, a strategy to further disrupt the uneasy alliance between her captors.

Paul's impatience shattered the precarious calm. "Hurry, Tom!" His urge to hasten their descent disregarded the perilous terrain of the mountain ravine.

Tom said, "I'm going as fast as I can. You want the horses to misstep?" Under his breath, he muttered, "We are not riding together. I can tell you that."

In this moment of tension and tired animosity, Isobel seized her chance, whispering a single word that would change the course of their descent. "Attack."

With that command, the dynamic of their perilous journey shifted, the balance of power upended by the will of a single, determined whisper.

The hawk descended, its talons aimed with lethal precision. Paul's initial shock gave way to a desperate defense. He flailed his arms, trying to create a barrier between himself and the avian assailant. Despite his efforts, the hawk's talons found their mark, leaving Paul to contend with the painful aftermath of the attack, blood streaming down his face as he struggled to regain control of his horse and his composure on the precarious mountain trail. The unexpected ferocity of the bird left him rattled.

Paul, his hands searching his pockets, retrieved a handkerchief, pressing it against the wounds that marred his forehead and cheek. The fabric saturated with blood, its bright red stark against the dusty backdrop of the trail. The blood flowed with a persistence that alarmed him, distracting his focus and weakening his grip on the reins. Forced to dismount, he struggled to access his saddlebags, cursing the inexplicable aggression of the hawk. "Damn! Why the hawk go after me?" he exclaimed, turning to Tom with a mix of bewilderment and frustration. "We're stopping."

Tom's response was swift, laced with irritation. "This is a stupid place to stop. Not enough room for us and the horses to stand on solid ground without sliding off a rock or something. After this stop, I'm leading." Dismounting with a grace that belied the precariousness of their situation, he approached Paul, his curiosity piqued. "What's wrong with you?"

Paul's situation was dire. "I'm bleeding, that's what. It's not stopping. Gotta find something else. Damn handkerchief is full of blood."

Tom offered his advice, and a soiled handkerchief from his own pocket. "Keep pressure on the cuts. It'll clot up... Yeah, like that."

Paul, in desperation, resorted to cutting a piece from his horse's blanket, a crude but necessary measure. Tom watched. "I don't know what to tell ya. I never saw someone bleed so much, but I've not seen a hawk attack someone like that. There's got to be some way to stop the bleeding. Can you just ride? How long to Virginia City? They got a couple of doctors there. You might need to be stitched up."

Paul's response was a noncommittal shrug, the uncertainty of his fate etched in every line of his face. As he mounted his horse, the pressure on his wounds lessened only for a moment, creating a fresh stream of blood staining his shirt—a grim reminder of the ordeal.

Tom's attempt at levity did little to ease the tension. "Don't worry, there's a Chinese laundry there, too. They can get anything out." His words, meant to offer some comfort, felt hollow in the face of their grim reality. "Just know, I still have problems peeing. Gonna be two of us at the doctor."

With Tom now leading, they resumed their descent, the trail offering no respite from its challenges. The hawk's attack, a savage reminder of the wilderness's indifference to their plights, had shifted the dynamic between the two men. Paul, struggling with his injuries, and Tom, burdened by his own ailment, found themselves bound by a shared vulnerability.

The surrounding landscape, a mix of stark beauty and daunting obstacles, mirrored the complexities of their journey. As they navigated the path, each man had to confront not only the physical dangers of their environment but the internal conflicts that the journey had unearthed.

In this moment, the wilderness watched in silent judgment, the hawk circling above a witness to their struggle. As they moved forward, the path to Virginia City and the promise of salvation it held loomed large, a beacon of hope in the shadow of their ordeal. The journey was far from over, and the true cost of their endeavors remained to be seen.

Isobel's situation, dire and desolate, left her with scant options for escape. The terrain, an expanse of open land punctuated by the daunting silhouette of mountains, offered no shelter nor hope for an opportune departure. She understood that her best chance lay in dividing her captors. The starkness of the landscape, while a barrier to her captors in their kidnapping endeavor, also meant isolation from any potential savior. In this vast wilderness, her cries for help would find no audience, her plight invisible to all but the uncaring sky.

The journey rendered her spent in body and mind, the relentless riding numbing her to the point of paralysis. Fear of attracting the malevolent attention of Tom and Paul kept her still, a statue upon a horse, her silence a shield against their capricious cruelty. Their focus on each other, their own grievances and bickering, provided her with a grim sort of respite.

As they descended the mountain's harsh incline, Tom and Paul's disregard for her well-being continued unabated, their stop at the base a mystery to her. Was it a brief respite or merely a pause before further travel? Hunger gnawed at her, a companion as constant as her hawk that shadowed their path. Their deliberate denial of sustenance was a strategy designed to weaken her, a ploy that seemed to succeed as she battled dizziness and an overwhelming desire to lie down and surrender to exhaustion.

Their journey resumed, her hawk a silent vigil, until they veered south at the next mountain's base, sparing her the ordeal of another ascent. The valley opened before them, a potential stage for her rescue, should fortune finally smile upon her plight.

By nightfall, they camped beside a creek, her new prison marked by a large leaf maple. Tethered once again, Isobel sought any position that might offer relief to her battered form, succumbing to the ground's stiff embrace. Thirst tormented her, a relentless affliction that made her mouth ache and her lips crack, mirroring the barrenness of her surroundings.

As darkness enveloped the camp, Isobel drifted into a fitful slumber. The stark reality of her situation—a plaything at the mercy of men driven by their darkest desires—cast a shadow over her dreams, leaving her to wonder if dawn would bring hope or further despair.

Chapter Forty Two

In the predawn gloom, shapes almost distinguishable against the dim light, John stirred from his restless thoughts, a sense of urgency pricking at his conscience. He roused Matt and Walter, their mission to rescue Isobel, pressing on his mind. The abduction taking place before sunrise on the previous day influenced his efforts. Gratitude filled him as his companions voiced no objections to the early start; their solidarity was a comfort in the face of the daunting task ahead.

The sun was making its way up, filling the sky with a beautiful palette of morning hues as they reached the crest of the mountain. The vast valley sprawled before them, a challenging expanse they hoped to traverse by nightfall. Matt's words, hopeful yet tense, broke the morning's quiet. "We might make it across the valley by evening. Sure hope we are making good time and catching up."

John, lost in a tumult of concern and fear for Isobel, acknowledged Matt's comment with a silent nod. The thought of failing her, of the possibility that he might never see her again, gnawed at him with a ferocity that mirrored the rugged landscape they traversed. Her presence had become a constant in his thoughts, day and night, and the void that her absence created seemed to widen with each passing moment.

Their descent was cautious, with John taking the lead. His experience as a horseman set the pace, mindful of Walter's apprehension amidst the precarious turns and steep drops of the trail. The hope was to regain lost time once they reached the more forgiving terrain of the valley.

At a pause to regroup, Matt rode up beside John. "Don't worry. We will find her." Walter's voice, fraught with frustration and self-doubt, interrupted their moment of camaraderie. "I can't do this. I'm holding you back. You go on without me." He maneuvered his horse around, intending to retreat.

Matt's response, though understanding, was firm. "That's fine. Be careful." They exchanged a wave of acknowledgment. As Walter turned back, John and Matt faced the valley ahead. Their resolve hardened. The mission was clear: to find Isobel and bring her home, a vow that each man carried with him as they pressed forward into the unfolding day.

Walter's uncertainty cast a shadow of concern over the group. John asked as he looked over his shoulder, "Are you sure he will be alright on his own?"

Matt's response carried a hint of regret, his words accompanied by a nonchalant shrug. "I hope so. Probably better he go home. I shouldn't have brought him along. But you know, he can't run the saloon by himself. He is a great person, loyal, trusting, but he gets overwhelmed."

"Yes, a nice man. I guess it makes it so we make better time, but I'll worry about him all the same." With that, John urged their horses forward, the trail demanding their full attention amidst the dangers of rattlesnakes and precarious footing. Each survey of the valley only deepened their disappointment, as their elusive quarry remained out of reach.

Once the descending sun filled the sky with twilight colors, they settled down on the valley floor to make camp. The approaching night brought a chill to the air, and the prospect of another day's hard ride loomed large in John's thoughts. The drive to rescue Isobel was a flame that burned within him, overshadowing all else.

John's mind often wandered to darker thoughts, fantasies of retribution against Tom and Paul for their transgressions. The injustice of Isobel's plight gnawed at him, a stark reminder of the flaws in their town's governance. Seeking personal vengeance tempted him, a counterpoint to his hope for lawful justice through the Marshal's intervention.

The thought of leaving the town that his parents had helped settle weighed on John. The possibility of starting anew, away from the shadows that enveloped their lives, was a consideration he could not dismiss. Isobel's safety was paramount, her well-being the cornerstone upon which he would build their future.

Yet, amid these turbulent thoughts, John's resolve remained unshaken. Rescuing Isobel, ensuring her return to his side, was his singular focus. The love they shared, a mirror to the enduring bond between his parents, was a beacon guiding him through the darkness. The journey ahead was fraught with uncertainty, but John's determination was unwavering. For Isobel, for their future, he would traverse any distance, confront any obstacle, for as long as it took.

Jane wrestled with an unwelcome sensation, an insistent nausea that pulled her from the embrace of sleep far earlier than she wished. The thought of preparing breakfast for her guests was a daunting task, as her stomach churned at the mere idea of food. She forced herself into the kitchen, setting about brewing coffee with a determination that belied her discomfort. The aroma, usually comforting, now tested her resolve, prompting her to consider if perhaps some toast might anchor her unsettled stomach.

From her vantage in the kitchen, Jane's gaze swept across the common area, where she spotted Henry, Isobel's uncle, surveying the hotel's interior with an unreadable expression. Concern fluttered in her chest—was the accommodation not to his satisfaction? She approached him. "How was your room, Mr. Perkins? Did you sleep well? Can I get you anything? Breakfast? Coffee?" Above all, she needed to ensure she met his needs before she could seek the answers to her own ailment.

Henry's response came with a warmth that eased her worry. "I slept like a baby. Or a rock. Before I can even think about coffee or breakfast, is there any news about Isobel?" His concern shifted the conversation to the one subject that gnawed at Jane's hope.

The mention of Isobel, and the dire circumstances she faced, cast a shadow over Jane's spirit. "No," she whispered. "I wish there was." The weight of her concern was a shared burden between them.

Henry's reaction, a mixture of concern and an unexpected confidence in Isobel's resilience, offered a sliver of comfort. "Oh my. I didn't mean to...ah...don't despair. Isobel is a strong young woman. She may not look it but boys learned quick not to pick on her in school. She would put them in their place. Physically, sometimes, not ladylike at all. I'll take some coffee and toast with jam." His request, simple and ordinary, anchored them back into a normal routine amidst the storm of worry that Isobel's disappearance had stirred.

As Jane navigated the complexities of hosting and concern, her movements through the hotel carried a weight heavier than the morning's duties. She addressed Henry with a blend of hospitality and care, despite the turmoil within. "Why don't you get comfortable in the dining room? Milk and sugar?" The simplicity of her query concealed the profound empathy she felt for the man, united in their sorrow over the loss of Isobel.

Henry shook his head, his response a silent testament to his current state of mind, and took a seat by the front window. There, his gaze could travel eastward, toward the path the Marshal and volunteers had taken, a physical manifestation of his worry and hope.

Jane, acknowledging his choice with a promise of swift service, "I'll get that right out for you," found herself once more battling the rebellion of her own body. The kitchen, with its array of scents, tested her resolve, teasing at the nausea that clung to her like a shadow. She was fortunate to stave off sickness for the moment, while she fixed Henry's breakfast and return to his side.

Delivering the toast to where Henry sat, lost in a gaze that seemed to stretch beyond the horizon, Jane felt a pang of shared sorrow. His expression, etched with sadness, was a mirror to the ache in her own heart. The bond of worry they shared over Isobel was a silent conversation between them, an understanding that transcended words.

Her own physical distress thwarted her intention to offer company, to lighten his burden with conversation. "I'm leaving this for you and I'll be back later. I have to make a visit to the doctor. But I'll be back." Her words, though leaving a promise of return, carried the weight of her concern for her own well-being.

Henry's response was a blend of concern and reassurance. "I hope it's nothing serious. Take your time. I know where the kitchen is." His dismissal was gentle, allowing her the space she needed, his wave a gesture of understanding as she moved past the window where he remained vigilant.

Henry cradled his coffee, its warmth seeping into his palms as he mulled over Isobel's letters, which spoke of Jane's generosity and kindness. Observing her now, her presence shadowed by a certain preoccupation, Henry recognized the complexity of human burdens, hers clearly extending beyond the immediate concern for his niece. His own heart ached with the prospect of a world devoid of Isobel, yet he understood his personal tragedy was but a thread in the tapestry of larger woes. Breakfast concluded, he carried his dishes to the kitchen.

Stepping outside, Henry found solace on a bench before the hotel, immersing himself in the quietude of Tin Creek—a stark contrast to the relentless pace of Chicago life. The stillness offered him a rare moment of reflection, though his thoughts drifted toward the void left by Isobel's disappearance.

Upon Jane's return from the doctor, Henry's attempt to engage her revealed her deep absorption in her own turmoil. "Jane, is everything alright? Do you have time to sit with me?" His inquiry broke through her reverie, a beacon of concern in her haze of distraction.

Jane, jolted by Henry's presence, confessed her longing for companionship in her moment of need. "Oh, I am sorry. I didn't even notice you there? Oh, my goodness. You know, I could do with a sit. And I'm fine. Really, I am. I just wished my husband was here. And Isobel. I need to tell them something and they are not here. Figures. Finally, can tell them and I can't." Her sigh, laden with resignation, settled between them as she took a seat.

Henry said, "If you need someone to tell your news to, you can tell me. As practice, I won't tell anyone. I hope everything is alright. Isobel has told me much about you. She adores you."

"I have never had a friend like Isobel. And she helped me with something I really wanted. And now I'm going to get what I want. Hard to believe." Her eyes met Henry's, sparkling with a mixture of disbelief and elation. "I'm going to be a mother! I can't believe it."

Henry's reaction was immediate and heartfelt, his hands enveloping hers in a gesture of shared joy. "Congratulations! Isobel will be happy for you. I am, too. I never had any children, but I think of Isobel as my own. You must be so happy. Fred will be happy too, I hope?" His words were a warm embrace, celebrating the new life Jane carried within her.

Jane's face lit up at the mention of Fred. "Oh Gad. Fred will be crazy happy. I can't wait to tell him." She turned to Henry, gratitude shining in her eyes. "Thank you. It feels good to tell someone. Now we'll wait for our loved ones to return. Hopefully, today." Together, they gazed down the path that held their hopes, their eyes searching the horizon for signs of Isobel and Fred.

The silence that followed was a comfortable one, filled with shared understanding and anticipation. Henry, however, steered the conversation into uncharted waters. "How well do you know Marisol?"

"Well, since Fred and I came to town and built this hotel. About 10 or 12 years, I guess. Why do you ask?"

Henry hesitated before he said, "She's a fine woman. I asked her to Missoula to help with Jack's case and got to know her on the way here from Missoula. Does she have anyone special in her life? She didn't say except that Jack was like a brother to her. Family. I don't want to step where I shouldn't."

"You're interested in Marisol? Well, I'll be. She is a straight shooter, that's for sure. I don't think I ever seen her with anyone. Most men are afraid of her. She runs her own business, and she's her own woman. She never acts like she needs a man. Independent. You'll get a run for your money. Better saddle up!"

"Saddle up? Whatever do you ever mean?" Henry's inquiry floated between them, tinged with both curiosity and a hint of amusement.

Jane, with a knowing smile, responded, "Marisol is a handful. I don't know you very well, but I don't think you're accustomed to a woman like her." As she spoke, her gaze shifted, catching sight of Gemma emerging from the general store. "Gemma, do you have time to sit for a spell?"

Gemma approached, her demeanor gentle, yet carrying an undercurrent of resolve. "Ah, yes, I do. You know you can't make Isobel appear by staring out there. She'll be back, I can tell you." Settling beside Jane, she turned her attention to Henry. "Good morning, Mr. Perkins. I hope you are enjoying your stay, even with the situation."

Henry offered a warm smile. "Good morning, Miss Gemma. I am trying my best. It is easier with the present company. And you're right, we aren't making things happen any faster. This is far better than dealing with the bank right now. Do you know where Isobel keeps the banking records? I need to take them with me when I visit Mr. Johnson."

Gemma's reaction was swift, her eyes widening with urgency. "I was told by a customer that they saw the Johnsons packing up their house. You might want to get over there, quick. I can get the paperwork. Sounded odd to me."

Henry rose, a newfound purpose igniting within him. "Please. I guess I will visit Mr. Johnson now. Thank you for telling me that. I can tell you later what is going on after my visit. Sounds like it is going to be more interesting than I expected."

As Gemma hastened back to the store, Jane said, "Oh, sure sounds like something is going on. Fred's been complaining about our bank account for a long time."

Returning with a stack of documents, Gemma handed them to Henry. "Mr. Perkins, these are for the loan, and these are deposits."

With a grateful nod, Henry accepted the papers. "Thank you. This is helpful." His farewell was brief, a nod shared between them as he made his way down the street towards the bank, a place now intertwined with his personal business.

Chapter Forty Three

In the bright morning sun, Mr. Johnson's steps echoed with urgency as he made his way to the bank, driven by desperation and a telegram's grim tidings received just the night before. The burden of sharing the revelations with his wife and the looming need to escape the consequences of his actions overwhelmed him. Tin Creek, once a refuge, now felt like a trap closing in around him.

As he unlocked the bank and hastened to secure the ledger—a damning record of his misdeeds—he could almost smell the stench of his own deceit. The combination to the safe was at the forefront of his mind when the sound of the front door creaking open sent a jolt of panic through him. Cursing his oversight for not securing the door upon entry, he peered from his hideaway, only to be met with a sight that rooted him to the spot—an older man, bearing a resemblance to George Perkins, stood there. The recognition sparked a flicker of fear; George Perkins had been a name synonymous with a past best left undisturbed.

Mr. Johnson's reaction was instinctual. With the ledger clutched like a shield, he emerged, attempting to gauge this unexpected visitor. The sight of the telegraph station, its last message a silent testament to his looming fate, only heightened his sense of urgency. He made a desperate bid to bypass the stranger, to escape the net that seemed to draw tighter with each passing moment.

But the man was quicker. Seizing Mr. Johnson by the collar with an authority that brooked no argument, he posed a question that held layers of implication. "Where are you going, Mr. Johnson? Don't you think you should see what I need? I might be a new customer. Or maybe..." His grip was firm as he steered Mr. Johnson toward the door, securing it with a click that echoed ominously through the bank. "I'm your new boss. I hear you're moving. Why would that be? I think you should stay."

In that moment, the power dynamics within the bank shifted, with the stranger asserting control over the situation. Mr. Johnson, caught fleeing, faced a reckoning he had sought to avoid, his plans unraveling at the hands of a man he had underestimated. The confrontation within the walls of the bank, once a sanctuary for his secrets, now became the stage for a tense and uncertain standoff.

"Moving? Oh, no. Are you the one who is buying the bank?" Mr. Johnson squeaked in a rising panic, seeking to wriggle free from the man's unyielding grasp. "Can you let go of me, please?" he pleaded, curling his arms over his head.

The stranger, however, remained steadfast, his grip firm as he issued his ultimatum. "When you hand me that ledger. We are going to close the bank for the day and do a full audit. And I'm going to tell you a little secret. The US Marshal is currently working on cleaning up this town. There are two arrests in the works and I hope for your sake there is not another. I hope I am making myself clear." His words carried the weight of law and order, a promise of reckoning for the shadows that lurked within Tin Creek.

Mr. Johnson surrendered the ledger, his gaze dropping to the floor in defeat. "Are you related to Ms. Perkins, by any chance?"

Henry's reply was firm. "I am. My niece. I am Mr. Perkins to you. And I have brought the receipts she received from you each time she came to pay on the loan or make a deposit. In addition, I have a receipt for the payoff on my brother's loan. We are going to start with that account first. Then we will go over all the other customers who have complained to me about their accounts." With the ledger now in his possession, Henry released Mr. Johnson, guiding him with a dismissive gesture towards the back room where truths long hidden would be laid bare.

As they delved into the Perkins account, Henry presented the evidence of deceit—the receipts from Isobel juxtaposed against the official loan payoff. The paperwork sprawled across the desk was a testament to the meticulousness with which Henry had prepared for this confrontation.

Mr. Johnson, now seated before the damning array of documents, was a portrait of guilt and fear. Sweat beaded on his skin, his hands quivering as he compared the incriminating receipts to his own fraudulent entries. The scheme he had crafted, borne of greed and underestimation of those he deemed powerless, was unraveling before his eyes. The illicit funds he had siphoned, driven by the insatiable demands of a dissatisfied spouse, now threatened to be his undoing.

Faced with the imminent collapse of his world, Mr. Johnson grappled with the reality that his choices had cornered him in a dire predicament. The thought of fleeing to Seattle, once a glimmer of escape, now faded into the realm of impossibility. The question of what would become of Carol and Betsy in his absence loomed large, a stark reminder of the personal toll of his actions.

Offering help with an almost sardonic kindness, Henry suggested, "Do you need some assistance, Mr. Johnson? I'm very good with numbers. Let me pull up another chair." He grabbed another chair with a deliberate slowness, setting the stage for their next moves.

Mr. Johnson, however, reached his breaking point, his resolve crumbling under the weight of his actions and their consequences. "I can't do this. You can have me arrested. Then you can go through the accounts yourself and deal with it your own way. I'm done. I just don't know what my wife and daughter will do now." His shoulder dragged low as he threw his hands up. A man defeated not only by the prospect of his imminent arrest but also by the personal fallout awaiting him—his wife's anger, his daughter's shame.

Henry, his lips twisted, stood feet wide, leaning on the chair. "What do I do with you until the Marshall gets here? I don't trust you to stay in Tin Creek on your own. I guess that means you will stay with me. Doesn't that sound like fun?" His words, heavy with irony, left little room for negotiation.

Resigned, Mr. Johnson agreed, pondering the message he needed to send his family. "Fine. Maybe someone at the hotel can send word to my family that I won't be coming home anytime soon." With that, he relinquished the ledger to Henry, a symbolic gesture marking the end of his tenure.

As Henry inquired about any belongings, Mr. Johnson's response was bitter. "Nothing I need where I am going." The surrender of the bank's keys, passed from his pocket to Henry's hand, was the ultimate act of capitulation. "The key to the door. You'll find the safe's combination inside the back cover of the ledger."

With the bank now secured under Henry's stewardship, they departed for the hotel, Mr. Johnson's steps heavy with regret. The path to the hotel was a somber procession, a man coming to terms with the price of his greed. "I guess this is what I got for giving my wife and daughter everything they wanted instead of teaching them to live with what they had. Now they would have nothing and I would lose my freedom and my family. Everything for ten percent." The echo of his footsteps was a stark reminder of the cost of his choices, a legacy lost for a fleeting gain.

Chapter Forty Four

Isobel's awakening was not only a return to consciousness but a reawakening to the magick that pulsed within her, an electric sensation that imbued her being with vitality and purpose. The sight of a majestic willow tree, its branches dancing in the gentle breeze beside the creek, greeted her as her eyes adjusted to the morning light. The tree, unnoticed in her exhaustion the night before, now communicated to her soul, speaking in the ancient, wordless language of the earth that she understood.

Tom's sharp tone shattered the morning's tranquility, his impatience a jarring contrast to the serene dialogue between Isobel and nature. "Why haven't you gotten coffee going? We need to get going, or do you want someone to find us first?"

Paul's exasperated response only added to the tension. "There you go. Complaining. Another day of you complaining. Fix your own coffee." Their bickering, a familiar refrain, filled the air, with Tom's muttering providing a bitter underscore to the morning's discord. "Of course. If you want something done, you have to do it yourself. Where's Walter when I need him? Dumb as a box of rocks, but he don't argue."

Isobel rolled her eyes. But within her silent dismissal, lay the seed of a plan, a strategy to exploit their weaknesses for her escape. She reached out to the earth, her request for aid sent through the touch of her palms against the soil, her head bowed in solemn entreaty.

The willow tree, sensing her plea, shimmered in response, a cascade of light flowing from its crown to the tips of its leaves—a signal, evidence of the alliance between Isobel and the natural world.

Rising, Isobel turned the tables with a suggestion so audacious it brought a momentary halt to the morning's turmoil. "Hey, Tom! Instead of that, why don't you cut some branches from that willow tree and you and Paul can take turns whipping me?" Her words, laced with a cunning that belied her apparent submission, caught Tom off guard, his reaction a mix of surprise and confusion.

Tom's pause, his raised eyebrow, a silent question to his accomplice, marked a pivotal moment in their power dynamic. "Did you hear that, Paul?"

"What?" Paul's oblivious inquiry underscored the shift in control, the first move in Isobel's gambit to use the forces that sought to subjugate her as the instruments of her liberation. Within the dance of light and shadow, nature's ally prepared to turn her captors' desires against them, the willow tree standing sentinel to the unfolding drama.

"She says we can cut branches to lash her with. I think the trip has been too hard on her."

Paul approached the willow, his gaze shifting from its majestic form to Isobel, with a knife in hand poised for an act of destruction. Tom, spurred by a similar intent, quickened his pace, his knife ready to carve through the tree.

Isobel, drawing upon her deep connection with the earth, whispered a silent plea to the willow, seeking its protection and intervention. Her request was not simply for resistance against the blades, but for a more active defense—one that would ensnare her captors and afford her a chance at freedom. Though bound by rope, her spirit remained unchained, her hope intertwined with the natural magick she commanded.

The willow, responding to Isobel's call, acted with a life of its own. Branches near Tom twisted and braided with an otherworldly agility, ensnaring his legs with a swift motion. *Swoosh*.

"What? Get me down." Tom's protests filled the air, his demands for release futile against the tree's embrace.

Swoosh. Paul, too, found himself caught suspended alongside Tom. His disbelief echoed in his cry. "Whoa! Damn, I dropped my knife. How are we going to get down?"

Tom, his world upended, accused Isobel with a pointed finger. "You did this. Just like those leaves. You're a witch. A damn witch."

Isobel's smile was one of vindication, a silent acknowledgment of the power she wielded and the justice she had rendered upon her captors. The sight of Tom and Paul dangling was a testament to her strength and the earth's allegiance to her.

A sudden disturbance among the willow's branches caught her attention—a clear signal from her avian familiar. *Attack. To scare, not to harm.* The hawk descended with precision, targeting Tom first. His screams punctured the tranquility of the scene, his movements frantic and futile. The bird, an extension of Isobel's will, turned its attention to Paul, who twisted to evade the talons aimed at him.

As the hawk perched atop the willow, its mission accomplished, Isobel stood witness to the power of nature's justice. Tom and Paul, ensnared and subdued, were at her mercy. In this moment, Isobel's bond with the earth was unbreakable, her resolve as steadfast as the tree that stood sentinel over her captors.

Isobel, drawing upon the serene presence of the willow and the latent energy of the earth, resolved to harness this power to rejuvenate her weakened state. Her sustenance would come not only from whatever meager provisions her captors had amassed, but from the essence of nature itself. The rope that bound her, once a daunting barrier to her freedom, now seemed a mere inconvenience.

Positioning herself on hands and knees, Isobel became a conduit for the earth's vitality. She reached out with her senses, tapping into the life force that thrummed below. The initial faint tingles of energy soon swelled into robust pulses, a testament to the earth's generous spirit. Gratitude filled her as she whispered, "Thank you for the blessing willow and earth."

Tom wiggled around and tugged on his shirt sleeves, brows drawing closer. "Did you hear that, Paul? She's a witch that talks to trees." His struggles against the willow's grasp only tightened its hold, eliciting a pained plea. "No. It hurts. Stop!" His defiance ebbed away, leaving behind a bitter admission. "She tricked me as soon as she stepped off the stagecoach. I've been tricked."

Paul retorted, "No. You're just stupid."

Isobel, turning her back on the scene of their defeat, focused her attention on the rope that restrained her. Clasping it, she closed her eyes, her mind reaching for the spell of decomposition.

With power drawn from deep within,
Let this rope's hold begin to thin.
By the magic of old, by the power of three,
Release me now, so mote it be!

The rope obeyed her silent command, unraveling, each strand breaking down until it vanished, leaving no trace behind.

Paul, jaw slack, arms wrapped around himself, said, "Tom, did you see that? She made the rope disappear."

Tom's response was a mix of fear and conviction. "I told you she's a witch." Their voices, a backdrop to Isobel's triumph, underscored the shift in power. No longer the captive, Isobel stood free, her bond with the earth and its elements a source of strength and a means of escape.

Isobel's wrists ached as she rifled through the saddlebags, her stomach a pit of hunger. Discovering a single piece of jerky, she didn't hesitate, her actions driven by the primal need to eat. With the two would-be captors hanging like peculiar ornaments from the willow, she abandoned all pretense of manners, devouring the jerky and sipping from Paul's nearly empty canteen. Tom's canteen, predictably, offered nothing but air.

Turning her attention to the horses, Isobel recognized needing to take both. Despite her inexperience and the extraordinary circumstances, she approached them with a gentleness born of necessity. Whispering words of comfort, she felt their warm breaths against her skin as they nuzzled her in return, a silent bond forming in the quiet morning.

With the horses prepared, Isobel faced the challenge of mounting. Choosing Tom's horse, driven by a sense of compassion for the animal, she struggled to hoist herself into the saddle. Her efforts were clumsy, her body not quite cooperating as she envisioned, but determination saw her seated, albeit unrefined. Below, Tom and Paul's laughter did little to diminish her spirit; they remained ensnared by nature's retribution, while she claimed their horses and her freedom.

Before setting off, Isobel allowed herself a last parting shot. "Bye, Tom. I hope the vultures find you soon. Do you want me to call them or let it happen naturally?" Tom's response was a weary resignation, a silent acknowledgment of his defeat. "Just go and I never want to see you again." Paul's retort, a single, venomous word, "Bitch," revealed the depth of his bitterness, their auras a stark contrast beneath them—violet and magenta shadows of defeat and disdain.

With a last glance at the captors and the willow that had been her unexpected ally, Isobel guided the horses away, her heart set on the place she called home. The trail before her promised a return to familiarity, to safety, and to a life untouched by the dark intentions of those she left behind. Isobel rode not only towards her home, but towards a future where her strength and her bond with the earth were undeniable, a future where she was no longer a victim but a survivor, returning to her roots and John.

John stirred from his uneasy sleep on the hard ground of the valley. Despite his discomfort, the urgency of their mission pushed any longing for his own bed to the back of his mind. Today, he dared to hope, might be the day he would reunite with Isobel and they could return home.

A peculiar sensation, the prickling awareness of being watched, roused him. John's gaze swept the campsite, landing on a group of horses nearby. Four horses! His heart leaped into his throat. Moving towards the animals, not wanting to spook them, he prepared for any sign of trouble. Instead, he found Isobel standing beside them, a weary but unmistakable smile gracing her features. Despite the weariness etched in her face, to John, she was as radiant as the day they had first met. Overwhelmed with relief, he rushed to her, lifting her off the ground in a whirlwind of joy. "Oh, you're safe! I'm so happy to see you. I was afraid I would never see you again and I can't live with that. How did you get away? Are they following you? We should go now." His words tumbled out in a rush, a chaotic mix of questions and declarations fueled by his surging emotions.

Isobel's voice carried the weight of exhaustion as she spoke. "I'm happy, too, but I need some water. I'm dizzy. How is Gemma? I've been worried." John noticed the weariness in Isobel's eyes, the spark that had once been vibrant now faded, as if drained by the adrenaline of her escape, leaving her to grapple with the exhaustion and strain on her body.

Guiding her to the remains of their campfire, John eased Isobel down, his mind racing to tend to her needs. "Gemma's fine. Don't worry. I'll get you some water and food. You rest. I gotta wake Matt."

Isobel said, "Oh, he came with you. I'm surprised. Why?" John noticed Isobel struggling to keep her eyes open.

In those moments, as John moved to fulfill Isobel's immediate needs, the reality of their reunion settled. They were together again, against all odds, their future a blank page waiting to be filled with their shared journey home.

John hastened to Isobel's side with water. He watched her drink, the relief in her eyes easing his worry. Without wasting another moment, he rushed to rouse Matt from his slumber. "Hey, wake up. Time to go home. Isobel is here, and she's safe. She's just had a hard time. No water or food all this time and she's been riding all night.

But we can go home now." The words spilled out in a torrent, each one underscored by a mix of relief and concern.

Matt stirred, his response immediate and resolute. "Yeah, let's pack up and get her home. Doc can check her out. No use staying here. Tom will follow her trail since he knows exactly which way she'll go." His words were a balm to John's anxious heart, a shared commitment to see Isobel home.

Isobel asked, "Why are you helping? You worked for Tom. I don't understand." Her exhaustion was visible, a heavy cloak that threatened to pull her into slumber then and there, despite the looming journey back.

"I worked for Jack and Tom threatened me when he showed up, so I couldn't leave. John said Jack is coming back and I am praying he is there when we get back. You're a gracious lady who Tom mistreated." His gesture of help, an offered hand and a bow, was a silent testament to his respect and apology for any part he played in her ordeal. "I apologize for everything that happened to you. Please know that Walter and I meant no harm to you. We were just trying to survive an unpleasant situation, as were you."

As Isobel expressed her understanding of the situation, implicating Tom, Paul, and Mr. Johnson as the root of her troubles, John noticed a shift in her demeanor when she addressed her next request. "Can I ride with you? I don't think I can ride by myself right now. I'm too exhausted." Her voice quivered, revealing a vulnerability that John had never witnessed. It was a moment of vulnerability, her exhaustion and the ordeal she had endured catching up to her in a wave of fatigue that seemed to physically bow her shoulders.

John, heartened by her trust, reassured her with a smile that could bridge any distance. "I wasn't planning on letting you ride by yourself. I want to hold on to you so I know you won't get away." He spoke with a tenderness intended to wrap around her like a blanket, offering comfort and security. As he helped Isobel onto his horse, and then mounted behind her, a protective urge surged within him, his resolve to get her home safely becoming an unspoken vow.

With Matt also prepared, they took the lead of the extra horses, their journey back to tracing the path of their outbound trek.

However, the encounter with the US Marshal and their own townsfolk, including Fred, several hours into their ride, introduced an unexpected complication. John could feel Isobel tense against him, her body rigid. She had a sharp intake of breath.

"Are you alright, Isobel?" As soon as John noticed, his concern was clear in the soft, worried tone of his voice. "Do you need more water?" His offer was both a practical attempt to comfort her and a gentle probe, seeking to understand the depth of her distress.

Isobel's assurance, "I'm... I'm alright. Just surprised, that's all," did little to mask the turmoil swirling within her. John could see her mind racing.

The Marshal's approach brought a formal air, his focus on justice unwavering. "Glad to see you are safe, Ms. Perkins. Your uncle is waiting in Tin Creek for you. I know he is eager to know you are safe. My mission is to bring Tom McCall and Paul Burke to justice. Where did you last see them, and how *did* you escape?"

Isobel's response was steady, but beneath the calm exterior, John detected the faintest tremor of tension. "I was fortunate. Two men came along traveling north and tricked them when they figured I was kidnapped. They hung them in a tree. Don't worry. They are hanging upside down, so they were alive when I took the horses.

Cross the valley and head south. Along a creek, you will find an enormous willow tree. That's where they are."

With the Marshal and his deputy on their way to confront Tom and Paul, the group turned toward Tin Creek, the atmosphere lightening as talk of celebration filled the air. But amidst the relief and plans for a town dance, John sensed Isobel's relief at the change of subject.

Fred's arrival and his words to John and Isobel wove a thread of warmth through the cool morning air. "I'm glad you're safe, but Jane is going to be so excited. You're like a sister to her. She is friendly to everyone, but not close to anyone until you came. When we get back, let's have dinner together. Plan?"

John, ever mindful of Isobel's wellbeing, interjected, "Yes. After we get Isobel some rest and the doc checks her out. I.. I mean, we would love to have dinner with you and Jane. Is that alright with you, Isobel?"

Isobel's smile was a ray of light. "I can't wait to see Jane. Yes. What else would I say?" Her simple acceptance spoke volumes, her resilience shining through the weariness.

As they journeyed back to Tin Creek, John experienced a tumult of emotions swirling within him. Relief and gratitude were paramount, the sight of Isobel safe by his side igniting a warmth that pushed away the chill of fear that had clung to him since her disappearance. Yet, beneath the relief lay a thread of tension of meeting Isobel's uncle and making a good impression. Every step towards home was a step away from the shadow of Tom and Paul, but also a step into the uncertainty of what awaited them in Tin Creek. The prospect of a celebration, of seeing Isobel embraced by the community and the joy it would bring to Jane, buoyed his spirits.

John found he looked forward to the simplicity of a shared meal, to the moment they could put the harrowing journey behind them. The path home was not just a return to the familiar but a journey towards healing and, perhaps, towards something deeper that had taken root in the space between them.

CHAPTER FORTY FIVE

As THE EVENING SUN dipped lower, painting the sky in hues of fading gold, Tom's world was an upside-down canvas of swaying branches and the ever-stretching valley below. The willow, a towering silhouette against the dusk, had become their unwilling host. From his inverted vantage point, Tom watched as two figures approached, their forms gaining clarity with each step. The sight of the Marshal and his deputy instilled a flicker of hope, though the rush of blood to his head made it hard to focus.

"Do you know who I am?" The Marshal's voice cut through the stillness, his badge glinting as he pushed aside the willow's branches to reveal himself. Tom pressed his palms to his eyes, laughing. His predicament laid bare before the law.

"You gotta help us. Some bitch hung us up like this. She is really shady, that one. She made it look like she paid me real money, but it was maple leaves. And then she told us to cut some branches from this tree for a lashing. Next thing we know, we are upside down like this. You got to go find her before she does any more of that stuff. She's gonna hurt someone. She's a sorceress or something." Tom's words tumbled out in a desperate plea, his body twisting to maintain eye contact with the Marshal. The absurdity of their situation, coupled with the disbelief likely painted across the Marshal's face, did little to assuage his fear.

Paul remained motionless. "Marshal, just cut me down and I'll come quietly. Tom. Shut up. You sound crazy. Oh, yeah. I forgot. YOU ARE CRAZY!"

The Marshal signaled to his deputy, who moved to release Paul from his arboreal prison. Tom, still dangling, could only watch as his chances of escape began with Paul's liberation, the irony of their situation not lost on him. Bound by the very branches he had sought to wield against Isobel, Tom was left to reckon with the consequences of underestimating the woman who had turned a tree into their prison, her magick—or whatever power she possessed—rendering them helpless in the face of justice.

As the deputy approached Paul, a glimmer of hope flickered in Tom's mind, only to be quickly doused by the sight of Paul crashing to the ground. Suspended and helpless, Tom watched as the deputy stood over Paul with a no-nonsense attitude. "I'm not picking you up or carrying you. But I will drag you. So you walk or I drag." Tom gasped, relieved it wasn't him on the ground, but a quiet moan escaped as the realization of his own precarious situation sank in.

Paul's struggle to rise was a painful reminder of their dire circumstances. The pressure building in Tom's head made it hard to focus, but he could hear Paul's labored breathing and the deputy's dismissive comments. "Follow me. I guess hanging upside down messes with your head, but your partner is bat shit crazy." The words stung Tom, a cruel echo of the judgment he saw reflected in the deputy's eyes.

The Marshal's words, however, cut deeper than any physical discomfort. His disbelief in their tale, his siding with Isobel's account, was a bitter pill to swallow. "I met Ms. Perkins on my way here. I can't believe she overpowered you and hung up in a tree by herself. So her story is certainly more plausible than yours." The recounting of their misdeeds, laid bare before the eyes of the law, left Tom feeling exposed and vulnerable. The Marshal's hypothetical musings on their fate, left to nature's mercy or the gallows, sent a chill through him.

Faced with the stark reality of his situation, Tom tried one last time to shift the blame, to paint Isobel as the genuine threat. "No, the real danger is that woman. Believe me. Maybe she's a witch. She's real sneaky. You won't know what you're facing and then wham, she hits you with some sorcery stuff. You got to get her."

As Tom dangled there, the world upside down, his pleas seemed to dissipate into the evening air, unheeded by the lawmen who saw through the facade he had built. The reality of his imminent capture and the possibility of facing justice for his crimes loomed over him, a shadow he could no longer escape.

Suspended and disoriented, Tom could only listen as the Marshal expressed his growing irritation with a chilling calmness. "You are really annoying me. I will not listen to your fables all the way back to Missoula. So shut up or I will gag you. You should hear yourself." The words were a cold reminder of his precarious position, the authority in the Marshal's voice brooking no argument. As the Marshal approached with his knife, Tom braced himself, a futile attempt at preparedness. "Watch your step." The brief warning preceded his abrupt descent, the branches giving way under the knife's edge. "Oops. Sorry." The ground met him with an unceremonious thud, the impact jarring yet almost welcome compared to the dizzying suspension.

Amidst the pain and the rush of blood recalibrating within his body, Tom grasped at any leverage he could claim. "Aw. I need to see a doctor. I have something wrong with my man parts. It's painful. I got my rights, right? I need a doctor. It would be faster to take me to Virginia City."

However, the Marshal remained unmoved, his actions methodical as he secured Tom in the saddle. The cold metal of the handcuffs was a stark reminder of his captivity. "You don't have the right to tell me where to go. Let's go." The finality in the Marshal's voice, as he led the way back to Tin Creek, left no room for negotiation. "Just remember. Too much talking gets you a gag. Fair enough?"

"Yeah, yeah. Fair enough." Tom's response was automatic, his mind racing with plans and counter-plans. Despite the desperation of his circumstances, a part of him remained defiant, certain of his own cunning. Glancing at Paul, Tom found a dark humor in their shared plight. The absurdity of it all lightened the weight of his fears for a moment.

As they traversed the valley, the reality of his situation pressed in on him. But Tom clung to a thread of hope, a belief in his ability to navigate the treacherous waters of law and retribution. His laugh, a brief escape from the gravity of his predicament, echoed against the backdrop of their journey back to Tin Creek, a place where the scales of justice awaited him.

Henry, perched on the edge of the hotel bench alongside Jane and Gemma, sensed a tight knot of anticipation in his stomach. His gaze drifted eastward, towards the mountains, each movement on the horizon a spark of hope. When Gemma pointed out the approaching riders, his heart leaped. Rising to his feet, he strained his eyes, seeking the familiar form of Isobel among them. As Jane stood beside him, her expression a mirror of his own anxiety, they embraced, their shared hope palpable. "Please let Isobel be with them!"

Jane's sudden decision to prepare for Isobel's possible arrival sent a ripple of activity through the group. "I need to be ready, in case." Her words were a catalyst, driving Henry and Gemma back into the hotel, though Henry's attention was diverted by Mr. Johnson's attempt at escape. "You're not going anywhere," he declared, steering the man into the dining room with an authority borne of deep concern for his niece. "Sit and don't move. Gemma, can you keep an eye on him?"

With Mr. Johnson now under Gemma's watchful eye, a wave of helplessness washed over him. Without Isobel in his immediate sight left him restless, yearning to contribute in any way he could. Henry's offer to assist Jane was driven by a need to be useful, to prepare for Isobel's return. Jane's plan was a simple one, but it provided a focus for his anxious energy. "Keep me company and listen for when they get here. I'm going to fix one of her teas for her, warm up some soup, and then put her upstairs for a good rest."

"I can fix the tea. That, I know how to do." As he set the kettle on the stove, his actions were more than just a gesture of hospitality; they were an offer of comfort, a tangible way to welcome Isobel back from the brink. In that moment, as he busied himself with the simple task, Henry found peace caring for his niece, a beacon of hope amidst the uncertainty.

As the kettle whistle pierced the air, a commotion outside drew Henry's attention. Gemma rose quick and rash, toppling her chair. She squealed, "Isobel!" but remained beside Mr. Johnson.

Stepping from the warmth of the kitchen, he was met with a sight that tugged at the very fibers of his heart—John, the young man from the stagecoach, was carrying Isobel with a gentle urgency that spoke volumes. Emotion welled up in Henry, tears threatening to betray the storm of feelings within. He hastened towards them, his voice catching as he spoke. "Oh, Isobel." His gaze flickered to John. "Is she alright? Jane is fixing some soup and has a room ready. And thank you for rescuing her. I am in your debt." In his heart, Isobel was as much a daughter as if fate had dealt them a different hand.

John's reassurance was a balm to Henry's frayed nerves. "Isobel's thirsty, hungry, and tired. But otherwise good. No worries." Simple words, yet they carried the weight of a safe return.

Isobel whispered with a weary joy, "Uncle Henry." The way she acknowledged his presence, coupled with her exhaustion, stirred a deep, protective love within him. As John set her down, Henry steadied the chair.

"I'm making you some tea. Be right back." Henry returned to the kitchen, his movements almost colliding with Jane's steady presence.

Jane's calm assurance, "Got it. Why don't you sit down? Everything is fine. It's gonna be fine," served as a gentle reminder of the care surrounding Isobel. As Jane set down the soup and tea, and returned with bread and butter, Henry took a seat close to Isobel, taking her hand in his. "I'm relieved you are safe. I'm sorry I sent you here." The apology was heartfelt, reflecting the guilt and relief that swirled within him.

Isobel's response, her weak smile as she sipped the tea, was a testament to her resilience. "I like it here." Her simple words spoke of acceptance and belonging.

From her post, Gemma clapped her hands. "I'm relieved you are back safe and sound."

Isobel placed her hand on her chest. "I'm glad to be back, too, Gemma. I was worried about you."

Jane's tenderness as she kneeled by Isobel, expressing her love and concern, was a poignant moment. "I was worried sick. I love you more than you realize. Eat a little and this is your tea for relaxation. Is that a good choice?"

"Yes, it is. I'm happy to be home surrounded by my friends and my fa... Uncle Henry."

As Henry watched Isobel interact with Jane, a quiet realization settled over him. Isobel's gentle acknowledgment of being home, coupled with the warmth in her smile towards him, filled his heart with a mix of relief and unspoken sorrow for the inevitable future. When Isobel's smile widened, a spark of curiosity lit within Henry, wondering at the cause of her sudden joy. In that instant, the depth of their connection, the shared trials and triumphs, bound them together in a way that went beyond mere words, a silent testament to the unwavering bonds of family and friendship that had carried them through the storm.

CHAPTER FORTY SIX

As THE EARLY MORNING sun cast its warm glow through the front windows of the hotel dining room, John, Henry, and Marisol gathered around a table, the quiet murmur of conversation filling the space between them. From their vantage point, Marisol's sharp gaze caught a disturbance at the far end of the valley—a cloud of dust rising at the base of the mountain, signaling an approaching party. Her observation drew both John and Henry's attention, who exchanged a quick glance before making their way outside to get a clearer view.

Standing on the dusty road, they shielded their eyes against the sun's glare, watching as the shapes of four men on two horses grew more distinct. John broke the silence with a conjecture, "Must be the Marshall."

Henry, squinting into the distance, confirmed his suspicion. "Yes, I believe it's Cam McDouglas."

At that moment, Walter emerged from the saloon across the street, his approach marked by nervous energy. "I need to talk to the Marshall so don't let him get away before I do. It's really important." The sweat staining the front of his shirt mirrored the anxiety in his voice.

John, sensing the urgency in Walter's plea, offered a comforting assurance with a supportive hand on his shoulder. "Don't worry, Walter. I'll make sure you talk to the Marshall. I know you have something important to tell him." Curiosity flickered within John, pondering Walter's distress, yet he felt certain it revolved around Tom—a suspicion enough to ensure Walter's message reached the Marshall.

As Cam McDouglas and his deputy arrived at the Sheriff's office, the trio from the hotel, along with a gathering crowd, followed in their wake, each step bringing them closer to the unfolding events that would shape the destiny of their small town. Expecting justice was a shared sentiment among those who watched and waited. As Tom stood there, gagged and the center of attention, Barnaby spoke loud enough for everyone to hear, "That's one way to shut Tom up!" His words rippled through the onlookers, igniting a wave of laughter that lightened the heavy atmosphere of the moment.

Marisol approached Tom with a measured stride, her presence commanding attention even amid the assembled crowd. At her approach, Tom's eyes, wide with a mix of fear and defiance, shifted towards her. The gag in his mouth muffled any retort he might have attempted, reducing his once menacing demeanor to a pitiable state of helplessness.

With her hands planted on her hips, Marisol surveyed Tom with a gaze that was both accusatory and triumphant. The feather in her hat, a vibrant contrast to the drab surroundings, fluttered in the breeze—a silent testament to her unyielding spirit. "Tom McCall, you thought you could frame Jack for murder and walk away unscathed. You believed your lies would hold up, that you could tear this community apart without consequence."

Tom, unable to speak, could only glare at Marisol, his eyes betraying the realization of his imminent downfall. The gag, once a physical restraint, now symbolized the silencing of his deceit, the end of his reign of terror.

Marisol, leaning in, whispered, "But you see, Tom, the truth has a way of coming out. Jack is innocent, and everyone will know it. And you? You will get exactly what you deserve." As she straightened, the feather in her hat catching the light once more, Marisol turned on her heel and walked away from Tom.

John sought Marshal Cam. "Excuse me, Marshall. But when you get those two in the cell, could you come talk to Walter and Matt at the Bitterroot Saloon? They have something to tell you. And I'm sure it's about this one." His gesture towards Tom was both an indictment and a plea for swift resolution.

Tom, meanwhile, muffled by the gag, attempted to assert his own narrative, his voice reduced to unintelligible murmurs. The futility of his efforts to communicate, to sway the tide of opinion against him, was manifested in the garbled sounds that failed to find sympathy among the gathered crowd. His struggles, a silent testament to his desperation, were lost in the broader clamor for justice and reparation.

Marshal Cam McDouglas nodded. "Yup, I can do that. How is Ms. Perkins?" His inquiry carried the weight of genuine concern, his seasoned eyes reflecting a myriad of untold stories from the frontier.

"She's going to be fine. She's resting."

"That's good. You wouldn't believe what this one said happened. Sorcery, magick tree, I don't know. He's a crazy one. I had to gag him. He wouldn't shut up. May have to keep him gagged and cuffed in the cell, too." Marshal Cam's recounting of Tom's fantastical tales, the absurdity of his claims, painted a vivid picture of desperation and deceit. As he secured his horse, the deputy escorted Paul into confinement.

"That one has been hiding the Wanted posters so no one would know. I'm going to recommend when someone goes to Hamilton to look at the Wanted posters there. At least, until you get a real sheriff."

John's agreement came with a nod. "That's a good idea. I'll let my father know. He travels to Hamilton every couple of weeks." The conversation, set against the backdrop of the Tin Creek's bustling main street, was a moment of calm in the storm of frontier justice, a brief interlude in the ongoing battle against lawlessness that defined their world.

As Henry made his way across the dusty street towards the jail, the boardwalk creaked under his determined stride. Reaching the entrance, he presented his case to Marshal Cam with a gravitas born of necessity. "Cam, do you have room for another arrest? I have an embezzling banker with documented proof."

Marshal Cam's response, a chuckle tinged with the irony of their situation, broke the tension. "Are we cleaning up here?"

Henry, catching John's eye, affirmed their shared commitment to the safety and well-being of his niece. "If my niece intends to stay here, we are." The statement, while simple, carried the weight of familial duty and the protective instincts that drove him.

John, caught in the moment, wrestled with his thoughts. His engagement with Isobel loomed large in his mind, a future he dearly wanted. The uncertainty of Henry's stance on the matter added a layer of complexity to his concerns. He realized he needed to speak with Isobel before approaching her uncle, keenly aware of how important Henry's approval was in their lives.

Together, John and Henry made their way back to the hotel. For John, the pressing issue now was navigating the delicate conversation about his future with Isobel. The path ahead was fraught with personal stakes, binding the fate of their small community to the resolutions of their intertwined lives.

When Walter saw the Marshal come through the door, his throat closed up, and his hands trembled. "Hey, um, Matt. He's here. I don't think I can..."

"Don't worry. I'll do the talking. You can fill in if I miss something, OK?" Matt tucked his rag into the waist of his apron. He came around the bar and walked up to the Marshall. "Sir, we have to tell you about a murder. Maybe we should sit down at this table."

The Marshall nodded and moved to the table. He paused by a chair. "You can call me Cam." He sat down, as did Matt and Walter. "So who are you saying was murdered?"

Matt looked down at his hands. "A lady that worked here. Her name was Shelley. I don't know what her last name was. Jack would know."

"I see. So why don't you just tell me what you know?"

Walter fidgeted and wiped the sweat from his face. He was thankful Matt was doing the talking because he didn't think he could even talk and he wouldn't be able to write it down since he didn't go far in school. His mother kept him home to keep him from being beaten by the other boys.

Matt took a big breath. "Shelley said something outside when Tom was, uh... making himself known to Isobel when she came off the stagecoach. Tom was furious, and they argued. Up there on the balcony. Then Tom had her by her shoulders and pushed her. She landed on top of a chair. Lots of blood."

Walter said, "I couldn't scrub it out."

Matt twisted his mouth while he patted Walter's back. "Tom had us paint a square over it and shove a table over the area." He pointed to the next table over.

Cam looked over and nodded.

Walter whimpered. "Tom made us bury her out back." He placed his head on the table while pulling a handkerchief out of his pocket. "No one deserves that."

Cam placed his hands on the table and used them to push himself up out of his seat. He leaned on his outstretched arms. "Gentlemen, I appreciate you telling me this. We will get her dug up and given a proper burial. My deputy will come by and get your information. You may be asked to testify or at least provide a written statement."

Walter blew his nose and looked at Cam. "Thank you. This has weighed on me terribly."

Cam stood up tall and pushed his chair in. "It weighs heavy on all good men. Now, if you will excuse me, I need to write this up and check on those two."

Walter watched Cam leave and let out a sigh that also released all the tension he held over the whole ordeal. Now he could wait for Jack to return and push all the nastiness of the last several months away. He never could handle it. Jack always took care of him.

CHAPTER FORTY SEVEN

As THE LATE MORNING sun stretched its fingers through the windows of the hotel, Isobel navigated the intricacies of the oak staircase, descending into a new day marked by recovery and revelations. Her entrance into the dining room was punctuated by a moment of levity, her gaze landing on the unexpected duo of Henry and Marisol, companions in coffee and perhaps more. The contrast between them was striking—Henry with his air of measured propriety, and Marisol, embodying the spirit of independence. Isobel released a soft giggle at the sight. "Is this a rendezvous? Should I sit at my own table?" she teased, a smile dancing on her lips.

Henry, caught in the unexpected spotlight, rose with a start. "How are you? Did you sleep well? Oh, yes, here..." His words tumbled over one another as he offered Isobel a seat beside him, a gesture that spoke volumes of his care.

As Isobel settled into the chair, the exchange of silent communication between her and Marisol was a testament to their bond—a wink, subtle yet laden with meaning, and an aura that shimmered with hues of chartreuse, a color of new beginnings and uncharted paths. Observing this, Isobel pondered the potential shift in their dynamics. With Marisol potentially stepping into a role far beyond a friend, the prospect brought a mix of curiosity and hope. What transformations had unfolded in her absence? And what would Marisol's influence as a step-mother entail? Isobel considered these questions, not with apprehension, but with an open heart, ready to navigate the changes that lay ahead.

As Marisol adjusted the glove on her hand, her voice carried the warmth of genuine concern for Isobel's well-being. "I am so glad you are safe and sound. I hope that scoundrel spends the rest of his life in prison breaking rocks for even thinking of harming you." Her movements were deliberate, each one imbued with a sense of purpose as she prepared to leave, granting Isobel and Henry a moment of privacy. "I'm going to leave you two so you can spend some private time together. I'll come visit later." With that, Marisol exited the room, her departure marked by an intentional sway in her step, a silent message meant for Henry alone.

Isobel observed this with a mix of amusement and curiosity, catching the subtle cues that suggested an unspoken connection between Henry and Marisol. The implications of such a pairing were still settling in her mind when Henry's confession drew her attention back.

Henry said, "Isobel, I have gravely harmed you by sending you here. When I'm truthful with myself, I didn't care what happened to George. That relationship never existed. I felt a family obligation that I shouldn't have. He stole your mother from me and I never forgave him for that. I am truly sorry. It's my fault." The blue sadness that enveloped him was a visual echo of his guilt and sorrow, a tangible manifestation of his inner turmoil.

Isobel, touched by his vulnerability, sought to offer comfort, her hand finding his. "You did what you thought was right. And it was.

I needed to come here as I regained my memories. I know who killed my mother." Her words, spoken with a gentle firmness, bridged the distance between them, her understanding and forgiveness a balm to Henry's troubled spirit. In this exchange, layers of past grievances and personal revelations unfolded, setting the stage for healing and the possibility of forging fresh paths from the pain of old wounds.

Henry's demeanor shifted at Isobel's revelation, his posture straightening as his eyes mirrored the shock of her words. "You do?" The question, laden with a mixture of disbelief and anticipation, hung between them.

Isobel's response was succinct, a single word that seemed to carry the weight of their shared history. "George."

Henry, struggling to process the implication, displayed a visible reaction that Isobel interpreted as violet contempt, a vivid representation of his turmoil. "But why?" His inquiry reflected a desperate search for understanding in the face of a bewildering betrayal.

"He thought she was a witch." Isobel sighed. "When insecure men envy wise and powerful women, they accused them of witchcraft."

Henry's hands pressing against the tabletop as he absorbed the full measure of George's transgressions. "I hope he suffered from his illness. George is no brother of mine." The vibrancy of his aura, now violet, underscored the depth of his anger and rejection.

"He did." Isobel's addition hinted at a deeper justice, one that transcended the mortal coil. The guilt she found in the notion set her hand reaching her neck, searching for the missing necklace. As a tangible link to her past and her mother's legacy, its disappearance sparked a flurry of concern. The realization that she had lost something so significant within the vastness of Montana weighed on her.

As she processed the loss, Isobel considered the true nature of the necklace. Had it been a source of constraint rather than protection? The freedom she felt in its absence suggested an unseen burden, perhaps a curse. The true enchantment lay in releasing the hold it had on her, allowing her to embrace a future unencumbered by the shadows of the past.

While Henry indulged in a moment of quiet reflection, his coffee providing comfort, the turbulent hues of his aura softened. The raw contempt he had harbored for his brother was dissolving into something less bitter, more contemplative. Isobel watched this transformation, granting him the space to navigate his emotions, aware that the revelations she had yet to share would demand even more from him.

Henry signaled a readiness to shift the conversation, pushing his coffee aside as he faced Isobel with a seriousness that underscored his intent. "I have something I want to discuss. It's obvious I'm old-fashioned in my views about marriage and careers for women. That I'm sorry for. I am working on it. You would make a wonderful nurse, and I want to pay the tuition."

Isobel, surprised and touched by the offer, responded with her own practicality. "But I have the money. I saved while working at the dress shop."

Henry said, "I am sure you will have need of that money when you finish school. You don't plan on living with Aunt Stella all your life, do you?"

Isobel hesitated. "Ah, no." The opportunity to share her engagement news loomed large, yet she pondered the propriety of speaking before John had the chance to discuss it with Henry. "Can you wait here while I get something from the shop?"

Henry's response was warm, his smile reassuring. "I have nowhere else to be than with you. You go right ahead."

Isobel's departure from the hotel marked a significant step towards unveiling a series of truths that had shaped her recent days. This next revelation, however, bore the weight of a profound change, one that promised to redefine the contours of their relationship. As she stepped out into the clarity of the morning, Isobel was aware of the gravity of the moment, the impending disclosure of her engagement to John, set against the backdrop of newfound truths and reconciliations.

A careful consideration marked Isobel's approach to the living area above the store, her knock on the door a gentle signal of her return, meant to temper any sudden surprise for Gemma. The moment the door swung open, the exuberant whirls of Shadow, the racoon's joyful dance greeted her. His antics, a mix of playful bows and spirited spins, were a heartwarming welcome back into the fold of home.

Gemma emerged, her ash blond hair being woven into a braid, her movement speeding up into a run as she caught sight of Isobel. Their embrace was a mutual acknowledgment of the worries and fears they had harbored during Isobel's absence. "I was worried about you being here alone," Isobel confessed, choked with emotion.

The concern in Gemma's green eyes mirrored Isobel's own. "I was worried about you being out there with those dangerous men and never coming back. I'm so glad you're here. Even Shadow missed you. Your hawk came to the window every day. I fed him, though

I know it's not the same." Her words, sincere and filled with relief, spoke volumes of the care she had taken in Isobel's absence, extending her kindness even to the hawk that kept vigil.

Isobel, touched by the gesture, offered a gentle reassurance. "Thank you for caring for him. I came to get something for my uncle and will be back later so we can catch up, okay?" Her hand ran over Gemma's hair, a silent expression of gratitude and affection.

As Gemma secured the end of her braid, she said, "That's fine. I have to open the shop. Your uncle is a nice man. He treats me like I'm not stupid. I like that."

Isobel retrieved the letter nestled within her grimoire in the top drawer of her dresser. "I'm sure he recognizes you are very smart. And he is really nice." With the letter in hand, she made her way to the door, offering a parting word. "See you later."

As Isobel made her way back to the hotel, her mind circled back to Gemma. The connection she felt with the young girl was undeniable, deeper than the simple bond forged by their shared circumstances. Isobel pondered the possibility of a familial link, a thread of kinship that tied them together in ways not yet understood. The resemblance in their resilience and the ease with which they understood each other sparked a curiosity within Isobel. Is there a hidden chapter in their family's history, a forgotten lineage that connected them? The thought lingered, an intriguing puzzle that added another layer to the already complex tapestry of her life. Despite the uncertainty, the idea of being related to Gemma brought a sense of comfort and belonging, a potential expansion of the family she cherished.

In the warmth of the hotel lobby, Isobel and Jane's reunion unfolded with an embrace that spoke volumes of the deep bond they shared. Their hug was a testament to the trials they'd weathered together, Jane standing as the sister Isobel had found in the unpredictable currents of life.

As they separated, Jane's concern washed over her features, a sister's worry etched into every line. "Are you alright? Nothing happened while you were with them? Those two are dangerous. They're murderers and train robbers and we had no idea while they were right under our noses."

Isobel, seeking to reassure her, clasped Jane's arms with a firmness that belied her recent ordeal. "Nothing happened but would have if we got to Virginia City. I'm fine. And they will go to jail for a long time."

Jane's response, a mix of vulnerability and relief, underscored the gravity of their shared fear. "I know." Her gaze lifted, hope rekindling in her eyes. "We are all together now and your uncle is waiting for you. He's so nice."

Isobel's laughter broke through the somber mood, a light in the aftermath of darkness. "That's what I heard." She brandished the letter, a bridge to the past and a key to understanding. "I have a letter from my mother for him. She wrote it sixteen years ago."

At the revelation, Jane's mouth dropped open, head tipped back as she took a deep breath. "Holey moley! You better get in there then." Her encouragement was a nudge towards the next chapter of

Isobel's journey, where the words of a letter penned long ago awaited to weave new strands into the tapestry of their lives.

Isobel made her way to the dining room with a purpose, her steps quickening as she neared the familiar figure of Henry seated at a table bathed in sunlight near the window. The sight of him, a cherished connection to her life in Chicago now present in Tin Creek, filled her with a sense of comfort and belonging. How she wished Aunt Stella could join them, but that was a hope for another day. For now, Henry's presence was the anchor she needed in the whirlwind of recent events.

Henry glanced up as Isobel approached, his eyes reflecting a tranquility born of the town's serene pace. "You're back. I've been waiting for some activity in town and there isn't any. The world moves real slow here. It's calming." He carried the ease of a man who had found a momentary respite in the quiet observation of life unfolding at its own rhythm.

Isobel took her place beside him, the difference between Tin Creek's tranquil existence and the relentless energy of Chicago not lost on her. "It differs from the hustle of Chicago. Other than a few miserable men, I have had a good summer here." With these words, she introduced the letter to Henry, a tangible link to a past filled with both love and loss. "My mother wrote this right before she died. It's addressed to you."

As the letter made its way across the table, a profound silence enveloped them, a space for Henry to brace himself. This was not only a letter; it was a bridge across sixteen years of silence, carrying messages from a world that once was to the reality they now inhabited. Isobel watched, a mix of anticipation and apprehension, uncertain of the emotions and revelations that awaited them both in the words her mother had left behind.

Henry's hand hesitated over the envelope, his touch reverent. This letter, unique in its enchantment, was meant for his eyes alone. With a deep breath, he unfolded the paper. But then he stopped. "I don't know if I can. The last time I read anything from her, it was the letter she left when she joined George in the middle of the night. That letter killed me, my heart and soul."

Isobel understood the depth of his pain but believed in the potential for healing. "I think this will be better. You won't know until you read it. Guessing will not help. Give her a chance. Maybe she is apologizing for everything." She fought the urge to reveal too much, to let the letter speak the truths Henry needed to hear.

With Isobel's encouragement, Henry resumed his task, spreading the letter open before him. Isobel watched, aware of the monumental nature of this moment. She could almost feel the weight of his apprehension, his hope mingling with fear as he read.

As the words took hold, Henry's aura, shrouded in the melancholy hues of blue, transformed. Isobel witnessed the gradual infusion of yellow streams within it, a visual manifestation of hope and perhaps forgiveness beginning to pierce the veil of his sorrow. She knew then that he was absorbing the heart of her mother's message, a revelation that held the potential to mend the fractures in his soul. Isobel's own heart ached in empathy, yearning for the letter to bridge the chasm of years of pain, to offer Henry the solace and answers he had longed for.

As Henry's gaze locked onto Isobel's, the gravity of the moment held them both captive. Isobel watched as the dam within Henry broke, tears welling in his eyes before cascading down his cheeks. He whispered, "You're my daughter?"

The question, so loaded with emotion, reached deep within Isobel, stirring a tumult of her own. Tears blurred her vision, rendering Henry an indistinct figure through the moisture. "Yes. I think so," she managed with a whisper.

In a shared impulse, they rose, drawn together by an invisible force that transcended their previous understanding of their relationship. Their embrace was years of longing. Tears mingled as they held each other, a tangible affirmation of their bond.

For Isobel, the embrace symbolized more than just acceptance; it was finding a place in the world where she was valued and loved without condition. It was an envy she had harbored, watching her friends bask in the warmth of familial love—a longing that now found fulfillment in the arms of the man she could finally, truly, call father. The revelation enveloped her in an overwhelming sense of joy and belonging, a profound emotional homecoming that marked a new chapter in her life.

CHAPTER FORTY EIGHT

ISOBEL STOOD BEFORE JOHN'S horse, Beau, a striking palomino whose presence reminded her of her recent ordeal. Despite her love for the majesty of horses, the memory of her arduous journey across the mountains lingered, leaving her hesitant. Her physical discomfort had faded, yet the reluctance to embrace the possibility of enduring it again shadowed her enthusiasm.

John pleaded, "It's a short ride, Isobel. I need you to come and see my surprise. I promise we will ride slow and steady. You'll like it, I promise." His voice was a gentle nudge, encouraging her to step beyond her apprehension.

With a soft sigh, Isobel reached out to Beau, her hand caressing the horse's side. "Be easy on me. I know I need to ride more and build up whatever it is that makes it bearable later. You sure I can't use a pillow?" Her words were light, tinged with humor as she addressed both John and Beau, finding solace in the shared moment. Beau's reaction, a flicker of understanding in his eyes, almost convinced Isobel he was laughing at her.

With John's steady help, Isobel mounted Beau, and soon after, John joined her, enveloping her in a comforting embrace as he took hold of the reins. The warmth of his body against hers, his arms wrapped around her, instilled a sense of safety and love that resonated within her. She yearned to experience it every day, but the thought of departing for nursing school cast a shadow over her heart. The prospect of being separated from John for two years tugged at her, igniting a turmoil of emotions. How could she endure such a distance, when being in his presence brought her an unparalleled sense of completeness?

As John's breath warmed the nape of Isobel's neck, she felt the delicate hairs there respond, a silent testament to the intimacy of the moment. His whispered inquiry, "Do you like that?" met with a soft, barely audible "Yes" from Isobel. The teachings of her youth, which extolled the virtues of propriety and restraint in matters of affection, clashed with the raw, beautiful emotions she felt in John's embrace. But she realized their solitude rendered these conventions irrelevant. Without prying eyes, the boundaries of propriety blurred, and she allowed herself to embrace the warmth of his touch. "I love your touch," she confessed, a declaration made even more profound by the freedom she found in their seclusion.

"Good. I have to get what I can before you leave. Two whole years. But then we will marry and no one can say a thing about us kissing or anything else." The prospect of their impending separation loomed over them, a shadow tempered by the promise of a future together, a future where their love could flourish unchallenged.

Silence enveloped them as they journeyed, Isobel's thoughts adrift in the sea of possibilities that "anything else" promised, a distant horizon of shared intimacies and whispered dreams. The reality of their long engagement, already taking shape in Anna's plans, anchored these dreams to the firmament of their current separateness.

As they crested a gentle hill, Isobel's eyes caught the sight of wooden stakes driven into the ground, markers of intent and purpose. "What's that, John?" she asked, her curiosity piqued, a momentary diversion from the intricate weave of emotions and futures unfolding between them.

As they approached the array of stakes jutting from the earth, John waved his arms out as he said, "This is my surprise." He dismounted and then extended his arms to assist Isobel down, guiding her towards the foundation of their future. "Step here. This is our new house. The kitchen is there. A fireplace over there. The stairs are here." He pointed up. "Two bedrooms." With each step, he painted the air with visions of hearths and halls, a spectral blueprint of love and life yet to be lived.

Isobel's curiosity bloomed as she navigated the invisible walls and corridors, her question echoing, "Two bedrooms?" The notion of space and its allocation stirred within her a mixture of excitement and inquiry. Their embrace, a physical affirmation of shared dreams and aspirations, was a moment of connection deeper than the footings of any home.

John's laughter, light and warm, carried his response through the air. "I thought you wanted children. You said so yourself." The conversation between them, playful yet profound, danced around the heart of their shared future.

Isobel met his gaze, her own sparkling with playful challenge. "Two bedrooms won't be enough. Maybe three. They can be smaller rooms. But I want more than one child. Your mother would love lots of grandchildren."

Surveying the stakes that marked the perimeter of their future home, John conceded, "I guess I need to rethink my plans." His laughter mingled with hers as he lifted her in a gesture that spoke volumes of his intentions and desires. "I want to have it finished by the time we are married, so I can carry you over the threshold."

As Isobel once again stood on her own, her eyes traced the outline of their home-to-be, her mind alight with visions of laughter and tears, of life in all its chaotic beauty. The realization dawned upon her that this was what she had been waiting for, not only the person who made it all seem right, but the future that person offered—a future where her dreams did not have to be sacrificed, but fulfilled and expanded in the embrace of love and partnership.

As the dust of their future home settled around them, Isobel turned her gaze towards John, a question burning in her eyes that reflected the yellow hue of the afternoon sun. "When are you going to talk to Henry?"

John's response came wrapped in a hesitance that tugged at the corners of his lips, his eyes darting away before finding resolve. "I guess it better be today. Over dinner?"

Isobel's agreement was silent, communicated through a simple nod, her eyebrows drawn together. Her nose wrinkled in a gesture that spoke volumes, encapsulating the nerves and excitement of the conversation that lay ahead. In this moment, nestled within the stakes that marked their future, the path forward seemed both daunting and bright, an adventure they were about to embark upon together.

In the soft glow of dawn's light, Isobel awoke with a heart brimming with joy and anticipation. The conversation between John and Henry regarding their engagement had set a cornerstone of hope and happiness in her life. It was as if all the pieces of her existence were aligning, creating a tapestry of love and belonging she had longed for. She found herself enveloped in the warmth of having a father's love and a fiancée's adoration, each a pillar of her newly constructed world. Gemma, young yet capable, had taken the reins of the store with a grace and efficacy that belied her age, her innate talents blossoming in ways that not only lifted the store's fortunes but also eased the burden on Isobel's shoulders.

As the morning unfolded, Isobel and Gemma engaged in a lively discussion about the store's future, Henry lending his wisdom from behind the counter, when Jane's presence at the doorway caused a harmonious greeting to escape their lips. "Hi Jane." The synchronicity of their voices mirrored the unity among them, reflecting the shared bond and camaraderie that had flourished in the heart of Tin Creek.

Jane entered with the grace of a dance, her steps carrying her to the counter, her smile so wide it painted her cheeks in vibrant strokes of joy.

Isobel said, "Someone is extremely happy today." The air around Jane danced with colors, her aura exploding in shades of yellow that swirled around her like summer's own embrace, a visual testament to the sheer bliss that radiated from her being.

With a playful shrug and a charming scrunch of her nose, Jane's voice rose to a squeal that filled the small store with an energy of its own. "I have great news!" she announced.

Gemma, caught up in the moment, bounced on her toes. "Tell us," she urged, her eyes wide with curiosity.

Isobel, harboring the secret like a treasured gift, felt a mix of impatience and delight at the impending revelation. The suspense had been a weight, a secret she bore with care, waiting for Jane to unveil the joyous news.

"I'm pregnant!" Jane's declaration was a burst of jubilation, her body animated with jumps and her hands clapping. "You helped me and I'm so grateful."

In an instant, Isobel moved, propelled by a surge of happiness. She navigated around the counter, her hip colliding with the corner in her haste, but the dull pain was a distant concern compared to the tidal wave of emotions. She enveloped Jane in an embrace, their tears mingling in a moment of shared joy and gratitude. "I'm happy for you. You're going to be a great mother," Isobel whispered.

Jane, overwhelmed by the magnitude of the moment, held Isobel tight. "You did it. I can't repay you for this." Her words were a testament to the profound bond between them, a connection strengthened by shared dreams and now, the promise of new life.

As Jane's news settled like a gentle summer rain over the group, Isobel noticed her father's presence at the edge of their circle, his expression a blend of confusion and curiosity. With a soft release from their embrace, Isobel turned towards him. "I gave her an herbal tea that helps with fertility."

Henry's reaction was a slow bloom of realization, admiration dawning in his eyes as he absorbed the significance of Isobel's words. "That is extraordinary. I'm impressed," he admitted, his head bobbing in a series of respectful nods, the gesture an unspoken accolade for the wisdom and kindness Isobel had shown. "Jane, congratulations. I'm happy for you."

Jane raised her arms in a jubilant gesture, her laughter mingling with the air of festivity that had enveloped them. "Time for cake to celebrate. I asked Marisol to join us. She doesn't know yet." Her laughter tapered into a contented sigh.

Gemma, with the unbridled enthusiasm of youth, proclaimed, "I love any opportunity to eat cake." She closed the ledger with a definitive slam, a signal that for now, business was secondary to celebration, and placed it beneath the counter.

Together, Henry and Gemma joined Isobel and Jane, a quartet woven together by the threads of unexpected blessings and newfound futures. With a turn of the key, Isobel secured the store, a symbolic gesture that mirrored the locking in of this moment of perfect contentment. As they stepped away, the click of the lock was a soft echo in the background, a reminder that, for Isobel, everything was indeed falling into place. Everything.

The End

If you enjoyed this novel, I ask two favors. One is to leave a review on Amazon, if possible, and Goodreads or share it with a friend or social media. Two is to join my newsletter here (https://www.anne ttegrantham.com/newsletter-signup/) to get notification when the next book, "Air Witch", is available.

Acknowledgements

The spark that ignited "Earth Witch" flared into life during a Deadwood binge on HBO, as I was gearing up for NaNoWriMo in 2018. I found myself musing over a tantalizing question: How would Al Swearengen react if Trixie or Calamity Jane wielded magical powers? Of all the novels I've crafted each November, this tale has been my favorite journey. Since that initial draft, the story has undergone three significant revisions, evolving and growing into the narrative that exists today.

The camaraderie and critiques from the Lewis County Writers Guild have been the whetstone for my skills, sharpening my ability to present you with a story worthy of your time. The collective wisdom of Amy Flugel, Margie Keck Smith, Wayne Wallace, Beverley Gowan, Johanna Flynn, and Kristen Franklin has been a blessing to my writer's journey. Their generosity of spirit is a debt of gratitude I carry, hoping to pay it forward with each word I write.

The vibrant community of 20Booksto50K has been a beacon, illuminating the path from manuscript to marketplace. The collective knowledge shared through Facebook interactions and annual congregations has armed me with the tools to bring this book to you, coupled with a dose of inspiration and an atlas of authorship.

Margie Keck Smith deserves a special mention for her role as a beta reader par excellence, whose insights have been crucial in refining the pages you hold.

To my children and stalwart cheerleaders, Rick Garza and Jennifer Swafford: their unwavering support and boundless enthusiasm have been my guiding lights. Their beliefs in my dreams fuels my courage to chase them.

At the heart of it all is Dale Grantham, my husband, who embraces my pre-dawn-bound writing rituals with love and understanding. And to Twilight, my faithful canine companion, who passed away while I worked to finish this novel. I mourn him daily.

Last, to you, dear reader—your journey through the pages to the end fills this endeavor with meaning. Thank you for your time, your thoughts, and, if you're so inclined, your reviews. They are the lifeblood of a writer's evolution. The tale continues, and Gemma's story awaits—her path brings two witches together to save her.

About the Author

Annette Grantham's life reads like one of her richly imagined fantasy novels—filled with journeys, discovery, and pursuing passions. Hailing from the bustling streets of New York, Annette's early years were a nomadic odyssey from the historic Northeast to the expansive heart of Texas. Her adventurous spirit found a home in the military, where she served with dedication and honor, before she embarked on a tech odyssey as a software engineer. However, beneath the code and uniform, a storyteller's heart beat with fervent imagination.

Annette's pen has always been mightier than a sword, and her lifelong dream to weave tales has come to fruition in her writing. She now crafts enthralling fantasy novels that stitch together her fascination with bygone eras and the mystical. Her four-book series, "The Frontier Witches," is where the grit of "Deadwood" (TV series and movie) meets the enchanting allure of "Practical Magic" by Alice Hoffman. Here, readers find themselves alongside bold and spirited heroines—witches who don't just navigate but flourish in the untamed frontiers of the Old West. The prequel to the series, "Dark Witch", sets you on the journey on how Mary and Stella end up in America after their mother, Lillian, is arrested and tortured for witchcraft.

Nestled in a snug cabin in Washington, where the wild whispers of nature are but a window away, Annette lives with her high school sweetheart under the watchful eyes of a lively squirrel congregation. Her home is not just a retreat but a wellspring of inspiration where she conjures her next spellbinding adventure.

Website: https://www.annettegrantham.com
Facebook: AnnetteGranthamAuthor
Instagram: annettegranthamauthor

ALSO BY

Dark Witch

Available at retailers here: https://books2read.com/u/4NgYxY

Fire Witch

Available at retailers here: https://books2read.com/u/mBABjy